Waking the Princess

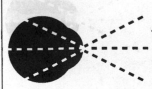

This Large Print Book carries the
Seal of Approval of N.A.V.H.

Waking the Princess

Susan King

WHEELER
PUBLISHING

This is a work of fiction. Names, characters, places, and incidents either are the product of the author's imagination or are used fictitiously, and any resemblance to actual persons, living or dead, business establishments, events, or locales is entirely coincidental.

Published in 2004 by arrangement with NAL Signet, a member of Penguin Group (USA) Inc.

Wheeler Large Print Softcover.

The text of this Large Print edition is unabridged.
Other aspects of the book may vary from the original edition.

Set in 16 pt. Plantin by Minnie B. Raven.

Printed in the United States on permanent paper.

Library of Congress Control Number: 2003070528
ISBN 1-58724-612-0 (lg. print : sc : alk. paper)

To my dear friend
Joanne Zaslow
with much love

As the Founder/CEO of NAVH, the only national health agency solely devoted to those who, although not totally blind, have an eye disease which could lead to serious visual impairment, I am pleased to recognize Thorndike Press* as one of the leading publishers in the large print field.

Founded in 1954 in San Francisco to prepare large print textbooks for partially seeing children, NAVH became the pioneer and standard setting agency in the preparation of large type.

Today, those publishers who meet our standards carry the prestigious "Seal of Approval" indicating high quality large print. We are delighted that Thorndike Press is one of the publishers whose titles meet these standards. We are also pleased to recognize the significant contribution Thorndike Press is making in this important and growing field.

Lorraine H. Marchi, L.H.D.
Founder/CEO
NAVH

* Thorndike Press encompasses the following imprints: Thorndike, Wheeler, Walker and Large Pr int Press.

Acknowledgments

I'm very grateful to my father, Mel Longhi, for information on civil engineering and methods of road construction, and for patiently explaining how to grade a road over a steep hill.

Also, thanks go to Meredith Bean McMath, Victorian costume expert extraordinaire, who found cool pictures of spectacular gowns and fetching little hats just when I needed them.

And to Mary Jo Putney for providing gracious sanctuary now and then, giving me a chance to write in peace . . . and kitty-sit too.

Prologue

Long ago . . .

She slept, her skin as pale as a river pearl, lips drained of warmth. Leaning down, he kissed her soft mouth and drew back. His heart broke anew to see her eyelids flutter without awareness, to see them close again.

Sighing, he touched the rippled dark silk of her hair. "Liadan." He whispered her name. "Wife of Aedan mac Brudei. Hear me." The faint pulse in her slender throat quickened as he spoke.

How little it took to keep her alive. Breaths as thin as ice on a spring pond, a heartbeat faint but steady. Each day, Liadan's serving woman fed her broth and water, which she would swallow even as she slept. Each evening, Aedan sat with his wife, the mother of his infant son, from gloaming until dawn, his grief eased a little in the strange serenity of her presence.

He rubbed weary fingers over his eyes and heard the fire crackle in the low stone hearth behind him. The hour was late, but sleep came hard. Aedan took Liadan's hand and frowned at the sight of the pink scratches on her forearms. He stroked his fingers thoughtfully over the marks.

A wild-rose briar had surrounded her that day of battle and strife, weeks earlier. She had not awoken since he had lifted her from her bed of thorns and blossoms. But he saw that her skin was healing, and the gash on her head had sealed. If her body could renew itself and breath flowed through her, life still existed — and so did hope.

She was gaunt now, a fragile shadow of the vibrant girl he had wed months ago, with his child great in her belly and the blush of it upon her cheek. Now he could count the bones in her hand, could set his thumb in the valley along her forearm.

He raised her tapered fingers to his lips, kissed them, replaced her hand on the covers. Raking his fingers roughly through his long, dark hair, he closed his eyes in anguish.

Druid priests and healers had spoken spells over her, using every potion, salve, and charm. Aedan himself, a warrior prince of the Dál Riata trained by Druids, had murmured incantations as well, tipping one infusion after another to her still lips. In dark of moon, he had swept his hands above her in magical patterns. He had even recited Christian prayers in an effort to stir her soul to awakening.

Yet Liadan slept on.

10

Aedan closed his eyes and thought of the magic he and Liadan had created together, their secret nights of sultry, magnificent love. He still yearned for her touch, longed to lose himself in her wild, bright spirit. Even now, exhausted and despairing, his body stirred at the memory.

Liadan was part of him — blood, heart, bone, and being. He could feel no greater torture than sitting helplessly while she drifted away. Though a warrior and a Druid, a man of secrets, strength, and resolve, he could not save the woman he loved.

With a fingertip, he traced a spiral of protection on her brow and murmured again the charm to guide a lost soul back to its forsaken body.

Journeying upward, come again down
Journeying outward, come again in
No peril shall befall thee on hill or in heather
Come again homeward, safe to me.

A frown passed over her brow like a ripple through water. Sensing her struggle to live, Aedan knew only he could help her.

Like drawing water from a well, he had the skill to tap the rhythmic force that flowed through every living thing. He would never give up. She would come back to him.

Liadan, hear my voice in the mist. Come to me, my heart.

The others implored him to set Liadan under the stars and allow her a peaceful death. They said his grief bound her to the earth like an iron chain. *Let her go,* they told him. *She will find you again in another world, and you will love once more.*

But he loved her now, here. She was a lark to his brooding hawk. Liadan would live, he vowed, if he had to reach into the Otherworld himself and pull her soul back with his own hands.

One method remained untried, though Druidic law forbade it. Yet any risk seemed small to him. The enduring magic of the written word, the tool of the Christian priests, was his final resort. A ribbon of words could fix a spell like a fireball on the wick of time.

Because of his Christian education, he could write down his spells in his own language. He would enlist eternity to call back Liadan's soul from its moorless wanderings.

Leaving her side, he went to a wooden chest to take out a parchment that he had used for another, more temporal purpose. The vellum sheet was filled with neatly inked words, and the wide margins would provide space for additional lines.

Aedan mac Brudei took the pot of lampblack ink and the feathery quill stored with it and carried them to Liadan's bedside. *Come again homeward, safe to me. . . .*

Chapter One

Scotland, Edinburgh
August, 1858

"I will not do it." Christina Blackburn folded her hands demurely but stubbornly and turned away from the window in Sir Edgar Neaves's museum office, which overlooked Edinburgh's sloping streets, crowded with shops and tenements. The National Museum stood in the shadow of the great crag that supported the castle, so that little sunlight penetrated the room.

"I cannot. Surely you both understand." She lifted her chin and faced Sir Edgar and the other man in the office, her brother, John Blackburn.

"My dear," Edgar said, rising from behind his enormous mahogany desk. He was tall and handsome in a cool, perfect way, his elegance suited to the richly furnished room. "Traveling to Dundrennan House to investigate the ancient walls found on that hillside would take only a few days of your time. You must go. This a plum, Christina."

13

"*You* think this is a plum, Edgar," she answered quietly. "You've long wanted to acquire Dundrennan's collection for the museum. If you go, you could make another offer to — Sir Aedan, is it?"

"Yes. Sir Aedan MacBride, the new laird and the late Sir Hugh MacBride's son. The great Highland bard left no poet in his heir, believe me. Sir Aedan is a blunt-spoken engineer who works on roadways like a common laborer. He seems uninterested in the historical importance of his estate." Edgar curled his lip in disdain.

"Perhaps, but since you know him, it would be more appropriate for you to go than for me," Christina said.

"Since I am not free to travel there just yet, I prefer that you take my place. The old wall that Sir Aedan discovered on his land, while blasting through rock for a highway, could very well be ancient. You could even publish a little paper about it. I will speak to Mr. Smith at *Blackwood's Magazine* on your behalf."

"You know that *Blackwood's* has already published four articles by my sister," John said curtly. "She's a well respected antiquarian in her own right, Sir Edgar, without your influence."

"Perhaps. But she needn't be concerned about this journey. It could prove worth her time."

"It is not the journey. I do not know how you can expect me to go . . . there." Christina paced in front of the window, her moss-green skirt and layered petticoats rustling softly.

"My dear, charming as usual, though somewhat irrational." Edgar smiled indulgently. "Please do this for me. I have promised to deliver a series of lectures at the British Museum, so I cannot go to Dundrennan for several weeks yet. You have the expertise to determine if this discovery is worth my time and the museum's interest. This stone wall could even prove to be Pictish in origin. You have a good understanding of that culture — Reverend Carriston trained you well."

Christina sighed, thinking of her elderly uncle, who now lingered in ill health. The Reverend Walter Carriston was an authority on the ancient history of Scotland and had taught his niece much of what she knew about history, literature, and scholarly technique. "I'm honored by your faith in me, Edgar. But surely someone else can do this."

Although she remained calm and cool, her heart thumped in protest. She could not bear to go to Dundrennan, of all places.

"Your uncle will be disappointed if you refuse —" Edgar's handsome brow crinkled, then smoothed. "Ah. Is it the painting?"

15

Christina felt her cheeks flame, a lamentable barometer of her thoughts. She had inherited her mother's auburn hair and the translucent skin that went with it. Glancing at her brother, she saw John watching her with perceptive concern. "Yes. The MacBrides of Dundrennan own the painting."

"I had nearly forgotten," Edgar murmured. "The famous Blackburn painters are too prolific, the lot of you. So Stephen's painting of you as the legendary Dundrennan princess is there? How very awkward."

"Christina is right," John said, standing slowly, his cane compensating for the weakness in his left leg. "Since the MacBrides now own the picture that caused such grief and scandal for her, she should not be expected to go to Dundrennan."

Edgar came around the desk toward Christina. "That was the one your husband completed just before his tragic death, isn't that so?"

Stiffening at the reminder, Christina nodded. "Stephen sold the painting, though he had promised never to part with it."

"He always was an unreliable fellow," Edgar murmured, watching her. Lean and dark, his long face chiseled perfection, his voice a mellow purr, he was an attractive man. Christina gazed up at him, yearning to feel comforted by his nearness. Yet she did not, and never had, although she told herself

16

that Edgar needed only to learn to show his kinder side.

Sir Edgar Neaves was a respected museum director, a sophisticated, accomplished gentleman a decade older than she was. A friend of her father's, Edgar made no secret of his growing fondness for the daughter of one of Scotland's most renowned painters. He had maintained a friendship with the Blackburns, and with her, throughout the humiliating scandal that followed Stephen Blackburn's death six years earlier. Widowed and snubbed by society, Christina was grateful for Edgar's continued loyalty, and for his support of her academic efforts.

Weeks ago he had asked her to marry him, and she had not yet answered while she still considered the offer. She hesitated, knowing that she did not truly love Edgar, nor did she feel any spark of passion for him.

Yet she had played with the fires of passion before in a wild marriage to her second cousin, and she had been soundly burned. A relationship based on intellectual interests would be safe and might even bring contentment. Edgar was a brilliant scholar who encouraged Christina's academic interests, although he made clear his conviction that a woman could never be a man's intellectual equal.

Now Edgar smiled, his cool blue eyes appreciative. "Dear Christina, no need to be concerned about that painting. No one would recognize you as the model for Stephen's princess. You are several years older now and thinner, not as . . . lush as you were then." He rested a hand on her shoulder. "Yet still attractive."

"Good Lord, Neaves," John burst out. "A little tact would be welcome. The lass was but seventeen then, and scarce twenty-three now. Christina is just coming into her beauty. Several artists would love to paint her, but she refuses to sit for pictures — even for the artists in her own family."

Slipping a hand into her side pocket, Christina felt the shape of her small spectacles tucked in a little tapestried bag. She generally wore them most of the day now, and it was true that she had grown thin and pale over the last few years. For all her brother's kind defense of her, she wondered if Edgar were right.

If she had become a dull little widow, bookish and prim, that was far better than the rebellious, wild girl she had been.

"No harm intended, sir. Some of you Blackburns have that fiery artistic temperament," Edgar remarked easily. "Your sister shares it, too, though she has a more academic bent."

John frowned and leaned on his cane, and Christina saw the pink stain of anger in his cheeks. Her brother, a striking young man

18

with glossy brown curls and an angelic face, rarely showed any bad temper, but she knew he disliked Edgar.

"Christina, you do not have to go to Dundrennan," John said.

"She will go if she cares about Walter's work," Edgar said.

"Uncle Walter?" Christina asked, turning.

Edgar nodded. "Someone else might overlook important details in this site. What of your uncle's research concerning King Arthur in Scotland? He was enamored of Sir Hugh MacBride's writings about the legends of Dundrennan. Think, my dear," Edgar urged. "An archaeological discovery in those hills could vindicate your uncle from his . . . ah, academic failures. And he has so little time left to him, sadly."

Christina caught her breath. Walter Carriston's theories of King Arthur's role in sixth-century Scotland, along with Arthurian links to Pictish tribes, had been ridiculed by Carriston's peers. A find of Pictish origin in the Strathclyde hills would add strength of proof to her uncle's lifework.

She straightened her shoulders. "You have a point about Uncle Walter," she conceded. "I will look at the site. I can keep away from Dundrennan House itself."

"Actually, Sir Aedan has invited our representative to stay there, sparing us hotel expenses, although we will tender the cost of your transportation. Do not worry about that painting, my dear," Edgar added. "It is part of the past, and it is best forgotten."

"Of course you're right," she agreed.

"Keep to your usual plain appearance, and no one will be the wiser. John," Edgar said, turning, "your sister will require an escort. I know you are free to go with her, having so few obligations currently." Edgar glanced at John's leg and cane.

John bristled. "I will gladly change my schedule for her."

"Thank you, John," Christina said.

While Edgar wrote a note for his secretary to arrange their transportation, Christina waited, her heart slamming. Dundrennan! She twisted her hands anxiously, dreading the sight of Stephen's beautiful picture again, with its unhappy memories.

Still, she felt an inner excitement, too. Perhaps curiosity compelled the scholar in her. The chance to uncover something ancient, to see and touch it, to learn more about it, was a plum indeed. Edgar knew her well in that regard.

"Sir Aedan thinks the site will yield nothing much," Edgar said. "I expect you to send word to me, of course. I will come as soon as I can arrange it."

Christina nodded, then turned away. Dread and anticipation swept through her, and the power of it made her hands tremble.

★ ★ ★

Startled awake, Sir Aedan Arthur Mac-Bride, baronet and laird of Dundrennan, bolted upright in his leather chair. Grasping at shifting reality, he soon recaptured it. The dream, which had seemed as real as life itself, faded swiftly.

That damned painting, he thought, had worked its way into his head while he dozed. Legends of briar maidens and Druid princes certainly had no place in his life, yet today had cluttered his dreams. Without glancing at the framed canvas over the mantelpiece, he shoved his fingers through his thick dark hair and tried to dispel a haunted feeling.

He never should have settled in the small business room off his bedroom to review the account ledgers. The air was too close and warm, the silence too deep, the columns of numbers too soporific. Imagination, given rein in sleep, had won.

Glancing at his pocket watch, he swore. Nearly time for tea. The ladies of Balmossie would fuss at him if he did not appear, to say nothing of the tempestuous reaction of their constant companion, Miss Thistle.

Unpleasant matters must be addressed with the ladies, issues that Aedan had postponed long enough. The preparations for the royal visit in October, which he dreaded more than welcomed, had made his life sheer hell. Now he must convince his charming but impractical kinswomen that the estate's finances could not support their continued enthusiasm for readying his house. He, too, wanted Dundrennan House restored to its full magnificence, but it was time for a stricter budget.

Before his father's death nearly a year ago, Aedan had promised to complete Sir Hugh MacBride's plans for Dundrennan. The famous poet, often called the Queen's own Highland bard, had gained an immortal reputation and a fortune writing epic poems of power and artistry — though a tad long and overblown for Aedan's own tastes, a fact he kept discreetly to himself.

Over the years, Sir Hugh had devoted time, passion, and cash funds to restoring and modernizing the family seat at Dundrennan. Refurbishing Dundrennan was an expensive longterm project, and after Sir Hugh's death, Aedan had discovered how much his father's fortune had dwindled. Yet the will specified that the work must be completed if Aedan was to keep the property.

Even with considerable funds drawn from his own accounts, Aedan found it difficult to repay the inherited debts. Honoring the tradesmen's fees incurred by his busy kinswomen proved an increasing challenge. The situation had to improve, or he stood to lose a great deal.

Rising, Aedan straightened his black brocade vest and snugged his dark blue neck-cloth, then slid into his black coat, settling the lapels. He brushed at the mud stains on his clothing, certain that his Aunt Lillias — Lady Balmossie — and his second cousin, Amy Stewart, would fret over his appearance. Dust and spatters were a daily result of his occupation as a civil engineer and builder of highways and byways in Scotland.

He sighed, feeling displaced somehow. Then he realized he felt an emotional residue from the dream, a keen pain of longing. The undercurrent spun in his gut, a yearning for something unfulfilled, like love.

Love. He huffed, low and bitter. For the lairds of Dundrennan, love was a waste of time — even a danger. He had fallen in love once, before he had become laird, but that had ended in tragedy. The Dundrennan curse lay square upon his shoulders now, continuing from the days of the first Aedan of Dundrennan to the current day.

True love had not done that ancient fellow any good, he mused, thinking of the legend of the princess lost in the briar.

A remnant of his dream returned: a woman's sleeping face, his hand upon her brow, desperation rife in him. He had actually been the ancient warrior from Dundrennan's legend, willing to do anything to save his princess. And she had been . . .

Absurdly, he had dreamed of the young

woman in the painting. Desire — a soul-deep longing — still burned in him like an ember.

Too much worry and too little sleep had brought it on, he told himself. He would have the gilt-framed thing moved elsewhere, and improve both work and rest.

Slamming shut the ledger with its frustrating numbers, he sighed. Nothing would improve those figures. The time had come to put his foot down with the ladies of Balmossie. For a start, he would suggest wall paint instead of hand-painted Irish wallpapers; he would point out that the old Turkish rugs, though worn, lent more character than acres of new plaid carpeting.

He must tell them, as well, that a museum representative would arrive on Thursday to stay at Dundrennan House while investigating the recent discovery on the nearby hill, Cairn Drishan, at the edge of Dundrennan's policies.

Two weeks earlier, Aedan and his crew had been working on the parliamentary highway that was to go over the slope of Cairn Drishan. Although Aedan's heart broke to cut through his own land, he understood the benefits of improvements in Scotland — an issue about which he and his father had often argued.

That day, the use of black powder had revealed dark stones protruding from the hillside cut like decayed teeth. Aedan and his foreman and assistant had uncovered part of an extensive stone foundation in the hill. Although he hoped the walls dated to the last fifty years or so, some deeper sense told him that the structure was much older.

If so, due to a provision in his father's will, he could very well lose Dundrennan in its entirety.

New or old, the discovery had to be examined by a representative of the national museum, according to a recent law of Treasure Trove, before road construction could continue. Frustrated by his father's legacy and delayed in his work for the Parliamentary Commission for the Department of Roads and Highways, Aedan had no choice but to comply with the museum's investigation.

Sighing, he flipped through the jumble of papers on his desk, and picked up a letter written by Sir Edgar Neaves of the National Museum. The man had informed Aedan that he was not free to come to Dundrennan yet, but would send a competent assistant, an antiquarian named Mrs. Blackburn.

Any old fuss-pot would do in Neaves's place, Aedan thought.

The man's covetous interest in the historical collections and objets d'art at Dundrennan House was more than annoying, it was disturbing. When and if Neaves did arrive himself, Aedan would instruct his housekeeper to lock up the plate and hide the keys.

25

Scowling, tossed the letter down and turned toward the door. Then he slowed, and approached the fireplace.

Centered over the mantel, the oil painting showed a young woman reclining among a scattering of wild pink roses. Her classic features and her graceful hands were peaceful, her skin was creamy, and her hair was a rippled auburn cascade. The translucent folds of her white chemise, touched with lavender and butter yellow in the folds, hinted at the pink fullness of her breasts and the sinuous curves of her body. Precisely detailed, its colors deep and rich, the painting seemed to glow.

The tiny brass plaque on the frame caught his eye: *The Enchanted Briar, Stephen Blackburn, 1852.* Any work by a member of the prolific, talented Blackburn family was a sound investment, and there were three such paintings in Dundrennan's art collection. Aedan had purchased this one at an exhibit at the Royal Scottish Academy in Edinburgh, not only because of the remarkable quality of the painting, but because the subject depicted Dundrennan's famous legend of the princess in the briar.

Aedan had hung the painting in his private rooms years ago, never admitting to anyone how deeply the image fascinated him, even haunted him.

That exquisite face and sensuous form seemed familiar to him now. She had become a soothing, alluring part of his life.

And now he had dreamed about her. That flaw in his solid practicality bothered him. Obsession and dreaming were for poets like his father, not engineers like himself.

He shoved his hands in his pockets, frowning. Tranquil and lovely, sensual and disturbing, at first glance the picture was all roses and luscious femininity. But the thorny mesh beneath the flowers added a subtle, wicked element. Each time he gazed at it, the painting seemed to seduce him.

She seduced him.

He rocked back on low boot heels. A force swept through him fast as a tide, leaving a trace of longing on the shore of his soul. God, how he wanted her, needed her. And she did not exist.

Stepping back, he shook his head. He would not indulge in fancies. His brilliant, idealistic father had made a fortune writing passionate epic poetry beloved by many. Pragmatism was sorely needed at Dundrennan now, and Aedan was its sole source.

Hanging the picture here had been a mistake, Aedan decided. The image was too dominant for this small room — no wonder it had invaded his dreams. He should consign it to some corner in this enormous folly of a house. Even better, he should sell it and pay off some of his father's debts.

But he could never part with it. He had

fallen in love, a little, with that briar-caught maiden. Part of him wanted to keep her near him forever.

Turning on his heel, he left the room.

Chapter Two

Gables and turrets rose above a ring of trees, a fairy-tale profile in honey stone. Looking out of the coach, Christina felt oddly as if she moved from her own time into an enchanted realm where objects were formed from the gossamer of dreams, and life was filled with wonder.

Fairy tales did not exist, she reminded herself sternly, and the open carriage was traveling far too fast to be a dream coach. Its breathless pace barely allowed a good view of the hills and moorland or Dundrennan House, which rose above some trees in the distance. And the light was already fading into twilight.

A brisk ride in an open carriage had left Christina breathless and unkempt. Strands of her auburn hair slipped loose from its thick knot, her cheeks were wind-stung, her gray skirt rumpled, and her steel-rimmed eyeglasses had slid down her slender nose. She pushed them up out of habit and looked around.

As the vehicle careened around another

steep curve, Christina gripped the inner door loop and leaned with the sway.

Through the twilight she glimpsed heather-bright hills and sweeping moors. Clamping a gloved hand to her black bonnet, its satin ribbons fluttering, she glanced at her brother.

John sat beside her, his left leg stretched out for comfort. He too held fast to his hat brim, but he smiled and seemed relaxed, clearly enjoying the reckless speed of the ride.

Then, jutting above a ring of trees, she saw towers, turrets, and balustraded roofs. As the carriage passed through open iron gates, Christina saw the house clearly at last.

All golden stone, blue slate roofs, and sleepy windows, the house blended medieval and later styles behind a façade of honey sandstone. The foundations were swathed in rosebushes scattered with pink blossoms, and more flowers filled a garden visible behind the house. A dense greenwood surrounded both gardens and house, and the arch of a church was visible in the distance.

Looking at the rose hedges and trees around the lovely old house, Christina thought of a protective briar around a fairy-tale castle, impossible to penetrate without magic.

Sitting forward, she felt her heart quicken in anticipation.

"Oh, my, they're here," the housekeeper

said, as Aedan encountered her in an upstairs hallway. Mary Gunn drew aside the lace curtain of the window overlooking the entrance and peered out. "The lady looks a bonny wee lass, and the gentleman is braw and fine!"

"Bonny wee lass?" Aedan asked. "Neaves is sending an antiquarian from the museum, but from what he said, I thought she would be an elderly sort, with a companion." Aedan had given it little attention, just glad to be spared Neaves's company.

"A young lassie, and she looks habbled by the wind. Auld Tam always drives like a madman." Mrs. Gunn's blue eyes sparked, and her face flushed beneath a lace cap with old-fashioned lappets.

Curious, Aedan approached, his boots quiet on the carpet. Mrs. Gunn stood back as he looked down over the graveled drive.

Tam Durie, the driver, lifted out some baggage with the help of a groom, while a gentleman in a bowler hat and umber jacket stepped from an open carriage with the aid of a cane. He turned to assist his companion, a woman, from the carriage.

In the lengthening twilight shadows, she looked slender and graceful in gray and black. Tucking stray wisps of curls under her black bonnet, she glanced up at the house.

She was indeed younger than Aedan had expected, and quite pleasant to behold, her face serene and lovely. He saw the surprising glint of spectacles on her nose.

Pewter-colored skirts billowed, full and plain, devoid of the flounces and fussy bits favored by his cousins. Wind stirred her short black cape and shivered the ribbons of her bonnet, tied over glossy dark hair. She was a vision of simplicity and grace.

The odd notion that he had seen her before pricked at him. Perhaps they had met at some soiree in Edinburgh or Glasgow. He and Sir Edgar knew a few people in common, including one or two artists called Blackburn — but he was sure he would have remembered this delicate, bespectacled young woman.

"A wee bit lass, as I told ye." Behind him, Mrs. Gunn peered down with vivid interest. "Is that her husband, I wonder?"

"I do not know," he murmured, frowning slightly. The young woman turned toward her male companion, her hand upon his arm. "Gunnie, since it's quite late, and Aunt Lill and Miss Amy are not here to act the hostesses, perhaps you would show the guests to their rooms. They can have a quiet supper and a chance to rest from their journey. The morning will suffice for introductions. Besides, I have a good deal of work to do in my study tonight."

"Very well, sir. Lady Balmossie and Miss Amy will ride over from Balmossie Castle in the morning, likely with that wicked Miss Thistle. The last time she was here, she hit me on the head with a sugar spoon," she complained.

"Thistle is dangerous at teatime," Aedan agreed.

Mrs. Gunn huffed. "Aye, well, let yer guests meet the dafties all at once, and have done with it."

Aedan smothered a smile. "It may be best."

"Mr. Stewart will be here, too, with his new bride, but they're nae so daftie as the rest." Mary Gunn's blue eyes twinkled. Aedan's widowed fourth cousin had served as housekeeper at Dundrennan for thirty years, and he had known her since he had been a small lad in skirts, before his mother had died. He could not imagine his household without Gunnie's competent, inquisitive presence. "Well, then. I'll go greet them and ask one of the Jeanies to bring them some supper, how's that?" Mrs. Gunn said.

"Very good." As Aedan watched, the young woman tilted her head to look up at the window. "My God," he murmured.

Seeing the exquisite, familiar curve of her cheek and the line of her throat, he felt as if he took a blow to the midsection. He had dreamed endlessly of that face.

Was he mad? Could she be the girl who had posed for the painting he owned? Her

33

name was Blackburn, he remembered quickly. The artist had been a Blackburn as well, and the model for the painting had been his wife — widow, now, he corrected himself, for that fellow had died a few years ago.

Heart slamming, he tried to dispell the astonishment of seeing her. The girl peered upward through her spectacles, and Aedan felt a sudden, unmistakable tug as their gazes met.

Dear God, he thought. Eyeglasses, black bonnet, plain dress and all, he knew her. Would know her anywhere.

"Oh, my," Mrs. Gunn said. "That lass looks . . . och, me, she's the one in that painting!" She clapped her hand on her broad bosom. "And the artist was a Blackburn, too! Och, me!"

"We do not know that she is the one," Aedan murmured.

"Are ye blind? What a kerfuffle this is! The ladies will be heart-roasted to have an . . . *artist's model* in this house, sir! *Heart-roasted!*"

He frowned at the flourishing drama of her reaction. "No need to decide too hastily what this Mrs. Blackburn is about."

"Och, if she's an artist's model, I can tell ye what she's aboot," Mrs. Gunn said ominously.

None of the pictures in the hallway showed

a half-naked princess on a flowery bed, Christina noted with relief as she and John followed Mrs. Gunn through a warren of upstairs corridors.

Mrs. Gunn showed John to his room first, then bustled onward, Christina in her wake. The walls were painted a warm pinkish color above dark polished wainscoting, Oriental rugs covered planked floors, and oil lamps gleamed on gilt-framed paintings — portraits, landscapes, and historical scenes, Christina realized, though she had no time to study them.

"Yer room is along here, Mrs. Blackburn," the housekeeper said. "It's in the oldest section of the house. 'Tis verra quiet here, and I thought ye might like to be near the library, being antiquated and all."

"Antiquarian," Christina said. "It's a wonderful house."

"Aye." The housekeeper stood back to allow Christina to enter first, then followed. "I think Andrew brought up yer baggage — aye, 'tis there on that bench," she commented. "I'll send one of the Jeanies to help ye unpack."

"Oh, what a lovely room." Christina turned. Snug and inviting, the bedchamber glowed with firelight. Floral draperies, bed hangings, and wallpaper complemented the faded patterned carpets, and an ivory counterpane swathed a four-poster bed. An old stone fireplace crackled with the sweetish, musty odor of peat. The window overlooked Dundrennan's policies, and through it Christina saw a far ridge of hills fading into the deepening twilight. "Wonderful. Thank you."

Mrs. Gunn smiled. "We call this one the Irish room for the wallpaper, which was hand-stamped in Ireland, long afore so many souls went starving," she said. "Miss Amy — she's Sir Aedan's cousin — wants to take doon all the paper and oot wi' the rugs, and cover tartan over everything. Sir Aedan says there's enough Scotchness in this bonny house, and so the Irish stuff stays."

"I like it very much just this way," Christina said.

" 'Tis a bonny house. Sir Hugh MacBride had grand plans for the place, but . . . well, he died afore the work was finished, and Sir Aedan is doing the best he can."

"It must be a great deal of work to keep this grand house."

"Aye, work and expense, but we love it. Is the fire lit in yer sitting room?" Mrs. Gunn peered into a tiny adjoining chamber that held two stuffed armchairs upholstered in worn red damask set upon a threadbare Oriental rug. "Aye." The little fireplace was cheerful, and a small window revealed the purple sky.

"This was a treasure room, long ago, where the lairds o' Dundrennan counted their gold," Mrs. Gunn explained. "There's a wee door behind the chair, see? It goes to the auld stair, which is dusty and dark, but ye can use it to go doon to the library anytime ye please, madam."

"Oh, I'd like that." Christina smiled.

"Just be careful in the dark. The laird and his brother shared this room when they were bairns, and they would take that stair to the great hall — the library, it is now — and off to the kitchens to steal a snap o' food at night from the stave-off cupboard. D'ye stay up late at night, that stave-off cupboard is a fine thing."

"Thank you. Sir Aedan has a brother? I suppose a very large family could live here in such an enormous house."

Mrs. Gunn sighed. "Only Sir Aedan now. Years ago, Sir Neil MacBride was the bonny heir o' Dundrennan, and Sir Aedan the youngest, with a sister atween them. But Sir Neil went wi' a Highland regiment to that war overseas. . . ." Mrs. Gunn frowned.

"The Crimean?" Christina asked.

"Aye, that's the one. Sir Aedan stayed at home, but Neil . . . ne'er came home." She sniffed, shook her head. "The grief set Sir Hugh on the road to his death and took something fine from Sir Aedan. He's nae the same man as he was then."

Christina felt a surge of compassion. "How sad. So much tragedy has come out of that war. My brother John was wounded there."

"The cane? Aye, I wondered. We lost others, too, tenants and so on. Sad, indeed. Well, one of the Jeanies will be here soon with yer supper and will fetch whatsoever ye'd like."

"Thank you, Mrs. Gunn."

"There's a bath, and a water closet, too, across the hall. Sir Hugh had new lavatories added years back. A shower bath is in the bathroom, with hot and cold spigots," she said proudly.

"I'll enjoy that," Christina said. "Who are the Jeanies?"

"There's Bonnie Jean, the upper maid, and Sonsie Jean, wha does a bit o' everything, and Wee Jeanie in the kitchens. We've always called the housemaids Jeanie, and the grooms and gillies are all called Andrew at Dundrennan. It's our way here."

"What a curious custom!"

"Aye, but Sir Aedan wants it changed, along with other things. He uses their own names, but old habits die hard, I say. We had a grand staff here when Sir Hugh wrote his poetry. Now 'tis Sir Aedan alone, though the ladies o' Balmossie often visit. Ye'll meet them tomorrow. I'll send Sonsie Jean to help ye dress, since ye didna bring yer own lass." Mrs. Gunn drew a long breath.

"I have no lady's maid," Christina admitted. "I live with my uncle and aunt in a small house, with only two servants, so I do for my-self in most things. If I need something, I'll ring the bell for . . . Sonsie Jean, is it?"

"Och, dinna ring the bell! I'd startle so! We dinna ring the bell here! Sir Aedan and Sir Neil did once when they were lads, and then they hid in a cupboard, those rascals. But I found 'em and chased 'em, and that were the end o' the bell-ringing!"

Christina laughed. "I promise never to pull the bell."

"Just come oot the room and call," Mrs. Gunn said. "We'll hear ye. Lady Balmossie shouts like a fishwife."

Christina tried not to smile. "I'll do my best."

"Tonight ye'll sup here, but other nights we'll have a fine dinner party, especially if the ladies o' Balmossie are here too. Though ye may have supper in yer room whenever ye like."

"Thank you. I expect that my brother and I will be here only a few days, but your wonderful hospitality is much appreciated."

The housekeeper narrowed her eyes thoughtfully. "That one's yer brother and ye live quietlike wi' yer uncle, ye say?"

"Yes, he is a kirk minister. My brother lives with our father in Edinburgh, but I now assist my uncle with his studies."

"Aye? But ye're a married lady by your name."

"I am widowed of my second cousin, who had the same name."

"Och, so young! I was widowed young, too. *Tch,* puir lass." She tilted her head. "D'ye have a sister, or . . . mebbe a twin?"

"A twin?" Christina frowned at the odd question. "I have a sister and two brothers, all painters."

"Aha, the sister is an artist! That must be it. Good night, mistress." Nodding, the housekeeper left the room.

Puzzling over the housekeeper's remark, Christina went to the window to gaze at the gardens. Soon Sonsie Jean, an elfin, red-haired serving girl with a breathless and pleasant manner, brought her a supper tray with a simple, good meal of hot broth, cold meats, and fresh bread.

Afterward, she sat down with a book in the little sitting room but soon dozed. She dreamed that she climbed a steep, heathered hill at night, toward a high tower that seemed made of bronze and silver. In a small window high up, she saw a girl looking outside, and curiously knew that the girl was herself.

A man approached the girl through translucent moonbeams, and took her into his embrace.

Christina awoke with a strange sense of longing. Unable to get back to sleep, she unpacked her things, and sat reading her own well-thumbed copy of Sir Hugh MacBride's early poems until nearly midnight, judging by the little clock on the mantel.

She felt eager to explore the hillside, which she hoped she could do the next day. Before leaving for Dundrennan, she had not found time to research its local history, but now she remembered that Mrs. Gunn had invited her to use the library if she wanted.

Thinking of Sir Hugh's extensive collection of books, she felt greatly tempted. Mrs. Gunn had said that the medieval stairway, just off her little sitting room, led directly to the old great hall, now the library.

Dare she go there tonight? Quiet reigned over the sleeping household, so she would not disturb anyone. She could find a book on Dundrennan's history, and return to her room unnoticed.

Earlier she had put on her dressing gown, but she quickly changed into a blouse, a dark skirt and flannel petticoats, and added a shawl, for the drafts in the old house were chilly. She slid into her black dancing slippers, which were comfortable and would be quiet as she moved about the house.

Taking up a flaming candle in its brass dish, she opened the narrow door, its hinges creaking, and looked into a dark abyss that smelled of must, stone, and disuse.

The pool of candlelight revealed stone steps curving around a slim central pillar. Christina drew up her skirts with one hand, balanced the brass dish in the other, and descended.

The narrow, wedge-shaped steps fanned steeply downward, and she moved carefully in the darkness. Since her room was on the third level, she guessed that the library must be on the second or even the first level, but she saw no door as yet. Moments later, she heard a squeak, and felt, over her foot, the breezy passage of what was surely a mouse.

Gasping, she jerked, and her thin sole skidded on smooth, worn stone. She reached out for the wall, losing her grip on the candle dish, and recovered her footing, but the brass dish clattered away, extinguishing. Blackness engulfed her.

Muttering under her breath, she turned to inch back up the steps. Hampered by her skirts, the darkness, and the steep, oddly shaped steps, she missed her footing again and fell hard to one knee. Gathering her skirts, she stepped upward, but tilted and then tumbled helplessly into the inky pit behind her.

Half sliding down the steps, bumping and turning, her shoulder and head knocked painfully against the wall, and her hip struck the edge of a step. Somehow she managed to slow her descent and soon collapsed in a breathless heap on a stone platform that felt blessedly large and squarish in shape.

Groaning, she sat up a little, then winced,

for her back and shoulder ached, and her head spun wickedly. She leaned against the wall and touched her head with a shaking hand.

A latch clicked, a light bloomed golden, and a man emerged from a doorway. Exclaiming softly, he crouched and reached for her. Strong, gentle hands took her shoulders.

"My dear girl," he murmured. "Are you hurt?"

Chapter Three

Woozy, uncertain, Christina wondered if she had been knocked cold and now dreamed, for she looked into the face of a warrior angel, and felt his arms harden around her.

Various small aches and pains soon told her that she was awake, and another glance proved that he was a man after all.

He was handsome enough to startle, with the strong, beautiful bone structure of a pure Celt, and a touch of thunder in his snapping blue eyes and in his straight, black brows, drawn together in a frown beneath a thick wave of raven black hair.

"Are you hurt?" he asked again.

"I'm fine." She winced and tried to sit up.

"Stay still," he ordered. "What the devil were you doing in this old stairwell? Don't move. Take a breath."

"I'm fine." She shifted awkwardly, feeling a sharp pain in her shoulder. "I'll just go back to my room — oh," she said, as she moved and her head swam. "Oh, my. Perhaps I'll sit here for a moment." She leaned against the

44

warm, powerful curve of his arm.

"Take all the time you need," he said.

Without a doubt, she was the girl in the painting. Her face was identical, though she seemed smaller and more fragile in person. Fascinated, Aedan studied her. If she had not modeled for that image, then she had a sensual, beautiful twin.

Behind spectacles framed in blue steel, her eyes were wide and beautiful. He had long wondered at their color: silky hazel, ringed in black lashes. Her overall appearance was demure and modest, not at all like the tantalizing, earthy goddess of the picture. But her graceful features, her lush lips, the long curve of her neck, all matched the model of that painting.

She sighed and leaned her head against his upper arm. A pulse beat under the creamy skin of her throat. Her lovely face, her swanlike neck, and her auburn hair spilling from its pins, she was the living image of the painting.

A little imagination brought to mind the exquisite details of breasts tipped pink beneath translucent fabric, the gentle swell of hips and abdomen, the long, smooth length of her thighs, all scarcely veiled from sight in the painting.

More than simple lust blazed through him in that instant. He felt a desperate, burning need to hold her, to save her, to love her. Leaning forward, he came close enough that her breath caressed his lips.

For one wild moment, he closed his eyes and very nearly kissed her.

She gasped softly, and he jerked back, saving himself from acting a damned fool. The urge still rushed through him, fervent and hot. Never had he felt such a shivering heat, like a deep force pulling at him. He actually trembled in its aftermath.

He cleared his throat. "I know everyone else in my house, but not you. Therefore, you must be the lady sent by the museum."

"I am . . . Mrs. Blackburn. Christina Blackburn."

"Welcome to Dundrennan, Mrs. Blackburn. I am Sir Aedan MacBride, laird of Dundrennan."

She blinked. "Oh! Sir Aedan!" She tried to sit up again.

"Relax." He grasped her shoulder to keep her still. "You are not quite ready for stair climbing."

"Perhaps not. Please forgive me for inconveniencing you, Sir Aedan. I only meant to go to the library this way — Mrs. Gunn said it would be all right — but I fell. I do apologize."

"Not at all. Had I known, I would have ordered the sconces lit in the stairwell. Generally only I use it. Can you stand, Mrs.

Blackburn?" He rose, keeping hold of her arm.

Lifting to her feet, she faltered, wincing.

"You're in no condition to go up or down, my lass," he murmured, and bent to scoop her up into his arms. She felt slender and fit beneath layers of clothing, and he picked her up effortlessly.

"Really, sir, I'm fine," she protested.

He shifted her against his chest, and she circled an arm around his shoulders. "That was a nasty fall, Mrs. Blackburn. Come inside. I want to be sure you're uninjured before you go wandering anywhere else tonight."

Mortified, Christina rode silently in his arms as he carried her over the threshold into a small, lamplit room. Her head ached, as did her shoulder and hip, and she was grateful for the reassuring strength of his arms.

His face was close to hers, his scent a pleasant mix of spice, wine, shirt starch, and subtle, earthy masculinity. Dressed in a white collarless shirt and a dark vest and dark trousers, the hardness of his torso pressed against her softer curves. She could feel the heat of her own blush, unseen in the dimness.

The room was similar in shape and function to her own little sitting room, although it contained one armchair and a desk. An oil lamp on the desk surface revealed an untidy pile of papers and open books. The fireplace housed a cozy peat fire. Sir Aedan MacBride set her in the leather armchair, her back to the hearth.

"Really, I am fine. I must go." She rose, and pain sliced through her hip and shoulder. Sir Aedan guided her down with a firm hand on her shoulder.

"Not so fine as she claims," he said, kneeling beside the chair. His earnest concern, his nearness, thrilled her unaccountably. He was a stranger, yet he seemed familiar somehow, and she found his quiet, relaxed, confident manner engaging.

"Really, I must go," she said reluctantly. "I should not be in your . . . private sitting room." Through a second door, she saw a bedroom with a canopied bed, its covers folded back, pillows plumped. A dark dressing robe lay on the bed. "This is very improper."

"More improper to send you away limping," he said. "No one need know about this but us, madam." His voice was low, his glance penetrating.

She subsided in the chair, and he dropped to his haunches to look up at her. Firelight flowed over him, and his eyes were dark blue and sparkling.

"Mrs. Blackburn, tell me where you are hurt, if you will."

She relented, shrugged. "My . . . left shoulder."

His hand slid up her arm, his fingers tracing over her shoulder, pressing lightly. Something elemental tumbled inside of her, and all she could do, when he asked what she felt, was nod dumbly or shake her head in silence. Withdrawing along her arm, he took her hand to move her fingers one by one.

Something wonderful surged through her, and her hurts seemed to lessen wherever he touched her. Feeling her cheeks heat like fire, she watched the grace of his hands upon her.

"Nothing seems broken. Where else does it hurt, madam?"

"My . . . head," she whispered. "And my . . ." She could hardly tell him that her hip and bottom felt bruised. "My . . . leg."

"I have a sister and female cousins. I've tended to twisted ankles before, without scandal, I assure you." He smiled.

She extended one foot, and he pushed her skirts above her ankle. Sliding his fingers over her foot, he flexed it gently. Shivers cascaded all through her.

"Those slippers," he murmured, "are not suited to a medieval staircase."

"So I learned," she answered, setting her foot down.

"Your head hurts, too?" he asked. She nodded, and he spread his fingers in a cap over her head, probing. She nearly groaned with the sweet pleasure of it. When his arm brushed over her blouse, her breasts tingled, tightened.

"Oh," she breathed.

"Does something else hurt?" He glanced at her.

"Oh, no," she murmured.

"There is a bump on your head, but all seems well, though I am no doctor. No doubt you'll feel some bruising for a few days." He rested his hand on her shoulder.

Even the simplest of his touches stirred a craving in her, a ready rush of desire. She had not felt like that in a long time. His warm hands, the rhythm of his breaths, the clean male smell of him, all tapped a well-spring of need in her. Sucking in a breath, she leaned away, knowing those feelings came from her lonely, aching, foolish heart.

She began to stand. "I really must go. Thank you, sir."

"Wait. I do not want you climbing those stairs just yet." Willingly, she sank into the chair again, glad for an excuse to remain, to feel his delightful, relaxing touch again.

"You'll need to rest tomorrow and use soothing packs on those aches, I think," he said.

She shook her head. "I came here to work, and I plan to go to the hillside in the morning. I'm fine, Sir Aedan."

"Stubborn lass." He rose beside her. "You could have broken your neck on the stairs in the dark, wearing those cumbersome skirts and little slippers. What was so important that you took the stairs alone, and at this hour?"

"I could not sleep, and I often study or read late at night, so I thought to fetch something from the library about the local history and geography before seeing the hill tomorrow. I'm sorry to be such trouble, sir. Thank you again." She stepped past him, wincing and stiff, feeling embarrassed and a little regretful, too, for she had enjoyed the quiet intimacy of their encounter.

Turning toward the door, she stopped, gasping.

The painting hung over the fireplace. She had not noticed it until now. Heart pounding, she gazed up at her own image.

She had forgotten what a masterpiece it was, exquisitely rendered, a passion of luminous color and sensuous shape, poignant and powerful. Lamplight and shadows heightened its astonishing dark grace.

"Dear God," she whispered.

He stood behind her. "You haven't changed."

So he knew. She turned to stare at him. "I wondered if it was here. Stephen said that he had sold it to the MacBrides of Dundrennan."

51

"Stephen Blackburn was a kinsman of yours?"

"He was my late husband," she said quietly.

"Ah." He nodded. "My condolences."

She tipped her head in gracious silence.

"I never met the artist. I bought the painting through the Royal Academy shortly after it was exhibited."

"That was just before he . . . died." Although she felt his steady gaze, she could not look at him. Tilting her head, she studied the painting.

"I was so much younger then. And a bit embonpoint," she added, looking up at her lush, rounded form in the painting.

"Not at all. Curvaceous and alluring, certainly. She is a beautiful young lass."

"A foolish young lass." She turned away. Sir Aedan stopped her with a hand to her elbow. Odd how his touch seemed so natural to her, she thought. So did being alone with him, although it was scandalous for her to allow any of it. But his touch felt right, so good, God forgive her.

"Do you dislike the painting?"

"It — reminds me of an unpleasant time in my life. But that was long ago."

"It's dated but six years ago. Not so far in the past."

"Farther than you can imagine." She felt a curious urge to cry. She lifted her head. "I've aged, changed."

"I would say that the model has only gained in beauty." A smile quirked his lips as he watched her.

"Oh, no, she's far plainer now."

"Hardly. Let me see. May I?" He slid free her eyeglasses and laid them aside.

Blinking at him, surprised, she did not protest. She wanted, selfishly perhaps, to hear his thoughts. Her vision softened around the edges but for his face, so close to hers. Studying him, she thought again of a protective angel, darkly beautiful, powerful in form and countenance.

He glanced from the framed painting back to her. "The earlier version has a pleasing roundness in the limbs, and the features are the same — elegantly classic. Yet the later version . . ." He touched her jaw with his fingers as if she were a statue and he an art critic. But her heart leaped.

"The later version?" she asked.

"Shh. I see a refinement in face and figure — some might call it slenderness — that enhances the graceful bone structure. The first version is lush and wild, but the second version has a strong and honest beauty . . . a vibrancy . . . that is far more attractive, though quietly so, than the first image."

"I do not know what you mean," she whispered. Spellbound, she felt no urge to escape or to stop him. Her pulse quickened as he tilted her cheek with his finger. "The first image has an innocence and wildness, but there is something . . . sad in the second. A caution in the eyes, a wariness in the mouth." His fingertip glided over her bottom lip.

She thought her knees would falter. "Yes, caution," she said in a spicy tone. "Afraid you might try to kiss me."

"Shall I?" His fingers stilled on her chin.

She stared at him, then roused herself. "Do not press your good fortune, sir."

"Shall I go on?" he asked.

She nodded, feeling as if they played a dangerous, delicious, secret game.

"The girl in the painting is a sensual creature, yet immature. She knows love but not . . . life. She's lost and tragic."

"She's a tragic princess," she said. "From the story."

"Aye, but the first image has something the latter does not. A sort of . . . blissfulness."

"Happiness," she blurted. "She was happy then, for a little while. She was adored." She knew she sounded wistful.

"Ah. And now?" His fingers traced her cheek.

Caught by his sultry magic, she closed her eyes, felt swamped by loneliness. Then she forced herself out of it, yanked her heart back, stepped away.

"I'm sorry," she said. "This was a mistake."

He picked up her spectacles, handed them to her. "She hides herself in the later version, I think."

"How silly." She straightened the metal frames on her nose. "A fun little game, like an *après-diner* amusement."

"Perhaps I shall suggest it to my Cousin Amy, who loves that sort of thing. She will have us scrutinizing everyone over coffee and brandy. Mrs. Blackburn, you did not tell me your assessment of the two versions." He folded his arms, regarded her.

"One is a painted rendition of a sleeping beauty," she said crisply. "A vision of innocence and untried passion. The other . . . is a plain and rather dull woman. All they have in common is the shape of the face, the color of the hair."

"You do not know, do you."

"Know what?"

"How lovely you are."

The words hung in the air. She glanced away. "I cannot compare to the girl in that painting. She is a confection, made from an approximation of my features and a lot of paint and fancy. She makes me seem beautiful for one moment in my life."

His steady gaze, the crinkling around his eyes, showed how carefully he listened. Already she felt that she understood his subtle expressions — a tilt of the head, a tightening of the lips, a flicker in the eyes. He seemed bemused and sympathetic.

"You need a new mirror, Mrs. Blackburn. You are every bit as lovely as that painting. More so. And I know, for I have enjoyed that painting for years."

She bristled, gathered her skirts. "Perhaps you like being closeted alone with a picture of a scantily robed woman. Many men enjoy that kind of thing, I suppose. Good night, Sir Aedan." She moved past him.

One long step placed him between her and the door. He leaned against it, folded his arms. "I meant to say that I greatly admire everything in that painting. Damn," he swore, shaking his head. "It does not sound right no matter how I word it."

She laughed in spite of herself. "Thank you. But the picture was never meant to be seen by anyone other than . . . my husband. He was not to exhibit it or sell it, but he broke his word to me. I cannot change the fact that you own it, unless you were to sell it to me. And I doubt I could afford it."

"I would never sell that painting. It means too much to me."

"I am sure it does. Please let me pass, sir." She sidestepped, for he still blocked her way.

"Before you storm out of here, all righteous fire and cold indignation, hear me out." He frowned down at her. "I am no lecher, Mrs. Blackburn, who bought a picture of a lady in her nightdress to appease some pru-

56

rient interest." He stepped toward her, resolute and close, and she went back, until her skirts crushed against the desk. "Nor do I think your morals or modesty are in question because you posed for that, once upon a time."

She sensed his anger and felt her own keenly. "Why hide this painting in your private rooms? Why do you even own it? And why do you . . . look . . . at me like that?" The words flew out.

"How is that?"

"As if you . . . care for me and would . . ."

"Kiss you?"

She watched him, then nodded slowly. He leaned toward her.

For a moment she thought he might indeed kiss her. She saw the intent flash clearly in his eyes and in the downward glance that took in her lips.

Feeling as if she were under some dreamy power, she leaned toward him and closed her eyes.

Her lips brushed his, warm and astonishing. She did not know who had touched first, but she let her lips move under his. Surely she dreamed. Her head whirled. Sliding her hand up his arm, she stepped in closer, drawn by some magical force, like sunlight spilling through storm clouds.

When she thought he would pull away, his

lips caressed hers, teased, drank deeper. His hand moved to cup her cheek, and a power that she could not stop filled her with the wild, raw ache of passion, long denied, bursting full. She gasped, and wanted to weep for the tenderness, the richness of the moment, for the sheer beauty of it.

His mouth parted from hers, and she sank against him, weak suddenly, trembling and stunned. He drew her to him.

"My dear lass," he murmured, his arm around her shoulders, "we must get you upstairs to rest."

"Sir," she said, gasping for breath. "I am not — please do not think me — because of the painting —"

"Not at all, Mrs. Blackburn," he said, guiding her toward the door. He reached for a candle, and they stepped out onto the landing. "My fault entirely. I am convinced that you are the most proper of ladies, caught in a rather odd circumstance."

"How very true," she murmured, and stepped out into the stairwell again, with even greater care this time.

He wanted to kiss her again, to never stop. Desire drove hard through him, startling in its demand, but he fought it fiercely, welcoming cool reason and his customary shielding of self and heart. He escorted her politely up the stairs, but felt like a thorough cad.

He was at a loss to explain what had come over him, simply because he had come face-to-face with the model of a painting he particularly admired. He was not one to give rein to imagination.

"Here is your door, Mrs. Blackburn. Good night," he said as they reached the higher landing. He forced himself to sound especially cool and reserved.

The girl had stirred him too deeply, come too damn close to touching dreams and pain. The only woman he had ever yearned to love stood before him now — and his longing was only a fancy.

As the laird of Dundrennan, he could never allow himself to risk the enduring passion of genuine love. According to the old Dundrennan curse, that was dangerous — particularly for the woman to whom the laird gave his heart.

"Good night, then," he said, inclining his head.

Christina adjusted her spectacles, frowning as she gazed at him. "Good night, Sir Aedan." Her eyes seemed full of yearning.

God, how he wanted to kiss her again. Falling in love had nothing to do with it, he told himself. One kiss could dissolve the spell that the woman in the painting held over him, and that Mrs. Blackburn seemed to share. With one more kiss he could prove that he felt only lust, and nothing more, for her.

"Well," he said, and he cleared his throat. "If you want to take these stairs again, be careful not to wear those dainty slippers. Though they are fetching," he added. "But I might not be here to help you the next time."

Her chin lifted. "I can take care of myself."

"No doubt," he murmured. Nodding in silence, he waited until she went into her room, then he turned and went back down the stairs.

For years her image had fascinated him, but the painting was a pale reflection of the model herself. Mrs. Blackburn might hide behind spectacles and sober colors, but he sensed real fire in her, and compelling sensuality in her wounded, smoldering gaze.

Suddenly he knew that he wanted to do far more than kiss her. He wanted to be the man who awakened the enchantress she hid inside. Loving Christina Blackburn would be rare and ecstatic, he thought — the sort of love that would last forever, days spinning into years, into a lifetime of passion and joy, fulfillment and companionship.

But loving like that was a risk he could never afford.

Chapter Four

A saucer hurtled past his shoulder, pale porcelain gleaming, to shatter against the wall. Aedan swept the toe of one black boot over the shards, recognizing a hand-painted view of the Great Exhibition of a few years earlier.

"Crystal Palace," he said.

"Not the one with the queen on it, I hope." His cousin Amy turned, a length of flowered fabric in her hands.

"The one with Prince Albert." Aedan glanced at the women in the room, Lady Balmossie seated, Amy Stewart standing beside her brother Dougal's bride, the renowned beauty Lady Strathlin — or Meg, as she had asked her new family to call her. The two young women stood holding yards of chintz between them. The cloth flowed over their belled skirts like a stream of cabbage roses.

"Oh, dear, Aunt Lillias gave that tea set to your father," Amy said. "A pity to lose a piece of it. Knickknacks and memorabilia lend such charm and tradition to a home."

"And images of the monarch are so verra

61

cheering to the spirit." His father's sister, Lillias — Lady Balmossie — peered at him from her place on the sofa. She leaned to pick up her embroidery in its hand frame and smiled at him, cheeks dimpling and lace cap bobbing, black taffeta skirt rustling as she moved.

"Cousin Aedan will have no nice things left at Dundrennan if Miss Thistle is allowed to run about." Amy turned in her flounced lavender gown just as a silver spoon sailed past her blond head and dropped to the floor.

"Miss Thistle, ye must cease tossing the whigmaleeries aboot!" Lady Balmossie snapped without looking up from her embroidery.

Perched on the arm of a chair, Miss Thistle chattered loudly in reply, showed her small teeth, then reached for another dish from the tea tray. Aedan took an abrupt warning step toward the little monkey. She retreated hastily, tail swirling beneath the frills of her peach satin gown.

"She misbehaves so," Amy complained.

Aedan gathered the saucer shards in his handkerchief and set them on a table with the spoon. "Thistle, fling the pewter instead. It will only dent up a bit."

"You missed tea again yesterday, Aedan," Amy said. "We waited it for you, but Aunt Lill was famished for her sweets." She pouted prettily, and Aedan mused that her gift of

62

true charm made her minor flaws, such as poutiness and willfulness, tolerable.

"Business at the work site, dear cousin," he said mildly.

Amy came near to brush dirt from his sleeve. "You should not work like a laborer. You are laird of an ancient estate now."

"A day's labor is honest means for many Highland men. And I use a shovel only now and then to help my crew."

"We did not see your guests at breakfast," Amy said. "Mrs. Gunn said they arrived last night."

"Most people take their breakfast a little earlier than you, Amy." Aedan smiled. "I didn't see the guests myself at breakfast, but I went early with Tam to fetch Dougal and his bride from the train station." He glanced at Meg, who returned an enchanting smile. In the months since he had met her, Aedan could easily understand why his cousin and good friend, Dougal, had fallen in love with her.

"I asked Mrs. Gunn to bring the guests here to the small sitting room for introductions," Lady Balmossie said. "Mornings are for visiting, after all. You can bring them out to your wee hill later, Aedan."

"That may have to be tomorrow. It's raining now, and it looks to continue much of the day. Thistle," he warned, seeing the little creature inch her paw toward the tray that held Lady Balmossie's cup of tea, which the viscountess enjoyed regardless of the time of day. The monkey chittered and folded her arms in imitation of Aedan. Lady Balmossie laughed.

"Aunt Lill, must we bring Miss Thistle with us when we come to Dundrennan?" Amy asked. "We should leave her at Balmossie."

"Dundrennan was her home when my brother Hugh was alive," Lady Balmossie answered, as Thistle crossed the back of the sofa behind her, tail waving.

"But she is so very tiresome." Amy went to the window to help Meg hold up the fabric. "Look. This would make lovely drapes," she went on. "And we should replace that rug with a tartan pattern carpet like the carpet we're putting in the corridors. The plaid would look so well with the flowers. What do you think, Aedan?"

He glanced at the blue draperies, the worn brocaded sofa, the faded but still handsome Turkey carpet. The furnishings in the sitting room were shabby and outdated, but they had belonged to his mother. He cherished the childhood memories and the feelings of comfort that he felt in this room. He did not want everything to change at Dundrennan.

"This room is fine as it is," he answered, watching Thistle's tail disappear beneath a chair.

"Fine? Dougal said the same!" Amy sighed in exasperation.

"How nice that they agree." Meg smiled. Aedan wrinkled his nose at her in amusement. He felt at ease with his cousin's wife from the beginning despite her impressive status as Lady Strathlin, said to be the wealthiest woman in Scotland. The pretty blond was honest and natural, totally lacking in guile or conceit, and he had quickly grown fond of her. He was fond of Amy, too, but keeping pace with her whims and moods could be exhausting.

"Where is Dougal?" Aedan asked, always glad for the bulwark of another male presence when the ladies of Balmossie were in a decorating humor. "I saw him in the garden not long ago."

"He's in the library working on some plans," Meg said. "He says they must go to the lighthouse commission in this afternoon's post."

"Hiding out, is he?" Aedan drawled. Meg laughed.

"Thistle!" Lady Balmossie said as the monkey clambered up the hangings. "She never acts so shoogly at Balmossie."

"That's because she stays in the conservatory there, climbing rhododendrons instead of curtains," Amy answered.

Aedan walked over to pluck the monkey off the drape, letting her swarm over his shoulders while he looked out the window. Although rain now fell in earnest, he could see the jagged contour of Cairn Drishan. His work crew had stopped all efforts there, not due to the rain, but due to the orders of the National Museum, citing The Treasure Trove Law. He sighed and stood silently.

Then he realized that he was listening for a knock on the door that would announce the Blackburns. Anticipation like that suited schoolboys, he told himself. Yet he felt on fire to see Mrs. Blackburn again, and in the clear light of day.

He could not easily forget his first meeting with her, nor the kiss he had boldly stolen from her.

"Thistle wants your attention," Amy said, startling Aedan out of his thoughts.

The monkey had begun to groom his hair. Aedan removed her from his shoulder, and she tumbled upside down, showing lacy pantaloons.

"Wench," he drawled.

"Naughty Thistle!" Lady Balmossie offered her a treat.

"If you spoil her, she will never behave," Amy pointed out.

"She was spoilt years ago, long before dear Hugh left her to me," Lady Balmossie said. "And he got her from a soldier who bought her in India, where she was ruined by Hottentots."

Aedan smothered a laugh, knowing it was no use to point out to his aunt that there were no Hottentots in India, or Oaten-toads, her term for Highland "savages" in Scotland, either. Although she had married a viscount in her youth, her upbringing was rustic Lowland, and she was inherently stubborn in her views.

"Well, when this antiquarian lady comes in, you must not scowl, Aedan," Amy said. "That glower you like to adopt would frighten anyone."

"He means to frighten her," Lady Balmossie remarked. "He isna keen on wicked Sir Edgar Neaves, who sent the antiquarian here, nor is he keen on the lady stopping his wee road."

Keen. Remembering that exquisite face, those delicious lips, he was far more than keen. His heart beat as if he were a boy about to encounter the object of a fervent crush.

"I'm sure Aedan will be very polite to her," Meg said.

"Certainly I will," he murmured.

MacGregor, the butler, looked old enough to be a great-grandfather, but Christina had to rush to keep up with him. Knobby-kneed and gnarly, wearing a red plaid kilt and black coat, tartan socks and creaky leather shoes, the old man led Christina and John across the foyer, up the stairs, and down a corridor.

As he picked up speed, Christina lifted her skirts to hurry, petticoats rustling. Behind her, she heard the rhythm of John's stride with the cane.

Their footsteps were muffled on green tartan carpeting, and the walls, warm salmon pink above polished oak, glowed brightly. As in the other corridors she had seen, paintings, antique furniture, and shining weapons were artfully displayed here, too.

The butler turned. "Are you having an umbrella, bonny sir?" His accent was the soft, precise English of a Gael.

She blinked, realizing he addressed her. "It's raining today, I know, but . . . we are not going outside just now."

"You will be needing an umbrella in here, bonny sir. Or a targe," he muttered, pointing to some round shields on the wall.

Christina followed, wondering if the old house leaked.

She saw a man nailing tartan carpet into place, which explained the thumping of a hammer she had heard. Down another hallway she saw a ladder, paint buckets, and brushes. She turned to wait for John, while MacGregor barreled onward.

"I should tell the laird that I'm a painter," John said. "He might let me paint some of the walls here with a brush and bucket. I'm that desperate for the work."

"Don't jest, John. You should not climb a ladder."

"No joke, dear. I've had few commissions since my injury."

MacGregor stopped before double oak doors. "Bonny sir. And sir." He bowed.

"*Tapadh leat, mac Griogair*," Christina said, thanking him.

He smiled quickly. "*Tha Gàidhlig mhath agad.*"

"What did he say?" John asked.

"He said I have good Gaelic," Christina replied. "Our mother was born in the Highlands," she explained to the butler. "She taught her children the Gaelic."

"I forgot most of what I learned," John added. "But my sister taught in a Gaelic school in Fife a few years ago."

"Helping Highland families?" MacGregor smiled. "Good, good."

He turned to knock on the door. A masculine reply sounded, and the butler opened the door to peer into the gap, his caution puzzling. Then he opened the door and waited for Christina to enter first.

Christina caught a glimpse of a sitting room, but she had no time to notice anything else. A blur of motion and sound whirled toward her, and a man's hand lashed out in front of her face. She heard the hard smack as he caught something. His fist brushed the tip of her nose, knocking her eyeglasses askew.

Gasping, she stumbled back against the doorjamb. A sun-bronzed hand clutched a teacup in long fingers. Broad shoulders in a black wool coat filled her view. Stunned, she looked up.

Aedan MacBride peered down at her from over his shoulder. "Why, Mrs. Blackburn," he murmured.

"Well done, sir!" John crowed. "Excellent catch!"

"It comes of practice. Madam, I do apologize." Aedan MacBride held a teacup, caught within an inch of her nose. Christina could not imagine why.

"Tcha," MacGregor said as he drew the door closed behind them. "You are needing that umbrella."

"Och, puir lass!" an elderly lady in black, seated on a sofa, called out. "Do come in and sit doon. Miss Thistle!" She snapped as something small and brown — a cat? — scurried under a draped table. Two young women, both blond, exclaimed, and one bent down to look under a linen-covered table.

Bewildered, Christina glanced at Aedan MacBride, who stood calmly beside her. "Welcome," he said. "Please excuse the rather unusual reception. I am . . . Sir Aedan MacBride."

Of course, she realized. No one here knew that they had met the night before. "Sir Aedan," she said, holding out her hand, "I

70

am Mrs. Christina Blackburn."

He took her fingers, his touch light but firm, his smile appealingly mischievous. In daylight, he was still astonishingly handsome, his eyes a keen blue, his thick hair so deep a brown that it looked black. His suit of black wool was neat but spattered slightly with mud, as were his boots.

"Sir Edgar Neaves sent me," she said, continuing her introduction. "And this is my brother, John Blackburn."

"I'm pleased to make your acquaintance, madam. Sir, it's very good to meet you." He gave John a firm handshake.

The laird took her elbow, his touch firm and warm through the cloth of her sleeve. Christina looked into his stunning blue eyes, and her heart pattered at a ridiculous pace.

His powerful maleness was distracting. She remembered the feel of his arms around her, the brush of his lips over hers in the darkness. Blushing, she allowed the laird of Dundrennan to draw her into the room.

With Christina Blackburn on his arm, Aedan faced a room swirling with chaos. Amy lifted her lavender skirts and stepped back as Miss Thistle scrambled behind a drapery. Lady Balmossie fluttered her fan over her bosom, while Meg bent over, cooing to the elusive monkey.

71

"Thistle," his aunt moaned, "how could you!"

Aedan calmly introduced his kinswomen one by one to the startled guests. Amy smiled brightly in welcome, then squealed as Thistle scuttled just under her skirts.

"Mrs. Blackburn, please have a seat." Aedan guided her to the sofa beside his aunt, who turned her fan to flap it helpfully in the young woman's face.

John Blackburn stood by, quietly laughing, while his sister blinked and glanced around, clearly bewildered.

"Mrs. Blackburn, can I fetch you a glass of water? Or smelling salts?" Aedan asked wryly.

"Oh no, I'm fine." She smiled up at him. "Quite fine."

"If flying teacups do not bother you, then you will feel right at home here," he answered, admiring her composure. She had not made a fuss about falling down the stairs last night, either, although she no doubt felt bruised and shaken.

"Such a kerfuffle!" Lady Balmossie watched the two young women trying to snatch the monkey. "Are ye harmed, lassie?"

"She's quite unbothered," Aedan said, amused.

"I'm so pleased to meet all of you," Christina said. "Thank you for inviting us here."

John Blackburn leaned on the ivory head of his cane. "Ladies, I'm utterly charmed.

What a delightful welcome." His wide smile was relaxed. He was a lean young man with dark brown curls, calflike brown eyes, and the added romance of a limp, all of which Aedan suspected would melt his kinswomen's hearts.

A bundle of peach satin skittered along the back of a chair. Aedan reached out but missed catching Miss Thistle.

Christina Blackburn stared. "Is that . . . a monkey?"

"I wondered when you would notice," her brother said, grinning. "Sir Aedan, where did you come by that beastie? I saw them in the wild when I was overseas, and a fellow I knew in India brought one home with him. This one's a female, by its bonny gown, I take it?"

"Aye. Miss Thistle came from India years ago. She was my father's pet. Now she belongs to my aunt," Aedan explained. The monkey leaped to his shoulder. Aedan sat on the arm of the sofa near Mrs. Blackburn and dipped down to let her see Thistle.

Reaching out, she tentatively touched the monkey's head. Miss Thistle leaped away, climbing loose limbed up the draperies to sit on the curtain rod and survey the room.

Christina stared upward. "I've seen them at the Edinburgh Zoo, but never up close before." She sounded astonished.

"My father left Thistle in his will to Lady

Balmossie," Aedan said. "He knew I did not have the patience for her."

"But you are quite kind and tolerant with her." She smiled at him with such fresh, yet sultry, beauty that his body stirred. No woman had ever had this sort of effect on him, throwing him off-kilter with a mere smile or glance. He frowned, straightened.

"Your rescue of my sister was gallant, sir," John said.

"With Miss Thistle about, one learns to move swiftly. And it was a pleasure to save Mrs. Blackburn." He watched her blush again. That hint of passion beneath her calm exterior fascinated him. He wondered how such a quiet little creature could have modeled for that sensual painting.

Meg held out her hand. "Mrs. Blackburn, please forgive our eccentricities. This is an odd welcome for you and your brother."

"Oh, not at all, Lady Strathlin. I rather enjoyed it."

"Miss Thistle is upset by so many changes at Dundrennan," Lady Balmossie explained. "She usually knows how to behave."

"She does not," Amy contradicted, and the others laughed.

"Mrs. Blackburn, I believe we met briefly last year in Edinburgh," Meg said. "At the opening of an exhibition at the National Museum of Antiquities. A display of some rather beautiful ancient Celtic pieces, as I recall."

Christina lifted her brows. "Oh yes! In all the commotion I did not realize . . . how very nice to see you again. We were introduced by a friend of yours . . . Mrs. Shaw, I think."

"Yes. Actually she is now Mrs. Guy Hamilton. She married my secretary just two months ago." Meg smiled. "That was a wonderful exhibit — am I right in remembering that you played a part in the discovery of those remarkable pieces, and in the arrangement of the displays as well?"

Christina nodded. "I accompanied my uncle to the site of that discovery, and then worked with Sir Edgar Neaves of the museum to identify and catalog the pieces. How kind of you to recall."

Aedan felt grateful to Meg for helping to make Christina Blackburn feel more comfortable after that raucous introduction to his family. Over Christina's head, he smiled privately at his cousin's wife. The sparkle in her aqua blue eyes told him that she understood.

"This is a marvelous house, Sir Aedan," John said. "We noticed some work being done as we came through the hallways."

"We are in the process of refurbishing the place, according to my father's wishes," Aedan answered.

"Yes, we want to capture Sir Hugh's grand vision for Dundrennan," Amy said. "The house was still unfinished at the time of his death." She rested a hand upon Aedan's shoulder, but he stood so that her hand had to fall.

"And we have another reason to finish up the house," Lady Balmossie said. "The queen is planning to visit us soon."

"Oh, how exciting!" Christina said.

"Och, aye." Lady Balmossie nodded. "Aedan, have ye had word yet when Her Majesty will arrive?"

"I had a letter from the queen's secretary in this morning's post," Aedan said. "The queen and her consort will preside over the opening of the Glasgow Waterworks on October the sixteenth, and then ride north over the new road — which had best be finished to allow for it," he added. "They will stay here for one night, and tour the Strathclyde hills the next day."

Lady Balmossie whisked her fan. "Oh, my! Will the house be ready in time? Will the painting and carpeting be done? And we must find an artist soon!"

"Artist?" John Blackburn asked quickly.

"For the dining room," Lady Balmossie explained. "Part o' my late brother's plan for the house — bonny paintings on the walls."

"Ah," John said, glancing at his sister.

Just then Amy leaned toward Aedan. "Dear Cousin, later you must tour the house with me. I so value your thoughts, even though you are determined to be a grumphie about the changes. We are planning the house together," she told the Blackburns.

That sounded uncomfortably matrimonial, Aedan thought. He frowned. "I'm grateful for the help my cousin and my aunt have been with the renovations."

"The house is quite impressive," Christina said. "John and I look forward to seeing more of it."

"We will give you the grand tour," Amy said.

"You might especially enjoy the library," Meg told her. "I'm sure Sir Aedan can answer any questions you may have about the book collection. He knows the library best."

"Oh? Are you a writer and a scholar, sir, like your father?" Christina asked.

"No, I am an engineer by education and by trade, although I helped my father maintain the library when I was younger. Feel free to use the library while you are here. As a scholar, you will want to make good use of it." He looked at her for a moment, thinking of her interrupted mission last night.

She thought of it too for he saw the flicker of awareness in her eyes. "Thank you, sir. Though I hardly consider myself a true scholar. I assist my uncle, the Reverend Walter Carriston, who is an accomplished antiquarian. I helped him to do some research for the museum. I occasionally help Sir Edgar, too, who asked me to examine the discovery on the hill near here."

He nodded. "Reverend Carriston wrote a history of Scotland, is that right?"

"Yes, his magnum opus, *A History of Celtic Scotland*, was published in four volumes," she answered.

"Ah. My father thought highly of his work."

"My sister is a fine antiquarian in her own right," John Blackburn added. "She aided our uncle in his research and writing. Her theories of Arthurian Britain helped shape his conclusions."

Mrs. Blackburn's cheeks were bright pink now, Aedan noticed. He reminded himself why she had come to Dundrennan. She had the power to ruin his career and lose him this house. He could not afford to forget that, despite her undeniable appeal.

"My sister is the last to admit her expertise," John went on. "But I am happy to show some braggadocio on her behalf."

"Please do, Mr. Blackburn," Aedan said, curious to hear.

"She can read and speak Latin, French, Greek, and modern Gaelic, and she is familiar with Old Irish. She can make sense of any old text, I think. She taught English in a Ladies' School in the Highlands, and she has published some articles of her scholarly work. And she is kind, sensitive, and modest in her view of herself." He smiled at his sister.

"John, really," Christina said, pinkening.

"What a paragon," Amy said coolly.

"Yet a green lass for knowing so verra much," Lady Balmossie said bluntly. "I thought a lady antiquarian would be a crabbit auld thing, like me." She chuckled.

"Mrs. Blackburn is young, but she is a married lady," Amy said.

"I am a widow." Christina Blackburn spoke softly. Aedan frowned, remembering her discomfort with the topic last night. "After my husband's death, I devoted myself to assisting my uncle with his work."

"I'm so sorry for your loss," Meg murmured.

"Thank you. Might I say, since my brother was kind about me," Christina said, "that John is a brilliant painter."

"I've certainly heard of the Blackburn family of artists," Meg said. "I own a beautiful seascape by the elder Blackburn, who is a very celebrated artist. . . . Would he perhaps be your father?"

Christian nodded. "Yes. I'm so glad to hear that you enjoy his work," she murmured.

"We have three paintings by Blackburn artists here in our own collection," Aedan said.

Christina blinked at him. "Three?" Her cheeks colored.

Damn. He had spoken without thinking. She seemed uncomfortable with the topic. "Aye, a picture of Queen Mary Stewart by your father, and one in the front drawing room signed only 'Blackburn.' The third is . . . in my study." He avoided mention of its subject.

"*That* one is quite improper," Amy said.

Mrs. Blackburn cast her brother a frantic look.

"The one in the drawing room shows Robert the Bruce crowned by Isabella of Buchan," Amy said. "*That* one is very nice."

"Robert the Bruce?" John said. "Why, I painted that one!"

"You, sir?" Aedan smiled. "What a marvelous coincidence to have you here. It's an excellent piece."

"Thank you, Sir Aedan. I did not realize it was here."

"John does not keep very careful records," Christina said.

"Aedan, you must ask Mr. Blackburn about painting the dining room walls!" Amy smiled.

"With a bucket and brush?" John gulped.

"No." Aedan smiled. "We have an unfinished mural in the dining room, started two years ago by a fellow who unfortunately died. Perhaps you would look at it. We hope to find someone to finish it for us . . . I wonder if you would be interested."

"Mr. Blackburn is a verra fine painter," Lady Balmossie said, nodding. "He could do a better job than what's there."

John smiled. "I would be happy to look at it."

"An artist! What wonderful luck!" Amy said. "Would you like to see it now, Mr. Blackburn? I would be delighted to take you there while Lady Strathlin shows Mrs. Blackburn the library. Aedan, will you come along?"

"I have a prior engagement with Miss Thistle," he drawled. At the sound of her name, the monkey chittered and skimmed down the curtain to leap onto Aedan's shoulder. He tickled her head.

"You rogue," Amy teased. "The lairds of Dundrennan never allow themselves to be smitten. There's a nasty old curse," she explained to the Blackburns.

"Curse?" Christina Blackburn asked.

Lady Balmossie leaned toward her. "They say that the lairds o' Dundrennan must never wed for love. 'Tis all nonsense, do ye ask me, but the men in this family like to believe it."

"Oh!" Christina blinked, clearly uncertain how to answer.

"Nonsense or not," Aedan said, standing, "it is tradition at Dundrennan to leave true love to those who can face its peculiar challenges." He bowed, making light of it, and turned to deposit the monkey on a tall stand, fixing her ankle with a small chain and feeding her an apple slice from a bowl. He turned. "Please excuse me. I have some correspondence that needs attention." With a polite nod, he went to the door.

"Aedan, do meet us in the library if you can," Meg said.

He looked over his shoulder. Seated amid the other ladies, Christina Blackburn seemed to bloom like a pale rose. He was fascinated by her, and knew he could not easily stay away.

"I will be there," he said, and he opened the door.

Chapter Five

The rainbow luster of the books made Christina gasp with awe as she followed Lady Strathlin into the spacious and beautiful library. High windows admitted silvery daylight, which gleamed on polished tables and leather chairs. Brass mesh shutters enclosed bookshelves that spanned the walls from floor to ceiling.

She turned, glancing around. A gallery walk skimmed the upper walls, accessed by steel staircases. More bookshelves were boxed in pillars that divided the huge room into private reading bays beneath the gallery level.

Above the fireplace hung her father's oil painting of Mary, Queen of Scots, for which her mother had posed. She smiled and turned with delight. Despite its size, the library seemed cozy, warmed by wood, leather, bright carpets, plenty of light, and the enticing smell of a wealth of books.

"Oh, how wonderful!" Christina felt enthralled. She had loved books all her life. In the years since Stephen's death, reading and studying had provided a much-needed haven of safety.

"This was once the great hall of the old medieval keep," Lady Strathlin told her. "It was used as a dining room until Sir Hugh had it renovated for his library. His study is through that alcove." She pointed to a corner with an open door. Christina peered through it at the mahogany desk, leather chair, and even more bookshelves.

"How many books are in the collection?" she asked.

"Over eight thousand." Aedan MacBride stepped out from behind a pillar in his shirt-sleeves and vest, his thick hair casually mussed, as if he had raked his fingers through it. Behind him she glimpsed a table scattered with papers, pencils, a slide rule, and a few maps. "This library was one of my father's chief passions, besides his poetry, and of course Dundrennan itself."

"Aedan!" Lady Strathlin said. "Is Dougal with you?"

"Here, love." Another man rounded the same pillar, his tall, powerful build and lighter coloring complementing Aedan Mac-Bride's lean, dark Celtic grace. He came forward to kiss Lady Strathlin's tilted cheek, then turned to take Christina's hand.

"I'm Dougal Stewart," he said, "Lady Strathlin's husband." His smile was beautiful, his handshake warm and kind. She liked him instantly.

"I'm very glad to meet you," she answered

84

when Lady Strathlin introduced her.

"Dougal is a lighthouse engineer," Aedan explained. "Perhaps you've heard of the Caran Lighthouse in the Western Isles."

"Yes, of course — it was completed recently," Christina said. "Quite an admirable feat, from what I understand."

Dougal shrugged, smiling. "My real fame is as the husband of the admirable Lady Strathlin — and of course as Amy's brother. And I'm Aedan's cousin, so he must occasionally put up with me here at Dundrennan."

Aedan MacBride huffed in amusement and leaned a shoulder against a pillar. "I hope you've come to claim your husband, madam," he told Lady Strathlin. "He is driving me mad with facts about the ratio of wave force to solid mass." He grinned and glanced at Christina. "If Dougal does not have some project to challenge him, he comes here and harasses me endlessly."

She laughed, glad to be included so naturally in their camaraderie.

"There is plenty to distract me these days," Dougal replied. "My wife and our children, who are at Balmossie with their nurse, all challenge me constantly." He tucked Lady Strathlin's hand discreetly and tenderly in his. Her fair skin suffused in a pretty flush as she looked up at him.

The warm glow of the couple's love and

respect for each other seemed tangible, Christina thought, and she nearly sighed with longing. Her own chance for an intimate, joyful relationship had been cast already, gambled, and lost.

Noticing Aedan MacBride frowning as he leaned against the pillar, she remembered Lady Balmossie's remark that the lairds of Dundrennan never married for love. Perhaps he did not approve of the happy display between Dougal and his wife.

Yet Aedan MacBride did not seem at all like a man opposed to love. Rather, he reminded her of a lost boy standing out in the cold, peering inside at a cozy family scene. His frown could not disguise the poignant hunger she saw for a moment in his gaze. Christina recognized it because she felt the same way.

"Mrs. Blackburn wanted to explore the library," Lady Strathlin said. "Sir Aedan can show you better than I can."

"I would be happy to do that," he murmured.

Smiling, Lady Strathlin took her husband's arm. "And I promised Mr. Blackburn that I would show him the marvelous books of art engravings kept here. He's with Amy and Lady Balmossie in the dining room. Come with me, Dougal. I want to introduce you. He's an artist, my dear, and you know I've been thinking about having our portraits done," she said as they left the library.

Aedan turned toward Christina. "What interests you most here, Mrs. Blackburn? History, art, literature, antique manuscripts? We have all those here and more."

You most interest me, she thought suddenly, gazing into his eyes, their brilliant blue guarding his thoughts within. He showed patience, humor, affection, but she sensed a trace of sadness, even bitterness, in him too, a contradiction that she found intriguing.

"All of it interests me, Sir Aedan. I've read all of Sir Hugh's poetry, so it's wonderful to see his collection of books. And my uncle and Sir Hugh corresponded on matters of history."

"My father spoke highly of him. Well, come this way, Mrs. Blackburn." She strolled with him around the library while he pointed out sections devoted to different subjects.

"Oh," she said as they walked along. "Scott, Shakespeare, Milton, Dante, Tennyson, Burns, Hogg, Carlyle . . . wonderful. Knight's *Pictorial History of England*, Chambers's *English Literature* . . . They seem like old friends to me."

"My dominie made me read them, too," Aedan commented, "though I can't say I was a willing scholar. I built bridges and towers with these books more often than read them." He grinned, and she glimpsed, fleetingly, a mischievous little boy.

"My brothers, John and William, were both like that," she said, laughing. "My sister, Marianna, and I were always readers."

"Then you will be in heaven here," he answered. "The books are organized in categories," he went on. "This bay, for example, holds folklore and mythology, that one books on the sciences. There are a great many books on the gallery level, too. If you wish to look at those, Mrs. Blackburn, you will want to call a groom, or myself when I am at home, to fetch books from shelves in the higher regions."

"I'm not afraid to climb ladders or walk the gallery, sir."

He glanced at her. "Not nervous at heights, then?"

"Not particularly."

"Good." She heard a grudging approval in his voice. "You will need that sort of fearlessness to climb Cairn Drishan. It's moderately high and still a rough walk in places."

"I am eager to see the discovery. May we do that tomorrow?"

"Depending on the weather, aye."

They had paused in the bay devoted to folklore, and she pulled a volume from the shelf to leaf through it. "It must have been marvelous to grow up in this place . . . even if you did use the books for building blocks," she added, chuckling.

"I did learn respect for books, should you

think me a complete boor." His mouth twitched in a smile. "We were raised on bards and poets instead of Mother Goose. We recited Sir Walter Scott and Robert Burns in our cradles, and we sang ballads about Border thieves before we could walk. And of course we learned our father's poems by heart."

She heard his teasing tone, but she sensed there was truth in what he said, too. She tilted her head, greatly curious about him. "Do you write poetry yourself, Sir Aedan?"

"Not a whit. I have a blasted fine memory for the stuff, though I lack an artist's soul. Our dominie despaired of me in the school-room when it came to writing essays and poems. My father always said I was made from numbers and steel — he meant it as a compliment, I hope. I took it as one." He looked down at her. "I beg your pardon, Mrs. Blackburn. Generally I do not go on about myself."

"I don't mind at all," Christina said. She enjoyed listening to him. Standing so close, she was keenly aware that they were alone together in the little alcove. The flexible bell of her skirts brushed his legs, enveloped him, allowed him to breach her outermost perimeter.

She should have shied away from such close proximity with a man she scarcely knew. But this man had helped her last night

89

when she was hurt, and he had kissed her, and she had not felt shocked at all. She felt at ease with him, and she found his animal grace exhilarating. She spent much of her time in the company of old books and older people in her uncle's home. She rarely socialized with men of her own age anymore.

And Edgar, for all his suave handsomeness and intellect, simply did not compare to this strong, earthy, genuine man. Edgar certainly did not stir her heart or her blood, and he had never kissed her as Aedan had. She did not think Edgar was capable of such passion.

"The books over here might interest you," Aedan MacBride said. As she followed him, she heard John and the others enter the library, murmuring quietly.

Aedan opened the brass mesh doors of a tall bookcase. As she moved closer, Christina's arm brushed his. She inhaled the clean spicy soap he used, heard the quiet rhythm of his breathing. She could hardly concentrate on the books. Nor did she understand the man's effect on her.

"Oh, yes, histories," she said quickly, scanning the spines. "Hume, Chambers, Carlyle — I've read most of these. And up there is Uncle Walter's *Celtic Scotland*." She pointed above their heads. "With the dark blue spines."

He fetched down the first volume and flipped it open. " 'To Sir Hugh, friend and fellow admirer of the ancient Celts, from Rev. Walter Carriston.' "

Christina traced her fingers over her uncle's familiar signature. Her finger brushed Sir Aedan's thumb, and she felt a sparklike sensation. She withdrew her hand quickly.

"My uncle translated some medieval manuscript pages for Sir Hugh," she said. "Some old documents found in family papers."

He shelved the book. "Aye, the Dundrennan Folio. We keep it locked away, though of course you may see it. You will want time to look at it, I'm sure, so we'll leave that for another day." He glanced down at her. "Does that suit you?"

"Of course."

"Come see my father's study." He led her to the corner room, allowing her to enter first. She gasped in admiration as she looked at the mahogany desk, the worn leather chair, the reference books on the shelves. A bowl of fresh wild roses sat on the desk.

"The queen's own Highland bard. You must miss him very much," she said softly.

"We do," he murmured. "So you've read his poetry?"

"Oh, yes. Wonderful epics, full of romance and adventure."

"He would have been pleased to hear that. He valued the opinions of his readers. Which one is your favorite?" He went to a bookcase that Christina saw held a full collection of his father's books. Opening its doors, he stood back.

"Oh, there are so many," she said. "*Children of the Mist* and *The Warrior* were such exciting adventures, and *The Wanderer* had a mythical, unforgettable power. But *The Enchanted Briar* has always been my favorite, I think." She touched the red leather spine with that title.

"Oh? Why so?"

"It is a superb study of how tragedy shapes character, how small mistakes can change the lives of many, and how a good man can be driven to desperate ends by love and grief."

He huffed. "Spoken like a scholar. Now tell me why Christina Blackburn likes it." He leaned against the desk, waited.

"Because . . . each time I read it, I cry."

"Ah," he said. "Honestly spoken, and kind praise. My father would have appreciated that. He wanted his poetry to stir the emotions — rend the heart and heal it again. What made you cry, Mrs. Blackburn, if I may ask?"

She tilted her head, thinking. "It is a beautiful, tragic love story. The Druid prince meets the daughter of a king, and they fall in love at first sight. Their meeting is heroic and poignant. Then her father forces her to marry a rival, and when she refuses, he imprisons her in a tower. Her only joy is when the prince comes secretly to her bower, but she will not disobey her father and escape with him." She shook her head. "And her anguish is so heartbreaking when she gives birth to their son alone in the tower, but for her old nurse. Even when she is released and defies her father at last, they cannot be together, for she falls under a spell cast by the prince's enemy."

"And so she sleeps forever," he said quietly, watching her.

"Forever, lost to her lover for eternity, yet always just within his reach. I . . . weep each time I read it," she said again.

"What touches you most about it?" he asked gently.

Her heart bounded as she returned his gaze. "The love they have for each other. He loved her beyond life itself and lost her. He never gave up, and he would not leave her side even when it seemed hopeless." She felt tears prick her eyes as she remembered the story.

"Aye." He watched her. "So stirring. True love."

She tipped her head. "Do you mock it? True love exists."

"Does it?" He raised his brows skeptically, gazed down his nose at her. Blue, blue eyes and his long, lean, powerful form distracted her, made her heart beat faster.

"I think so," she said, returning his gaze defiantly.

"Have you known it yourself, Mrs. Blackburn?"

She looked away. "That is a very personal question, sir."

"So it is, and I apologize. If it soothes your ruffled feathers any, I do believe true love exists for some. Just not for everyone." His gaze remained steady.

"Love is essential, sir. Through that miracle, human beings thrive. Surely you have known —" She stopped, remembering his kiss, his hands warm upon her, arousing wickedly sensual feelings, so that her cheeks heated in a rising blush.

"The lairds of Dundrennan do not risk love as a rule. We certainly have affection for the fairer of our species — the MacBrides would have died out otherwise." He smiled, a impish quirk of his lips, yet his gaze held a smoldering quality. "But we do not indulge in true love for particular reasons of our own."

"Indulge? Sir, real love is extraordinary and irresistible. It is thunder and lightning, a — a hurricane," she went on, gesturing. "The blaze of the sun and the shine of the moon. A force of nature, powerful and inexplicable. It cannot be stopped or denied. It is not an indulgence, like . . . like chocolate!"

"For a bookish wee thing, you have a romantic soul." His eyes sparkled, and she felt her face go even more fiery. "I suppose you believe in love at first sight and a whole rasher of other nonsense."

Christina lifted her chin. "I see you refuse to be convinced of true love's worth."

"Are you trying to convince me of it, Mrs. Blackburn?"

"Not at all. The argument is merely an intellectual exercise."

He laughed easily, and she sensed no malice in it. "Remind me to tread carefully next time you are in a mood to exercise your brainpan, madam. You will want to argue the worth of sonnets or valentines. I cannot keep up."

"Laugh if you will, sir. But true love and love at first sight do happen. I wish —" She stopped.

"That you might find it?" he finished gently.

She shrugged. "Your cousin and his bride have found it. I admire that."

His smile sobered. "So do I. But I will leave it to them. Extraordinary love is . . . extraordinarily dangerous at Dundrennan."

"What an odd thing to say."

He regarded her for a moment. "Your name ought to be Miss Burn, I think. You blush like fire, do you know that?"

She put a hand to her warm cheek. "Oh!"

"I meant it as a compliment." He spoke affectionately, his tone gentle. "You may be a cool little scholar on the exterior, my dear

Miss Burn, but you have a fire of the spirit. My father would have liked you very much, I think."

"Thank you," she said in surprise.

"Not at all." He stood. "Shall we see if the others found those engravings?"

"Amy has expensive taste, I will give her that," Aedan said. He glanced at Amy's older brother, Dougal Stewart, who chuckled as he walked beside Aedan. "Dundrennan would not be as fine a place as it is without her advice, and Lady Balmossie's as well."

Dougal Stewart nodded, glancing up at the back of the house as he and Aedan walked along a graveled garden path. "Amy said you've taken a sudden liking to plain color on the walls."

"I also told her I like old, threadbare rugs rather than new carpeting." Aedan grinned. "Ultimately, it may save some pounds."

He could be honest about financial matters with his cousin and childhood friend. He and Dougal had attended university together, along with their friend Evan Mackenzie — lately the Earl of Kildonan. All three of the men were engineers. Dougal, always a daredevil vying to prove himself, had gravitated to the dangers of lighthouse construction. Aedan, used to striving for practicality in an impractical household, had chosen to design highways. And Evan had applied his talents to creating beautiful bridges.

Dougal's latest feat of daring was his recent marriage to Lady Strathlin, surprising everyone who knew him — except Aedan. He had long hoped that his cousin would settle down once he found a woman as passionate and as brave as Dougal was himself.

Although he was happy for Dougal and Meg, Aedan felt a twinge of envy. Privately, he longed for love like that in his own life. Having lost his fiancée three years ago, he was older and wiser. He realized that he had mistaken friendship for love.

True love was not in the cards for the lairds of Dundrennan, he reminded himself. He had no business yearning after it.

No business kissing a delectable stranger, a guest in his own house, late at night, either, he thought sternly.

He cleared his throat. "I'm doing my best to afford the work my father wanted done in this house. But I cannot fault him for poor accounting. A good part of his fortune went to grain shipments to feed Highlanders and Islanders ousted from their homes in the clearances."

"Aye, it was good work he did. My wife did the same when she had the chance. By the way, Meg would be glad to help with Dundrennan's expenses, should you need it," Dougal added quietly.

Aedan shook his head, aware of Meg's

enormous personal fortune as well as her giving nature. "I'm touched by her generosity, but I can bear the costs here for yet a while."

"At what personal cost to you? Fund the rest of your father's whims here, and you will soon be out of pocket."

Aedan looked at him. The morning light gleamed in Dougal's brown hair rich with sun streaks, and his calm green eyes reflected his steady character. Aedan trusted his cousin as he did few others. "I have the resources, Dougal," he answered. "I have the income from road contracts, and my investments in jute and whisky have been profitable. And lately I have invested in silver darlings."

"Herrings, whisky, and jute are good business for Scotland. But you cannot funnel all your available cash into Dundrennan."

"My father's will specifies that the improvements in the house be completed by year's end. We have only a little more to do."

Their steps crushed out a rhythm on the stones of the garden path. A cool breeze, hinting of autumn to come, ruffled Aedan's thick, dark hair and fluttered the lapel of his mud-spattered black jacket. Nearly autumn. Time had him fast by the short hairs.

"This place is marvelous," Dougal agreed. "It has become a veritable museum, an homage to Scottish history."

"Aye — jammed with paintings and artifacts, swathed in tartan, thick with old swords."

"Luckily for you, the ladies of Balmossie have an unnatural fever for decorating." Dougal smiled.

"True. I am confounded by such things," Aedan said.

"I agree, you can get through all of it — because you love this old place."

Aedan nodded in silent agreement as they walked.

"The antiquarian . . . is not quite so antique as expected, is she," Dougal commented. "Rather lovely, your Mrs. Blackburn."

Aedan smiled faintly. "A . . . pleasant surprise," he admitted.

"I wonder what Neaves has in mind in sending her."

Aedan sighed. "I wish he would stay away entirely, but I doubt it. I recently had a letter from the museum's advocates. They wish to assert a claim to the clause in my father's will that favors the museum." He glanced at Dougal. "Neaves drools at the mere thought that this house could revert to the care of the National Museum, as my father stated in his odd provision. If the house is not restored like the setting of some damnable Highland play, they win the lot."

"Either you comply, or you lose damn near everything."

"Exactly."

"And if your little antiquarian finds something of real historical significance on that hillside?"

"Then I have a problem indeed. The Treasure Trove Law will dictate, and the museum could take it all."

"Even if it was treasure enough to save this house, and pay off the debts?"

"Even then." Aedan glanced up at the house as he and Dougal walked through its shadow. Seeing that massive, familiar, beloved silhouette, he felt a deep wrenching in heart and gut. He did, indeed, love this old place.

"Mrs. Blackburn seems an astute scholar," Dougal said. "If there is something in that hill, she will find it."

"Aye. And God help you."

Aedan nodded, while he listened to the crush of quartz stones beneath their bootsoles, pressing into the earth of his ancestors. He looked at the foundation of the house, surrounded in thick wild rose hedges, still sprinkled with late summer flowers of pale pink.

Generations of MacBrides had lived here — though they had not often loved here, in keeping with their peculiar family tradition. And his father's poetry had been written here.

The briars of Dundrennan had always protected this place. Aedan would protect it too, however he could, no matter the price. He could not bear to lose Dundrennan.

Chapter Six

Hearing the faint creak of the door and the gentle rustle of skirts, Aedan peered over his newspaper. Christina Blackburn crossed the sunny, oak-paneled breakfast room, her figure neat in a skirt and trim jacket of dark gray wool. He nodded in silent greeting, and she smiled shyly.

In the plain skirt and jacket, with her hair winged back in a low knot, her spectacles perched on her nose, and her cheeks a delicate pink, she looked demure and scholarly. Yet a sensual, delectable quality seemed to emanate from her, and each time he saw her, desire rushed through him, hot and strong. He found it difficult to remain detached whenever the museum antiquarian was in the room.

He was beginning to wish that Sir Edgar Neaves had come after all. Aedan rose to pull out a chair at the table, near his own chair. "Good morning, Mrs. Blackburn."

"Sir Aedan," she murmured. He caught a waft of lavender. "This is a lovely room," she remarked, looking around.

He glanced at the rose chintz draperies, the flowery seat coverings, and the green tartan carpet. "Nearly everything was redone in here a few months ago. I suppose it is nicer than before," he added, perusing his newspaper.

"It's cheerful and relaxing. What was in here before, sir?"

He frowned. "Dark drapes . . . I don't recall the color. Leather chair seats — worn, but comfortable, I thought. The wood floor was creaky, but needed only some polishing. It seemed fine as it was, but my father had already begun some changes in here, so I left it to the ladies of Balmossie to finish the room. Apparently the queen likes chintz," he said dryly. "I know Cousin Amy does."

"The flower patterns complement the marvelous view of the gardens at the back of the house."

He glanced through the floral-draped window at the lawns, neat pathways, and beds filled with late-summer blooms. The stone arches of an old ruin soared above the orchard trees. "All this flowery nonsense in here does look well with the garden view," he murmured. "I had not noticed before."

Mrs. Blackburn smiled, ducking her head a little. Scowling, Aedan flicked his newspaper upright and went back to reading.

Sonsie Jean sailed into the room in a breezy hurry, her appearance fairylike with her wispy red-gold hair and her small build.

After efficiently pouring coffee into a china cup for Mrs. Blackburn, she refilled Aedan's cup and set a packet of mail beside his elbow.

"Thank you, Muricl," he murmured. Smiling, the little maid bobbed her head and left the room.

Christina looked at him. "I thought she was Sonsie Jean."

"She is, but her given name is Muriel, so that's what I call her. My father called all the maids Jeanie to save himself the trouble of learning their names. He was a brilliant poet, but a featherhead about names. It was his custom, but it is not mine." He turned the newspaper page. "I call her Muriel."

"I see," she said. "What about Bonnie Jean and Wee Jean?"

"Bonnie Jean — that happens to be her name. And Wee Jeanie, who scrubs in the kitchen, is actually Eliza."

"So that's what you call her."

"Aye." He sipped his steaming coffee. "I think it fair to show respect for the servants in that way, though Mrs. Gunn still calls the maids the Jeanies. She clings to my father's rules out of habit and perhaps because she misses him a great deal. It gives him more of a presence here, I suppose."

"His presence and influence are everywhere here."

"True." Aware that she watched him

steadily, Aedan held the newspaper up like a shield and tried to concentrate on a column that reported Queen Victoria's public schedule. The royal family would soon arrive at their Highland home of Balmoral, he saw, and the queen and her consort planned to attend the opening of the Glasgow Waterworks on October the sixteenth.

Scarcely two months, he thought, before his highway must be completed. He lowered the paper to glance at Christina Blackburn. How remarkable that this petite, lovely creature had the power to prevent him from meeting his obligations.

He turned the newspaper page, and when Christina rose to go to the sideboard, he stood when she did, then sat again to read the paper. He had eaten his fill earlier of the variety of foods arranged there. She selected fruit, porridge, eggs, and toast and carried her plate toward the table, pausing at the window.

"What's that?" she asked. "Beyond the trees — that arch of stone in the sunlight?"

Aedan looked up from his paper. "That's the Remembrance. It's a monument to the ancient princess of Dundrennan."

"How wildly romantic! It looks like a medieval ruin."

"It's five hundred years old. And it may be wildly romantic, but it's a maintenance problem — crumbling stones, mildew, grassy areas and hedges to trim, and so forth."

"Still, you must be very proud to have it here."

He stood to hold out her chair while she sat again. "It is rather picturesque," he admitted, glancing through the window at graceful arches surrounded by trees and roses. Odd how Christina Blackburn made him see familiar things with a fresh perspective. "My father hired stonemasons to restore the cloistered arcade and engrave some new designs in the stone. You must go see it while you are here." He sat and took up his newspaper again.

"I think my brother would love to sketch it," she said, "if that would be allowed, Sir Aedan."

"He may draw it to his heart's content, madam," he murmured, and he turned another page. He knew he was acting coolly toward her, but he felt the need to distance himself. Since her arrival, he had revealed too much of himself. Now he must reel in any lines he had cast out. The woman was only a business acquaintance, and in a few days she would be gone.

Yet he felt as if he had known her all his life, as if she were a missing puzzle piece, newly discovered, that fit neatly and essentially into a space he had not known was empty.

Frowning, he told himself not to entertain

fancies. But he could not resist peeking at her over his newspaper.

She ate discreetly but with good appetite, something he liked in women, who sometimes ate like birds due to silly notions about appearance and propriety. Amy regularly skipped breakfast and nibbled at luncheon and dinner, and fainted, albeit prettily, now and then, from hunger or tight stays.

He sipped his coffee and began to read his mail, finding a frantic plea from the Parliamentary Commissioners for a firm date on the completion of the road. Frowning, he pocketed the letter.

"Sir Aedan," Christina said, "am I late this morning? There is no one else about. My brother will be down soon, but I thought others might be breakfasting. It is nearly eight o'clock."

"You and I are the early risers this morning, but for Mr. Stewart, who has gone into Glasgow. Lady Strathlin has gone back to Balmossie to be with her children — they have a little boy and an infant girl. My aunt and my cousin are rarely seen before ten-thirty when they are here, and then they eat lightly, so that Cook's fine spread often is wasted. Mrs. Gunn is a good and practical soul, and she sees that what remains is wrapped and delivered to those who may need it. I am glad to see that you are a woman of honest appetite," he added.

Her cheeks colored as she sliced a muffin to butter it, and she nodded, spreading marmalade on it, then taking a bite. If he had said the same to Amy, she would have stopped eating for the rest of the day, he thought. "Do you suppose Tam Durie could drive me to Cairn Drishan this morning?" she asked. "My brother would like to go, as well."

"I would be glad to drive you there myself, if you can be ready to leave within the half hour."

"Thank you. I thought to walk the distance, but John is not comfortable with rugged walks."

He nodded. "May I ask whether his injury is temporary, or something more permanent?"

"My brother was in the Crimea," she answered quietly. "He was injured at Balaclava. He has regained much of his strength and abilities, and we hope for further recovery, but . . . well, he accepts his infirmity with his usual good humor."

Aedan frowned slightly and set down his newspaper. "My older brother, Neil, was at Sebastopol," he said. "He did not return."

She stared at him. "Oh, Aedan," she breathed impulsively. "I am so sorry."

He nodded curtly, fighting a sudden, unexpected onslaught of grief brought on by the tenderness in her tone, a grief he did not want to feel, not now. He fingered through the envelopes beside him without seeing them. "Well," he said. "Well. As we were saying, I would be happy to take you and Mr. Blackburn out to Cairn Drishan this morning. You may walk another day, or you may take ponies if you wish. We keep two garrons for hill terrain. Though you may need to go out to the hill only once."

"I expect to visit there several times. I have to examine it carefully and prepare my report for Sir Edgar."

"I confess that I was surprised he sent you here rather than coming here himself."

She sat straighter, her backbone curving away from the chair. "Sir Edgar intends to come here as soon as he is free, if that eases your doubts about a female's expertise and authority."

Aedan pressed his fingertips together and hid his smile. "I do not doubt your capability. I suspect you might be more competent than Sir Edgar, who likes very much to boast about his accomplishments, from what I recall. When does he intend to come here?" He nearly ground out the question.

"Not for a few weeks yet."

Aedan shrugged. "Well, I expect that both of you will find little of real interest on Cairn Drishan. We uncovered an old wall, common enough around here in defining property boundaries."

"Sir Edgar feels that a Pictish ruin might be on that hill."

"I was there that day. I assure you it is an ordinary wall."

"Oh? Were you hunting, or walking the hills?"

"My work crew did the blasting, madam. I am the civil engineer for the Highland Highway in this region, appointed by the Parliamentary Commissioners of Roads and Highways."

Her eyes widened. "Oh! I knew you were an engineer, but I did not know . . . Sir, I apologize for my ignorance."

"No matter. Are you familiar with the highway project?"

"Yes, it is the prince consort's current favorite development to promote tourism and healthy industry in Scotland."

"Creating more roads is a good scheme, though some feel it will spoil Scotland. I support industries that increase Scotland's finances and provide work for those who have lost their means."

"Do you support Scotland's growing tourist industry?"

"To some extent. I do not want my own estate to become a well-trodden symbol of the romantic Highlands. My father regarded Dundrennan as a historical treasure and would have thrown open our doors to the public, but I prefer that it stay private."

"Yet you allow a public road through your property."

"The estate and deed are mine, but most of the land in Scotland belongs to the crown. The landowner's permission is sometimes only a legal formality. Parliament takes precedence in matters like public roads, and the road would have been brought through here regardless. At least this way I have a say in how it cuts through my property."

"I see. What if the wall on that hillside proves to be a national treasure, Sir Aedan? You cannot deny access to it."

"I believe you will find that wall rather ordinary and a disappointment. There is no horde of treasure, no carved Pictish stones, nothing to indicate an ancient site."

"There does not have to be something fantastical sticking out of the ground for it to prove ancient. According to Treasure Trove, the National Museum must evaluate any discovery that might be historical, regardless of how ordinary it may appear."

"I am aware. But it is merely a legal exercise in this case, I think."

"We shall see, sir. Surely you know the legend that King Arthur himself buried gold in those hills."

He lifted a brow. "You know of that legend? Ah, you have succumbed to my father's magic. I almost forgot."

"I am not certain I take your meaning."

"He invented that tale of a golden horde and added King Arthur to the cast of characters in his poem, *The Enchanted Briar*. Many think his tale was factual, but it was mostly fiction."

"Sir Hugh based his verses on legends founded in history."

"He took thin tales and fleshed them out in his imagination. Do not waste your time, or your museum's time, on fancies, Mrs. Blackburn."

He stood, aware that she stared up at him and regretting his sharp tone. But he was impatient where his interrupted road was concerned — and he could not soften any further toward her. He found her simply too damned intriguing.

"I will wait for you and your brother in the foyer, madam." With a courteous nod, he left the room.

A dark net draped over her neatly tipped black hat lessened the sun's glare as Christina followed Aedan's long-legged stride down the front steps. John made his way more slowly behind them. In the drive, Tam Durie waited beside a two-wheeled carriage harnessed to a huge bay with white feathered feet.

"Yer gig is ready, Sir Aedan," Tam said after greeting them. "Andrew Mor came doon frae the hoose to say ye wanted it,

111

though we had Pog saddled for ye. D'ye want me to drive?"

"Thank you, Tam. I'll drive the gig, and Pog can follow on a lead. Unless, Mr. Blackburn, you would like to ride the mare." He indicated the gray horse walking up the drive in the care of a young groom, a slight blond lad in a shabby kilt and jacket.

"I'd be happy to ride her," John said, grinning.

Tam tipped his hat and departed while John vaulted into the saddle. Christina accepted Aedan's assistance into the high seat of the gig. "I promise you that I will drive a bit more sedately than Tam," he commented, taking the reins.

"I found his driving rather refreshing," she answered.

"Somehow that does not surprise me." They moved ahead, while John, mounted on the gray, rode beside them down the private lane to the wide public road. Aedan kept the huge feather-footed bay to an even pace. Perched on the springy, cushioned bench, Christina glanced at him.

"You needn't creep along for my benefit, Sir Aedan."

"You're an impatient lass," he murmured, glancing at her. "I was considering my horse, Mrs. Blackburn. Pog is not accustomed to walking beside a vehicle, nor is she used to different riders, though your brother handles

112

her well. She's a temperamental thing."

"Pog?" she asked, curious.

"Short for *pògach*." He glanced at her. "You know Gaelic, Mrs. Blackburn, do you not?" His eyes twinkled, and a smile played around his flexible lips.

"*Pògach?* What does it mean?" John asked.

"Fond of kissing," Christina answered. "Did you name her?" She slid Aedan a slanted glance, and he grinned at her.

"Tam did. He kisses her on the nose each night, and has done so since she was a colt. He was present at her birth, and she's almost more his horse than mine. Tam swears she cries without her good-night kiss."

John hooted, and Christina giggled. She sat close to Aedan on the narrow seat, and although her skirt and petticoats were a barrier, she was pleasantly aware of his long thigh beside hers and his arm brushing hers.

The road was a clean ribbon over the moor. "The route is in good repair," she observed. "So many Highland roads are rutted and rough, or have alarming curves and steep slopes."

"This is an old drover's track, which we rebuilt and surfaced. I've been overseeing the roads and byways in the western regions for about two years. This part is level, but it climbs once we near the hills. Steep gradients are impossible to avoid in the Highlands."

"Tam Durie showed us just how steep they

can be," Christina said, and Aedan chuckled.

Soon he pointed to a farmhouse nestled at the foot of a high, bleak hill. "That's the home farm, which produces much of what we need at Dundrennan House. Parlan Mac-Donald, who tends the farm, is also our factor, and he helps see to the welfare of our tenants. His brother Hector is my foreman on the road crew, and Hector's daughter and grandmother do the laundering for us at the house. Our tenants are fewer now, but there is still work for the factor, and we will find work for every tenant who needs it. My father always insisted on that, despite the troubles of the last seventy-five years or so, and I am determined to honor it."

"Were homes cleared here for sheep grazing, as they were all across the Highlands?" John asked.

Aedan shook his head. "Not here. My father and grandfather would not tolerate it. We were forced to sell off some of our land, though, and those homes were cleared to make room for sheep and hunting preserves. We could not stop it once our rights were sold. Some of the people left homes they had occupied for generations, and some were evicted by the new tenants."

"Did many of the men on the estate go to war?" John said.

"Aye, many of them joined the Highland regiments to gain some income for their families. A good number were killed in the Crimea and India, and many have gone on to other posts in India. Some of their widows and families left to live with kinfolk, and some have left Scotland entirely. Some are still here, though."

Christina sighed. "The sweeping away of the old ways."

"Scotland has seen war and strife throughout her history, but never change on such a scale as the last few generations. We are not at war, yet the enemy is at our gates."

"What enemy?" John asked.

"Poverty, sir, and greed. Ignorance and prejudice. Even tourism, greedy to see romantic settings, but disrespectful of our customs."

"There are groups who work to preserve Gaelic culture, sir," Christina said. "I belong to a few of them myself. Your father revived Scottish heritage in his poetry, like Scott and Burns and some others."

"All worthy efforts. I agree that our culture must be protected, but Scotland needs to enter the modern age in order to survive. The Highland culture, and the Highland people, would benefit from a little modernization. I support improvements and growth, rather than destruction, and the blending of new methods with the old. At the same time, I admire Highland history and culture and wish to do my part to protect and preserve them."

"What of the roads you build all over Scotland? Do you see that as protecting your country or interfering with it?"

"Inroads, Mrs. Blackburn. New pathways into the heart of an ailing nation. Roads and railways will bring new lifeblood into Scotland and help save it."

"Then you are as much a crusader for Scotland as I am," she said, glancing at him.

"I do what I can," he said. "And Dundrennan, a small part of Scotland entirely in my hands, is of chief concern to me."

The gig sped along the road, and John cantered ahead. The hills thrust dark shoulders into a blue sky, their rounded slopes tough with stones and grasses. Heather spread gorgeous plummy color over the inclines. Christina looked around, admiring.

The finished road ended just ahead, and a raw earthen track curved up a hill, its path marked by wooden stakes. "The black powder was discharged up there," Aedan said, pointing.

Peering through her veil, Christina saw a dark gash along the right side of the hill. It seemed unremarkable, just as Aedan MacBride had said.

Clearly he thought the museum's investigation was little more than an inconvenience.

But Christina was intrigued about whatever lay inside Cairn Drishan. What if some long-forgotten ancient treasure did exist there, as legend said? Suppose her uncle had been right about the presence of King Arthur in this region after all, and some proof of his theories could be found?

Imagination or not, Christina could not wait to explore the mysteries of that hill.

Chapter Seven

"The sleeping king," Christina murmured. "Do you see him in the shape of the ridge?"

"What?" Aedan glanced at her.

"A Celtic tradition tells of a great king trapped under a mountain, held by magic," she explained, then pointed. "If we could see through the crust of the earth, we would see him lying there, asleep. His head is to the left, below that his shoulder, and the lesser slopes of his hip, knee, and so on down to his feet."

"Ah, now I see it. Though I wonder how you can see anything at all through that netting. You look fetching in that hat, madam, but it isn't very practical."

"It cuts the glare of the sun. You should try it for yourself. Perhaps you would not scowl quite so much."

He chuckled low, and the sound tempted Christina to smile herself, which she did secretly behind her veil. "So the king sleeps under a spell. And when he wakes?" he asked.

"Then all will be well in the land again, or so they say."

"We have a similar legend at Dundrennan, but ours is about a sleeping princess."

"And when she wakes, will all be right in the land?"

"So they say," he murmured. "But she will never wake, for no one can break the spell."

She slid him a curious glance. He halted the gig and jumped down to walk around. "Well, Mrs. Blackburn, since the crust of this hill is already broken, let us see what sort of pie it is." He grasped her by the waist and lifted her down. She very much liked the iron press of his fingers against her waist, and she gripped his forearms for support as he lowered her.

"We walk up the hill from here," he said. "It's easier than taking the gig until the road is cut and topped. Tell me," he added, glancing at John, who was leashing Pog to a nearby tree. "Will the climb be difficult for your brother?"

"It may be, but he is doing better lately. He will rest if his leg bothers him. Thank you for your concern."

"And you? Will you have any difficulty?"

"None. This way?" Gathering her skirts, glad she had worn sturdy boots, she took the dirt pathway quickly. Above, along the zigzagging course, she saw the raw cut in the hillside.

"The highest of these hills is a thousand feet at the summit," Aedan said, walking behind her, John a little farther back along the earthen path. "You can see where we halted work beneath that rocky cliff, about three hundred feet up."

"Hopefully your roadwork will resume shortly," John said.

"That depends on your sister, sir." Aedan slid her a glance.

She frowned without reply and hurried ahead. A little farther up, she stopped to gaze at the jagged pile of rocks.

Seeing Walter Carriston's books in Dundrennan's library had reminded her again of her uncle's controversial theories concerning Celtic Scotland. Sir Edgar Neaves had hinted that she might even find something to support her uncle's research. If that were true, then her ailing uncle could regain his tarnished reputation before he died.

She felt a surge of hope, or perhaps only wishful thinking. Her work with Uncle Walter had been fascinating and rewarding in many ways, yet disheartening in the last year, for he had endured the academic ridicule of his dearly held ideas, and it had affected his health. If her work here revealed a Pictish presence, her uncle's reputation would benefit.

Her eagerness renewed, she climbed faster, pulling ahead of the men. As she walked, she lifted the hems of her gray woolen skirt and four petticoats, including one of red flannel that flashed fiery color with each step.

The path cut through the heathered slopes and led toward the site of the blasting. Turf had peeled back, exposing raw earth and sheer rock. Despite her sturdy boot soles, Christina nearly stumbled on the stone-littered path.

"Be careful," Aedan MacBride said, coming up behind her. He extended his hand to help her jump a mucky puddle. His fingers were firm on her gloved hand. "The mud can be very bad here after a rain. We made drainage ditches, but a fierce storm could start a mud slide. One more reason to finish this road quickly." He turned to her brother. "Mr. Blackburn?"

John had stepped off the path to sit on a boulder. He held a small sketch book. "I'll come up soon. I want to sketch some landscape and make color notes on the light."

Christina looked at Aedan. "He may need to rest," she murmured. "He lost some muscle from the gunshot wound and lacks full strength in that leg. He never complains outright, but it still causes him some pain."

He nodded, frowning. "The hill is quite steep and rough from here on, madam. Would you like to rest, as well?"

"No," she said decisively. The sunlight was strong, but her veil obscured her sight. She pushed the netting back and twisted it behind her hat, fastening it with a long hatpin.

"You could command armies with a weapon like that," Aedan commented.

She sent him a little glare and resumed her steady ascent. Each breath came a little dearer now, and she cursed the whalebone stays beneath her blouse and jacket, although she was glad for her shorter walking skirt and her tough-soled brogans, which allowed her to take sure strides.

Aedan went ahead and reached out a hand in assistance. He kept hold of her gloved hand to help her along the steep, winding track, his grip firm and pleasant. When he let go, she missed that comfort.

"Why does the road curve like this?" she asked, putting a hand to her side, pausing to draw in a few breaths.

"To allow for the steep grade of the hill. The road cannot go straight up and over. We cut it this way, so that it rises a little, then swings that way, rising again" — he gestured as he spoke — "gradually moving up and then down the hillside. That way the ride is not so steep in a carriage."

"Going on foot, I feel as if I have climbed a veritable mountain," she said, still breathless. "Why not cut the road around the base of the hill?" She looked down. The slope fell steeply away from the edge of the path, shored up by boulders.

"Do you see that wide burn on the moor below? It cuts close to the hill, so the lower slope can be very boggy. And the land on other side of the burn no longer belongs to my estate, and we could not obtain the owners' permission. They prefer to keep it for hunting privileges."

"You said the government could take precedence in the case of a parliamentary road."

"The owner of the lease happens to be the queen," he said. "They rent the land out for hunting. So we could not argue the rights of the road for our project."

"I see. Oh, Tam took us this way in the carriage," she said, looking around. "The view is stunning. Look — there's an eagle!" She pointed.

They stood so high on the slope that the great bird glided beneath them, the sun bright on its outspread wings. Below, the moorland spread out like a golden quilt, meeting the heathered hillsides, the sky above sweeping and clear. Christina smiled, sighing with admiration at the beautiful landscape.

"Aye, it's lovely and peaceful," Aedan agreed, watching her. "I came here often as a lad. It is one of my favorite spots."

"Then why take blasting powder to it?"

"Black powder, madam," he corrected. "There was a great deal of rock, so we had little choice. And we thought there would be nothing of historic value here, for there was no sign of anything."

"My uncle always believed something might

be found on Cairn Drishan," she said. "There are ancient ruins elsewhere in these Strathclyde hills."

"My father shared that hope."

"But you do not," she said astutely.

"Not particularly. Can you continue, Mrs. Blackburn, or do you need to abandon your stays?" He lifted a brow.

Her cheeks grew hot. "That is none of your concern."

He smiled in answer and offered his hand again. She took it and they moved upward, soon reaching a large cluster of rocks, which they clambered over. The wind fluttered Christina's hat ribbons against her cheek and billowed her skirt.

"Careful, lass. My crew has not yet cleared all the rubble from the explosion. I must ask you never to come up here alone. It is not safe." He pulled her upward.

She stepped up beside him and faced him. "I am not helpless, sir. I would do fine here by myself."

He stopped to glare down at her. "Christina Blackburn," he said sternly, "it is dangerous up here, and you will not come here alone. Either I will come with you, or some of my men will do so. Never alone. Is that understood?" He frowned, his brows straight and black over blue eyes of a brilliant clarity.

She considered arguing, then nodded. "I understand."

His hand tightened on hers as he drew her over more rocks. "Just a few feet more. Good," he said. "And there it is."

She looked around, then stared.

Dark with age, irregular in shape, the stones upthrust like teeth in a monstrous jaw, savage, primeval, but with underlying structure. They had not been shaped by nature or blasting powder, but by tools, and had been stacked in a deliberate pattern. Many had fallen out of the set, resulting in a jumble.

She released Aedan's hand and walked forward, heart pounding. The wall was in shambles, black with age, strangely glossy. Beyond its staggered line, she saw a gaping hole in the hillside, like a mouth opening to show fierce teeth and bones.

"Oh," she said. She dropped to one knee, touched a few stones. "Oh, my."

"I hope you are not disappointed, having come so far."

Neither disappointment nor thrill described her reaction. Dismay was closer to the mark. Unable to make sense of the puzzle of stones at first, she did not know what to say. Aware that she was touted as an expert, she hid her uncertainty. She had expected a ruin, but not utter chaos.

After a moment she pulled a small notebook from her reticule and knelt on the cushion of her skirts to make quick notes and sketches. Then she rose to her feet.

MacBride moved toward her, stepping over the toppled barrier.

"Be careful," Aedan warned behind her. "It's unstable."

Nodding, she made more sketches, trying to puzzle out the relationship of turf and stone. How long had this been here, and what sort of structure was it? Were there clues buried in the earth here? Toeing the dirt, she turned over a few small stones.

Kneeling, she traced the stones of the tumbled-down wall with her hand. Something in their appearance was very odd, but she could not think what it was. She frowned, examining them.

"No cache of gold, as you see," Aedan said. "Little to recommend further investigation. I'm sorry."

She hefted a small, dark stone thoughtfully in her hand. "Do not apologize, sir. This place may indeed be very old. My uncle's research on the Celtic tribes in this area indicates that there was a settlement in the area of Dundrennan."

"Well, there is a hill fort a few miles from here."

"Indeed, I know of that one. And where there is a fort, there are often homesteads in the vicinity. I will not dismiss this pile of stones out of hand just yet."

"Not yet?"

"Not just yet." She looked up and saw him

frown. Wind lifted his hair, fluttered his shirt and gray vest, for he had left his jacket in the gig. Muscular, handsome, intriguing and secretive, he seemed part of this place, somehow — strong and bold, earth-wrought and mysterious. Even his black hair and blue eyes, his black clothing and gray vest, seemed to blend harmoniously with the iron-gray stones that surrounded him.

"Mrs. Blackburn, do not be misled by your ideals and by your great desire to find something here."

"Sir?" She stood, heart pounding, but she reminded herself that he could not know her hopes for her uncle's work.

"There are no miracles to be found here, no treasure, no ancient tombs waiting to be discovered. This is most likely a collapsed black house, covered by a landslide decades ago. Luckily it was deserted before then, for we saw no bodies among the stones. I beg your pardon for mentioning so unpleasant a topic."

"But I would be fascinated to find an ancient body entombed here. It would yield wonderful information about the past. If you wish to persuade me to abandon this task, or if you doubt a woman can be of use here, you are mistaken."

He narrowed his eyes. "I do not care if Sir Edgar sent man, woman, or bogle to examine this hill. Surely you can tell a black house from a hill fort."

"I can tell you, sir, this is no black house," she snapped.

"A shieling, then. Just a lot of old, dirty stones to be moved out of the way."

"I am no archaeologist — that is a fairly new science — but I will not dismiss this as unimportant. Not yet," she repeated. "I mean to assess it carefully."

"Be as careful as you like. Just be quick about it."

She stood, brushing off her hands. "What is the rush?"

"The road must be completed by mid-October. Your assessment must take only a few days at most."

"You wish to be rid of me."

He inclined his head, and she could see that his temper and impatience were sparking hot. "You and your brother are welcome to stay at Dundrennan as long as you like. Just be quick about your work here — so that I can get on with mine."

"I will not be rushed, nor will I allow you to tell me what I think about this place," she said furiously.

"I would simply appreciate your . . . efficiency, madam." He stepped backward. "We must go, if you please."

"If you please, sir, I will stay for a while. Go about your day. I will be perfectly safe here with my brother."

"Well." He frowned. "My crew is working

on the moor on the other side of this hill, and I will be there if you need anything. I will leave the gig for you and Mr. Blackburn, and I will take the horse. Mrs. Gunn expects you for luncheon at one o'clock. Good day, Mrs. Blackburn."

"Before you leave, there is a matter to discuss." She knew he would not like it, but that suited her well just now. "You know all construction on the hill must cease for now."

"I am aware of that," he said curtly.

"Sir Edgar wants the nearby roadwork halted until he can come here to make his determination. That includes any work on the moor, if it is within a mile or so."

He narrowed his eyes. "That is ridiculous."

"The use of black powder or machinery could set up vibrations that would disturb this fragile find."

"There is no find," he said bluntly. "That is slate and sandstone behind you, not bone china, for the love of God!"

"There is no need to swear. You are a civil engineer. Do not pretend that you do not understand the danger of tremors."

"Of course I do."

"As for the rest, the law of Treasure Trove dictates —"

"What treasure?" he demanded. "Are you now judge and jury to dictate the future of my career and my home, as well? If I lose Dundrennan because of —" He stopped, turned away, as if holding his temper and protecting some private thought.

"Lose Dundrennan?" she asked. "What do you mean?"

"Nothing." He frowned. "Mrs. Blackburn, this road must go through, no matter what you find here." He turned on his heel and walked away, nimbly clearing the rocks until he disappeared around the sloped curve.

"Aedan MacBride may indeed be right, Christina," John said later. "This may be one great, useless pile of stones." He sat on a boulder, having slowly climbed the rest of the hill to join her after Aedan left. "But I suspect you will not surrender to him on that point."

Christina surveyed the confusion of rocks around her, feeling discouraged. Realizing the enormity of her task, she felt almost ill. MacBride's angry outburst bothered her more than she wanted to admit. She understood his dilemma, but she could not give in to his will. "Sir Aedan wants me to dismiss this, but I must continue."

"Aye, you must, over and above Treasure Trove Law." John nodded. "You hope to find something to support Uncle Walter's theories."

She nodded. "There must be some clue here — we are in the right area, and this might well be from an early century."

Bending, she picked up a broken bit of the dark rock that had tumbled from the ruined wall. Frowning, she turned it in her hand. Something eluded her, something she could not quite pinpoint in her mind.

"So you do not think this is a black house, as Sir Aedan suggested?"

She shook her head, examining the rock thoughtfully. "I do not agree with him on that," she said. "I'm not sure exactly why quite yet. I just have a feeling."

John nodded and returned his attention to his sketchbook. Christina turned, and a fast, cool wind whipped over the hills, rippling her veil, her ribbons, blowing her skirts back. She surveyed the chaotic rubble all around her, then looked out over the rounded, bleak hills.

Something was here in this place, something of importance. She felt it, knew it, but could not yet define it. A trace, an artifact, even the smallest inscription or carving might mean the difference between a simple ruined wall and a historically significant ruin.

Years ago, the Reverend Walter Carriston had translated documents that had referred to a specific location, a place close to Dundrennan, and had hinted at a connection with Arthur, the great warrior-king who had become the stuff of magnificent medieval legend but who had apparently lived during the sixth century. Her uncle's discovery of some early references to Arthur had become the basis for his life's work. Carriston had strived to prove that King Arthur, a warrior-king in a warlike society long before the Middle Ages, had links to Celtic Scotland — indeed, might even have come from Scotland himself.

His theories had been ill received, and he had suffered in reputation and health. But he had never doubted his conclusions. Christina respected her uncle and his work and believed that his theories were based on historical truth.

Now that this wall had been found on Cairn Drishan, there was hope. She was certain of one thing. The wall was exceedingly old. Turning the stone in her hand, looking at its glossy, greenish black surface, she nodded to herself. Indeed, very old.

King Arthur at Dundrennan. An even more astonishing thought was that Dundrennan's own princess might have been the great king's contemporary in history. A find in support of that, her uncle's most cherished conclusion, would be astonishing. It would change understanding of Arthurian scholarship. It could even alter the interpretation of the Arthurian legends.

No wonder so many scholars rejected Carriston's theory. His work threatened what they regarded as gospel truth, that the Arthurian tales had roots in the Welsh, English, and Cornish traditions. Scholarship allowed that the historical Arthur, the sixth-century warrior briefly mentioned in early chronicles, may have crossed into Scotland to conquer it.

But her uncle had suggested that Arthur came of a Scottish Celtic tribe himself. A scandalous, unacceptable suggestion, despite his convincing evidence.

"If I could find some material proof of his theory," Christina said thoughtfully, looking around, "his work would be redeemed. The truth is here somewhere. I know it."

"You are very stubborn." John got to his feet and came to stand beside her. "A stubborn nature is a fine asset, but do not demand the impossible from yourself."

She looked at John. "I must. You know I must."

He sighed and after a moment nodded. "Well, if you are so determined, I will help you if I can. But you'll have to find your proof before Sir Edgar arrives to take this over from you."

She nodded. "I suppose I should ask Sir Aedan for a shovel, then." She laughed bitterly. "He'll either expect me to dig here myself — or he will refuse me even the loan of a shovel and just tell me that this is unimportant and I should be on my way. But it *is* important, John." She looked at the little piece of rock in her hand. "I'm sure of it."

"I don't think he's that much of a Mr.

Scrooge. And besides, he does have a full work crew. . . . Do you suppose he's using all of them down there?" He smiled a little.

"John Blackburn, you are a genius! Are you ready to go down the hill, or would you rather rest here until I get back?"

"I'll wait. It was a long walk up that hill, and I'd like to make some sketches here. Where are you going?"

She shook the glossy rock. "I mean to convince Sir Scrooge to loan me far more than a shovel!" Hitching up her skirts, she hastened down the earthen incline.

Chapter Eight

Earth and rock sundered open, spitting debris into a blue sky as the blast shivered through the heather. Standing two hundred yards away, Aedan felt the vibration. He had witnessed countless explosions as a civil engineer, but this time the world — his very being — seemed to tilt. Swift as a shadow, a foreboding rushed through him and faded.

Just a routine blast, he told himself, a safe and necessary phase in the construction of the parliamentary road under his supervision. His contract with the Commission for the Department of Roads and Highways required the timely completion of this Highland project, and he was determined to honor that commitment.

Since the highway cut through the edge of the property where he was laird and baronet, he felt uneasy ordering permanent alterations in the land. Still, he agreed with the merits of improvements across Scotland, and he would do his part to help bring those benefits about.

Underfoot, the wide road was topped with a

tightly packed layer of crushed stone that stretched south over the fells toward Glasgow. Northward, the road met a line of hills that crossed the moorland for miles. Marked by wooden stakes, a rough earthen path zigzagged up the incline of Cairn Drishan.

For two years Aedan and his crew had inched this gravel-packed route along the Highland Boundary Line, through rough terrain and unpredictable weather. Only seven weeks remained before the queen's visit to Dundrennan, when the government expected the new route to be completed. But the recent delay posed by the discovery of stone walls on Cairn Drishan had halted work on the vital hill section of the road.

He glanced toward Cairn Drishan, over a mile away but easily visible as part of a curving chain of hills. The rounded top sat slightly askew, like a tilted hat. Notches halfway up one heathery slope marked the road cuts, and a deep gouge indicated the site of the ruined wall.

Christina Blackburn was up there now, he thought, examining those stones. The very thought of her made his heart beat a little faster, he realized with a frown. She was so lush and spirited behind her gentle, bookish exterior that he felt all the more fascinated by her. He wanted to see her again soon, wanted to learn more about her, be with her —

No, he cautioned himself. It would have been far better for Dundrennan and its laird if the museum antiquarian had turned out to be an old fusspot after all.

He fervently hoped that the wall would prove to be recent and unremarkable enough to allow his work to continue as planned. An alternate route was plausible, but more complicated to execute.

As the explosion's thunder gradually subsided, Aedan felt the wind, warm and dusty, though still fragrant with heather. He stepped out from behind the protection of a roadside boulder and saw members of his work crew doing the same near the side of the road. One of them, a young blond man, approached Aedan.

"A touch of black powder reduced that cluster of boulders and saved days of hard labor," Aedan said. "Well done, Rob."

"Thank you, sir." His assistant engineer, Robert Campbell, smiled. Rob looked more like a towheaded schoolboy than the most promising student in Rankine's classes in modern principles of engineering at Glasgow University, Aedan thought. "I know your plan calls for grading by hand digging whenever possible to preserve the landscape, Sir Aedan, but once again we found more rock than anticipated."

"Blasting was the best solution." Aedan brushed earth dust from his shirtsleeves and dark brown linen vest. "You placed the charges cautiously, and kept the damage to a minimum."

"Hector MacDonald watched me like a nursemaid." Rob turned to grin at the lanky, sun-browned man who approached them.

"I made sure the lad didna pluff the cap off Cairn Drishan, too, and he dida fine job there," Hector said as he approached. "Although the blasting that day exposed that wall up there. Did yer lady antiquarian decide if 'tis a historical place yet?"

"Not yet. She's still up there, looking around." Earlier, Aedan had told his assistants the reason for his late arrival that morning. "My father always believed something of historic significance would be found on Cairn Drishan. I hope he is not going to be proved right in that."

"Is that why Sir Hugh protested the highway project so strongly?" Rob asked. "I thought it was because he loathed improvements in the Highlands."

"True. He preferred an unsullied Scotland," Aedan said.

"I was thinking that a landslide, even an earthquake, might have buried that wall years ago," Hector observed, glancing at the range of hills behind them.

"Aye," Rob agreed. "The Drishan ridge runs into the Highland Boundary, and tremors are not unknown in this part of

Scotland. I studied a semester in the new science of geology," he added.

"Perhaps a mud slide took doon that wee house," Hector mused.

"Wee? Those walls are six-feet thick," Rob said. "And I think it will prove to be a very ancient site."

Aedan sighed and rubbed a hand over his face wearily. He felt a sense of dread, knowing that Christina Blackburn had authority over part of his life just now. His own instincts said that the wall was ancient, although he did not want to admit it.

He stood to lose everything — road, career, estate, and ancestral home — if those humble stones proved historic, thanks to a troublesome codicil in his father's will.

"Damn," he whispered. He was anxious for Christina to come down from the hill and make her pronouncement. Glancing in that direction, he thought he saw her walking down the slope, but the figure disappeared behind an outcrop of rock.

"The route has to go through that hill," he said, turning back. "We cannot afford to lose any more time on this project."

"Still, there's no choice but to wait a bit," Rob said. "The Treasure Trove Law requires investigation when something of possible historic significance is found in Scotland."

"Treasure! Aye, that would be fine!" Hector rubbed his hands in delight.

139

"It would belong to the government, not us," Aedan said.

"I've heard that ancient kings lived in this area centuries ago," Rob mused, looking at the hill. "I wonder. . . ."

"Aye, those walls could be part of the auld castle in the legend," Hector said.

"Exactly," Robert nodded. "Sir Hugh MacBride wrote about the legend of Dundrennan in one of his poems, *The Enchanted Briar.* I learned the verses as a lad. It mentions hidden gold."

"Every schoolchild learned those verses, including the poet's own brood," Aedan said. "My father based that poem on our old legend, but the tale is fictitious."

"The auld traditions say there's treasure somewhere in those hills, hidden by magic, just waiting to be found," Hector said. " 'Tis King Arthur's gold, they say."

" 'Deck'd in raiment of the sun,' " Rob recited, musing. " 'A mighty horde of treasure bright. . . .' "

"A fine wee poem." Hector nodded approval.

"That thing is ten cantos long," Aedan said. "And this is nonsense. No treasure exists up there. Just a lot of old stones."

"King Arthur's gold is there somewhere," Hector insisted. "It will be found when the princess wakes from her magic spell."

"That will be never," Aedan pointed out.

"It's a child's fairy tale. My father invented most of it."

"Part of the legend is true," Hector pointed out. "And if there is gold ye'd have nae more troubles, sir."

"I'd have new troubles," Aedan snapped.

"Dundrennan House and its grounds would become a famous touristing site," Rob said.

"Tourists!" Aedan shook his head. "I just want this damnable business over with quickly. Well, nothing to be done now but tend to the tasks at hand. Hector, ask Angus Gowan to survey the new gradient, if you would."

Nodding, the older man turned to walk toward the crew that worked farther down the road.

Extracting a leather memorandum book and a stub of lead pencil from his pocket, Aedan made a quick sketch and scribbled some notes. He crossed the graveled road toward the work crew and equipment, while Rob walked alongside him.

"Rankine recommends the use of black powder wherever the rock is sufficiently dense to merit it over handwork," Rob said as they walked. "But it's clear that we cannot blow willy-nilly through any part of this route, no matter how hard the rock."

"It's important to follow instinct and logic, as well as rote." Aedan glanced at his apprentice. "Oh, I have a message for you, Rob. My aunt and my cousin Amy wish to thank you for taking tea with them a couple of weeks ago when I was away. And they asked me to invite you to a small dinner party at Dundrennan House tomorrow evening. I didn't even know about it myself until this morning. They'd like to welcome the museum antiquarian and her brother."

"Welcoming the enemy?" Rob grinned.

"So it would seem," Aedan replied grimly.

"Please tell the ladies that I would be honored to attend," Rob said. "I look forward to meeting your antiquarian. And I'm curious to see what surprises are in store at Dundrennan House. Last time I was there, Miss Stewart was keen to drape new curtains on your window poles, so I helped her."

"Amy is still in the throes of decorating madness," Aedan muttered. A curious noise threaded through his awareness. Turning, he pointed toward a huge red steam engine secured on a platform wagon drawn by two oxen. "That great metal beast is rattling again."

"And Donald is waving for assistance. I'll see to it," Rob said, and sprinted away.

Giant pistons and shovel arm pumping, the steam engine hissed and clicked loudly as it drove a huge metal scoop into the ground to dig a new section of the road. The machine dominated Aedan's attention as he watched Rob leap on the cart to adjust the controls.

Dust mingled with smoke to form a cloud around the work site. Along the earthen track over the moorland, men wielded picks and hand shovels, clearing debris in the wake of the steam engine. The metal beast, rented from a Glasgow firm, was powerful and very useful, though finicky and often bothersome.

When Hector shouted over the noise, Aedan scarcely heard him. Looking around, he saw Hector pointing in the direction of Cairn Drishan. Aedan glanced there.

And swore, loud and sharp.

Heading toward them from the hills, his own gig and bay came tearing down the road, raising dust. Christina Blackburn was at the reins, going at such a mad pace that he could see the black ribbons of her hat and a tail of skirt flapping in the wind.

Realizing that the vehicle hurtled straight toward the work site, seeing his men drop their tools and scatter, Aedan broke into a run and hurried toward the gig's path.

He shouted, waving Christina away, but the vehicle was going far too fast. Galloping onward, the bay whinnied and lurched sideways, and the gig turned, leaning dangerously.

Dashing behind the canvas tent where he had tied Pog to keep her away from the dust and commotion, Aedan leaped into the saddle and raced toward the vehicle. As it careened wildly across the moor, he saw Christina pulling desperately on the reins.

Chapter Nine

Galloping alongside, Aedan reached out and grabbed the bay's bridle, pulling steadily and rode in tandem, guiding both horses as they slowed and stopped. As the gig clattered to a halt, one of its two wheels struck a rock. Christina nearly flew out of her seat, landing with a smack on the bench, grabbing the side bar as she uttered a small shriek.

Settling the bay horse, Aedan shifted Pog and faced the driver. She gathered herself from a sprawl and sat upright, showing a glimpse of slim ankles and calves in pale stockings and the flare of a red petticoat among white frills before she shoved her sober gray skirt down. She sat up, righting her hat, adjusting her jacket.

How on earth she had kept that hat and veil in place, he could not imagine. Her face was pale beneath the filmy fabric. Her spectacles glittered faintly, and a few auburn curls danced free over her shoulder. She tucked them somewhere and faced him.

"Have you been taking driving lessons from Tam Durie, madam?" he asked calmly.

She glared at him from under her net and lifted her chin. He wanted to laugh, but even more, he wanted to shout at her, shake her for being a fool and scaring the wits out of him. Crossing his hands on the saddle pommel, he returned a hard stare.

"Your quick action saved me," she said. "Thank you."

"And it saved the gig and a valuable horse." He regarded her. "I believe I have saved you three times in twenty-four hours. In primitive cultures, that means your soul is mine."

She tilted her chin, adjusted her gloves. "Thank heaven this is not a primitive culture."

"This is the Highlands, where the Gaels were long considered to be savage tribal creatures. And I am fully Gael by blood, if somewhat civilized by Lowland standards —"

"Somewhat," she said tersely.

"So you may well owe me your soul in return for the rescues," he said sternly, striving to keep his temper. His heart still hammered with fear and concern, not for the expensive Clyde-bred horse and the London gig, but for what might have happened to Christina had he not intervened.

She brushed at her skirt. "There is no need to be sour with me, Sir Aedan."

"Fine. Then I will be direct. Why in the name of all the devil's henchmen did you

145

drive my gig like that and push that horse in such a manner?" He nearly shouted this, but he glanced away and drew a hissing breath to gather his composure. He looked back. "Is there some emergency? Is your brother hurt?"

"No. He's fine. I apologize. I am not used to driving country distances, and I lost control of the horse. Something frightened it. Her."

"Him. That would have been obvious, had you taken care to observe your horse, like a responsible driver. Do you handle a cart like that in Edinburgh? I should be wary of being near the High Street on one of your shopping days."

"Stop it," she snapped, startling him. "You have cause to be angry, but you need not be harsh. The horse bolted. And I am grateful to you for perhaps saving my life, sir. Please accept that in lieu of my soul, if you require something of me. And do not stir a needless argument. It suits neither of us."

He drew his brows together, puzzled, mollified — and impressed at how easily she had cut through his angry response. "I beg your pardon. I was unfair. But I was . . . alarmed."

"Then just say so." She looked past him. "The horse was startled by the explosion as we came down the slope, and then again that thing over there. What is it?"

"That? A steam engine. Surely you have seen them."

"Certainly, but never with a . . . scooping thing on it."

"It holds a shovel, Mrs. Blackburn. We are hurrying to finish the road, and the beast expedites the digging."

"Digging . . . Sir Aedan, I came out here to ask a favor." She folded her gloved hands neatly in her lap and looked at him through the veil as primly if she were a guest at tea.

He studied her face behind the seductive shadow. The finely spun thing was damnably alluring, he thought, for it enhanced her wide eyes and the fine bone structure of her face and gave him thoughts a man should not entertain in the presence of a lady.

"Aye, what is it?" He patted the shoulder of the big bay horse, calming it. What was so important to Christina Blackburn that she would race to speak to him? Waiting, he glanced at her.

"I think the site on Cairn Drishan merits closer investigation," she said.

"You do." He waited, wary.

"Yes, I believe there may be an ancient structure there. If only a small part is exposed, the rest could prove an astonishing find. It must be excavated."

"What would that entail? Apart from having no roadwork done near it, of course." His tone was acerbic.

"Careful digging must be done there to clear the area."

"And you raced here to borrow a shovel from me, is that it?"

"Several shovels, and men to use them."

He scowled. "My men have a great deal of work to do here."

"They are needed on Cairn Drishan for a few days only. The turf layer must be cleared away so that I can properly examine the walls."

"A few days of digging will hardly make a dent up there."

"Longer, then. But I need a crew of men to do the labor. Or do you expect me to do the digging myself?"

He raised a brow. "Do not tempt me, Mrs. Blackburn."

"I cannot make my report complete until I have some idea what is buried in that hill."

"It is just more rock, and lots of it," he said firmly. "Digging up there would exhaust my men unnecessarily and use days of good weather that we need for roadwork. Please try to be realistic, madam. That pile of stone up there was created by the hand of man, I agree — but not ancient man. Drystone walls are common in the Highlands. Black houses, we call them, after the color of the interior from the smoke of peat fires —"

"I know all about black houses. I lived in one for a year. I have not forgotten the experience."

"You what?" He blinked at her.

"I lived in one. My mother was of a Highland family, and she went north to spend a year teaching English to Gaelic children. My father went to Italy at the time to paint and teach. He took my brother and half the house staff, and Mother took my sister and me. She taught in a Ladies' School, and we assisted her, and we lived in a rented crofter's house. My mother wanted to do something useful, rather than sit idle in Italy while my father painted and socialized."

"So you lived in a black house?" He had thought her the product of an elite cosmopolitan upbringing, but now he looked at her in admiration. She was a constant surprise to him.

"Yes. I know exactly what a black house is, sir. And that, on Cairn Drishan, is not one."

"Then what is it?"

"My guess is that it may be a Pictish house of great antiquity."

"Most Pictish houses are of great antiquity," he pointed out logically. "Do you have grounds for supposing this, other than fervent academic hope?"

She glowered behind the veil. Then she reached down to the floor of the gig and lifted something in her hand — a dark rock the size of her fist. For a moment he thought she was going to lob it at him. "The walls are vitrified," she said.

"They are what?" Knowing what she

meant, he was simply surprised by her once again.

"Vitrified. The process of burning timbers inside a stone structure, resulting in a fire so intense that the stone melts and forms a vitreous, glassy surface, rendering the walls impervious to damage by missiles. Either the place was burned, or it was purposely set afire to increase its defensibility. As an engineer, you must be familiar with the term."

"I am."

"Then why did you ask what it meant?"

"I did not —" He sighed, exasperated, and reached for the rock, turning it to look at the dark greenish glaze. "You may be right, Mrs. Blackburn. This has a glass surface. Odd."

"The entire wall seems to be like that, but on the inside portions only, indicating a fire inside the structure. I found it everywhere that I scraped away dirt."

"A black house or shieling could have burned, resulting in vitrification of the stone. But it's not proof of an ancient house and ancient inhabitants."

"I expect to find proof of that, too, with time to dig there. This rock is highly suggestive. Even you must admit that."

He sighed, realizing that she had the advantage as the museum's representative and could order as long a delay as she pleased. "Very well, then. You will have your crew, but only for a few days. I assume the museum will pay their wages for the work." He looked hard at her.

"I will recommend to Sir Edgar that they be compensated. Can they start tomorrow morning?"

"You are not shy about your requirements, are you? Not for a few days yet. If you decide you want the loan of the behemoth, too, I must refuse."

"That is not —" She stopped. "Oh. You are joking."

He smiled fleetingly, then turned, waved. "Meet my foreman," he said when Hector arrived. "Hector MacDonald — Mrs. Blackburn."

"Aye, mistress, I saw ye coming o'er the road like a fireball. So ye've seen the great gawpin' hole in the hill?"

"I have, and I find it very interesting, Mr. MacDonald."

"There's king's gold on Cairn Drishan somewhere, mistress." He grinned. "Arthur's gold, they do say."

"So I've heard. Perhaps you would be so good as to help me find it." She smiled. Watching Hector's beaming face, Aedan knew that his foreman was already lost to her charm.

"Hector, the lady would like a crew to do some digging under her supervision. I want you to choose two or three men to start work on Cairn Drishan in a few days."

"Aye, sir. Mistress." Hector tipped his hat, then walked back toward the men to speak with them.

"Thank you, Sir Aedan." Christina's smile flashed through the veil. Quick, hot, certain lust clenched inside him. He frowned, aware of just how easy it was to fall under her spell.

"Aye, well," he answered. "Where is your brother? Disinclined to travel with you, is he?"

She had the grace to chuckle. "John stayed on the hill to make some landscape studies," she said, as she gathered the reins. "I should go back to fetch him. Good day, sir."

"Mrs. Blackburn, do me one favor. Allow your brother to drive back to Dundrennan. My day would proceed more peacefully if I did not have to chase my gig and bay again."

Her eyes sparked behind the veil and the spectacles — he saw their flinty fire. "Or rescue me again?"

"That, as well."

"I assure you it will not be necessary, Sir Aedan." She snapped the reins and turned the gig.

Watching her go, Aedan realized he was smiling. Wholly aside from her resemblance to the girl in that painting, Christina deeply intrigued him. Prim and scholarly, sensual and lovely, she also had no small talent for calamity. With all that wit and spirit, she was

152

far more seductive than she could possibly know.

Frowning thoughtfully, he watched the gig travel toward the sloping hillside.

Pog turned her head, blew softly, and Aedan gave the horse a distracted pat. Then he guided her back toward the road and his crew. Some of the men hastened to busy themselves, while others — like Hector — stood grinning openly at him.

"Halloo, Effie MacDonald!" Aedan called as he approached the croft house. In the afternoon light, the whitewashed walls and heather-thatched roof were bright against the hillside. "Halloo, the house!" he called again.

The door was flung open. "Och, 'tis the laird himself, come to see auld Effie! Dora, here's our laird!" An older woman grinned at him and waved him inside. Tall and buxom, her gray hair drawn tight beneath a white mutch, her apron spotless over a dark, striped dress, she waited in the doorway.

Aedan dismounted and led Pog into the shelter of a thatched-roof byre that protruded from one end of the house. A goat looked up, blinking its strange yellow eyes, while the black cow occupying most of the space hardly moved.

"Pardon me, Flora. Hello, Hamish, you old devil," Aedan said affectionately as he lifted a burlap sack and spilled oats into a manger for the animals to share. He walked toward the house while Effie MacDonald stood, holding the door open for him.

"Come in. Come in," she told him. He greeted Effie and entered the dim, smoky interior. A young woman stood silently beside the fire. "Bide a wee, Sir Aedan," Effie said. "We've just made tea, and there's scones with currants and cinnamon. Ye like those well."

"Dora," he said. "I'm here, lass." He walked toward her, and the smiling girl held out her hands. She wore a brown dress, and her hair had a pretty bronze sheen in the firelight. He took her hands, her fingers calloused but slender and graceful. Her face was a pale oval, and her lovely eyes, once wide brown pools, were clouded and unfocused.

"Aedan," she said, accepting his gentle kiss on her cheek. "Sit by me." He settled beside her on a long wooden bench.

"What brings ye, Aedan?" Effie said while she served steaming, fragrant tea in two delicate china cups for them and poured her own serving into a plain mug.

"The scones, my dear," he answered. "I could smell them across the moor — it's four o'clock, and Effie MacDonald's making cinnamon scones again, I told myself, and I leaped on my horse."

Both women laughed. "I'll get them. They're just out of the oven," Dora said, rising, trailing her hand along the edge of the table until she reached a cupboard. She fetched a covered plate, which she laid on the table near Aedan.

"I just wanted to visit, really," he said. "It's been two weeks since I was here last." He accepted a plate with hot, buttered scones on it, while Dora sat beside him.

"I'm so glad you've come," Dora said. "I wanted to tell you the news. Mrs. Farquharson said she'd take more of my crochet work in her ladies' shop in Milngavie and sell them for a good price! She said the shawls and dainties I made sold, all of them, and she had requests for more. I must work quickly to finish the new things." She indicated a big basket beside the bench, filled with lacy crochet work and a ball of creamy wool.

"That's excellent, Dora," Aedan said. "I've seen Mrs. Farquharson's shop in Milngavie. It does a brisk business."

"And now that Grannie Effie does laundering and starching for the new English families that live on the other side of the glen, we'll soon be feeling rich as the queen." Dora smiled.

Aedan sipped his tea. "Effie MacDonald, you know there's no need for you to do that much work," he said quietly. "I'll always take care of you. I promised your husband that I would see to your welfare when he went off to war, and I mean to do that."

Effie shook her head. "I've done the laundering hereabouts since I was a lass, and now I'm an auld widow. What would I do wi' my time and my hands, otherwise?" She held them up. They were gnarled and strong, the kindest hands, powered by the kindest heart Aedan had ever known.

"You and Dora can come stay at Dundrennan. Put up your feet, rest your hands, and tell Gunnie and the rest what to do," he suggested lightly.

"Huh," Effie said. "I'll ne'er leave this auld hoose. I was born here and I'll dee here. Dora will leave one day to wed some braw lad, and I'll be alane wi' me washing and me visitors. I do like visitors." She gave Aedan a reproving look.

"I'll try to come more often," he promised. "Perhaps I'll bring some new friends. We have an antiquarian and an artist staying at Dundrennan House."

"Auntie Queerie? Who's that?" Effie demanded.

"A historian, Grannie," Dora said. "A scholar. A lady, too, this one. Rob Campbell told me, when he visited the other day."

"He didna tell me aboot it — he talked only to ye, my lassie, wi' yer heads togither by the fire." Effie smiled, and Dora's pale cheeks turned pink. "An artist, too? Huh, Miss Amy is scheming to fix that hoose the way she likes it, and then she'll snag ye in wedlock!"

Aedan suppressed a smile. "Amy is just doing what my father asked. And the antiquarian lady came to look at the hill for the museum. The artist is her brother. I hope he'll finish up some of the painting my father wanted done."

"Ah." She leaned forward. "Aedan, if ye find King Arthur's treasure in that hill, dinna let Dundrennan's gold go to a mooseum." She sniffed. "And dinna wed Miss Amy. She's a guid lass, but daftie as yer auntie, wha keeps that scunnersome wee beastie!" She made a face.

"Thistle is practically part of the family," Aedan said, chuckling. "And Amy will do fine for a laird's wife someday."

"Aye, but nae for ye," Effie said, while Dora rose to refill Aedan's cup with steaming brew from the teapot. "Ye could be the one to break the curse over Dundrennan. The one meant for ye is named True Love. Wait, lad. Ye'll know her when she comes."

He split and buttered another scone. "Oh, you know that's a bit of a risk," he said as lightly as he could. "I'm done with true love, after . . . well, I took on the curse of the Dundrennan lairds and after Elspeth died."

Effie leaned close, her face serious. "Ye're nae done yet, I'm thinking. There's a love for ye — a love of all time. A love like they write them poems aboot. I'm thinking ye'll be the one to break that ill curse. One day, true love will land on yer doorstep like a wee birdie, and ye'll know. Ye'll know."

Aedan stared at the old woman. The image of Christina Blackburn, who had dropped on the landing outside his study, came to him clearly. But that could not be, he told himself; that must not happen now that he was laird of Dundrennan.

He shook his head. "I think you're a bit of a poet and dreamer, like my father." He took a bite of the scone while he gathered his wits, then turned to Dora. "I was in Edinburgh last week, and I saw my sister, Mary Faire, and her husband. They asked me to convey their greetings to you and Effie. You'll remember Connor MacBain?"

"Aye, a bonny braw man," Effie said. "Doctor MacBain."

Aedan nodded. "Connor has a medical practice in Edinburgh, and he has made it his life's work to study and treat the diseases and conditions of eyes in particular. He said he would be happy to examine your eyes, Dora."

She looked toward him, her eyes unfocused, her brow puckered. "Thank you, Aedan, but . . . well, none can help me. Mr. Johnstone said so after he tried all those spectacles with me, and the eye potions, too."

"Mr. Johnstone is an itinerant merchant," he said. "He sells eyeglasses out of pasteboard boxes. And God only knows what is in those potions of his."

She wrinkled her small, uplifted nose. "Doctors are so costly." She lifted her chin a little. "If God wants me to be blind eventually, then it will happen. There are worse things."

"True, but let's talk to Doctor MacBain." He took her hands, felt her initial resistance. "Please, Dora. I told him that I would pay his fee, but he insisted that he would charge you nothing for his services." He glanced at Effie, who watched them silently and seriously, leaving the decision to her granddaughter.

"It's verra nice, but — I do not think 'twould be of any use," Dora said.

"But I think we must at least find out if there is a chance. We would travel on the train to Edinburgh. Effie must come, too, of course," he said, glancing at the old woman.

Dora smiled. "I do like the train, and so does Grannie."

"We could stop in Milngavie and bring your baskets to Mrs. Farquharson's shop."

"Rob Campbell offered to drive me for that. But what if — Doctor MacBain canna help me?"

"Either way, he will be honest with you, and he'll give you the best medical attention you could have. Besides, I think you would both enjoy a couple of days in Edinburgh. I'll bet Effie would like to try some fruit ice creams there." He grinned.

"Ice creams? I'll go, even if Dora willna," Effie said, and she gave Aedan a conspiratorial wink.

Laughing, Dora nodded assent.

Chapter Ten

Reluctant to shout into the corridor for a maid's help with dressing as Mrs. Gunn had suggested, Christina opened her wardrobe to find something suitable among the gowns and outfits she had brought for her first dinner party at Dundrennan House.

Sighing, she realized that she had packed only one dinner gown — a lavender-blue satin which seemed too formal for that evening, the third since she and John had arrived at the house. Since she had not expected to stay more than a week or two, her clothing choices were limited. As neither a social guest nor an employee, she was not certain what was appropriate.

Most of her clothing was dark or somber, though she was no longer obligated to wear black, or even shades of gray and purple, as a widow. Deciding on an outfit that was dressier than a day gown, she chose a skirt of brown plaid silk and a high-necked blouse of ivory lawn, so fine it was nearly translucent.

After tying black slippers on her feet, she quickly pulled a lace-edged camisole over her

corset and stays and stepped into cotton petticoats and a full but lightweight crinoline.
Dropping the brown plaid silk skirt over that,
she snugged a black velvet waister around
her slender middle.

Her hands, she noticed, were trembling.
Just a genteel dinner party, she assured herself, though among relative strangers but for
her brother. Aedan MacBride was better
known to her, but he had been furious with
her earlier in the day, and she expected to
see the same tension in him that evening.
Her own feelings toward him hovered somewhere between deep attraction and sizzling
exasperation. Since a lady could express neither, she would show him only quiet dignity.

At the mirror over the washstand, she
smoothed her bronze-sheened dark hair,
knotted at the nape of her neck. After adding
a black net snood and jet earbobs, she bit
her lips for a little color, remembering that
Aedan had called her "Miss Burn" for her
tendency to blush easily. That thought
brought high pink into her cheeks whether
she wanted it or not.

Remembering their surprising kiss on the
first night of her arrival, she felt her cheeks
and throat grow even hotter. She ought to feel
scandalized and insulted by his advances, she
told herself. Instead, a fresh, wild excitement
tingled all through her. His unexpected tenderness that night had made her feel lovely,

made her feel desirable again. She wanted to see that side of him again, instead of the curt, cold man he had been at other times.

Do not be a daftie, she told herself. Nothing he did or said should matter to her. They would certainly share no more kisses. He was not looking for love or courtship, and neither was she.

If he entertained other intentions toward her simply because she had posed for that painting, then he could just rethink it, she thought crisply.

Yanking on ivory kid gloves, she resolved not to fret over him any longer. Nor should she anticipate his touch or his deep velvet voice at her ear. He was certainly capable of kindness, but he could be moody and bad tempered, too, especially regarding his infernal road.

Besides, she had found safety in her spinsterish, scholarly life. If she ever changed her status, it would be to marry Sir Edgar Neaves, who expected only intellectual passion from her. Her tempestuous marriage to Stephen Blackburn had been a heartbreaking folly. She would never again make the mistake of thinking herself in love.

Grabbing her needlepointed reticule, she gathered her skirts and went to the door.

"Mrs. Blackburn!" Dougal Stewart smiled as he bowed over her hand. "You certainly are not the fusty antiquarian Sir Edgar led us to expect. Quite charming, madam."

"Thank you, Mr. Stewart." Her voice sounded slightly hoarse, Aedan noticed as he listened, as if she had a head cold.

And well she might catch cold, he thought sourly, in that thin film of a blouse. She was far too fetching — even happily wed Dougal was flirting a little. What man could help it, Aedan thought, in the presence of so beguiling a young woman?

Subtle feminine allure emanated from Mrs. Blackburn in veritable waves, he thought, but she seemed ignorant of her effect on the men in the room, particularly on himself. A siren indeed, but an innocent sort, her appeal guileless and genuine.

She looked at him, and he glanced away, straightening his shoulders, keeping his expression neutral.

"Aedan, you've said little enough." Dougal glanced at him. "Surely you agree Mrs. Blackburn looks a picture."

Unfortunate choice of words. "Hm? Aye," Aedan said casually. "A picture, indeed." He saw a quick blush stain her cheeks.

"Surly lad," Dougal told Christina. "Scarcely notices bonny lasses and winsome dinner gowns."

Oh, but he had noticed. Ever since Christina had entered the room, skirts floating, mahogany hair knotted at the curve of her nape, he had watched her from the corner of his eye. He knew exactly how that sheer blouse veiled her creamy skin, how it revealed the delicate grace of her shoulders and the tantalizing swell of her breasts above a lacy undergarment. He had gauged her trim waist, snug in black velvet, and had imagined spanning his long fingers around her. Would have imagined more, if he had not forced himself to look away — only to look again.

Frowning, he rocked back on his heels. Normally he did not register what women wore except when he was appreciating smooth shoulders, quivering cleavage, the pretty curve of a waist or an ankle. Now he realized that his cousin Amy wore pale blue with a fall of lace over her slight bosom, Meg was sleek in dark green satin, and his youngest cousin, Sarah, Amy and Dougal's adolescent sister, wore a flowery pattern that swallowed her whole. Lady Balmossie wore her habitual dowager black.

His glance strayed again to Christina Blackburn. Somehow she was prim and seductive all at once, like a confection of chocolate, cream, and whisky. He craved to taste her again.

Clearing his throat, he told himself he was just hungry for dinner. No doubt MacGregor would announce the meal soon enough. Turning, he nodded in response to whatever John Blackburn had just said to him.

"Er, aye," Aedan answered, hoping that applied to the topic.

"I want to thank you again for inviting me to work on the mural, Sir Aedan," John said. "Miss Stewart showed it to me the other day. It would have been a grand thing — a pity the fellow could not finish it."

"He began it after talks with my father, but weeks into it, took ill and died quite suddenly. Awful, of course, for so many reasons. Please feel free to make your own judgement on the scheme. You may want to complete his design, or you may start again."

John nodded, his blue-gray eyes steady. "I'd like to incorporate his work with my own ideas and style. I've been making some sketches and thinking about it."

"I apologize for the lack of time. We do not want to rush you, sir. I'm honored and grateful for the stroke of luck that brought you here, by the way. We despaired of finding an artist who could complete the wall in a timely and economical way. And being familiar with your work, I'm especially thankful. You're a talented man, Mr. Blackburn." He indicated John's framed painting, which they had owned for years, on the far wall.

"Thank you," John said quietly. "I'd like to take a closer look at that painting, sir. I haven't seen it for years." He turned with Aedan to stroll across the room, passing Christina, who chatted with the Stewart sis-

166

ters and Lady Strathlin. "Come see the *Isabella*," John told her.

Christina excused herself to glide between the men, her wide skirt swaying, her gloved hands riding on the swell. Aedan repeatedly glanced down at her.

What the devil was happening to him? First secretly smitten by the painted image of a girl — now smitten a thousand times harder by the one who had posed for it. Without expression, he stood with the Blackburns to gaze at the gilt-framed painting.

The jewel colors of John's picture caught the firelight's glow. Its simple composition showed a seated knight and a standing young woman with long blond hair. She held a shining crown in her uplifted hands, and a halo of light suffused the couple, giving them a mythic ambience.

"*Robert Bruce Crowned by Isabella of Buchan*," Aedan said, reading the brass tag on the frame. "My father favored scenes from Scottish history and particularly liked this one of yours, Mr. Blackburn. I understand you trained in the Pre-Raphaelite circle for a time. Any work of art out of that group has a rising value these days."

"I was fortunate to live for some time in London after I left university," John said. "I studied with Rossetti and then Millais and began to form my own style apart from my father's, although he tutored me initially."

"Father is best known for history paintings in the grand style," Christina told Aedan. "John enjoys historical and mythological subjects, but his pictures have less pageantry and a more intimate emotionalism." She smiled.

Rob Campbell, Aedan's engineering assistant, came to join them and regarded the painting. "Excellent piece, Mr. Blackburn. May I ask if the female figure is intended to resemble your lovely sister? Or is that my imagination?"

Christina stood quite still, and Aedan felt her tension. He too had noticed the resemblance.

"Christina did model for Isabella," John answered. "She was about sixteen years old then. How astute of you to notice."

Rob nodded. "A wonderful likeness, Mrs. Blackburn, aside from the difference in hair color. A remarkable testament to your brother's skill and to your own loveliness."

She had gone pale, Aedan noticed.

"Thank you, but it was years ago, Mr. Campbell. I was scarcely out of the schoolroom, and John was actually still at university then."

"Your gifts were evident at a young age, sir," Aedan said.

"It is a joy to draw my sister's classic features. She modeled for my father, too, and for our siblings. Our cousin Stephen, as well — her late husband."

"He was also a painter?" Rob asked.

Christina colored passionately, Aedan saw, but she need not have worried, since Rob had never seen the painting in Aedan's private rooms. "Yes, he was," she told Rob. "I often sat for the artists in our family. It gave me an excuse to daydream."

"Miss Burn" was an accurate name, Aedan thought. Christina blushed like a living ember, searing heat just below the surface. She tempered it with elegant dignity and perfect composure. "Ah, MacGregor is here to call us in to dinner," she said. Aedan turned to see the butler opening the door.

"Good. Rob, you're to escort the Misses Stewart," Aedan told his assistant, "while Mr. Blackburn will escort Lady Balmossie." They nodded and walked off to fulfill their duties.

Christina glanced around, her skirt floating, as she clearly looked for her own escort.

"Mrs. Blackburn," Aedan said quietly, extending his arm.

She accepted, the touch of her gloved hand light on his forearm. Her silken skirt rustled against his thigh.

Only that, and desire struck through him like lightning. Her flowery scent and the whisky husk of her voice, the sway of silk, the hint of skin through delicate fabric, all mingled with the memory of their passionate kiss. The girl in the painting was but pale cardboard compared to this vivid creature.

Yet he must not forget that Christina Blackburn was poised to destroy his road, his career, possibly more. He must maintain aloofness — though that already proved a challenge.

MacGregor held open the door while the others followed Aedan and Christina into the dining room. Crystal and silverware gleamed under candlelight, and the muted colors of the unfinished mural danced over the walls. As they walked, Aedan leaned down.

"Do not fret, Mrs. Blackburn," he murmured. "No one will see that other painting."

She glanced up. "No one, sir?" she whispered.

"Only myself," he said, and he drew out her chair.

Tasting little of the dessert of raspberry tartlet and lemon ice or the excellent fare of lamb cutlets, roasted potatoes, and vegetables that had preceded it, Christina set down her spoon. She had no appetite, and her thoughts distracted her so much that she could scarcely pay adequate attention to the dinner conversation around her.

Throughout dinner she had sat next to Aedan MacBride, but had said little to him. After his murmured reminder about the painting, she had remained too aware that he saw her *en déshabillé* daily. The picture hall-marked a time when she had been wild, passionate, beautiful, happy . . . and terribly unwise.

To his credit, Aedan had been quietly considerate and attentive to her throughout dinner, despite her near silence. She sensed no lascivious glimmer in his eyes, no residue of that day's anger, either. On the contrary, she had sensed admiration, even concern. Touching her wine goblet to her lips, she glanced at him again.

Framed by a high-backed chair whose Jacobean strength suited him, he wore Highland dress — a pleated kilt of the red tartan preferred by the MacBrides of Dundrennan, with a black jacket, a vest, and a white shirt. In the drawing room, waiting for dinner, Christina could not help but notice his taut and powerful bare legs. Along with the golden tan on his high cheekbones, his strong physique revealed his time spent out-of-doors, active in his work.

He had the savage appeal of raw masculine beauty, enhanced by the rugged elegance of formal Highland dress. Once again she felt the undeniable pull that had swept her away on the night she had allowed him to kiss her.

Blushing, she told herself to finally forget that kiss. But she could not. Sipping her wine, she smiled at the chattering company around her, nodded as if listening and agreeing, and made an effort to abandon her unladylike thoughts.

"You are indeed quiet this evening, Mrs. Blackburn."

She met Aedan's direct, steel-blue gaze in the candlelight. He toyed with his own half-eaten dessert, she saw, his silver spoon resting in long, sun-browned fingers.

"I am a little fatigued," she admitted.

"No doubt so, after your adventure today, madam," he said. She flashed him a sour look, but saw only a twinkle in his eyes. "No harm done, I hope. Please do not feel that you must stay if you would rather retire."

She shook her head, though she did long to escape. Her head felt stuffed with cotton wool — too much wine, too little sleep, too many thoughts.

"It's really very good work," John said, turning to look at the partly completed painting on the wall behind him. He was seated opposite Christina, beside Amy Stewart, who swiveled to look with him, though she must have seen it a thousand times.

The others murmured agreement, and Christina looked up. In shadows and candlelight, she could make out some lightly sketched areas of landscape and a few figures on a whitewashed background that swept around three walls.

"Sir Aedan, do you know the ground?" John asked.

"Ground?" Aedan looked puzzled.

172

"The support for the mural," Christina murmured.

"Ah. The artist asked the housepainter to apply a coat of whitewashed plaster before he began his sketches. I remember that he insisted it dry thoroughly first."

"Good," John said. "Then he knew what he was about. Wall murals done in *buon fresco* — where the paint is applied on damp plaster, essentially — do not endure in the British climate, unlike hot, dry Italy, where the fresco technique of the Old Masters was so highly developed. My father and some others did a fresco mural at Windsor for the royal family a few years ago. It was a disaster, saved only by altering the technique to *fresco secco,* or painting upon dry plaster."

"That makes sense, since our weather is often damp in any season." Aedan leaned toward John. "Is there a chance you could complete this within a few weeks, Mr. Blackburn?"

John raised his eyebrows. "I cannot guarantee it, Sir Aedan. Is there a particular reason you would like it done so quickly?"

"The verra queen is coming in October," Lady Balmossie commented from her position at the other end of the table.

"Ah, that's reason, indeed," John said. "I will do my best."

"Pray do not rush it, Mr. Blackburn," Amy said, tilting prettily toward him, "if haste

173

would spoil the effect."

"Of course, Miss Stewart," John said with a ready flush. "Sir Aedan, do you have an idea what you'd like to see done on these walls?"

"The murals in this room were my father's dream," Aedan said. "A codicil to his will dictates his plans for each part of the house. Aside from fabric choices and so on — which I've primarily left to Amy," he said, smiling down the table at his cousin, "his list must be honored and the work finished by the end of this year . . . if we wish to keep the house in the family."

"Oh!" Christina looked at him in surprise. "Oh, my."

He lifted a brow in silent agreement and sipped his wine. "Still, it can be done. My father's codicil is so precisely detailed that Miss Thistle could oversee the work," he said. "Most of the changes were already underway when he died. I have the responsibility to see them done."

"The mural is the one of the last projects," Amy said. "Uncle Hugh chose the subject himself. We will leave the rest to you, Mr. Blackburn."

"I hope I am up to the task. What is the theme?"

"Dundrennan's legend," MacBride said. "The tale of the princess in the briar."

A chill ran through Christina. Glancing at

Aedan, who looked steadily at her, she searched the sketchy wall images for the elements of the story. She saw only landscape and a few figures.

"Certainly you must make the mural your own, regardless of what is already there," Lady Balmossie said.

"I am fortunate to have come here with my sister, then," John said, startling Christina. "Since she is an expert in the history and lore of Celtic Scotland, she has advised me before on authentic detail for my paintings."

"Perhaps she could model for the princess," Rob suggested. "She was perfect as the medieval heroine in your other painting."

"What a marvelous idea," Lady Balmossie said.

Stunned, Christina frowned at her brother, who blithely ignored her, while Aedan MacBride continued to gaze at her.

"Actually," Aedan said, "I think it a fine suggestion."

"I absolutely agree," John said, smiling.

Christina took up her spoon and dipped it savagely into melted lemon ice.

Chapter Eleven

"You've seen most everything in the house now," Amy said, "but for the gardens and that old monument out in the back garden." She led Christina, John, and Lady Strathlin into the foyer after a thorough tour of Dundrennan House. Although the Blackburns had been at Dundrennan for a week, Amy had declared the rainy day perfect for a complete tour of the house and its collections.

"With such rain, you will have to look at the gardens another day," Lady Strathlin said. "But here in the foyer you can see the stained-glass windows that were recently added. They're beautiful, Amy," she added with an approving smile.

"They give the foyer a nice medieval feeling, I think," Amy said. "Sir Hugh wanted a design that featured a briar-rose vine — the flowers are a theme throughout the house." She pointed to the tall, narrow windows flanking the door and another window on the landing of the stairs, all of which featured briar-rose vines in colored glass.

Christina turned, looking with delight. After luncheon with Lady Balmossie, who had retired to nap, the four of them had strolled through the rooms while Amy pointed out the redecorating effort. They had lingered over Sir Hugh's extensive collection of historical artifacts, some objects hung on the wall and others protected in glass cases, and John had been fascinated by the art collection displayed in various rooms.

"The house is beautiful," Christina said. "Quite unique. It must be a wonderful place to live." Beside her, John murmured his agreement.

"Only Cousin Aedan lives here now, though we visit often," Amy said. "Eventually he will marry and the house will be busy again, I hope."

"I'm sure he will," Christina commented, wondering if Amy were interested in the position herself. "Thank you for showing us the house, Miss Stewart. And Lady Strathlin — so kind of you to take the time. I know you must be anxious to return to your children at Balmossie."

"Their nurse takes very good care of them. I'm planning to go back after tea. And please call me Meg — the other makes me sound so stuffy." She smiled.

"And of course, it's Amy," Aedan's cousin added.

Christina smiled her thanks and offered her

first name to both young women.

"Are your plans for the mural proceeding, Mr. Blackburn?" Meg asked, for John had paused to look at a Scottish landscape painting in the foyer.

"I've been sketching ideas for the program, and I hope to begin some painting soon," he replied.

"Wonderful!" Amy smiled, spreading her hands on her blue crinolined skirt as she glided toward the main staircase. "Come with me, if you please. There is something I want to show you upstairs, on the uppermost floor."

They climbed to a landing that split in two directions to lead to the dining room and drawing room on one side and the billiard and breakfast rooms on the other. Christina knew now that the rest of the rooms in the central tower section were bedrooms. Amy and Meg then led them upstairs to the highest level, where they had not gone earlier.

Throughout the house, dim hallways were brightened by wood wainscoting and vibrant walls in salmon pink or ochre. Paintings glowed in lamplight, as did neat rows of weapons — shields, swords, axes, and halberds glittered overhead.

"That sword up there was used by Robert the Bruce." Amy indicated a longsword with a worn leather hilt. "And that small dagger is said to have belonged to MacBeth himself. Those two swords were lost by English knights at the battle of Stirling. The long axe over there belonged to Rob Roy Mac-Gregor."

"Dundrennan is a sort of museum," Christina said.

"In a way," Meg said. "Sir Hugh catalogued much of the collection before he died, and he discussed the provenance and value of several pieces with Sir Edgar from the National Museum. There was some discussion of buying the collection, but Aedan refuses to consider it."

"The sale of a few pieces would ease the cost of the repairs and refurbishments," Amy said. "I wish Aedan would reconsider. We do not need all these old weapons. Some of them are quite vile." She wrinkled her nose. "One of the swords still has blood on it."

"I'm sure Mrs. Blackburn is aware of the museum's interest," Meg said.

"I know little about it," Christina replied. "Such dealings are kept private. I am merely a Lady Associate of the Society of Antiquaries, although I do some research and other work for Sir Edgar."

"We're grateful for the good fortune that brought you both here," Meg said, and she smiled.

They reached the uppermost hallway, where Amy opened a door. "This is the long gallery. Once it was used as a schoolroom, but no one uses it now. Sir Aedan thought that you might like to use it for an artist's studio, Mr. Blackburn."

"This would be excellent," John said when they entered. The long gallery was a huge room with whitewashed walls and dark wood floors. Rainy daylight streamed silvery through the windows. Sparsely furnished with a cupboard, bench, long table, and hard chairs, it looked like the schoolroom it once had been.

"The light is good, and from the north, clear and even," John said. "And that huge table is ideal, since I'll be working on very large sketches for the wall."

"Then it is yours for the duration," Amy said, handing him a key. "My cousin said you will be going to Edinburgh for a day or two to fetch some supplies."

"Yes, I'll leave tomorrow and return shortly with trunks full of paint and so on, even some costumes and props."

"Oh, costumes! It sounds like great fun!" Amy said as they all left the room together.

"I hope so. Does that lead out to the roof?" John asked as they passed a door at the far end of the hall, where there seemed to be no space for another room.

"Yes, come and look," Amy said. "The view is marvelous." She opened the stout door and led them into the cool, damp air on the balustraded roof. "Centuries ago, sentinels would post up here. There is an overhang, so our gowns will not get wet."

Christina smiled, feeling the clean kiss of the wind on her face and stirring her skirts. Rain pattered the stone wall walk and half walls.

Dundrennan's policies extended in all directions, miles of heathery hills, golden meadows, and thick forest, the whole softened by mist. The arches of the Remembrance, the medieval monument beyond the orchard, thrust upward.

"That's so beautiful," she said, feeling a powerful urge to see the romantic old monument to a lost princess. "I wish we could go see it."

"The Remembrance is a gloomy place, especially in the rain," Amy said. "I think it's eerie and morbid. It should be closed off. Not even the lairds of Dundrennan will go there."

"It's romantic and picturesque," Christina said.

"I agree." Meg glanced at the drizzling skies. "Oh, more rain starting. Shall we go inside? It's nearly time for tea, and Aunt Lillias will be expecting us. And Thistle, I suppose."

"This may be Miss Thistle's last tea at Dundrennan for a while," Amy said. "Cousin Aedan thinks the paint fumes could disturb the beastie's health, and suggested to Aunt Lillias that she keep Thistle at home in the conservatory. May we be so fortunate as to be without her company," she added.

Laughing, John opened the door for the ladies and made a quiet comment that set Amy to giggling.

At teatime, Miss Thistle's antics left Christina convinced that Aedan was wise to urge Lady Balmossie to take the monkey home. By the time they had finished tea, two saucers and a teacup lay broken on the carpet, a plum cake had been smashed on a footstool, and Lady Balmossie wore a shortbread biscuit on top of her lace cap until Christina plucked it free.

For some reason, Miss Thistle clung to Christina with utmost affection, pausing only to fire crockery at family members or at the door each time it was opened. Thistle's attachment to Christina made John laugh, and even Amy, who disliked the creature, giggled with delight.

"Sir Hugh always said Thistle had a keen eye for good people," Lady Balmossie said. "We must tell Aedan that she's approved Mrs. Blackburn. Where is Aedan today?"

No one knew, and when Christina realized that she watched the door closely, she turned away. He did not come to tea, and his kinswomen surmised that he was busy with his roadwork, although rain generally halted much progress, they explained.

After tea, Christina sat in her room, reading and writing a few letters, then fell asleep, dozing so deeply that she did not wake until she heard a persistent knocking at the door.

"Ye slept through supper, mistress." Sonsie Jean carried a silver tray with covered dishes as she entered the room. "Mrs. Gunn sent me to bring ye soup, toast, and tea. She told Sir Aedan ye was tired, puir lassie, but she thought a bowl o' Scotch broth would restore ye."

"Thank you, Muriel," Christina said, recalling Aedan's considerate use of the girl's real name. She rubbed her eyes and glanced at the little mantel clock, astonished that she had slept so long. Muriel set the tray in the sitting room, and Christina tasted the soup while the serving girl poured tea for her.

"Och, I nearly forgot, mistress. Sir Aedan said to tell ye that the lamps will be lit in the library tonight, d'ye want to work there on yer books and such. He might be there himself, he said, but he'd have work to do and wouldna disturb ye."

Her heart raced. "Thank you." Muriel nodded and left.

After finishing her meal, Christina combed her hair with trembling fingers, then smoothed her simple gown of dark green brocade, taking time to put on her sturdy brogans.

She might read for a little while in the library, and perhaps, if the weather permitted, she would stroll in the gardens. She was curious to see them, and the thought of the old monument in moonlight piqued her curiosity. Adding a lightweight tartan shawl, she descended the narrow stair to the library, taking care to go slowly. This time, unlike her last calamitous venture down the old steps, lamps in the wall recesses illuminated the way.

The laird had said the lamps would be lit for her. She wondered if he would be there himself. Her hand shook as she pulled on the door latch leading into the library.

Entering to discover herself alone, quelling the disappointment she felt, she chose a few books from the shelves. Then she found a comfortable chair in a quiet niche and settled down to read.

She was there, just as he had hoped. Golden lamplight pooled over Christina as she sat in a leather chair, her head bowed over a book and her feet curled beneath the folds of her skirt. She looked more like an adolescent girl than the seductive woman in the painting of the briar princess.

Yet when she glanced up at Aedan's approach, her simple, natural beauty was more alluring than any image. Her eyes were wide behind her little spectacles, her mouth a small moue as she closed her book at the sight of him and sat primly. Her shoes were brogans, he saw, not the slippers of the other night.

She would not lose her balance in those sensible things, he thought. While that was reassuring, he would have enjoyed another chance to catch her.

"Sir Aedan! I did not expect to see anyone here so late."

"Mrs. Blackburn. I came to check on the last things."

"The what?" She looked puzzled.

"Last things for the evening," he explained. "Or so we call it here. I take care of the lamps, the doors, check the hearths, make sure the dogs are all in for the night, and so on."

"One of the dogs is there, asleep." She indicated a corner under the gallery, where a white terrier lay curled on a worn leather chair. "She has been a sweet companion while I've been sitting here, though she was asleep most of that time."

He smiled, gazing at the dog, who had scarcely lifted her head at his entry, so familiar was she with the rhythm of his step and the sound of his voice. "That chair she's in was my father's favorite spot for reading. Gracie was his devoted pup and has not forgotten him. We let her sleep there now — even Mrs. Gunn does not object. She keeps a blanket for her on the chair. Gracie's getting

185

older now and seems soothed by this place." He glanced around. "I have one more dog to find, our cairn terrier. She prefers a warm spot by the kitchen hearth. I'll check there before I finish up."

"Do you round up Thistle, too, when you do the last things?"

"When they are here, my aunt and her lady's maid take care of that." He made a wry face. "As did my father, who fancied Thistle. Gunnie would send the beastie back to India if she could. I heard that you made a friend of our wee Thistle today at tea." He smiled.

Christina smiled, too. "Somehow I did," she answered. "I would have thought the butler would take care of the lamps and such at the end of the day, Sir Aedan."

"MacGregor is a feisty old rogue, but forgetful sometimes. And it is tradition at Dundrennan for the laird to see to the last things."

"You honor many traditions here, as the laird, I think."

"Some I honor, and some I forego. I was not raised to be the laird, though now that I am, I tend to my responsibilities. If you would prefer to read a bit, madam, I'll come back after I see to the rest of the house."

She stood, set down her book. "I thought I might go for a walk in the gardens before I went up to my room."

"Now? In the rain and the darkness?"

"The rain has cleared, I think, and there's some moonlight. I wanted to see the gardens and the monument . . . the Remembrance."

"Very well. I would be glad to show you."

"Oh, no, I cannot inconvenience you. Besides, if we were seen together so late, we would have much to explain."

"Does that matter? We both know it's perfectly innocent to go for a little walk at night."

"Truly, I can find my way. It's just through to the back of the garden. Shall I use the side door past the kitchen?"

"Aye, but do not wake Cook, who sleeps nearby — she can be disagreeable. Take the path straight back; do not veer left, for that leads to an oakwood. We would not want you to get lost. Go through the gate at the end of the path, and follow the yew walk out to the Remembrance."

"Thank you. I thought it might be nice to see the Remembrance in moonlight."

"It might indeed. You are a romantic, Mrs. Blackburn." He thought it would be nice to view the monument in moonlight, too — if he was with her. And he did not like the idea of sending her out alone, even within the grounds. "You may want to bring a lamp with you, for the path is overgrown with tree roots in some places. But the view at night is well worth the trouble."

"As Scott said, 'If thou wouldst view fair Melrose aright . . .' "

" 'Go visit it by the pale moonlight,' " he finished.

"You know it!" She smiled, and he shrugged modestly. As she crossed the room, he admired the sway of her skirt. She turned at the open door. "Good night, sir."

He waved nonchalantly. "Keep watch for wildcats."

She paused, stared. "Wildcats?"

"We see them occasionally. They've been known to perch in the trees — though never close to the house, so far. Luckily, the wolves that used to harry this place are extinct now."

That last was heartless, he knew, but he could not resist teasing her a little. She was so very serious and so very damnably appealing.

"Wolves? Oh —" Christina bit her lip. "Perhaps I should take a lantern, after all."

"Stubborn bit lass," he muttered walking toward her. "Look here, Mrs. Blackburn. As host and laird, I do not want a female guest to wander about in the dark alone and on unfamiliar grounds."

"I assure you that I will be perfectly fine."

"And I assure you that I am a trustworthy escort."

"I just thought . . . that we should not be seen together at this hour, walking alone in a

. . . well, a romantic setting."

He leaned a hand on the doorjamb above her head. "Everyone is asleep but you and I, so no one would know. It would be our secret. We already have one or two between us," he said, leaning closer, "do we not?"

She gazed up at him. "We do," she said. "But we do not need this one as well."

"Fair enough," he murmured, and he reached beside him to take up a small oil lamp. He handed it to her, then swung the door open for her, bowing his head in silent farewell as she left the room and headed for the kitchen corridor.

Chapter Twelve

Walking through threads of moonlight, Christina saw the monument at the far end of the path. Its slender, roofless arches rose upward to create a magical silhouette. Thick, flowering hedges of sweet briar grew to either side of the tree-lined path. The blossoms, spare now, gave off an applelike fragrance.

Rosa eglanteria, the true wild rose grew in abundance at Dundrennan, she realized; the dense, lovely briers, so fitting to this place and its legend, surrounded the medieval monument ahead and encircled the foundation of the house, as well.

She felt a sudden sense that she was not alone, and turned, expecting to see Aedan behind her. The path was empty. Hearing again the faint rustle of movement, she paused, listened. Nothing.

Had Aedan been joking or serious about the wildcats? She looked around, wishing she had accepted his offer to escort her after all. Assuring herself that she was alone, she moved ahead toward the silent, soaring Gothic ruin.

Nearing the structure, she gasped in awe. The Remembrance was a small and simple cloister, an arcade of slender columns and pointed arches forming four sides, enclosing an open, grassy area. Out of a wild, magical tangle of sweet briar, ivy, and moss, the ruined arches rose into the night sky.

Hesitating at the arched entranceway, Christina stepped inside to walk across the grassy atrium. At the far end stood a rectangular block, a bier or a tomb, placed before the elegant backdrop of columns. All else was empty, silent, and mysterious, a place of moonlit stones and inky shadows.

Looking around, she felt distinctly that she was not alone, as if someone, or something, watched her — or watched over her, for the sense was not threatening. As the magic of the place overwhelmed her, she turned in delight to take in its beauty.

A carved frieze ran above the slender stone arches and columns, cut with words that were difficult to decipher in the darkness. She went toward it, tipping her head back.

" 'She sleeps,' " she read aloud, softly. " 'Nor . . .' "

" 'She sleeps, nor dreams, but ever dwells, a perfect form in perfect rest,' " Aedan murmured. His voice shivered like silk through her soul. She whirled.

He leaned against the doorjamb, arms folded, watching her. The loneliness of his

191

silhouette struck her.

"You came," she said.

He inclined his head a little. "I came," he said, "to make sure the wolves and wildcats did not come."

"How kind of you." She looked up at the words carved in the frieze again. "It's from Tennyson."

"Aye. When Lord Tennyson heard from my father about his plans to restore the Remembrance, Tennyson suggested those lines from a poem he was working on — a sleeping-beauty tale."

"Lord Tennyson knew of the Remembrance?"

"Nearly everyone knows about Scotland's own Sleeping Beauty." Aedan put his hands in his pockets and stayed in the doorway. "Many would like to make this place a sort of pilgrimage spot, because of our legendary princess — and because of my father, who was a bit of a legend himself. The Glasgow City Commissioners and the directors of the National Museum — including your Sir Edgar — want me to open this to the public. It has great cultural value, they claim."

"But you do not want to share it?"

"My father did not want to share it — not this place. The house, aye, but not the Remembrance. It would be full of tourists hauling travel rugs and looking for picnic spots. I want it to remain private."

"Then I am privileged to be here with the laird himself," she said, smiling a little.

"You are special, indeed, since himself should be asleep at this hour," he drawled.

Smiling, Christina walked closer to the pale granite block. It stood waist high, like a tomb but lacking the recumbent sculpted figure so common in medieval monuments. Only a stone pillow, carved with tassels, lay on the flat surface. She swept her hand over the stone, which was smooth with the slight grit of age and exposure.

"Is she here?" she asked quietly.

"No," he said. "We do not know where she is. It's an empty memorial."

Seeing another frieze of words carved around the upper edge of the bier, she bent to look. " 'What thou see'st when thou dost wake, do it for thy true-love take,' " she read. "Shakespeare, from *A Midsummer Night's Dream*."

"Exactly so." His voice was rich as cream in the darkness.

Feeling a touch on her shoulder, a comforting caress, she straightened and turned, thinking Aedan had joined her.

But he still stood in the doorway, a dark, lean shadow. She sucked in a breath and stepped back. Clouds shifted, and cool moonlight veiled the granite bed and the gleaming pillow.

A form shimmered on the stone, and

Christina saw — for one fleeting instant — the delicate figure of a girl. She lay still and beautiful, so translucent that the hard shape of the pillow showed through her shoulders.

Then she was gone. Christina widened her eyes, but she saw only stone, empty and flat.

Heart pounding, she stepped backward, then whirled and crossed the grass toward the door, toward Aedan and safety. It had been her imagination, she told herself, only that.

She hurled out of the cloister so fast that she collided with Aedan on the doorstep. He took her by the shoulders.

"Ho, was there a wildcat in there after all? You look as — what's wrong?" The amusement left his voice, and his hands tightened.

She shook her head. "Nothing — may we go now, please?"

"You're trembling. Are you cold? Give me your hands." He chafed warmth into her bare fingers. She had a habit of forgetting her gloves, and had done so again. He wore none either, and the direct, heated contact was both comfort and distraction.

Holding her hands, he regarded her with a frown. "Did something frighten you? This place can be eerie at night. I should not have let you come out here."

"I am not faint of heart. But I saw —" She half laughed, shook her head. "I *imagined* that I saw a girl lying there. It was just the

194

trick of a moonbeam, but it startled me."

Concern flickered in his eyes. "Are you all right? Do you need to sit down or go back to the house?"

She shook her head. "I am quite fine."

"Bonny Mrs. Blackburn," he said, smiling. "Always strong and stubborn, no matter her calamities."

"I am not generally given to fancy," she said. But she was glad he held her hands, glad he stood close enough to warm and reassure her. The bell of her skirt enveloped his legs, and she leaned toward his strength.

He bowed his head toward her, and she thought suddenly that he might kiss her. Heart still pounding, she felt weak with distraction, with anticipation. Nothing else existed just then but the two of them. Propriety seemed a dim and unnecessary idea, easily ignored. She stared up at him, realizing that she stared at his lips, with their whimsical upper curve, a hint of impishness in an overly serious man.

"You saw her," he said. "Some do, or think they do. There have been a few stories of it over the centuries."

"If she is not buried in there, why would she haunt this place? She . . . lay there," she said softly, remembering, "so peaceful. So very delicate and beautiful."

"Aye." He watched her for a moment. "At least, so I've heard. You must be a sensitive,

195

or perhaps you have the Sight in your family line somewhere. It must have been a shock to see."

"It was." She lifted her chin. "But I do not have the Sight that I am aware. It was only a trick of moonlight in this romantic, pictur-esque place. I am not about to swoon over it."

"Pity," he said. "Then I could catch you."

Her heart bounded to hear his soft, inti-mate tone. "Perhaps you should go catch your wee ghost," she said lightly.

"I would, but I have never gone inside."

She blinked. "You what?"

"The lairds of Dundrennan never set foot inside the Remembrance. My brother and I were not allowed here as boys. And as an adult, I have never gone inside."

"Why? It's so beautiful in there."

He glanced through the arches. "They say that if a laird of Dundrennan sets foot in the Remembrance . . . he will fall in love."

"Oh," she said, looking up at him. "Is that bad?"

"Madam, that is disastrous."

"I see," she said, a little indignantly. "That is a part of the legend I've never heard."

"We keep it to ourselves," he murmured. "The Remembrance was built in the twelfth century." He dropped her hands, took a breath, as if summoning himself from a spell. "One of the lairds of Dundrennan commissioned it as a memorial to his lost wife."

"Just as the Druid in the legend lost the princess tragically," she said. Aedan nodded. His closeness in the dark, even without his touch, made her knees wobble strangely.

"Because of that ancient tale, it is said that no laird of Dundrennan can marry for the sake of true love. It is a plain danger."

"How is it dangerous to the laird?" she asked, puzzled.

"Not to him, but to his love, should he marry her. Each time the lairds in our line marry for love, the wife dies."

"How awful!" She rested her hand on her chest. "But — can it really be true, in practice?"

He shrugged. "It seems to be the case through our generations. So we take care not to wed the women we love."

"But you marry, or your legitimate line would not exist."

"Aye, we marry for friendship, for companionship. For procreation and survival. We wed, but we do not fall in love." He looked at her. "And that is our private legend, Mrs. Blackburn. Not exactly the stuff of fairy tales, is it?"

"It's touching, and very sad." She studied his moonlit face. Like a piece of a puzzle, the revelation made him easier to understand, somehow. "Surely some of your ancestors must have married for love."

"Of course. My own father adored my mother, and they wed for the sake of real, passionate love, defying the tradition."

"So the curse does not always come to bear."

"They were married ten years, a long time in Dundrennan terms. Then my mother died. So the curse won. It's said that when a Dundrennan laird follows his heart, tragedy will out."

"For the wife only?" She frowned. "There is something misogynistic in that."

He laughed a little. "I assure you I have the utmost respect for your fair gender, madam. The legend of the princess repeats itself. She died tragically, and the prince survived, doomed to live without her. Our relationships echo that pattern."

"Is that a curse at work, or is it part of the natural course of life? Women give birth — women take chances, and very often they do not survive their spouses."

"Men take chances, too, in war and other ways. You have a point, of course, though Dundrennan's tradition says this happens each time the laird truly loves his wife. Who can say if it's always the case — it could not be traced, even with complete family records. Nonetheless, the lairds of Dundrennan are raised to believe that a marriage based on love will end tragically. Consequently, each of us who inherits this place faces that risk. We, of course, have free will to decide." Quiet words, his gaze so steady that Christina caught her breath.

"Where there is a curse, there is always something that will break the spell. A charm, a miracle, a . . . kiss." She watched him.

He moved toward her, and her heart thudded hard. "They say our curse will be lifted only if the princess's true love awakens her. Not very likely, is it?"

Suddenly Christina felt a flood of compassion and a rich sense of affection. She wanted to touch Aedan, console him, love him herself, this lonely, strong, intense man. She wanted him to be free to reach out for the love he deserved but thought he could not have.

Why did she feel so deeply toward him? She scarcely knew him. While she found him undeniably attractive and fascinating, he could be equally infuriating at other moments.

"You are not a man who follows beliefs blindly," she observed. "I think you are a strong-willed man who goes his own path in all things. Why let the old curse bind you? It is sad to give up a precious dream without knowing if you could ever have the passion of true love, without allowing yourself to try —" She stopped, blushed in the dark. "Do forgive me."

"Speak out. I enjoy your honesty. Until a

few years ago, I never gave the curse much credence myself. I thought it would never affect me, since I was not the heir. Then my older brother died, and I learned the strength of our tradition."

"What do you mean?"

"You were wed, Mrs. Blackburn. You have known love."

"I thought I did, once. But I was very wrong, and it ended — in sorrow." She paused. "Have . . . you ever been in love?"

"I had a fiancée, four years ago," he said, surprising her. "Elspeth was a bright and cheerful girl. You would have liked her, I think. She took a fever a few weeks after I became heir to Dundrennan. She died but two months after we had word that my brother Neil had been killed."

"Oh! I am so sorry," she said in a rush.

"I did not believe in the curse until then."

"You loved her," she murmured.

"I was very fond of her. I do not think it was the sort of love that . . . that fills the heart like sunshine floods a dark place. But I cared for her very much."

"Love has many degrees of passion," Christina said.

"So I hear." He looked at her piercingly. "But I cannot explore it. I will not risk a woman's life. Falling in love is . . . unthinkable for me."

Her heart thumped very fast. "I thought

you and Miss Stewart might wed someday. I had that impression."

"My cousin and my aunt like to think so. Amy thinks she will reform me and end Dundrennan's curse. I might consider marrying her. She is young, but she is a pleasant lass, and it would not be an unhappy union. I do not love her in a romantic sense, but I am fond of her, and that is enough."

She regarded him thoughtfully. "And she would always know that. That is . . . very sad."

"It is," he agreed. She glimpsed something raw, something lost, in his face. "Well, Mrs. Blackburn, you have seen the Remembrance in moonlight, a rare treat and only for you. I hope you have enjoyed it." He inclined his head.

"Are you not curious to venture inside?" she asked.

"Curious, aye," he said. "But I will not cross that step, in order to protect the life of someone . . . I may not even know." His gaze remained steady on hers.

"How gallant," she murmured. "And it protects you, as well, from the sting of Cupid's arrow."

"I think I am impervious to that by now."

She tilted her head. "Are you?"

He moved closer. "I suppose I could test it."

She tipped her head. "I think you should," she whispered.

He bent down and his lips touched hers lightly, then with a heat like clear fire plunging through her. She grasped his arm for support. His hand rose to cup her cheek, his lips moved over hers in a deep, slow kiss. She faltered, sank a little, clutched at his coat.

When that kiss abated, she went hungrily into a new one, and he groaned low, pulling her to him. Circling her arms around his waist, tilting her head, she drank in his strength, his mystery, his tenderness. She knew, with exquisite clarity, that she had wanted this with him, needed it desperately.

Wrapping her in his arms, he gathered her close, kissed her again, and she could feel, even through layered petticoats, the rock-hard certainty that he desired her. Her own craving intensified, shook through her.

Had he urged her for more, beyond an extraordinary kiss in the moonlight, she would have surrendered willingly, given of her very soul. Desire filled her, astonished her, so powerful and genuine that she trembled to her core.

She moaned softly, and he pulled away, stepped back. Cool air woke her from the kiss, dissolving the hold that passion had over her. She blinked as if coming out of a dream.

"Madam," he said, his voice hoarse, "I took advantage of you to test my own limits. That was not chivalrous."

"Not at all." She watched him, wary and breathless.

"I promised you that it would not happen again, but it has. I am at a loss to explain why this seems to happen between us. I assure you that I do not behave like this normally."

"Nor I." She straightened her shoulders. Why did she yield so easily to his slightest touch? He was a stranger to her, yet she felt as if she had known him and understood him forever, as if he were a part of her. "This — it's like madness. Perhaps it is the moonlight."

"It may be. We should go back, Mrs. Blackburn."

"Christina," she whispered. "I am Christina."

He murmured her name, and it had never sounded so wonderful to her before. "Aedan," he offered in return. He took her arm and guided her toward the path, then took his hand from her elbow.

She walked ahead of him through the tunnel of yews and into the gardens. Entering the house by a side door, they walked silently down a dark corridor to the foyer. Moonlight streamed through the stained-glass windows there.

At the foot of the main staircase, she turned. "I must know," she said quietly.

"Know what?" His voice was gentle. He rested a hand on the newel post, waiting for her to continue.

"What you discovered when we kissed. Were you . . . impervious?"

He leaned close. "I am a laird of Dundrennan, and I cannot risk falling in love," he murmured, so close that she could smell the faint spice of his soap, feel the warm caress of his breath. Lifting his hand, he brushed his fingers over her hair, where some strands had drifted loose.

She watched him, enthralled, silent.

"But if I ever did" — his fingers caressed her chin — "it would be with you."

She sank her eyes closed, sighed.

Then he drew her into his arms and kissed her again, swift and hard, kissed her until her knees went weak and she grabbed at the lapels of his coat. He kissed her so exquisitely and thoroughly that she felt her heart blow open like a rose in sunlight.

Then he let go of her and stepped back, though she lifted her hand toward him. He bowed his head, either in apology or farewell. Then he walked away, turning down the shadowed hall that led to the library. She heard the door open, quietly close.

Christina stood by the staircase, her hand flattened over her chest, legs trembling beneath her skirts. A strange buttery weakness filled her. She sank to the step in the satiny pool of her skirts, her heart pounding.

If I ever did, it would be with you.

Chapter Thirteen

Christina climbed the slope of Cairn Drishan, using the walking stick that Mac-Gregor had insisted she take. Learning that she planned to walk to the hill alone — John had returned briefly to Edinburgh — the old Highlander shook his head.

"Bonny sir, you are needing this on those hills," MacGregor had told her, handing her a sturdy polished stripling nearly as tall as she was, with a leather strap set three-quarters high. Christina soon discovered it to be a practical aid on the steep parts of the slope.

The morning sky was pearly, and mist veiled the moor and the hills, bright with heather. At the top of the ridge, four men awaited her. MacBride was not with them, and she felt a keen disappointment, for she had not seen him at breakfast, either. And the poignant memory of the night before lingered in her.

Hector MacDonald walked toward her, a long, lanky man with a gaunt face, vivid blue eyes, and gray hair with heavy sideburns.

"Mrs. Blackburn! Good morning to ye." He dipped his hat.

"Good morning, Mr. MacDonald." She walked up to the site alongside the foreman, where the three other men were waiting, shovels and picks in their hands. Dressed in shabby trousers, nondescript coats and hats, and muddy boots, she would not have thought them to be Highlanders. But she heard the Gaelic they spoke and saw their Celtic heritage in their high-cheekboned faces, their height and strength, their ruddy coloring and intelligent gazes.

A brown and white spaniel ran toward her, tail wagging, and Christina reached out to pet her. "Who's this?" she asked.

"That's Cailin," Hector said. "She belongs to auld Angus Gowan, there. Those are his sons, Robbie and Donald."

She nodded to the men, who touched their hats respectfully. Then she bent to rub the spaniel's shoulders. "Hey, girl," she said, as the name translated in Gaelic. "And a thousand welcomes to you, too, on this fine day." She laughed as the dog licked her bare wrist above her glove. Christina murmured to her affectionately in Gaelic.

Angus stepped forward. "You know the language, mistress? Good! Cailin is coming with us when we are working on the roads. She is coming with me for years when we are herding cattle in the hills. She is a good lass, and she is not minding if we herd, or hunt, or dig — she is happy to be out with us."

Christina nodded. "You no longer herd cattle, Mr. Gowan?"

"No, mistress. Our farm was taken from us years ago, but Sir Hugh gave us a home on his estate. When part of his land was sold, we lost our land again, but now we work on the laird's road crew. Cailin is happy whatever we do. People can learn much from dogs about contentment, I say."

"Oh, yes." She nodded. "Thank you for coming up here when you have so much other work along the highway. I know Sir Aedan is anxious to finish his road."

"Aye, mistress, the laird has much responsibility there," MacDonald agreed. "But he can spare the Gowans for a few days."

"He can dig with that metal beast," Robbie Gowan said. His kinsmen laughed. She noticed that the men spoke English in the same soft accent and odd speech patterns as MacGregor the butler.

"Hopefully this will not take many days," she said. "It is easy to see where earth and rock cover the old wall. I would like the earth carefully cleared away from the top layer, if you will." She pointed as she spoke, and the men nodded.

"What about the wall?" Angus asked, eyeing it dubiously, hands folded on his shovel.

"Leave it undisturbed. I will mark the loose stones with chalk — blue chalk if the stone should be removed, white chalk if you are to leave it." She opened her reticule and removed two pieces of broken chalk that she had borrowed from her brother's wooden box of soft pastel sticks.

"They'll grub the hill — clear the brush and bracken away," Hector explained, "and then start where the wee wall appears and dig across to the opposite wall, there. How far back into the hill, mistress?"

"As far as is safe, Mr. MacDonald, or until the wall ends."

"Aye." He spoke to the men, who walked off to begin their task. Hector whistled to the dog, who came to him for petting. "That split in the rock, there, is from the explosion, when Mr. Campbell set the black powder in the hill. It is not so safe here, I'm thinking. I will come here with the Gowans while there's digging to be done here. Sir Aedan asked that ye ne'er be alone on this hill."

"Oh, did he? It is not necessary to protect me, Mr. MacDonald. I am neither foolish nor incautious. You can tell that to Sir Aedan."

"Aye well," he said, wiping his forearm over his brow, "ye'd best tell him that yerself. I willna come atween ye. There's fire in ye both, and I dinna care to be burned by it." Hector grinned so engagingly that she had to laugh.

★ ★ ★

Sunshine split the cloud cover later, and
the damp earth dried in the sun, making digging easier. While the men worked steadily,
Christina knelt on the ground, her skirts
tucked around her, and bent to examine the
stones in the wall, marking some of them
with the chalk. In the warm, bright sun, she
dropped the veiling over her black bowler hat
and removed her jacket, under which she
wore a crisp linen blouse.

She brushed her fingers over a stone, intrigued by cut marks along the side. Pulling
her hatpin from the netting, she scraped at
the dirt embedded in the stone. She paused
to pencil her observations in a small memorandum book, then took up the hatpin again
to scrape delicately at the rock.

"If you are going to use that thing to clear
all the dirt from these stones," Aedan said,
"you will be up here forever."

Startled, she looked up, her heart leaping,
as it always did when he was near. He stood
tall over her, his back to the sun, his legs
long, shoulders wide, his stance powerfully
masculine and assured.

Last night, they had shared astonishing
kisses, and though she should not care, she
longed for that warmth from him again. Now
he frowned down at her, his mood cool and
impenetrable.

And he did not look inclined to kiss her

ever again. He only looked annoyed.

"Good day, sir," she said, forcing herself to sound pleasant. "You are right, of course. Perhaps it is futile to clean the rock with my hatpin." She opened her reticule to take out a small implement that she had brought with her.

"What the devil is that?" He looked down.

"A toothbrush, as you can see." She waved it.

"An odd time to be polishing your smile."

She displayed a sweet grin and began to scrub at the stone.

"For the love of God, woman! Scrubbing those rocks like a scullery maid will not improve their appearance or their value. And will only prolong the time wasted here."

"There is no need for oaths," she retorted. Wielding the little brush diligently inside a crevice, she blew at the loosened dirt. A few marks were visible on the stone, and she picked up her pencil to sketch them in her notebook.

"Only a few weeks are left before this road must be finished. Mrs. Blackburn, are you listening to me?" He dropped to his haunches while she worked. "Why the devil must you do this?"

"My uncle once discovered Pictish carvings of great antiquity while cleaning some stones in a field with his old toothbrush," she explained. "The science of archaeology has made great strides since Uncle Walter was a lad digging flints in his kailyard. Even fifty years ago, fossil bones were still thought to be the remains of dragons and monsters. Celtic knives were thought to belong to fairies."

"Oh, and they don't?" he asked dryly.

She scowled up at him. "We are learning much about the past from careful digging. Now we know the value of caution and cataloguing, and we can unravel early history more accurately. Time has its layers, just as the earth has its strata. Both will yield their secrets if treated with care and respect." She wiggled the toothbrush to make her point. "We cannot dig willy-nilly in this place."

"You may not be an archaeologist, but you seem to know what you are about here," he said, and she heard grudging respect.

"I have assisted with other finds. But I am primarily an amateur antiquarian. My main interests are history and literature. But this must be done here, and I must do it."

"You will find no Pictish carvings here, nor is there time to search for them."

"*You* may not have time, sir, but I do. Clearly you are an impatient man." She brushed at the stone, then blew.

"Not in all things, but in this, aye."

"It is senseless to hurry through the work here without thought for what may be destroyed."

"In other words," he ground out, "what you propose to do will take a long time."

"What I propose," she said crisply, "is to be careful, observant, and organized. If you were impatient with your road, what then? The quality would be poor."

"I generally know what we are digging into and laying down and how much time is required, give or take the weather and some other factors."

"Like Pictish walls?" She brushed a stone close to his booted toe. He shifted his foot.

"And stubborn little antiquarians."

She sat back on her heels to look up at him. "We have something in common," she pointed out. "We both dig into the earth and take it apart. You create roads, I resurrect history. While I shepherd the past, you shepherd the future. We are not so different in what we do, and neither of us knows what we will find. Look what you discovered with your blasting powder."

"Aye," he said, staring down at her. "Just look what I discovered."

She thought of his remark last night, when he had tested himself against the onslaught of love — and found himself invulnerable. Feeling the sting of that, she lifted her chin. "Since you are so very busy, Sir Aedan, perhaps you should get back to the moor and to your great metal beast," she said petulantly.

"Mrs. Blackburn, the commissioners are

breathing down my neck. I had another letter from the queen's secretary, inquiring as to when this road will be ready for Her Majesty's wee jaunt from Glasgow. By the way, you have a letter from Sir Edgar in the same postal bag," he added. "He probably wants to know what you found and if it will benefit him any. Of course I am impatient and demanding. There is no leisure time for polishing stones."

"I am collecting information to report to Sir Edgar. No doubt he wrote to ask after my progress. I cannot just tell him that the stones are old and he should come see them. He and the other museum directors expect something specific."

He glowered. "Tell him not to come look at all."

She regarded him through the shadow of her veil. "Have you always been so obtuse, or is it a skill you foster through incessant practice?"

"Have you always been so stubborn and willful?"

"Yes," she said, and she turned to blow on the cleaned stone.

He turned, muttering something under his breath, and strode away to speak with Hector and Angus. Christina resumed her work, scrubbing furiously.

No one could ever guess that they shared delicious secrets, she thought. Wild kisses, tender embraces, coveted paintings, and hidden stairs apparently were to be conveniently forgotten in favor of snarling and snapping. Regardless of what sort of exchange they shared, she always felt sparks between them, like flint and fire, compelled to ignite each other.

Christina chewed the end of her pen, deep in thought, then applied nib to paper and added to the reply she was composing to Edgar. Each word had to be carefully chosen, for Edgar had a sharp nose for the scent of an antiquity. He would come to Dundrennan quickly if he thought there was merit in the hillside find.

The clearing and digging is coming along well and may yield interesting results, she wrote. *But it is too soon yet to declare it worth your valuable time and mental energy.* She had to have enough time to search for any sort of Arthurian connection. After the digging of the last two days, she was now certain the walls had once belonged to a Pictish house.

She was unsure how to end her note — she wanted to avoid encouraging Edgar's interest in Cairn Drishan and his interest in courting her. She re-read his letter to her. *I remain your faithful friend, my dearest Christina. I know you think of me with the same affection I tender to you.* He had signed it, *Your devoted Edgar.*

"Oh, dear," she murmured. The tone of the letter was very like Edgar himself — assuming and haughty. Lately his arrogance had begun to irritate her. She realized that she had to gently disentangle herself from his affections. Giving him permission to court her had been a mistake, she realized now, and she was glad she had not yet agreed to his marriage proposal.

After the thrill she felt in Aedan Mac-Bride's arms, she realized she could never bear to marry Sir Edgar Neaves. No future existed with Aedan — she was no fool and would not let herself hope — but the life of a bookish widow seemed preferable to one spent with Edgar. She would forever compare Aedan's kisses, his depth of spirit, his humor and strength, to Edgar's cold kisses and colder personality.

She would have to tell Edgar soon that she could not in good conscience accept his proposal or his courtship. She would suggest that they remain colleagues and friends.

But she could not bring herself to write the words just yet. The pen in her hand shook, its drop of ink spattering her hand and her white cuff.

Sighing, she looked with dismay at the black spots spreading across the fine cloth of her undersleeve, made of delicate white lacework in *broderie anglaise*. Her aunt Emmie had carefully made the pieces for her as a

Christmas gift, and now carelessness had ruined one of the cuffs.

After folding her letter and setting the pen down, she left the library, intending to go upstairs to the black-and-white-tiled bathroom to scrub her sleeve with soap and cold water.

The housekeeper was in the foyer as Christina entered it. "Good afternoon, Mrs. Blackburn. Ye seem in a rush, mistress."

"I've spoiled my sleeve with ink." She held up her arm.

"Och, such pretty work, too! Let Effie MacDonald tend to it. She's the laundress, and it's her day to be here, in the washhoose. Go oot the side door by the kitchen, and go past the herb garden. Ye'll see a stone building. Having it oot there keeps the smell o' the bleachin' away frae the hoose," she explained, wrinkling her nose. "Show yer sleeve to Effie MacDonald, and she'll make it right. She's a guid woman, and she likes a wee chat." Mrs. Gunn smiled as Christina thanked her.

She found the washhouse easily enough, a small building in a far corner past the walled enclosure where herbs and flowers grew in profusion.

Opening the door to the washhouse, she was immediately assailed by heat and dampness and the scents of lye, bleach, and soap. The huge room, white and filled with light,

216

held several large tables and a huge brick hearth where enormous copper urns boiled. The high ceiling was hung with racks draped in snowy linens. Two young women and a third older woman wore aprons, their faces flushed as they worked at various tasks.

The older woman came toward her, tall and gray-haired, wiping her hands on her apron. "May I help ye, mistress?"

"Yes. Are you Effie MacDonald?" Christina asked.

"Aye." The woman's eyes were deep brown and penetrating, her cheekbones pronounced, her dress dark and plain. But her earlobes gleamed with gold hoops — a gypsy's face, Christina thought.

Introducing herself and showing her sleeve, Christina explained her errand. Effie nodded and efficiently removed Christina's under-sleeve, then scrutinized the spots.

"Gunnie was right to send ye here. If that ink sets, yer bonny lace would be ruined, aye." She took it to a large tub with brass spigots and flowed cold water over the spots. Then she reached overhead to a shelf filled with small bottles, taking down a bottle and a slender brush. "Some use chemists' potions for their laundry now, but I say old and cheap works best. This will take it oot," she said, uncapping a bottle.

"What's that?" Christina asked, watching as Effie dipped the brush into the liquid and smoothed it over the stained cloth.

"Horse piss," Effie said, "and lemon."

"Oh!" Christina said. Within a few moments, the delicate cloth whitened again before her eyes. Effie then rinsed it with soap and water and added a liquid from another bottle.

"Lavender water," she explained. "Did ye think I'd have ye smellin' o' horse piss?" She laughed and folded the piece inside a linen towel. "Now we'll dry it wi' the flat iron, and 'twill be guid as new. Dora," she called, "here's a wee bit o' lace for the iron!" Effie crossed the room, and Christina followed.

A pretty young girl turned, flat iron in her hand, and took the lace cuff from Effie. Christina watched while Dora carefully ironed the half sleeve inside the toweling. Her nimble fingers kept just out of the flat iron's hot range as she guided the heavy thing over the towel, steaming the dampness out of it.

Watching her, Christina realized with a small shock that the girl was blind, or nearly so. Glancing at Dora's face, she saw a strong resemblance to Effie.

The older woman poised her fists on her hips. "Mrs. Blackburn . . . Ah, ye'll be the laird's guest frae the mooseum, come to look at his great hill. He told me aboot ye, mistress."

"He did?" Christina asked, surprised.

"Och aye, when he came to tea last week — Sir Aedan comes to see me when he can, guid lad. I've known the laird since he was a bairnie in skirts," she confided, leaning forward. "Hector's my son. This is Hector's daughter, Dora MacDonald."

"Oh! Mr. MacDonald mentioned both of you. I did not know —"

"That I'm the laundress? Aye, and my mither and grandmither afore me. We've ay worked for the lairds o' Dundrennan. And Dora here, she makes bonny crocheted things, shawls and whatnot. Sells 'em, too, in Milngavie," she added proudly, while Dora smiled.

Dora handed Effie the newly cleaned and pressed sleeve, and Effie slipped it over Christina's hand and wrist, tying its ribbons snug under her sleeve, the cloth fresh smelling and warm against her skin.

"Thank you so very much, Effie," Christina said, relieved.

The woman smiled, her eyes shrewd. "So ye're the mistress o' that mountain, giving orders to the laird, I hear."

Christina laughed. "I doubt Sir Aedan would take orders from me or any woman."

Effie laughed with her, and nearby, Dora and the other maid chuckled as they worked. "Well, he wouldn't listen to anyone when he was engaged to my niece Elspeth, and he's still that stubborn," Effie said.

"You knew Sir Aedan's fiancée?" Christina asked.

"Och, aye. She was my niece, and Dora's cousin. She and the laird knew each other when they were babes in arms together, and they were always good friends. 'Twas natural for them to come to marrying. Pity she took ill," Effie said, shaking her head sadly. "But sometimes 'tisna meant for such blithe souls to live long in this world, and it may be he wasna meant to be content. The lairds o' Dundrennan dinna wed for love, y'see."

"So I've heard," Christina said.

"But I do hope it proves different for Sir Aedan. He's had too much loss, too many troubles, that lad, and so bonny and braw a man, such a guid heart, always caring about others, and caring so much for his home. I like to think there's a special love for him — I feel that there is. Perhaps he'll be the one to break that wicked curse someday." She smiled at Christina, and a peculiar wisdom seemed to glow in her crinkled, keen eyes.

Christina nodded and felt sudden, surprising tears prick her eyes. Just the lye in the air, she told herself. But she, too, wished that Aedan MacBride could defeat the curse that doomed the brides of the lairds of Dundrennan. Suddenly, she desperately wanted him to be happy. And she did not even know why it meant so much to her.

"Oot wi' ye, noo, for I've work to do, and

so have ye." Effie opened the door, and Christina thanked her for her help and stepped outside. Cool air blew over her damp cheeks and through the freshly curled hair along her brow.

She gathered her skirts and hurried back to the house, wondering if she would see Aedan that day.

Chapter Fourteen

"*Tableau vivante,*" Amy said in a tortuous French accent, "is a game like charades, but played as living statues. We usually mimic artworks, but tonight we will act out scenes from literary works."

Lady Balmossie peeked dubiously from her needlework. Seated on the sofa, Aedan smothered a smile, although he agreed with his aunt. When Amy had suggested parlor games after dinner, he wanted to flee to his study. Her parlor games were usually tedious, but the temptation of playing any sort of game involving Christina Blackburn overruled his initial impulse.

"We'll use the hallway for our stage and the doors as our curtains. When your tableau is ready, knock on the door and we'll open it." Amy waggled the slip of paper in her hand. "Now, we've all drawn partners and have been assigned literary works from the papers in my basket. A pity that Meg and Dougal are not with us this evening, for they are both very good at this game."

"Amy, dearie, they wanted to be with their

bairns," Lady Balmossie said. "We canna expect them to come with us to Dundrennan nearly every day."

Amy shrugged. "The more the merrier, Auntie. Well, Cousin Aedan, I believe you and I have the first turn."

Aedan glanced at the slips of paper in his hand. One named a Shakespearean play and the other named his partner — Christina Blackburn. Pleased with his good fortune in the draw, he looked up. "According to this, I am partnering Mrs. Blackburn." He saw Amy's expression falter.

"But you and I were supposed to — oh, mine says John. Very well," Amy said, and she had the grace to smile at John Blackburn, who had returned from Edinburgh that afternoon. "Aedan and Christina will go first, then."

Aedan rose and bowed to Christina. She stood, blushing, and he tucked her hand in his elbow. "Give us five minutes," he told the others. "Or a bit longer. This may be complicated." He led her toward the double doors.

Lady Balmossie grumbled. "Rob Campbell, you and I are partners. We may as well forfeit now, for I willna be verra guid at playing taboo." Rob laughed.

"Remember the rules," Amy called to Aedan. "You must pay the forfeit if you take too long out there. You'll stand in the corner

223

until someone gives you a kiss to set you free!"

"A silly rule and a silly game," Aedan murmured to Christina as he escorted her into the hallway. She chuckled. He slid the pocket doors shut behind them so that they were alone in the dim, lamplit corridor.

"Here is our assignment, Mrs. Blackburn," he said, showing her the paper. "Romeo discovers Juliet in her tomb. Not very merry, I'm afraid, but Amy made the choices. It is her game."

"I suspect she wanted to be your partner and hoped for a good faint in your arms."

"Ah, well. I believe you've done that yourself, madam. Was it worth the trouble?" He cocked a brow.

"Mm, perhaps." Her hazel eyes twinkled. "We'd better hurry, or we'll pay the forfeit."

"We'll win. I never lose, actually."

"No? You must have been insufferable as a lad."

"Quite possibly." He looked around the hallway. "Shall we use a bench or chair for Juliet's tomb?"

"According to Amy, we can use only our imaginations and ourselves. And I cannot lie on the floor in this gown." She indicated her crinolined skirt of gleaming lavender blue satin.

"Very well." He dropped to one knee, raising the other, his thigh straight and firm.

"Sit on the floor and lean against me."

"Oh, I must not —"

"Mrs. Blackburn, what is not otherwise permissible is encouraged in parlor games. I suspect that is why they are so tediously common. Lean on me, madam."

She sat carefully, her skirt spreading around her in a billowing, airy cushion defined by the crinoline. A frothy hint of petticoats peeked at the hem. She leaned against him.

"I doubt Juliet reclined like a Roman empress taking dinner," she said.

"Relax, madam, you look quite enchanting that way." He slid his left arm beneath her shoulders. "Comfortable?"

"Quite." She tilted her head, closed her eyes.

"I doubt Juliet wore spectacles," he drawled.

She slipped them off, and he tucked them away in his coat pocket. "Are we ready now?" she asked.

"Not yet," he murmured, cupping his fingers around her bare shoulder. Her lavender satin gown had a deep fall of lace across a low-cut bodice that revealed her upper shoulders and chest, and a demure strand of pearls looped her throat. Touching her soft skin, Aedan gazed at the lace edging that rode the luscious swells of her breasts.

A lightning strike of desire tore through

him, and he drew a breath against it. Leaning forward, he rested his other hand at her slender waist, snug in black velvet. He felt the gentle rise and fall of her breath.

Lowering toward her, his face mere inches from hers, he kept his movements slow and studied, fighting inwardly for control. He had promised to act with better chivalry toward her — and he had promised himself to be impassive toward her.

But he was not. When he had kissed her several nights ago, he had discovered, to his astonishment, that he felt far more than lust. What poured through him when he touched her, when she was near him, was different from any feeling he had ever known and difficult to define. Hot and exquisite like lust, but deeper, expansive, as if he felt the heat and spark of his own soul.

Realizing that he could not stop that feeling, and aware that he was vulnerable to her, he felt an odd sense of alarm.

She wiggled a little in his arms, settling herself, tipping her head back. Her breath was fruity and gentle upon his cheek. He wanted to taste her mouth and her creamy skin, wanted to round his hands over her firm, soft breasts. Holding her, even so innocently as this, worked a strange, hot magic on him.

"Are you ready, Romeo?" she said lightly.

He could not answer. She was close

226

enough to kiss, her mouth luscious, her breasts rising, falling provocatively under the lace. Leaning toward her, he closed his eyes for a moment.

She sagged in feigned death against him, trailing her outer arm to the floor, tilting her head drastically. "Here lies your Juliet, awaiting your heartbroken soliloquy."

"Mm," he said, and he could not think of any quote to utter — he whose memory for poetry never failed him. He kept still and ex- pressionless, fearful that if he moved he would lose his restraint. Playing this game with her had been a lapse in judgement, he thought. He should have begged off entirely.

Christina moved her shoulders, and the sweet quiver of her breasts sent desire plunging through him. He frowned.

"Romeo, do try to look passionate," she complained.

"I would, if you behaved more like dear Juliet on her tomb and less like Miss Thistle, twitching about and chittering."

She scowled, and Aedan chuckled. Some- times when he was with her, he felt at ease enough to be playful, something he had all but lost in the last few years.

Obediently, she folded her hands at her waist, dropped her head back more decorously, and waited in silence. Aedan saw that she adopted, unwittingly, the pose of the girl in the painting. She lay expectant, wholly trusting, no

227

longer only a fascinating image to him, but rapidly becoming familiar, part of the fabric of his daily life now. And what he had learned of her — sweet yet seductive, stubborn and calamitous, quick-witted and perceptive — fascinated him even more than before.

And what rushed through him then had all the force of pure desire, yet it was deeper and far more profound. He feared to name it.

"Sir." Christina opened an eye again. "Are you ready?"

"Aye," he muttered, aware of the tension of a particular readiness mounting in his body. "Somehow you land again in my embrace. It is the strangest of coincidences."

"I promise never again to tumble upon you or step into the path of a flying teacup, and I will certainly never again have you for a game partner. Is that acceptable?"

"Indeed." It was not. He leaned over her.

She tilted her head farther, exposing that glorious swan's neck. In her playful mood and her satiny, seductive gown, she was bewitching and innocent all at once.

"Passion," she reminded him in a whisper, opening one eye.

Passion. Suddenly he was filled with it, dark and strong and ripe with it. She roused him, haunted him as no woman ever had, ever could. But he could not let himself fall in love with her.

"Miss Burn," he replied, "you know not what you ask of me."

"Take the mood," she said.

"I have the mood. I cannot think of the words."

"Say this, then, as Romeo did — 'O my love! my wife! Death, that hath sucked the honey of thy breath, hath no power yet upon thy beauty.'" She quoted from the play, then leaned her head back on his arm, closing her eyes.

He stared down at her, his heart slamming. He understood just how Romeo felt and how the ancient Druid prince had felt when his princess had faltered in his arms, lost in endless sleep in a briar.

Love battered the gates of his soul. He began to tremble.

Aedan cupped her cheek. "'O my love . . . my wife.'" Whispering that near slayed him. This was no longer a game.

"Mm, better." She looked at him, then smiled. He melted.

"Aye," he said, and then he kissed her.

She caught her breath, then opened her mouth under his, and he knew her hunger matched his own. Resting her hand on his neck, she welcomed his tongue inside her mouth, where she was wet and delicate. Wrapping her close, moving his lips with hers, he felt himself fill to bursting, felt his heart awaken.

His left hand cupped the gentle warmth of her shoulder, and the other was spread fingered on her high black velvet waister. She shifted in his arms, turned, and his right hand slid upward over lavender satin to touch the swell of her breast. She moaned breathily, undulated so that his fingers easily slid beneath the upper edge of her corset and lacy chemise and found her nipple, soft, warm, stiffening under his touch.

Deepening the kiss, mounding his hand over her breast, he touched tongue to tongue, and finger met nipple, and he began to sink into a whirlpool from which he feared — he knew — there was no escape but one. And it would demand the price of his heart.

A little knock came on the other side of the drawing-room doors. Christina gasped, jerked, and Aedan straightened, settling lace and satin into their previous arrangement.

"Oh, dear God," she whispered raggedly. "What is this between us?"

He had no time to answer — and could think of none — for Amy called and threatened forfeit. He felt stupefied by Christina's extraordinary effect on him. He could not explain it. He certainly did not know what to do about it.

"Ready, you two?"

"Aye, one moment," Aedan answered. Swiftly Christina adopted her pose, eyes shut. He did, too, and stayed motionless.

The doors opened. While the others batted names about, laughing over whether the tableau represented Tristan and Isolde, Lancelot and Elaine, or some other tragic literary couple, Aedan held Christina in the shadowed hallway. Remaining completely still, he hardly listened to their banter, for he had come to a staggering conclusion.

Against his will, despite resistance, the laird of Dundrennan was falling dangerously, disastrously, in love.

Steady rain pattered against the library windows, filling the room with a peaceful susurration. At a large table, John and Amy looked at books of ancient costumes, Amy turning pages while John sketched in a notebook. Meg and Dougal shared a big leather chair beside the fireplace, their heads close in private conversation. Above the mantel hung the painting of *Mary, Queen of Scots* by John Blackburn the elder.

Christina sat alone in a small bay beneath the gallery, a stack of history volumes on the little table beside her chair. Over the top of her open book, she glanced at Dougal and Meg, whose devotion and respect for each other was evident. Though she was glad for their sake that they had found love and treated the gift kindly, she felt a cold trickle of loneliness within.

Once she had thought to have true love in

her own life, but her idealistic, romantic dreams had turned to sorrow and guilt. Now she remembered slow, surprising kisses with Aedan MacBride and thought of what she had allowed him to do. She had craved it shamelessly.

She told herself that it was only her infatuation for him. His actions no doubt originated from healthy masculine urges. Aedan had made it clear that he was uninterested in love, yet he was certainly not uninterested in caressing her — and each time he touched her, she wanted him more desperately.

Loneliness and long-stifled passions vied in her for release and satisfaction — that was all. She had known loving and had enjoyed it with Stephen, when he was capable, when he was not too inebriated or simply too exhausted from pushing himself in his painting frenzies. She had enjoyed their bed play together, especially when he remembered to give her some attention, and brought the thrill into her body.

Aedan, she sensed, would help her find that thrill with care, with tenderness, wanting her to feel pleasure as he might in her. A sudden demand tightened in her body, as if he had actually touched some sensitive, secret part of her.

Her cheeks flamed with heat. She had to stop her imagination from this rampant behavior. *Stop,* she told herself. *Just stop.* These were impossible dreams that served no purpose.

Sighing, she turned her attention to one of her uncle's volumes on Celtic Scotland. She did not hear footsteps until Aedan stood in front of her.

"Sir Aedan." She set down the book. "Good afternoon."

"Mrs. Blackburn." He inclined his head. He was dressed in a neat black suit, a tall silhouette in front of a window. "I hoped to find you here. The library seems to be the place for rendezvous today," he added as a trill of feminine laughter floated across the room from where John and Amy sat together.

"John has asked Amy to pose for a figure in his mural," Christina said. "She is very pleased."

"So I see." Rocking on his heels, hands behind his back, he paused. "We've had a bit of rain this week, more than usual for this time of year. The moorland road is awash with mud, and the hill is a mire, too. I sent the men home for the day."

"Yes, Hector MacDonald got word to me. Surely you did not seek me out to discuss the weather," she added warily. He looked awkward, as if something else was on his mind.

"No. I . . . realize that I have been remiss, Mrs. Blackburn."

She thought of kisses stolen in the dark. "R-remiss?"

"I have not yet shown you the Dundrennan Folio."

"Oh." She almost felt disappointed. Had she expected him to fall to his knees and profess his worship of her? "Oh, the folio! I had nearly forgotten. I would love to see it."

"Come with me."

She rose and followed him to his father's study. Inside, he partially closed the door and went to a tall mahogany cabinet behind it. He inserted a key and opened the lock then removed two cases and brought them to his father's desk.

Red ribbons secured two collapsible boxes, and Aedan began to untie the first one. "The Dundrennan Folio is a collection of family documents and writings by family members, stored as two volumes," he explained. "The pages range from some loose early parchments to papers belonging to my father."

"Yes, I know. Uncle Walter visited Dundrennan years ago at your father's request and translated some medieval pages from copies Sir Hugh made. I have always wanted to see the originals."

"I believe Reverend Carriston saw the old poems. They are in this box." He opened the first volume. Velvet-lined box sides flattened to reveal several packets wrapped in white silk. "There are some old medieval poems and documents."

"Sir Edgar Neaves also came to Dundrennan, interested in acquiring some of the collection," she said.

He shot her a grim look. "He did not acquire any of it. Especially not this. These are family papers and will not be sold." Aedan opened the first silk packet. "I believe your uncle translated these pages."

"Oh, they're beautiful." She gasped to see a sheaf of loose vellum sheets, clearly very old, judging by the style of calligraphy and the ink color. "These are several poems by an ancient Gaelic poet, the Dundrennan Poet," she said.

The parchment page was unevenly shaped, tattered at its edges, slightly foxed with pale brown stains. Neat rows of text filled the page, and the brown ink lettering had the distinctive rounded, controlled elegance of old Celtic script.

"The Dundrennan Poet wrote about battles and some mythical and historical Celtic heroes," she said. "Oh, it is fascinating to see the original pages." The decoration was sparse, with the largest initials intricately illuminated in brownish black ink. Tails and finials swirled into vines and animal heads, the drawing style sure yet delicate.

"I believe the poet wrote in the sixth century," Aedan said. "The language is Gaelic, and family tradition says he was an early laird of Dundrennan, so we keep them in the folio."

"The language is Old Irish, the earlier form of our Scots Gaelic. There are Latin phrases mixed in here, too, I see, which would indicate a Christian education."

"I assume you are familiar with your uncle's translation?"

"Of course. I am delighted to see the originals."

"Examine them at your leisure. Spend as much time with them as you like, madam. The privilege is all yours." He smiled.

"Oh, Aedan, thank you," she breathed.

"You are welcome, Christina," he murmured.

She leaned closer to see, her shoulder brushing his arm. He turned the page to a parchment sheet covered with columns of neat words. More cramped, tiny writing filled the wide margin.

"This is not the poet's work," he said. "If I recall, it is an ancient register of households. Is it of interest to you?"

"My uncle translated this, too. It's a muster roll, listing the names of warriors available to fight for some Pictish king. Look." She traced her finger down the page without touching the vellum. "Your ancestor is listed here. Aedan mac Brudei."

"Oh, aye! I'm his namesake, apparently. A mysterious warrior — we know little about him or his people, but they settled here in the Dundrennan area and were part of the earliest members of what became Clan MacBride."

"This Aedan would have been of the Dál Riata tribe that inhabited this region of Scotland around the sixth century A.D.," she said. "Since we know so little about the Picts, this list of names is a rare and valuable historical document."

"What are those odd notations in the margin? Some clerk's afterthought?"

"My uncle told me that the roster had some marginalia that he could not decipher, and he never copied it. He thought the lines were added by a later hand." She shrugged. "Marginal notes sometimes occur in old manuscripts. Writing surfaces were scarce, so book pages had to serve for paper when needed. The book's owner might jot something down in an old book — for example, how many cows were sent to market that month, or how many cheeses were bought from the local farm."

Aedan smiled. "Maybe it's a list of Pictish cheeses."

She laughed with him. "I wish I knew. I'd like to study the inscription more closely sometime."

"Anytime." In the sudden silence, with his gaze upon her, she felt a blush warm her cheeks.

She looked away, wanting to protect her secret, fervent feelings for Aedan, which seemed very strong today, fed by the last few days and evenings in his company. "This is indeed a treasure. Thank you. I would love to spend a little time with these pages."

"If it continues to rain with such frequency, you will be translating instead of digging," he said, wrapping the pages in the silk again. She helped him tie the ribbons.

After replacing the cases in the cabinet, he closed and locked the narrow doors, then held out the little key to her. "Here. Keep this, and examine the folios whenever you like."

She came toward him, standing near him in the wedge of space behind the door. "Oh, I cannot accept your key."

"Nonsense. Take it." He pressed the bit of iron into her palm, let go of her hand. "I trust you, Mrs. Blackburn."

"Thank you." Her gaze held his, skimmed away. "The folio is extraordinary. No wonder Sir Edgar wanted it for the museum."

"Huh," he grunted. "He wanted more than the folios. He offered to buy the collection, even offered a blanket sum. My father . . . well, he refused to sell. So have I."

"Edgar is very impressed with the whole of the Dundrennan collection — the art, the books, and the historical memorabilia. Would you ever consider parting with some of it? The museum would be an excellent place for any of this collection, and you could share

238

these wonderful things with the entire world."

"I do not mind sharing them one day, perhaps," he said. "But I will not share them with Edgar."

"Edgar is a superb scholar, and he is a director of the museum."

"Edgar," he said sharply, "is sly as a snake."

"Really, sir, I do not understand your attitude toward him. You have made insinuations before this."

"I do not insinuate. I know. Edgar is a snake in the grass. He made repeated attempts to wheedle and manipulate my father's dearest possessions out of this place."

"He negotiated," she said.

"He wheedled," he insisted. "He cajoled. He made offers that were insulting. My father was unwell, and Sir Edgar would not leave the man be. He endangered my father's health with his damnable, heartless persistence. I believe he caused the last fatal attack. In fact, I am certain of it."

"Edgar has a cool and businesslike manner, and at times he seems to be a little . . . well, insensitive to others' feelings, which can be mistaken for hauteur. I assure you, he is simply a very high intellect who is at heart a decent fellow."

"Hauteur, madam, hardly describes it. I will not sell a single thing to him, and if I had my choice, he would never come here again — but for the hole in that damned hill."

"Do not swear. And I believe you are wrong about Edgar."

"I think you are the one mistaken about him." He frowned. "Edgar, is it? Are you on such familiar terms with him? You are usually formal with me, though we have enjoyed some . . . intimate acquaintance."

She felt the heat grow fierce in her cheeks. "I have known Edgar since we were young. Our fathers were friends."

"I see," he said thoughtfully. Something shuttered in his eyes. "But you and I should keep things formal."

"I . . . It might be best. I will not be here much longer, and . . . well, I am not quite certain what happened between us those few times." She spoke softly, looking away. "I do not know if it is something that should continue."

"I am equally confused, madam. But I know one thing — it is extraordinarily pleasant to be confused over you. Christina," he said in a low, gentle manner, "you and I have not behaved improperly. We both responded in a most natural way to natural appetites. Such things happen."

She blinked. "That was not something that occurs naturally between acquaintances."

"I am aware," he murmured. "And I am at

a loss to explain it. But I know I pressed too far with you, and I am very sorry."

Christina looked up at him in silence. She urgently wished he would kiss her again. But her heart foundered, nearly hurt. She realized she had been foolish to give her feelings rein.

This had to end — she knew it, and he seemed to know it, too. She felt it plummet through her, a cold, sad, lonely certainty.

"Perhaps it is best to forget what happened, madam, and consider it . . . a prelude to friendship."

Disappointment punched into her at his tactful rejection. "I understand." She glanced away. "Of course we should overlook it."

He nodded. The pull and the need in her was so powerful that she nearly threw herself into his arms. But he had made it clear that she was not really welcome there. Dalliance was fine with him, apparently, but attachments of an emotional sort were not.

What a simpleton she had been. In mere days, she had lost her heart to this intense, beautiful, exasperating man. For six years she had restrained her feelings, hiding her heart and her needs from herself and others. She had vowed never to fall in love foolishly again and always to be cautious and sensible.

Yet she had fallen like a rock from a high cliff, and now she was lost in the flow of feelings she could barely control.

"Aye," he said. "Perhaps we should forget this, then."

She watched him. "Can you . . . do that?"

"Not easily," he whispered. "But I will try." His face was close, his lips a breath from hers. His finger crooked her chin, lifted her face. She closed her eyes as his touch melted through her. How could she forget what was unforgettable?

Yet she made herself step back, embarrassed, afraid she might cling.

He reached over her shoulder for the door. "Shall we go, Mrs. Blackburn? It is nearly time for tea. And a pleasant interlude it will be, for Miss Thistle is happily plucking plantains at Balmossie today." He chuckled, and it sounded hollow. She did not laugh at all.

She moved past him in silence, chin high.

Chapter Fifteen

"I have an idea," John said as he entered the breakfast room, limping with his cane. "And I think you will love it."

Christina glanced up, coffee cup lifted. She had come to the breakfast room early the next morning to find Aedan already seated at the table, reading his newspaper. After politely murmured greetings, they had eaten in silence. She was on the verge of asking his thoughts when John arrived, his evident enthusiasm like a fresh breeze whipping through the tension in the room.

"Not 'Good morning; and how did you sleep, dear sister,' but simply 'I have an idea,'" she said, amused. "John, that's a sure sign that inspiration has you fast."

"It does." John gave her an impish grin and went to the sideboard to pile his plate with food. Rising, Christina carried his plate and a cup of fresh coffee to the table while John managed his cane.

Aedan folded his paper. "What has inspired you, my friend?"

"I know just what to do with the mural,"

John answered, buttering a slice of toast. "And I began the preliminary sketches last night, while I worked late, up in the long gallery. I think it will work very well."

"Excellent. What might it be?" Aedan placed his elbows on the table, joining his fingertips in a pensive arch.

"I will tell only you two," John said. "And it must stay between us for now."

"It will remain our secret until it is revealed in glory on the dining-room walls," Aedan said.

John nodded. "Good. I've decided to use the landscape that is already in place on the wall. Then I'll add scenes from the legend. I want to arrange several scenes in a medieval fashion, with past, present, and future happening all at once, in the foreground, middle ground, and background of the landscape."

"Very fitting, I think," Christina said, and Aedan nodded.

"First, on the wall beside the dining-room door, there will be the prince arriving with his Celtic warriors — golden torques, armbands, plaid cloaks, shining weapons. Then the meeting of the prince and princess in her father's hall, and another scene where the Druid prince teaches the princess to write — that is where they fall in love, you see, so it needs to be a tender image. Then her father imprisons her in a tower when she refuses to wed a rival king. The prince climbs up to meet her there in secret."

"You could place that scene on the wall beside the window," Christina said.

"Exactly what I was thinking. As we come to the last wall, the princess holds her newborn son, then escapes from the tower. She is caught by the evil rival, who casts a sleeping spell over her, and then the prince discovers her fallen in the briar. The last scene will show his grief, his desperation and devotion as she lays asleep forever on her bed." He waved a hand. "And the entire mural will be bordered in a pattern of Celtic knot work and rose-briar vines."

"I can imagine it all vividly," Christina said, smiling. "And I quite love it." She glanced at Aedan.

Aedan nodded. "A wonderful concept. And we will certainly keep it to ourselves until you finish it. If you like, we can ban everyone from the room until you want the work to be seen."

"Thank you. At first, I will be doing sketches in the long gallery, before I begin work on the walls. I've asked some of the others to pose — Miss Amy and Lady Balmossie, and Lady Strathlin and Mr. Stewart, too, along with household staff."

"A good idea to include the likenesses of family and household staff in the Dundrennan mural," Aedan said.

"I would like both of you to pose for the

prince and princess," John said.

Christina stared at her brother, then glanced quickly at Aedan. He frowned slightly, and neither replied.

"Please. You are perfect for this couple," John urged. "I knew it the night you played Romeo and Juliet together. That scene gave me the idea for the last image in the mural."

Christina shook her head. "Oh, John, I could not."

Aedan glanced at her. "Sir, your sister seems uninterested, but you have other choices. Cousin Amy would leap at the chance."

"Miss Amy was disappointed not to be asked for the princess," John said. "But she has agreed to model for sister of the princess — I'll invent one for the mural — as well as some of the faces in the court. She seems pleased with that."

"Because she will be a princess also." Aedan smiled.

"Aye. But the two main characters in the piece must have the perfect models, or none of it will seem as good as I think it could be," John said. "You want to see most of the mural done in several weeks, sir. Now that I have my scheme, I could do the sketches, the overall design, and have the figures roughly painted in that time, and attend to the details at leisure."

"You would have to work very fast," Christina said.

"With the right models, the work will be much easier."

Aedan looked at Christina. "He has a point. Mrs. Blackburn?"

She shook her head mutely.

"Stephen's painting of the princess is here, too, do not forget," John said.

"How could I forget?" Christina asked quietly.

"If both images of the princess agree, it enhances the romantic appeal of both, and even adds a sense of reality to the legend, something that would be magical, here at Dundrennan."

"Another excellent point," Aedan commented. John nodded.

"I do not think I can do this," Christina said.

"No one else could do this but you, Christina," John said. "Sir, will you agree to pose?"

Aedan studied her. "If the princess will agree, the prince is willing."

She scowled at Aedan, then at her brother.

"We could begin today," John said. "It would take only a few sessions on your part."

"Evenings might be best for both of us," Aedan said. "That is, providing Mrs. Blackburn agrees." He waited.

"Really, I cannot —" She felt trapped, desperate, with both of them watching her. The thought of posing for the briar princess again made her breath catch uncomfortably in her throat.

Looking away, she suddenly remembered Stephen's gaze, hungry and critical upon her while she lay half clothed. She had been so very young, so naïve and willing to please, easily succumbing to his charm, believing in his talent, believing in the ideals of true love — and fooling herself.

But when she thought about posing with Aedan, she wavered and nearly gave in to her brother's fervent request. Hours shared with Aedan, perhaps even in his arms while John drew them — that would be a small heaven. There she would find solace, comfort, and some secret joy to keep for her own when she left Dundrennan.

Biting her lip, she looked at her brother and nearly agreed. But then she remembered that others would see the pictures. She shook her head. "I cannot."

"Christina, please," John said. "This time it would be different. It would be wonderful. Please try to realize that."

"Different?" Aedan frowned, watching them both.

She turned. "You may as well know, Sir Aedan, since you own the original painting. I brought about tragedy and scandal when I modeled for that picture. My . . . husband's death, the painting itself, brought scandal and sorrow and embarrassment to my family." She stood, slapped her napkin down on the table. "Sit, both of you," she snapped when they began to stand out of courtesy. "Decide who shall be your princess, for I do not think it can be me."

She fled from the room, slamming the door behind her.

"Stay, sir," John said, when Aedan rose to pursue her. "It is no use talking to her now. Let her cool a little."

"Believe me, I am acquainted with your sister's temper," Aedan said. He subsided into a chair, shoving a hand through his thick, dark hair. "I knew she did not like the original painting, but I had no idea she felt so strongly about it."

"Later, perhaps you could talk to her about this. She might listen to you, Sir Aedan. I hope that between us we can convince her to model for the mural paintings."

"It's Aedan — I prefer it, to be frank. 'Sir Aedan' makes me sound fond of cigars and shooting parties." John laughed and offered his first name in return. "If your sister is so opposed to modeling for the princess, why press the matter?"

"She *is* the princess — there can be no other, in my mind. Even when I was a lad and read your father's poem for the first time, before Stephen ever painted her, I imagined Christina as the briar princess. It might be her natural elegance, her quiet, dark beauty, or the way she can seem both fragile yet strong."

"I think it's all of those. I understand. Believe me," Aedan said. "But what happened to Stephen Blackburn? I already knew that he had died and that she posed for the picture. When we bought it, we heard that there was some scandal surrounding the artist. I thought perhaps the picture shocked polite society, but truly, it is a beautiful thing, a noble and exquisite work of art. And scandal is not uncommon among painters, sir, begging your pardon."

"Of course. You're correct, Aedan. The female body is not considered scandalous in a work of art. But posing for it, then seeing it exhibited, with the model's identity widely known, followed by the artist's death — it created an uproar for a while. Nothing we Blackburns could not handle, mind you. But Christina took it all very hard. She lost her husband, her dignity, her ideals, all at once. She lost faith in herself."

"What happened?"

"Stephen drowned," John said bluntly. "He was found in the river within a few months of his marriage to my sister, just after the painting was exhibited at the Royal Academy — it took a prize that year, as you no doubt know. The police said his death was an accident, perhaps a suicide. I believe he fell in, coming home late one night. Drunken fool," John muttered.

"Intoxicated? Was that a usual state for him?"

"Unfortunately, it was. He said liquor freed his artistic genius. He had a Saturnian temperament, if you know what I mean."

"I do. Passionate, addictive, rather unpredictable."

"Exactly. He was brilliant but troubled, and that inner darkness intensified his art. He was twenty-three when he died; my sister but seventeen, scarcely more than a child. And she was willful and passionate, too, and brilliant in her own way."

"Not always a bookish wee thing, then?"

"Always intelligent and keen on her studies, but a hotheaded young girl, eager to be independent. And Stephen was older, more worldly, already known for his genius. He fascinated her, and she fascinated him. He began *The Enchanted Briar* just after their marriage. It is his most sublime work, I think."

"Did your sister know about his difficult nature when she married him?"

"Not really. She was young, impulsive, headstrong, and so was he. They eloped. He was our third cousin on the Blackburn side, and they were not complete strangers. He was very charming, and she fell rather desperately in love — I think he did, too, as much as he was capable. Our families were furious. By the time she realized she had made a mistake, it was too late."

Aedan went to the window, shoving his hands in his pockets. He saw Christina hurrying along the garden path, black bonneted, her gray skirt swinging like a bell. "So she married for true love," he said thoughtfully.

"She thought so, but she was wrong. True love betrayed her. She said she would never wed again, though she has allowed someone to court her recently."

Aedan half turned. "Court her?"

"Sir Edgar Neaves, sir. He's been helpful to her in her academic pursuits and has been very attentive to her. She gave him permission to court her. The fellow wants to marry her."

"Does he?" he murmured, narrowing his eyes, gazing outside.

"Aye, but I wonder if it is wise. She . . . can be too trusting, my sister. With Stephen, with Edgar. She married young and mourned Stephen grievously, and she has little experience with men."

Aedan's frown deepened as he watched Christina in her solitary walk. He felt John's remark like a blow to his gut. All he had wanted was to protect her, cherish her, finding her irresistible himself. Had he only taken advantage of her? Was he no better than the other two, in his way?

"She felt responsible for Stephen's accident, you see, and has blamed herself, cloistered herself. It was especially hard for her because he lingered so long afterward."

Aedan felt a cold chill. "He what?"

"He lay in an unconscious state for weeks before his death. She nursed him selflessly and compassionately, but she has never been the same. She went from a fiery, vibrant girl to a quiet, sad wee thing. I have rarely seen that bright lass in her since."

Aedan watched as Christina left the garden gate and advanced over the meadow. "No wonder she refuses to pose for you."

"Aye, the memories are painful for her."

"Then why insist?" Aedan glanced over his shoulder.

"I believe posing might help . . . heal her."

Instinctively he knew what John meant. "Posing for the same thing, under different circumstances."

"Aye. She protects herself with books and intellect and one task after another. In the years since Stephen's death, she has devoted herself to Uncle Walter and his work — he welcomed her into his home after Stephen died, when our father was cold to her. And now that Uncle Walter is unwell and suffering a fallen reputation as a scholar, Christina wants to help him somehow. She takes that responsibility upon her shoulders."

"A serious wee lass, your sister."

"I asked her to pose because I care about her. I want to see her happy again, to see her filled with dreams again. But she must come out of her bookish tower first."

"Aye," Aedan murmured. "I understand entirely."

He watched Christina climb a low hill, the distance between them increasing. He felt a deep tug within, as if his heart were a tightly closed flower straining to open, petal by petal.

"John," he said, "do you believe true love exists?"

"I do. I think it could come to all of us, but it's often overlooked and not always plucked up when it appears. Love is very real. It helps us all, heals us, clarifies our lives. Oh, indeed, I believe in it. And no one deserves it more than my sister," he added fervently. "Why do you ask?"

Aedan shook his head. "Excuse me," he said, turning toward the door. "I really ought to head out for the day. If I run into your sister, I will do my best to convince her . . . to pose for the mural."

"Run into her? You might have to run her down to convince her of that, Aedan," John said dryly.

Aedan stood beside his horse at the base of Cairn Drishan as Christina approached. He held the reins in one hand, the other hand casually fisted at his waist. He waited for her, but she stepped to one side, intending to pass him entirely.

"Why, Mrs. Blackburn," he said pleasantly.

"How did you get here so quickly?" she snapped.

"Pog and I used my road," he said. "It's a fine wee road." He tied Pog's reins to a nearby bush and turned. "You took the route over the moor and the hills. A longer route, though well suited to contemplation."

"If John sent you here to plead with me, you can just take that fine road of yours somewhere else." She began to move past him, but he reached out and caught her arm.

"Christina —"

"I will not pose, even for John. He can ask someone else, and his mural will still be wonderful. It is his talent and vision, not the model, that will make it so."

"Listen to me," he said. He did not let go of her arm, and she made no effort to pull away. Though she wanted to be left in peace, she did not want to break this rare contact with him — not yet, when they had both agreed to keep their distance and be only friends.

"Please do not tell me how it would please my brother, or whatever it is you agreed to tell me," she said. "Because then I would appear utterly heartless when I refuse."

"Christina," he said. "I know all about Stephen's painting."

"You do not know. No one truly does," she said. Though something in her cried out to stay, she jerked free from him and began to climb the hill.

"Listen to me, you wee fool," he said, stepping after her, taking her shoulder, turning her to stand in the middle of the earthen path between the wooden stakes.

"What?" She looked at him impatiently. "I have work to do."

"So do I. But this is more important. Christina, I know about Stephen and the scandal of the painting you posed for."

"So John told you. I never wanted you to know the whole truth of it," she said. "I should have realized you would find out. Not that it makes a difference, since you care for me . . . only as an acquaintance." She glanced away. "And the more you know about this, the less you will care to know me at all."

"Don't be ridiculous. I care very much about you."

She glanced up at him, wary, watchful. "You do?"

"I feel we have made great . . . inroads in our friendship."

She huffed and looked away. Aedan rested his hand on her shoulder, then slid his fingers down to encircle her arm. "Christina, I've known since the beginning about the so-called scandal — the artist's death, the shocking picture he painted of his wife. I'm sorry for your tragedy, my dear. But none of the rest matters a whit to me. It never did."

She looked up at him. "You are not shocked by my behavior?"

He shook his head. "No. You had your reasons. And the result is . . . breathtaking." He rubbed her arm gently. "Undeniably a credit to the artist as well as the model."

"But if you know why I cannot pose for this figure again, why pursue me on this?"

"I agree with your brother. You are perfect for this. And it would not be the same thing at all, since John would never ask you to sit without your clothing or assume a . . . suggestive pose. His vision is very different from Stephen's. The first version is that of . . . a seductress. An innocent siren."

She gazed up at him, remembering the sultry game they had played that first night in his room, when she had fallen and he had seduced her with kindness and earthy charisma and a simple, exquisite kiss. "And the later version?" she asked, tipping her head a little, tentative, hopeful. "What of that one?"

He smiled, his thumb brushing circles on her arm, raising shivers in her. "The later princess," he said, "is still vividly beautiful, and she does not know it. What we speak of now is a third version. And that one . . . well, John's vision will be magnificent, I think. Quietly brilliant. The entire tale told in a sparkling sort of narrative. And I want you to be part of it — to be its focus, its heart."

She sighed, shook her head, looked away, so she would not have to meet his eyes, blue as the bright summer sky behind him.

"When I saw that painting in your room," she said, "so much came back to me — all the broken promises Stephen made to me, all his fits of temper, the days and nights that he painted and did not eat, only drank. . . . There are things no one knows, not John, not anyone. Only myself."

"My dear lass," he murmured. "I'm sorry."

She drew a breath. "He liked to paint at night, and he would drag me out of a sound sleep to pose for him if he did not have something just right. He would tear my clothing off to get me out of it — he never had patience. He said we would buy new things for me. We could never afford them."

"Did he . . . harm you?" Aedan asked in a low rumble.

"Not that way," she answered, shaking her head. "He was fierce about his work, selfish with it, but not cruel beyond it. He loved me . . . in his way. But when John asked me to pose for the princess again," she went on, "all the fear, the unhappiness, the broken dreams, came flooding back. So many long nights when he left me alone and came staggering back, drunk, to lock himself in his studio." She blinked back tears. "My wild, haunted artist. He could not be anything but what he was," she said.

"You loved him?"

"I thought I did. I certainly cared very deeply, and tried to be his helpmate in all things. But I learned . . . how wrong I was about love. And then he died. . . . My God, he struggled with that, too, just as he fought with every force in his life — genius, love, even death itself —" She gasped a little and lowered her head.

"And you were always there for him, weren't you?" Aedan drew her close, wrapped an arm around her. She leaned her cheek on his chest, pressing against the sturdy wool of his jacket. He felt so solid and strong, so reliable and earthy and real, so deeply attractive. His heart thumped slowly, his hand kind on her back, his silence patient.

She wanted to be in his arms so much, wanted to be held and protected there, wanted to lean on his strength until her own returned full force. He did not take her into his embrace as he had done at other times. That hurt deeply, secretly, but she stood still and did not show it.

"Later I realized that I had not loved him so much as pitied him," she said. "I wanted to save him, foster his genius, but he was beyond it. And I have lived with the regret and the shame ever since. I do not want to go through it again."

"Christina," he murmured. He tipped her head up. "This time it will be very different. This time, if you pose for the princess, all will end happily. You will be pleased with the result and proud of it for the rest of your life. I promise it."

She looked at him, blinking back tears she refused to shed. "How can you promise that?"

"Because," he said, brushing at a wayward strand of her hair, "I will be there as the prince. Will you trust me at my word? And trust your brother's vision for this mural?"

Christina sniffled. "I . . . Let me think about it."

He smiled and brushed his hand over her cheek slowly, his blue eyes intent, deep and sparkling, so that her heart pounded fiercely in her chest. "Good," he said. "Take some time to tell yourself that you are safe in this. Perfectly safe, my dear lass." He kissed her on the cheek, only the cheek, but so tenderly that her knees melted beneath her.

Slowly he let go of her, and though she desperately wanted to step into his arms again, she watched him, let him step away. Her heart felt heavy, hollow, and sad.

"Perhaps there will be a happy ending for this princess, at least in this one matter," he said, and he reached for Pog's reins.

"Perhaps," she said quietly.

He bounded into the saddle and then looked down at her. "Mrs. Blackburn, good day."

She watched him go, and she knew that there would be no happy ending for her, no matter how wonderful it would be to pose in Aedan's arms, no matter how magnificent John's mural would be when it was done.

Because when it was done, she would have to leave.

Flowers everywhere she went. Lavender stems filled a tall vase on the table beside her bed, while marigolds and daisies glowed in a glass beside her place at breakfast. Heather bells tied with ribbons brightened the stone wall when she arrived on the hill in the morning. Blowsy pink roses floated in a glass bowl in her little sitting room when she returned in the afternoon, filling the air with sweetness.

Now, a chain of daisies surrounded her dinner plate, and a posy of wild roses lay on the table beside it. She knew who was responsible. Smiling, she looked at him across the table.

"John," she said, "enough. You will give me hay fever."

Seated at the head of the table adjacent to her, Aedan chuckled.

"Will you do it?" John asked eagerly.

She half laughed, half sighed, glancing at Aedan. He lifted his brows in silence. They were only three for dinner that night, as the ladies of Balmossie had stayed home to nurse colds, and Meg and Dougal had gone to Glasgow.

"How did you find so many flowers in September?" she asked.

"Sonsie Jean — Muriel — helped me," he said. "And Sir Aedan suggested the wild roses."

Quickly she met gazes with Aedan, then looked away.

"I do hope you'll agree, Christina. Those flowers were a good deal of work," John said, grinning sheepishly.

"Sir Aedan helped, too, did he?"

"Certainly," Aedan said. "I get to be the prince, after all." His lips twitched in a little smile.

Twirling the little posy of wild roses, she finally nodded. "Very well. But you will have to sketch like mad to capture me, John Blackburn, for I will not do it again."

"Pity," Aedan commented. She sent him a little scowl, but he only raised a brow.

"We'll start tonight, then, after dinner," John said. "Meet me in the long gallery."

"Tonight, madam?" Aedan murmured, his gaze steady as he waited for her answer. A thrill of pleasure and anticipation slipped down her back.

"Tonight," she said, and she took a sip of wine.

Chapter Sixteen

"For now, let's start with the meeting of the prince and princess," John said. Seated at an easel that held brownish paper, he picked through a box of charcoal sticks, chalks, and pencils. He glanced at Aedan and Christina, who stood side by side. "Face each another . . . Yes, like that. Good. Now, Aedan, take Christina's hands in yours, as if you have just met."

She offered her hands to Aedan, her fingers quivering slightly. His clasp was warm and firm as Aedan raised their linked hands toward his chest. "How is this?"

"I like that," John said. "It shows both tenderness and fascination, as if these two sense they are meant for each other. The overpowering strength of love at first sight will be part of the theme of the mural."

"Ah," Aedan murmured.

Silent, Christina felt delicate shivers ripple through her. Love at first sight, indeed. She was very much afraid that she had succumbed to that already. The laird of Dundrennan was far too enticing for her lonely, needy imagination to resist.

"Excellent. Hold that," John said, sketching with a bit of chalk, his arm moving in long, loose strokes. "I knew you two would be an excellent match for this. Your complementary coloring and trim figures, your classic, balanced features — all perfect. And there is something . . . quite indefinable between you," he went on as he drew them. "It fairly sparks around you."

"That might be due to our arguments over Cairn Drishan," Aedan said wryly. Christina frowned at him, and he raised one eyebrow without changing his expression.

"Whatever it is, it's perfect for this mural." John worked quickly, folding back the paper to begin a new drawing while they kept still in the pose.

"This will be the first meeting of the briar princess and the Druid who came at her father's request to teach her to read and write," John said. "I shall use MacGregor for the Pictish king, Mrs. Gunn for his queen, and I thought Lady Balmossie would make a wonderful Celtic priestess."

Aedan chuckled. "She'll want her familiar on her shoulder. Did Druids keep monkeys?"

John snorted with laughter. "The focus of each scene will be the developing love between the prince and princess," he said. "I'll fade the other characters using washed color, so that you two will stand out in brighter colors, with strong linear touches. Now, gaze into each other's eyes — oh, aye, just like that! I'm nearly done with this, and then we'll go to another pose, if you are not tired."

"Not in the least. Madam?" Aedan pressed her fingers.

"I can continue," she answered. Head tilted upward to look at Aedan, Christina flexed her shoulders a little.

John looked up. "Christina, your eyeglasses —"

"Oh!" She set them aside, and Aedan took her hands again.

"And your hair — it must be long and loose," her brother said. "And your skirts . . . well, I did hope to draw you in costume. I brought a trunk of art materials and some costumes with me from Edinburgh on this last trip. I have the gown Mother wore for Father's painting from the tales of Ossian — you know the one, Christina."

She nodded, looking at Aedan. "Father won first place for it at the Royal Scottish Academy. It's a stunning picture, nearly as large as one of these walls, filled with gorgeous figures in a misty, magical setting."

"Christina and I were among the models for that picture when we were bairns," John added, intent on his drawing.

"My father owned an engraving of that painting," Aedan said. "It's quite a stunning piece. Very dramatic. You must show me where to find you and John in the engraving. I'd like to see you as a wee lass."

She smiled, surprised and warmed by his interest.

"If Christina wears a costume — Aedan, would you mind wearing a tunic? Seeing the drapery would help speed my work along. You are accustomed to wearing the kilt, sir. The tunic costume I have in mind is similar to that."

"Certainly," Aedan said. "Shall we change now?"

"Please. Christina, the costumes are over there." John pointed to a large steamer trunk that servants had lugged up the stairs for him days earlier. Its lid was propped open.

"There is a sitting room through that door, where you can change privately," Aedan said.

She hesitated, frowning. "Oh, very well," she conceded. "But I'll pose in costume only if no one else is allowed to see us."

"Really, Christina, we are not running a brothel up here," John remarked. "And besides, the human body expressed in art is a beautiful thing. It is something to admire, not leer at."

"Absolutely," Aedan murmured.

Frowning at them, she turned and went to the wardrobe to choose the long, pale gown that her mother had worn years ago. She saw the red tunic that John had in mind for

Aedan, and she draped that over the trunk lid for him.

"Christina," John said. He came close to her. "What I want to capture in the princess is elegance and extraordinary beauty. The fluid drape of clothing over the human form will help create that. The Pre-Raphaelite women — Jane Morris and Lizzie Siddall and the rest — often favor a medieval style of dress: long, loose, flowing day gowns." He hesitated, shrugged. "This may be a sensitive topic for a lady to discuss, but I am your brother. Jane and Lizzie go without stays and the thickness of several petticoats. I rather like the look," he confided. "The antique waist, I believe they call it."

"Wretch, thinking only of your art," she said, half teasing. "Very well, then. So long as I'm fully dressed," she muttered.

"Of course," he said. "And thank you."

She nodded, glancing at Aedan, who leaned against the table, arms folded. He wore the kilt and black jacket he had worn at dinner, his bare legs hewn and strong, knees tight, arms and shoulders broad and appealing.

The thought of slipping into that silken gown without her supporting undergarments did not shock her as much as John supposed — or even as much as she might have thought herself.

Instead, she felt secretly excited by the tacit permission to be in Aedan's embrace without the layered barrier of her formal clothing. She craved being near him for as long as she could, and so it felt more welcome and enticing than shocking.

Perhaps Aedan and John had been right after all, and posing for the mural would be enjoyable for her, rather than something she would regret. Draping the dress over her arm, she went into the adjoining sitting room.

Accustomed to doing without a lady's maid, she removed her dinner gown and crinoline quickly, aware that the men waited for her. Standing in corset, chemise, drawers, and stockings, she paused, taking a breath as if about to jump into deep water.

She had not called such boldness out of herself for years. After popping the hooks and eyes of her snug stays, she removed them and laid them aside. Taking a deep breath, she stood in a simple chemise and long drawers of light, embroidered cotton and picked up the medieval costume that her mother had once worn.

The heavy, creamy silk slid fluidly over her body, free and comfortable, designed with a low neck, long bell sleeves, and a trailing hem edged in gold embroidery. As she ran her hands down the natural curves of her torso, revealed under the gown, she felt an exhilarating sense of freedom, even independence.

She loosened her hair from its braids and pins and combed it with her fingers until it flowed in a thick, soft cloud over her shoulders. Tying a golden fillet across her brow, she spun around. The light, easy drape of silk and cotton against her skin felt sensual and wholly delightful.

When she opened the door and walked into the long gallery, Aedan and John turned to stare at her.

In turn, Christina stared at Aedan, who wore a tunic of deep red, embroidered in golden thread at neck and knee-length hem. A plaid cloak draped over one shoulder, fastened on the other shoulder with a huge paste brooch of Celtic design. His legs were bare, his feet in soft leather boots, and the heavily muscled skin of his forearms and neck gleamed in the lamplight. She could easily see the taut shape of his torso and wide shoulders beneath the soft woolen fabric.

She moved toward him dreamily, feeling as if she had stepped into the misty surround of another place and time, a world of legends and magic.

"Beautiful," Aedan murmured, drawing her toward him at her waist. He took her hands and lifted them, clasped with his to form a knot between them.

Her heart quickened, and she was lost, taken up by love and held fast. Unable to

269

look away from his gaze, for a moment she forgot why they were there, what they were doing, even forgot that their devotion was feigned. It felt so real.

"Excellent — hold that," John said, taking up his chalk. "The prince and princess falling in love, entirely focused on each other, so that the rest of the world disappears for them." He shifted the easel. "The profile view of this pose is striking — like some Celtic god and goddess, drawn together by love and destiny. Perfect," he murmured, drawing.

"Comfortable?" Aedan squeezed her fingers affectionately.

Christina nodded and felt the sudden prick of tears in her eyes. Neither Stephen nor Edgar would ever have shown her this sort of kindness, couched in quiet, iron strength.

"Relax for a moment," John said after they had held the pose for a few minutes. "This is going very well — you are both such a pleasure to draw. I have an idea for the next pose — Aedan, would you help me move that small table over here?"

Aedan nodded and helped John shift a compact, sturdy table near Christina. Then John showed them the first of his sketches, and they admired the deft, fluid line with which he had captured their pose.

"Now, the prince comes to his princess through the window of her tower. She welcomes him with open arms," John directed. "Aedan, use the table as if it's a window ledge. You must look as if you have just come over the windowsill."

Lifting one knee to the table as if climbing, Aedan kept his other foot firm on the floor. When he beckoned, Christina moved toward him like iron to a magnet.

"My apologies if this makes you two feel awkward," John said, "but this next pose needs a rather impassioned embrace. You must go into his arms, silly lass," he went on when Christina hesitated. "Aye, and see how he welcomes you."

Resting his hands at the back of her waist, he pulled her toward him. Her breasts, draped in silk and cotton, brushed against his chest. Even in pretense, the pose felt so natural, and his touch upon her so compelling, that she had to close her eyes for a moment and simply breathe to maintain her composure.

Aedan leaned his forehead against hers, his breath soft on her cheek. Supported in his arms, Christina thought she might dissolve, then and there. She was thankful he did not know the wild track of her thoughts or how hard her heart was beating.

"What were their names?" John asked as he sketched. "The prince and princess?"

"Aedan mac Brudei and —" Aedan paused.

"Liadan," Christina finished.

"Liadan, aye! How did you know?" Aedan murmured. "I thought that was known only to the family. My father did not include that in his poem, keeping the detail for the family."

"I've been studying the old parchment in the Dundrennan Folio, remember? It's written in the margin."

"Is it?" he asked. "I want to see it."

She nodded, and her nose brushed his. Again she closed her eyes, for a secret, burning ecstasy built steadily within her. She wondered if he felt it too, for his fingers at her waist grew hot through the thin layers of her clothing.

"Hold that. It's wonderful, very loving," John said, absorbed in his work.

Aedan sighed low, so that only she heard. Keeping her eyes closed, not daring to move or speak, Christina felt very much afraid that she was falling deeply, rapturously in love.

"What was that opening verse, where the princess and prince meet for the first time?" John mused while he sketched. "Ah, now I remember it —

'A glance, a murmur, a touch of hands,
Their souls entwined, and the need began:
Storm-fierce, falcon-swift, deep as time.'"

Love at first sight. Christina realized suddenly what she had felt in the moment she had looked up to see Aedan silhouetted in the window when she first arrived — and the moment she had looked into his eyes when he had discovered her fallen on the stairs outside his door.

The inexorable, dynamic pull of one soul toward another, one twin seeking the other, compelled to find its own perfection and completion. She had fallen in love with Aedan MacBride the instant she had seen him, and she tumbled deeper with every encounter.

But if it stirred in him, too, he would refuse to allow the possibility — and she ought to do the same herself. She sighed, sad and low.

"Are you tired?" Aedan whispered.

She shook her head mutely.

"Don't move. That's perfect," John murmured as the silence spun out, filled only with the scratching of chalk. "Perfect."

"Damn it all," Aedan swore softly, shuffling amid the papers and maps scattered on the library table. Two days had passed since he and Christina had modeled for John, and in the midst of that pleasant distraction — he wondered when John might require their presence again — Aedan had arranged to meet with his assistant engineer to discuss the roadwork. "There has to be another solution. Hand me the other map — the Ordnance Survey for the region of the moor."

Rob Campbell, his sun-bleached hair gleaming gold in the sunlight that poured through the library windows, slid the map across the table. "We've both gone over the maps many times, sir," Aedan's assistant said quietly. "There are few good options. We can take the road over the other side of Cairn Drishan, or take it around the base of the hill —"

"Straight through Effie MacDonald's kailyard," Aedan finished. "And I refuse to do that." He bent down to peer at the area, measured carefully on the most recent Ordnance Survey map. He traced a fingertip over it thoughtfully.

"Effie has said she would not mind," Rob said.

"She felt obligated to agree, I'm sure. She would certainly mind losing the only home she's ever known. And I would mind, too. I promised my father that I would never oust our tenants. Even if the queen demanded it, I would have to refuse."

"Sir, it is by far the better route to go through Effie's property. The second option, on the other side of that hill, would take us through even more rock than we've already encountered. It would require considerable blasting, and the museum has banned our use of black powder, for now, at least." Rob glanced across the library, where Christina

Blackburn sat curled in a leather chair, reading.

"I know." Aedan dragged over another map to compare it to the first. He took up a pencil to sketch the profile of the hill again, although the table was littered with drawings of various angles of Cairn Drishan. "If we make cuts here and here," he said, indicating the sites with arrows, "using black powder in modest amounts for a minimum of rubble and debris, we could cut through quickly. But this route would be longer and steeper than the one I originally designed."

"We could vary the gradient with slight adjustments as we take the path up the hillside and down again," Rob said. "It would be on the other side of hill, a safe distance from the site of the old wall."

Aedan nodded. "If we are to finish the route by the time the queen makes her jaunt from Glasgow to Dundrennan, we will have to start the work immediately."

Rob nodded. While his apprentice engineer studied the drawings and maps, Aedan took a moment to glance toward Christina.

Lately he had spent more time working in the library. He preferred the larger table and brighter natural light there — and he liked it even more if Christina was also working there.

He now had a habit of looking for her whenever he entered the room, feeling a little fillip of excitement when he saw her and a tug of disappointment when he did not. He liked hearing the scratching of her pen on paper if she sat writing letters, liked looking up to see that she was there somewhere, tucked in a chair reading intently or sitting at a table with the folio open before her.

When she was there, the room seemed warmer and more inviting, regardless of the quality of weather or lighting. Sometimes he caught the faint fragrance of roses and lavender mingling with the familiar scent of books or heard the whisper of silk and skirts.

Most of all, he liked it when she put down her pen or her book and glided toward him. She showed genuine interest in his work, in the maps he used or the careful drawings he made, which were precise and clean rather than artistic. In turn, he asked her about the progress of her translation, or which book she was reading and what she thought of it.

He did not particularly care about this or that book. They did not hold the magic for him that they had held for his father or his sister or for Christina. He asked because he wanted to hear her thoughts and listen to her melodic, slightly husky voice. He asked so that he could study her face, with its fascinating blend of purity and allure.

Once, the library had been dominated by his father's vigor, his intellect, his powerful memory. But Christina's quiet presence made subtle, enervating changes in the way he saw the room. Now he associated the place with her almost as much as with his father. Somehow he did not think Sir Hugh would have minded that. The poet would have approved of Christina, her love of books and stories and history, her talents and her thoughtful nature.

"What do you think?" Rob asked.

Aedan blinked, looked at him. "Oh. The hill. We should begin working there as soon as possible."

"That's what I just finished saying. We can send a crew of men up along that way to begin the grubbing of that side of the hill, removing shrubbery, heather, roots and rocks, and so forth."

"Aye. And we can send the behemoth that way to shovel the new path until we can begin blasting."

"Right." Rob stood, gathered some of his papers into a leather case. "I'll go talk to Angus Gowan about doing a new survey of the other side of the hill. Are you coming back out to the work site with me, sir?"

"What? No. I have some charts to do for the new plan. I'll work on them now." Aedan nodded as Rob left the library.

Sitting back, chewing his pencil's blunt end thoughtfully, Aedan watched Christina, curled reading in his father's favorite leather chair, with his father's terrier asleep at her feet. He noticed the rich, dark fire in her hair as the afternoon sun spilled over the crown of her head. A long while passed before he could focus his attention on his maps again.

Chapter Seventeen

"Mrs. Blackburn," Hector called, "ye should come see this."

Clouds covered the hot morning sun as Christina looked up. She was perched on a rock, writing another note to Edgar to tell him that the foundation stones of a Pictish house now seemed to be emerging from the earth. Several days of digging had exposed more of the structure.

"Yes, what is it, Mr. MacDonald?" she asked.

"I believe we've found something here, lass."

"Oh!" She set aside the writing box that held her paper, pen, and ink pot and nearly stumbled in her haste to reach the spot where the foreman and Angus Gowan stood. The Gowans, who had been working diligently all morning, stood back, shovels in their grimy hands, dust smudging their faces.

"One of the stones shifted a bit when we were clearing here, mistress," Angus Gowan said. "That flat one in the flooring there. Rocked, it did, and seemed loose."

"We pried it up," Donald Gowan said. "See what we found."

She saw a dark hole in the earth, filled with curious shadows. Sinking to her knees, she peered inside. The cavity was cleanly cut and walled with fieldstone. Round shapes, apparently pots and vats, were stacked two deep along the far wall.

"Can you move the stone any more, Mr. MacDonald?"

"Aye, lass. The thing is on a lever stone, as if 'twas meant to be opened. And look. There are steps for going down. Is it a tomb, d'ye think? Och, we'll find a king's ransom now," Hector said gleefully, rubbing his hands.

She brushed earth from her hands and stood back as the Gowans heaved the great stone to expose more of the square opening. Angus lit and held an oil lantern for her, shining it down into the gap. Looking into the gloom, Christina saw the shapes more clearly. Several large clay pots were stacked against a wall.

She smiled as she turned toward the others. "We might find vats of wine or tubs of grain, but not gold, Mr. MacDonald. This is a storeroom. It's called a souterrain, an underground room. Like a butler's pantry."

"A sootie— a what? A pantry in the ground? They had suchlike, them that lived here?"

"Aye, they had surprising sophistication in their homes, with luxuries like wall cupboards, shelves, even private lavatories."

"Och, mistress, dinna tell me that." Hector turned pink.

"Storerooms like this one are fairly common in this sort of house, from what I understand. Food would have stayed fresh and cold in here. They would have kept grain and so on in those clay jars." She stood, gathering her skirts. "I'd like to go down to see. Can you move a ladder in there for me?"

Hector beckoned to the Gowans, who hastened to bring her the wooden ladder they had brought to use while clearing the taller sections of the wall embedded in the torn hillside.

"Ye want to see grain and auld stale cheeses that's been doon there for a thousand years?" Hector asked, and he shrugged. "Ye'd best wait, lass. We'll send Donald doon first, in case there's danger. He's a braw laddie. Donald," he directed. Christina handed the young Highlander the lamp, and he carefully descended the ladder into the hole.

"Souterrains are not very exciting, I suppose," Christina said. "I have read about them, though I have not yet seen one myself. They were often used as storerooms and were simple chambers cut into the earth, lined with stone blocks to retain the coolness.

281

Sometimes there are several chambers linked together, and when they are filled with stone and pottery vats, it can prove quite exciting."

"Oh aye, pots. Verra interesting," Hector said, sounding unconvinced. "I'd rather find pots o' gold!"

"So would I, Mr. MacDonald. But this will do." She waited anxiously, looking over the edge as Donald wandered about. Although she tried to act scholarly and detached, she felt very excited, for she had secretly wondered if the site would yield anything other than crumbling stone partitions.

Donald looked up. "Nothing here but auld jugs and chamber pots!" As he came up, Christina moved to step down the ladder.

"Mistress, dinna go down there," Hector said. "The laird wouldna want that."

She looked around. "Why would he care? Does he worry that I'll find some gold and steal it away for the museum?"

"Och, dinna get in a kerfuffle. He cares aboot yer welfare, I'm thinking," Hector replied. "He told us to watch everywhere ye set yer bonny foot and sweep the verra earth where ye walk, and make sure the stones were clean where ye set yer cup o' tea and where'er ye rest."

"He said that?" she asked in surprise.

"Nae exactly, but near enough," Hector admitted.

Angus nodded vigorously. "Himself said to

me, 'Angus Gowan, you are never to be leaving the wee lassie alone up on the hill, and she is never to be wanting for anything, or it's I will be hearing of it.' "

"So if I let ye doon there the noo, and something were to happen," Hector said, "a scratch to yer finger or dirt darkening yer wee nose . . . och, the laird will be after me for it."

Christina stared at him, her thoughts racing. Although Hector was making something of a joke, she wanted to believe that Aedan could care that much about her. "I'm sure the laird is concerned about a further delay to his road, or something interesting turning up here in his absence," she replied primly.

"It's ye he thinks of, and nocht else. I canna let ye doon there, lass, 'til the laird says it's safe."

"Do you think it's safe?" she asked bluntly.

Hector shrugged, looked at Donald, who shrugged.

"Well, then," she said, gathering her skirts and stepping down, "I shall take responsibility. If the laird does not like it, send him to me." She moved into the shadows.

"A muckle fuss over stale oats," Hector muttered.

After carefully descending the ladder, Christina reached the earthen floor of the storage chamber. She noticed that the clay jars stacked against the wall were painted with various animal and abstract designs, in a primitive yet elegant style.

A closer look confirmed that they were all sealed with thick wax. She wanted desperately to discover their contents, but she did not want to disturb the centuries-old dust on their shoulders, nor spoil the peace and the mystery of their secrets. She turned and looked up at the men waiting.

"This is truly marvelous," she said, her voice echoing in the cool, musty space.

"Is it gold?" Hector asked hopefully, peering down. The lantern he held poured light over her.

"Old pots, Hector, my friend!" She felt giddy with delight. "Come down and see!"

"Och," he said with resignation, stepping into the opening. "Only for you, lass."

Yet more mud. This road was cursed, Aedan thought. He shoved a hand wearily through his hair and gazed around the work site. Another night of thundershowers had created even more muck. His men toiled along the side of the road, picks and shovels making sloppy noises, the work going slowly. The steam engine, garish red in the cloudy light, huffed and spat in a forceful rhythm, straining to lift the heavy earth. One of the men hopped up on the wagon that supported the great beast and checked the gauges, keeping an eye on the machine.

Rob Campbell sauntered toward Aedan. "We've made progress, despite all, sir," he commented. "Another half mile or so yet to grub out and dig, and we'll reach that long stretch of road from Glasgow that was completed last year. Then the top layer of crushed stone goes on, and after that. . . ." He shrugged, looked at Aedan. "We have nearly a month left. We may make it."

"Aye, perhaps — if we can cut through the other slope of Cairn Drishan in an efficient manner," Aedan said.

"Providing that we find no other ancient sites," Rob said dryly. He glanced at the incline of the great hill nearby. "Has Mrs. Blackburn had word from Sir Edgar yet?"

"She had a letter from him, and I presume she will answer, but I do not know what they discussed. I'll be going to Edinburgh myself in the next week or so, but I intend to avoid him."

"I understand you intend to escort Miss MacDonald and her grandmother to see the doctor. Dora — Miss MacDonald — told me about your offer. I want to thank you for your generosity."

"No thanks needed. I imagine you would have done the same, given the opportunity."

"Oh, aye. I'd accompany you if I were not needed here in your absence. I'd like to give Miss MacDonald my . . . support."

"I gather that your friendship with Miss MacDonald has grown close. Effie mentioned something of the sort."

"It has. And I'd like our friendship to become closer, sir. I hope Dora feels the same way, but I feel I must wait a bit."

"Perhaps if the treatments improve her eyesight, you might wish to court her," Aedan suggested carefully.

Rob frowned. "Do you think it makes a difference to me if she can see or not? I'd court her now if she'd allow it."

"Ah. The last time I was there, I mentioned your name, and Dora blushed a fine pink. Then she wanted to hear news about Robert Campbell and none at all about the laird." Aedan grinned. "Even talk of our trip to Edinburgh did not interest her as much as hearing that you posed for an ancient Scottish warrior in John's mural. I told her that you wore a tunic and carried a large shield and a sword from my father's collection. And I made sure to say that you looked as fine as a warrior from the ancient Fianna. The young lady seemed very impressed."

Rob laughed. "Thank you. That may help my case. I'm not quite sure of her feelings yet, so I've been cautious."

"My friend," Aedan said, "caution is wise around fires and steam engines. But matters of the heart sometimes require courage and boldness, rather than caution."

"You sound like a man who knows whereof he speaks." Rob studied him calmly.

Aedan shrugged. "I've learned that some men have courage for everything but love. They might regret that caution later in their lives. Do not be one of those."

"Are you saying Dora might like to know how I feel?"

"Just so, sir."

Rob nodded. "That might take bravery, indeed."

"I have faith in you." Aedan glanced toward the steam engine, which had begun to sputter. "Rob, go turn off that infernal machine, if you would. The behemoth has had enough exercising for one day."

"Aye," Rob said, and he strode away.

Frowning, thinking about his own lost chance at love, Aedan looked toward the high ridge of Cairn Drishan, far up the moor. Earlier, he had noticed a small figure perched near the site of the old wall.

She was there now, her dark skirt billowing behind her, her white blouse and straw hat pale in the gray light of a gathering rainstorm. He narrowed his eyes, watching her intently.

Her small figure was fragile compared to the massive hillside, yet she was determined, undaunted by the task ahead of her, undeterred by rising storm winds. He admired her strength and stubbornness, even though it conflicted with his own goals, his own determination.

He shaded his eyes with his hand and wondered if she could see him now — one still dot upon the moorland — as he could see her. He wondered if she sensed his spirit or felt the same pull he felt, like an invisible gossamer thread spun out between them.

A great, aching need rose in him to go to her, to declare his feelings, to take the advice he had just given Rob Campbell. He wanted her desperately — the intensity of it shook him, astonished him — but he dared not acknowledge that need.

If the curse of his forbearers held true, declaring his feelings for Christina would doom her. He was not a superstitious or fearful man by nature, but that risk he could not take.

Hearing a rumble, he looked up, seeing greenish gray clouds gathering from the west. He muttered a low oath, realizing that yet more rain would bring fresh mud and further delays. He shook his head at the prospect.

More thunder. The air felt alive, charged with the power of the storm. What drove through him in that moment felt even greater, capable of shifting his life out of its habitual track.

Change. He felt its inevitable strength, dreaded it, unsure where it would sweep him. He did not particularly like change, but he was a realist. He knew it had already entered his life. Whether he would continue to resist it, or if he would surrender to its power, remained to be seen.

Fat drops of water pelted his shoulders as he whirled and marched off, calling to his men to cover the great metal beast before the thing began to rust.

"I would rather you were not alone up here, Mrs. Blackburn," Aedan said. "There is a thunderstorm brewing. There were some raindrops not long ago, and those clouds look ominous."

Startled, Christina glanced up through the fall of black lace fringing the brim of her straw hat. She was kneeling, so that Aedan's spare, muscular form silhouetted against the pewter sky seemed vastly tall. Glowering, hands fisted at his waist, he did not look pleased.

Resuming her task, she stretched a measuring tape across part of the souterrain's stone cover. "Good afternoon to you, too, sir. I will not melt in the rain," she said stiffly.

"Nevertheless, there is a danger of mud and potential rockslides up here. You should always have someone with you on this hill. I saw Hector down on the moor just now, as I was coming from Dundrennan." He looked up as thunder rumbled. "He said you wanted me to come up here. I thought you might need me urgently for something, so I hurried."

Need him, she thought. Yes, she did, heart and soul, but she could not let it show — she had only begun to admit the possibility to herself. "I am perfectly fine alone up here."

He glanced around. "Where are the Gowans?"

"If you must have a count of heads, Mr. MacDonald has gone to take luncheon with his mother, and Angus and his sons went with him. I was invited as well, but I thought to finish this part of the work before going down the hill." Picking up her memorandum book, she recorded the measurements, then pulled the ruled ribbon over a long edge of the stone, stretching to reach.

Aedan took the metal-tabbed end and drew it out to span the stone. "You might come to harm here alone, with a storm on its way. Six and one-half feet," he said, releasing the tape.

She wrote down the number. "I am not helpless, sir. I can find shelter if I need it. And since you're here, you can save me if I faint from the exertion of using my sewing tape," she snapped as she yanked the tape outward.

He huffed at that and silently helped her stretch the tape over another section of stone. Christina jotted the numbers down and made rough sketches, all the while aware that

Aedan stood just beside her. She glanced at him from beneath the brim of her lace-trimmed hat.

One booted foot propped on the stone wall, his black jacket draping from his hand, resting on his shoulder, he seemed all earthy strength and ease. A slight breeze ruffled the rolled sleeves of his white shirt and lifted his dark, wavy hair. He looked far cooler and more comfortable than Christina felt.

Gloved, bonneted, and swathed in several layers, she longed to be half so unencumbered. Because of the day's warmth and the nature of her work, she had worn only three petticoats beneath her dark gray skirt, and had done without her stays, which had made the long climb to the excavation site easier and had proven cooler. Although she had opened the top button of her linen blouse, sweat trickled between her breasts and ran down her back beneath her chemise and camisole.

She picked up a little fan to flutter air over her face and throat, glad for the shade of the straw hat.

"A little rain will give us some relief from this heat," Aedan said. "You look rather warm, Mrs. Blackburn. I have some lemonade — not so cool as when Mrs. Gunn gave it to me this morning, but at least it's wet." He handed her a silver flask wrapped in leather.

Accepting the flask, she drank the sweet, tart liquid gratefully then handed it back.

"The men have made a good bit of progress since I was last here," Aedan said, glancing around. "Have you found anything in particular? Hordes of gold, chests of silver, that sort of thing?" His tone was amused rather than sarcastic.

"We've exposed more of the walls, which I think are the foundation of an ancient Pictish house. And this hole here is a storage chamber." She stood, smacking earth from her hands.

Aedan frowned. "Ancient Pictish house? Are you sure?"

"It's nothing modern, I can assure you of that. The walls are rounded and nearly six feet thick in stacked stone. Not so large as a fortress, but fine enough for its day. Over there is the entrance of the house or tower, with the fallen lintel — do you see that long stone, there?"

In silence, Aedan walked toward the ancient stones and touched them thoughtfully. Christina followed.

"That square niche over there is a stone cupboard. Along there are three beds built into the thickness of the wall. And in the center is a hearth." While she spoke, he went there to look.

"Cozy," he said. "This is no black house at all, is it? I see I must admit defeat, Mrs.

292

Blackburn." He looked at her over his shoulder.

"We were never at war," she said quietly, and he lifted a skeptical brow. She went on. "The house has certain features in common with Pictish habitats. My uncle studied ancient ruins in the north while writing his history of Celtic Scotland, and I traveled with him to examine some of them. These are very like what we saw."

He walked toward the storage pit. "And this hole?"

"A souterrain, an underground chamber." She followed him. "We found it this morning. A storage cellar, lined in stone. There are over a dozen tall clay jars inside."

"So I see." He crouched and peered into the opening. "Do you know what they might contain?"

"Grain, most likely oats or barley. Perhaps oil or wine. It's an exciting find, and I think that Edgar and the other directors will be pleased. Dundrennan could become famous for this site alone."

Aedan rubbed a hand over his eyes, then sighed. "So that will be the end of it," he murmured.

"The end? Aedan, this is only the beginning." She wondered what troubled him. The wind picked up, rippling her skirts and her hat ribbons, and she put a hand to her hat. "I hoped you would be pleased by this."

293

"Pleased?" He gazed down into the dark gap and did not answer further. Fat raindrops began to spatter the earth and the stones, quickly dampening their shoulders. "Well, you may as well show me this storage chamber of yours. It will give us some shelter from the storm. We've stayed out too long, and now we're caught." Thunder rumbled as Aedan held out a hand to her.

Glancing at the ominous sky, Christina saw lightning strike silver through the clouds. She accepted his hand in assistance and proceeded ahead of him down the ladder, while the rain began to pound in earnest around them.

Chapter Eighteen

Whether grain or gold filled those vats, his chances of cutting a road through this part of Cairn Drishan were done. Even worse, his hope of keeping Dundrennan House was sorely jeopardized.

Aedan sighed and leaned back against the musty stone wall, one knee raised as he sat gazing around the little storage chamber. Two rows of waist-high, round-bodied clay vessels stood in the shadows. Painted linear designs graced the dusty, untouched shoulders of the clay jars. Eerie and silent, filled with secrets, those simple containers had the power to stop his project cold and send changes rippling through his life.

His father would have been delighted by the potential of a few humble pots in an earthen pit. Sitting in the darkness, Aedan smiled sadly, wishing Sir Hugh MacBride could have seen these. As for himself, he had no choice but to accept the significance of the site with all the implied consequences and carry on as best he could.

He glanced at Christina, who was scribbling in her little notebook by the light of an oil lamp that she and his men had left there earlier. They had also left behind a few candles, a canvas tarpaulin, a ladder, and a couple of plaid blankets, on which Aedan and Christina now sat.

Rain pounded on the stone cover that partially roofed the souterrain, and drizzle slipped down one wall, muddying a patch of the earthen floor. Aedan rose and took the tarpaulin, climbing up the ladder to drape the stiff cloth over the opening.

"If this place is truly ancient," he said, "we do not want it soaked."

"Thank you," Christina said, putting down her little book and her pencil. She wrapped her arms around herself and shivered. "It was warm on the hill in the sun earlier, but it's quite chilly down here."

"Well, it is a cellar," Aedan pointed out. "And we're both damp from the rain. We should sit over there, away from the leak." He moved with her to a dark corner, closer to the pots and away from the opening. Christina spread out both plaids, and Aedan settled into the corner while she sat beside him.

From the inner pocket of his jacket, he produced a small silver flask. "We finished the lemonade, but there's some whisky in here that should warm you nicely." He offered it to her.

He half expected her to refuse, but she took it and drank, swallowing twice and gasping a little before handing it back to him. He sipped and set it aside.

The chamber smelled faintly of ancient earth and stone, and the rain drummed steadily on the stiffened canvas draped overhead. Somewhere outside, thunder rumbled low and faint. Christina shivered slightly, her shoulder pressing against him. He lifted an arm to encircle her and share the warmth of his body. Neither of them spoke.

Listening to the rhythm and rumble of the storm, Aedan felt his earlier impatience dissolve, and a sense of contentment wrapped around him like magic. Here in this dark, ancient place, being alone with her felt wholly right, without impropriety.

Thunder boomed again, followed by a sharp crack of lightning. Christina leaped a little in surprise, and Aedan pulled her gently toward him. She did not protest, but nestled against him naturally, turning her body slightly to fit to his, her gloved hands folded demurely in her lap. Beneath layers of skirts, her legs stretched out beside his longer legs, the leather toes of her sensible boots peeking out. Aedan lifted his knee and rested his other arm there, keeping one arm tucked around Christina.

Her straw hat poked into his jaw, and he angled away his head. "Madam, I beg you, divest yourself of that bonny thing before you put out my eye."

"Oh!" she said in apology, and she reached up to untie the black satin ribbons, drawing the hat away and setting it down.

Aedan brushed his hand over her hair, where strands were mussed from the hat. She allowed that touch, and he felt the echo of his innocent caress like thunder down to his toes. With her head lifted, his lowered slightly, her breath fell sweet upon his cheek. There was a waiting sense to that breath, soft, receptive.

The need to kiss her pulsed boldly through him, but he resisted its strength. Days earlier, they had agreed to be friends only. Posing with her for John each night was temptation enough, he thought — sitting here with her could be devastating to his resolve. With luck, the storm would be short-lived.

And yet he hoped it would go on and on, trapping him here with her, just the two of them, away from the outside world.

A lightning crack sounded again, and she jumped. "I'm sorry," she said.

"Do not apologize," he said. "Not everyone likes storms." He rubbed her outermost arm. "Thunderstorms in these hills can be quite fierce. They come fast over the moorland from the west and hit the hillsides with a good deal of power. The lightning up here has struck solitary trees and killed sheep and has even started rockslides. Now you know why I did not like to see you alone here with a storm in the offing."

She nodded vehemently and leaned closer into the circle of his arm. The warmth between them deepened, penetrated through him, turned to ease and comfort. She felt so good in his protection, as if she belonged there, as if he had long searched for her, wanting to keep her close like this.

He remembered how she had felt under his hands when they had posed, the luxury of warm silk sliding over her body, thin fabrics separating his hands from her waist, her hips.

Nearly groaning at his thoughts, feeling his body surge of its own accord, he tipped back his head and tried to simply relax in the darkness beside her. Mellowed by a few sips of whisky, the drowsy patter of rain, the pervasive sense of comfort and peace between them, he deepened his breath.

Christina leaned against him and rested her cheek on his shoulder. Her palm lay on his chest, and an alluring pool of heat grew and spread.

Keenly aware of how alone they were, he was even more aware of her body beside him, swathed in layers of clothing. He sensed her heat, felt the burn of her beneath his hand, which was cupped over her shoulder. As he thought about tracing his palms over her skin and remembered the taste of her lips, his fingers began a gentle sweeping pattern over her shoulder. That simple touch felt like fire and sent a crackling sensation through him from head to foot.

They had agreed to be acquaintances only, but the lusty track of his thoughts took dominion over him now. He could not endure sitting here with her much longer, exercising restraint. If the rain did not soon stop, he would be testing his willpower again to see just how impervious he was to the spell of love.

But he already knew how vulnerable he was — at least where Christina Blackburn was concerned.

"I suppose," Christina said, looking around the little chamber, "the museum will send someone else to supervise this site just as soon as I tell Sir Edgar about the pots we found."

Aedan shifted a little, almost relieved by the remedy of a potential dispute. "Edgar? He'd better keep away from Dundrennan himself. I do not want to see the man. And I suppose both of you will be eager to close down my road forthwith."

"Edgar will decide if your road will close, not I."

He cocked a brow at her, and she returned the glance. Behind those delicate blue steel spectacles, her hazel eyes were soot lashed and dusky green. He noticed how stubborn her chin was, how lush and soft her lips were, and he knew that her cheek was the softest he had ever touched, creamy pink.

Think of the road, he reminded himself, *and the house and blasted Edgar.* Thinking about her softness, her lusciousness, would be disastrous. He lifted his arm from around her shoulders, and she sat up. "Mrs. Blackburn, I think you do not realize how serious it will be if the highway cannot go through this ridge."

"I do not mean to challenge you."

"You challenge me, Christina Blackburn," he replied quietly, "far more than you know."

She watched him silently, and he felt his heart pound hard enough to be heard. "Aedan, this site is a magnificent find," she said then. "Cairn Drishan will be regarded as a national treasure. I thought you would be pleased — and proud."

"Proud to lose my home and my career?" he demanded.

She frowned. "I do not understand."

"You know there is a codicil to my father's will."

"Yes, concerning the house and the restorations. It appears that you will meet those conditions easily. What does that have to do with the hill?"

"The restoration to the house is not a problem, now that your brother has agreed to do the murals. But there is another ad-

301

dendum. If something of significant historical value is discovered on the estate, nearly everything — the house and some of the land — could revert to the care of the museum unless certain other conditions are met."

She tilted her head in concern. "What conditions?"

"In effect, Dundrennan would become a museum. I would have to arrange for exhibits and tours, and every room would be opened for viewing, with only a few kept for private use. Tourist pathways and seating would have to be provided for the sites on the estate. There would be a constant stream of people here, between the attraction of these ancient discoveries, my father's own extensive historical collection, and his legacy as a poet."

She nodded slowly. "In that case, Dundrennan would scarcely feel like your home any longer. You deeply value your privacy."

"And the privacy of my kinfolk and our home. I do not want to comply with this request, but if I do not, the house and a portion of the estate will be under the control of the museum."

"So either way, Dundrennan becomes a tourist attraction."

"Exactly. And if I do not agree, the treasures my father collected and whatever treasures might be found here" — he gestured toward the clay pots — "will be taken to the

National Museum for permanent display. To Edgar's unending delight, of course. Surely he told you about this."

She shook her head. "He never said a word about it. I did not know."

"Neaves has been drooling after this property ever since my father's will was read. He was present that day."

"He never told me," she said. "But he never had reason to. I did not know you then."

"True," Aedan replied. He thought of the painting he had looked at daily for six years, her image that had become part of him. In a way, he felt as if he had known her for years — forever somehow.

"Why did Sir Hugh want such a strict addendum?"

Aedan sat back. "He always believed Cairn Drishan would yield something significant one day. He wanted to ensure that it would be protected if it was discovered."

"Apparently he was right about the hill." She frowned. "But I do not understand the reason for the codicil. It's as if he did not trust his heirs to handle the situation as he wanted."

"Perhaps he thought I would put my road first."

She watched him. "Was he right about that?"

He inhaled, blew out the breath. "My father and I never agreed on the matter of the highways and byways in Scotland — or this road in particular. But I have always done my best to cope with the needs of both the roads I must build and the estate I've inherited. I have always done my utmost for both. I care about my small role in improving Scotland, and I care about Dundrennan, too — very deeply."

"But he never realized that, did he?"

Aedan shook his head. He looked away from her to glance at the old dusty pots. "He intended Dundrennan for Neil," he said quietly. "Not for me. My father had no doubts where Neil was concerned. My brother and my father agreed on every matter to do with the estate. In fact, Neil was a writer himself, and some of the pieces in the collection were his acquisitions — military pieces were a particular love of his."

"What was he like?"

"Neil? A fine man," he murmured. "More handsome than I and less of a grumphie, as Amy likes to say. He had a ready laugh and a generous heart. He was quite knowledgeable about history — I believe he actually read many of the books in our library," he added wryly. "You would have liked him."

"I'm sure I would have. Though I like the current laird rather well," she said, smiling a little, her voice soft. In the amber lamplight, he saw her cheeks pinken, and he felt warmed by her words. "He sounds like a wonderful man, and a great loss."

He nodded. "Neil went off to the Crimean shortly after Father bought him a commission. He wanted to purchase one for me as well, but I did not want to join a regiment. I had finished four summers of apprenticeship and years of study, and I had just been awarded a grant for a road in Ayrshire. Sometimes I think . . . had I gone to war as my father wanted, I might have been with Neil the day he died — I might have been able to help him. I would have taken the bullet for him if it had come to that," he said low and fierce. "He might even now be laird of Dundrennan, as he should have been."

"Aedan." Christina leaned toward him. "You are a fine laird, perhaps best suited to Dundrennan now, since you understand so well the necessity of improvement in order for Scotland to survive. If I had been your father," she murmured, "I would have trusted you to do the right thing, no matter what the situation."

He looked at her in surprise, not expecting that depth of loyalty. "Would you?" He tipped his head, watched her curiously. "You, who like to argue with me on certain issues? I would have thought you might agree with my father. You are of like mind with Sir Hugh in many ways — like Neil was."

"That may be," she answered, "but I know

how deeply you care about Dundrennan. You would never compromise its integrity as both a home and a historical site."

"Thank you," he murmured. "That means more to me than you could know. And you are right, Christina. I will not lose Dundrennan. I will do whatever I must to keep it whole and intact — even turn it into a museum." He frowned, thumped his fist on his upraised knee.

"The codicil exists, and now this place has been found. What if we find something more, Aedan? A tomb or another ancient structure, for example?"

"Or Arthur's gold?" he drawled. He shook his head. "Whatever we find, no road can go through here now. I am aware of that."

"What can we do to ensure that Dundrennan is protected, as you want, and that the terms of the will are also met?"

"In order to make sure that the museum — and Sir Edgar — get their just due out of this?" he asked quietly.

"I am not thinking of Sir Edgar," she said crisply, "and you should know that."

"Why," he said, leaning forward, "should I know that?"

Her expression was wholly intent as she angled toward him. "Because you should just know it."

He huffed. "That is charming, madam, but obscure."

"I . . . do not care for Sir Edgar . . . as I once thought I did," she said carefully.

"Aye?" Aedan leaned still closer, his arm brushing her shoulder, his face inches from her own. Her gaze locked with his.

"I was . . . swayed by his kindnesses to me, just as I have been . . . swayed by yours," she finished on a breath.

"I have not meant to sway you, madam," he whispered, "or to persuade you to anything you do not want for yourself."

She inclined toward him as he spoke, tipping her face upward, her lips a breath away, her eyes closed. Then she leaned another inch and kissed him.

He gave in to that sweetness readily, hungrily, taking her by the waist to draw her to him while she looped her arms around his neck and pressed against his chest. Her mouth moved under his, warm and heavenly. When their lips parted for an instant, she kissed him again — he was sure that she initiated it, as she had the first one — and he leaned back against the wall, taking her onto his lap and wrapping her in his arms, her skirts billowing over their legs.

He had maintained control and behaved himself, yet she had surprised him utterly, and he surrendered completely, gratefully. He kissed her with fervor, traced a hand over her fine-boned, stubborn jaw, finding the shell of her ear. She sighed, and her lips opened under his. He slipped his tongue outward to meet hers, and that sweet and delicate contact made him burn so hot for her that he thought he might be unable to bear it.

Pausing to tip her face upward, he gently slid her eyeglasses from her nose and set them aside. She blinked widely at him, the lovely purity of her face both innocent and seductive. He leaned close and took her into his arms again.

Her hands slipped up his back to clench at his shoulders. Sliding his hand up her slender back and down again to span her waist, he shifted his fingers and found the tiny buttons at the front of her blouse. She arched her body against him, and the full globe of one breast filled his palm, her nipple stiffening through the soft fabric.

He kissed her again, and she brought her fingers up to frame his jaw. The soft kid of her gloves slid over the rasp of his beard, and he turned his head, used his lips to gently bite at the gloves, pulling at the leather fingers playfully. She laughed, soft as air, and slid them off, tossing them aside. Then she took his face in her bare hands again and came close to kiss him, opening her mouth under his.

Her openness and boldness, her ease in touching him and being touched by him, let him know that she felt comfortable with him in this secret and ancient place, as he felt with her. As their kiss lingered, he slipped his hand over her clothed breast again, and she sighed, moving slightly, allowing his fingers to cup and gently caress.

Some of the upper buttons of her blouse were undone — he had noticed earlier the creamy skin that peeked through — and he slipped another button free, then more. As her upper blouse fell open, she caught her breath on a sharp intake and arched against him again. He slid his fingers inside, encountering fragile lace and cotton, and her breast, warm and exquisitely soft, spilled into his hand. She gasped when Aedan found the nipple and took it in his fingertips. Feeling her heart slamming under her rib cage, he kissed her deeply, lingering his lips on hers, while his fingers brought first one breast, then the other, to life. He could feel tiny shivers on the surface of her skin.

She moaned and leaned back in his arms, allowing him greater access, and he dipped his head, mouth slipping along the arch of her throat and down, until he tasted the warm pearl of her breast with his lips, teased it with his tongue until Christina shuddered and sighed and undulated against him. He lifted his head to kiss her mouth again, tasting her sweet and eager tongue, then kissed her cheek where the heat of her blush had grown so strong.

"Why, Miss Burn," he whispered against

her lips, his fingers undoing more buttons, pulling gently at delicate, beribboned fabric, "my beautiful Miss Burn — no stays?"

"None," she said, on a little gasp. "You were right. I could not breathe well when climbing the hill — and it was so — so —"

"So hot," he finished for her, his lips moving over hers as he loosened her chemise. The flimsy fabric was slightly damp with rain and perspiration, redolent with the warm, floral fragrance that seemed so natural to her.

He lowered his head and took her nipple with his lips again, feeling it tighten while his hand encircled and teased her other breast. She cried out softly, a kittenish, needful cry as she arched across his lap. The subtle rubbing of her rounded bottom over his sensitive, hardened erection nearly drove him mad.

Capturing her around the rib cage with both hands, he rolled his thumbs over her nipples while he sought her mouth again with his own. When she sucked delicately and quite deliberately on the tip of his tongue, he knew that she wanted and needed what he had to have, knew she felt all the desperate intensity he himself felt. The enticing thought that she might allow it to happen made him as hard as rock, as hot as fire.

He shifted, holding her, kissing her, driving her mad, for she bucked gently in his embrace. He pushed at her skirts and slipped his hand up her leg, found her knee, poised there.

She did not stop him; indeed, she pressed against him with a little whimper, so that he lowered his head again to her breast and kissed her there, slipped his tongue into the hot crevice between her deliciously full breasts. He breathed in her fragrance, closed his eyes, trembled for control.

Though she wore long cotton knickers over her stockings and garters, he knew from previous experience with ladies and their undergarments that the long garment might open quite easily, and he let his hand slide slowly over the soft fabric that covered her lean leg. Amid the folds, he found the opening he sought, a slitted gap in the cloth, and felt the warm female nest hidden there. He traced his fingertip delicately over the tender crevice, taking his time, giving her every chance to protest.

She cried out, gasped, and took his head between her hands, drawing him upward to meet her mouth. But she did not kiss him, only hovered, lips to his, as if waiting.

He waited, too, ready to withdraw his hand. She made no sound, did not move, but her breaths came fast and her heart pounded through her back, where he supported her with one hand.

His own heart thundered, and somewhere outside — far beyond, in the world he had forgotten even existed — he heard the crack of lightning, and the increased sheeting of the rain on the tarpaulin overhead.

"Someone might —" she whispered.

"No one will find us here," he murmured. "We are safely hidden. . . . No one . . . But if you do not — please, my darling lass, tell me now, before I —"

"Oh p-please," she murmured, her voice shaking, and she pushed gently downward, so that his finger, still resting motionless upon her intimate entrance, slipped inside, into exquisite heat, and she whimpered from what he knew was splendid, unmatchable joy.

He groaned, a low rumble, as he touched her there, where she was hot and honeyed and ardent, already swollen for him. She trembled as he moved his fingers slowly, easing her toward her release. He did not know how long he could endure it, but he was determined to give her this pleasure, though he strained against the searing demand in his own body, felt passion burn a path through him, but he held back, denied himself release.

He found her nipple again — she offered it, asked for the touch of his mouth there with the arch of her body — and he tasted there while he touched and teased her elsewhere with his fingertips. She turned in his arms as the thrill finally shuddered through her, and she whimpered a little in his ear.

Closing his eyes, he felt the delicious undulations of her body, heard her soft cries. He could scarcely bear it, nearly groaned aloud, nearly spilled himself out without fulfillment, just for the intense excitement of touching her, wrapping himself in her embrace.

Somewhere in the midst of heat and passion, even while she rocked with the final easing of the thrill that she had felt, she shifted in his arms and he felt her fingers eagerly upon him. He was surprised, for he had not expected or anticipated her help, her boldness. Her palm fitted to the hard bulge he could not conceal, and she worked the buttons and the drawstring of his trousers. Silently, swiftly, he opened his belt, nearly losing his control entirely when her fingers, slim and heaven soft, captured him, velvet over hot iron.

Her caresses turned up his passion like the wick of a lamp, bright, hot, flaming fast through him. Closing his eyes, he let the storm engulf him, and it slammed through him like thunder.

He came shuddering and vulnerable and needful in the generous fire of her touch, and he gasped out, drawing her tightly to him. For one moment, he let go of every lock he had ever had upon himself, just this once, just for her, only for her.

Chapter Nineteen

"You haven't seen this bedroom since we finished it," Amy said to Aedan. She opened a door along the hallway. "Come look. The queen should stay in this one, I think."

Aedan stood back, allowing Amy to enter first and careful to leave the door open while they were alone in the room. "Ah, dark green," he commented, looking at the newly painted walls. "Stylish — and economical," he added wryly.

The room had been used by his mother when he had been a child, and the gleaming maple furnishings had been hers as well. This had been her private bedroom, but Aedan remembered that when he had been a lad, the adjoining door separating his parents' bedrooms had always been open. Now it stood closed.

"The other bedroom will be used by the prince consort," Amy said, seeing his glance. "Because that was your father's, we left it just as it is."

He nodded approval, then looked at the bed with its coverlet of ivory damask and an overhead canopy in floral chintz. The same pattern draped the windows. "That flowery stuff seems to be your signature mark, Cousin," he commented. "If there is chintz on the windows, Miss Stewart has been here." He gave her a quick, amused smile, and she laughed, clearly pleased.

Aedan walked around the room, noting the silver brushes and the mirror on the dresser, the bowls of fresh flowers, the high polish on the furniture, the little framed paintings on the walls and the silken cushions on the chairs, all the lovely touches that made the room both cozy and beautiful.

"Ah, more Scotch carpet," he said, looking down. "We must have acres of it throughout the house by now."

"It mixes so nicely with the flowery stuff," Amy said, with a little twinkle in her blue eyes. "And the term is Scottish, if you please, Aedan. Your father always insisted that 'Scotch' was a vulgar Anglicization."

"And so it is. Even we Scots are guilty of it at times. What is this?" Aedan walked toward the marble fireplace. "John Blackburn's painting of Robert the Bruce with Isabella is here now?"

"For the time being," Amy answered. "It looks so handsome in this room, and I thought the picture would please the queen."

"True, it's a good expression of the noble

Scottish spirit, which the queen seems to admire."

"It's such an excellent work," Amy said. "So smoothly painted and highly detailed. I hope the dining-room mural proves half so nice as this one."

"From what I've seen of his preliminary drawings, I'm confident of the outcome," Aedan said. "I think even Aunt Lillias will be pleased."

"There is some Pre-Raphaelite influence in his work," Amy said, studying the painting for a moment. "Though Mr. Blackburn is a better draftsman than some of the Pre-Raphaelite Brotherhood, I think."

"I didn't know you knew much about their work."

"I do now," she said. "Mr. Blackburn has been educating me. We've been looking at the books of engravings that your father added to the library. John — er, Mr. Blackburn's technique is precise, yet he has a lovely decorative flair. He had classical training under his father, which shows in his disciplined drawings. He's a remarkable talent. And you've said yourself that anything by a Pre-Raphaelite artist, even of the outer Scottish circle, will prove a solid investment."

"And might even pay for more carpeting," Aedan remarked.

Amy wrinkled her nose playfully. "You could always sell some old something-or-

316

other out of Dundrennan if you had to."

"Never, my dear cousin, and you know it well."

"I do understand. Auntie says you will have a tussle with Sir Edgar Neaves when he arrives."

"No doubt," Aedan agreed, and he left it at that.

"Aedan — that picture you keep in your study, painted by that other Blackburn," Amy began. "That's a beautiful thing, if rather shocking, as I remember — I haven't seen it since you moved it to your rooms a few years ago. It's far darker and more passionate in mood than John Blackburn would paint, I think. Christina posed for that one as well, did she not?"

"Aye, but that was several years ago. Her late husband, Stephen, painted it. He was a brilliant artist, though of a callous and troubled nature, from what I gather."

"How sad," Amy said. "Is that why she seems such a sober little thing? She keeps herself in somber colors and is usually quiet and bookish. I get the sense that she is hiding her true self, her true strengths. Perhaps it is her spectacles that lend that impression. I think Christina could be a dazzling beauty, if she would ever wake up to that fact."

"I agree. That's an odd way to put it, waking her up, but somehow . . . very apt."

"I suppose I was thinking of that painting. The girl is asleep in that one, like the fairy tale of Briar Rose, or the legend of the princess of Dundrennan." Amy smiled. "Christina is such a dear girl, with a good heart and a pleasing manner. I will be sorry to see her go when she finishes digging on that hill."

He gazed at the painting, which held Christina's precise likeness as the medieval woman with Robert the Bruce. "Aye," he said. "She has become . . . a favorite of all of us here, I think. But she's not always . . . sober and bookish."

"No, she's not," Amy said. "When she's with you, she fairly sparkles. I think you are much improved in her company, too."

He raised a brow. "I am?"

"Oh, yes, not nearly the grumphie you can be with me. Auntie Lill says Christina has put a polish to your tarnished old soul, and it does you good. You smile more than growl these days."

Aedan studied his blond, fair cousin thoughtfully. "I do?"

"Definitely. I think you do not know, do you?"

"Know what?"

"That you're . . . well, thunderstruck, Dougal says."

"Thunderstruck?" He made sure to glower a little. "Me?"

"Yes, and what are you going to do about it?" Amy asked.

"Do about what?"

"Do not be a daftie, Aedan. What are you going to do about your interest in Christina Blackburn?"

"What interest?"

"Aedan!" Amy pouted, then paused. "I have been wanting to speak with you about something, but I . . . hesitated to bring up the subject."

"What? Are you perhaps thinking of doing the library in flowery stuff? Or, God forbid, my own apartments?"

"I wouldn't touch your apartments," Amy said. "No, it's another matter. I thought . . . well, that someday we might . . ."

"I thought so, too," he said gently, "once upon a time."

"Aedan . . . I am truly fond of you, but I do not think I could ever marry you."

He stared at her. "You what?" He frowned as if he did not comprehend what she had said. A rushing began in his ears. "You do not . . . want to be my wife?"

Amy shook her head. "I am so sorry, dear Aedan. I know this means a great deal to you, and I do not mean to disappoint you, but . . . well, I think we are just not suited to each another."

"Not suited?" He felt not thunderstruck but dumbstruck. This revelation was an unexpected gift, he realized. He had never been keen on courting and marrying Amy, as fond as he was of her.

"You are a little dull, my dear, sweet Aedan," she said. "I suppose it is because you are so very practical and economical and so involved in your work. You do not mind dirt on your jacket or long days in the sun that brown your cheeks, and you never seem to quite know what color the drapes are in your own house."

"Is that dull? I'm sorry if it's so," he said. "It's just how I am. My father called me all steel and numbers. I suppose he found me a little dull, too." He shrugged, feeling a little bewildered suddenly.

"He might have, because he was a poet and you are a man of the earth. Your strengths are very different than his. And he was right. There is a good bit of steel in you — which I have always liked very much." Her eyes sparkled. She leaned closer, hands clasped. "May I confide the entire truth of my feelings?" she whispered.

Aedan nodded warily.

"Well, you see, I am rather fond . . . of Mr. Blackburn," Amy said. "And I think he likes me in return. He might wish to court me, but he will not if he thinks I am promised to you."

"I see," Aedan said slowly. He felt a sudden, unabashed relief. "You know I am very fond of you, Cousin, but you may be right — we may be better off as friends. If that pleases you, your happiness is all I care about."

"Well, of course you care," she said. "You want me to finish the rest of your house." She dimpled prettily.

He smiled. "You have done a marvelous job with the house, and I know you will continue to do so. I think it's wonderful that you have found someone who is more patient than I am, who will be more interested in colors and whatnot."

"You loon," Amy teased. She gave Aedan a radiant smile. "It is far more than his interest in talking about colors. He is a very talented man, a brilliant artist, really. And he finds me something of an artist, too, in my way."

"And so you are. You're very talented and very lovely, and he is a lucky man to have your affection. I'm sorry to lose my chances with you, but glad to see you happy."

Amy tilted her head, considering him. "And I'm glad to see you happy," she replied. "I know you hoped I might be a safe sort of wife for the laird of Dundrennan — because you do not really love me in that way."

"Oh come, now," he said. "I'm very fond of you, dear."

She leaned forward and gave him a quick peck on the cheek. She was soft and fragrant, and he loved her very much in that moment — loved her as he loved his sister, loved her as he might love a friend. He smiled at her, and rested his hand on her shoulder.

"Aedan," she said, "if you do love Christina in that way, what will you do? The laird of Dundrennan must never fall in love, they say. Not truly, not forever."

"My dear," he said, turning to escort her from the room, "I'm not that much of a daftie."

But he was, and he knew it, and he did not know what he would do at all.

Footsteps, quiet and close by, startled Christina as she sat at a table. Turning, she saw Aedan standing there. He smiled, warming her inside — but she immediately remembered their encounter in the souterrain the day before. Her cheeks flamed hot, and she ducked her head, nearly dropping her pencil.

She was not certain, a day later, how to respond to him now, whether affection was appropriate, or whether she should pretend that impulsive, secret interlude had not happened. They had been interrupted from further passionate exploring by the arrival of Hector and the Gowans. Both she and Aedan had hurried out of the souterrain and had not seen each other privately since.

"Christina," he murmured.

"Oh, Sir Aedan," she said, glancing around to determine if they were alone. The library was quiet and golden in the afternoon sunlight. "Aedan," she said again, looking up at him.

"I don't mean to disturb you. I came here to pick up some maps and saw you working. You were so involved that you did not hear me."

"Yes, I — I've been translating parts of the oldest pages in the Dundrennan Folio," she said, indicating the parchment sheets spread out on the table.

Aedan came around the table to stand behind her, leaning over her shoulder to glance at the pages. "You mentioned that you had seen the princess's name here somewhere," he said.

"Yes." She reached for one of the two parchments and pointed with a gloved fingertip. "It's there, along the margin. You may need the glass to see it clearly."

Leaning his hand on the table near her arm, he took up the magnifying glass and bent to examine the script that she indicated. His jacket brushed her shoulder, and she caught the scent of spice, soap, and the earthy musk that seemed part of him, a scent that always excited her subtly whenever he was near.

"Ah," he said. "Liadan. What does that line say?"

She leaned close. "Liadan nighean Math-ghamhainn. It means 'Liadan, daughter of the bear.' "

"Bear? Odd. The legend says her father was a Pictish king, but no name is given. He was this . . . *Math-ghamhainn?*" He pronounced the Gaelic hesitantly.

"Apparently. It may have been his nickname, or even a title of some sort. Animal names were common among Picts, it seems. Old poetry contains references to proper names attached to epithets like wolf, bear, eagle, raven, hawk, and so on." She tilted her head. "For example, if you had lived then, you might have been called . . . 'Aedan the Raven,' for your coloring. Or 'Aedan the Hawk,' for your keenness of vision and your decisive air."

He half sat on the table, looking amused and relaxed, folding his hands on his thigh. She could easily imagine him as an ancient warrior, exuding a powerful presence.

"And you might be called . . . a lark. Or a swan. A dark swan." He smiled a little.

"Darkling swan," she said quickly. "How did you know? I just translated those words yesterday from the marginal text."

"I did not know. I was only naming your . . . grace and beauty."

She stared at him, entranced.

Instead of coming closer to kiss her, as she rather hoped would happen, he looked down at the parchment. "Liadan. This is really quite a discovery, you know. I did not know her name was in these documents. My father told me her name, but it was hearsay, passed down along generations. Now there is proof."

"The name has been there all along, but no one had translated it in recent memory, I suppose. And there are a couple of poems in these marginal notes as well."

"Poems? Truly? My father would have loved this. He would have adored you simply for that, Miss Burn," he said, looking at her keenly.

She blushed, wishing she could control it, but he only smiled. She traced her gloved fingertip down the margin of the parchment, glad to share with Aedan what she had recently discovered through translating the old text.

"The verses are lovely. And I think these words may have been written by your ancestor, the prince himself."

"The prince?" He looked pleased. "What makes you say so?"

"His name is on the roster, and it appears again in the margin. *Aedan mac Brudei à Dùn Droigheann* — Aedan MacBride of Dundrennan." She pointed to the name on the list, then the marginal notes. " *'Dùn Droigheann'* means 'the place of the briars.' This is your ancestor, the one who loved and lost the princess of Dundrennan."

He nodded slowly. "If his name appears in the margin, it may have been overlooked all this time as part of the roster."

"I think so. And I believe he wrote these additional scribblings with his own hand."

"Fascinating." Aedan bent forward and used the magnifying glass. "I cannot read the text myself, but there's no doubt this is a brilliant discovery." He sat back, regarded her. "Sir Edgar will be very pleased. Have you written to tell him?"

"No," she said, looking down. She had been avoiding that, knowing Edgar would hurry to Dundrennan once he knew.

"You must be very proud of this."

"I feel honored to be trusted with the folio pages."

"My father would have been delighted with this. It brings Dundrennan's legend to life."

She nodded. "It's coming to life in other ways, too, isn't it? John is painting the legend on the walls, and now we've found something on Cairn Drishan."

"Odd that it's all happening at once. I wonder if the hillside is actually connected to the legend."

"It's possible, since the dates may be similar, but it's too soon to say. The structure on the hill may be of a later time."

"I see. Tell me about Prince Aedan's poems in the margin."

"There are a few verses scribbled there,

similar in pattern to Highland charms or prayers, which are a very old tradition among the Gaels. I haven't finished translating the lines yet."

He peered at her penciled notes. "Would you read some of it?" he asked.

She nodded, traced her finger over the page. " 'Liadan, my darkling swan . . . thy promise was as the sun to me,' " she read quietly. " 'Thy kiss was bright as the moonbeam. I will follow after thee and bring thee back.' "

"My God," Aedan said in a hushed tone. "May I see?"

She gave him the notebook. "You may read it, if you like."

" 'Smooth thou, soft thou; well I love thee under the plaid,' " he murmured. The quiet richness of his voice sent shivers down her spine. " 'Thou are splendid; thou shalt be wanton.' " He looked up, and his glance met hers, keen as fire.

Her breath caught. She watched him in silence. His fingers on the notebook were spare and strong, and she remembered how his hands felt upon her body. *Wanton, indeed,* she thought.

In that moment, she burned so for him, wishing desperately that he would take her into his arms. He made no move to do so, simply leaning forward to look at her page of notes.

"Beautiful stuff," he said. "But I thought Celtic poetry was all heroics and bloody battles."

"Much of it is. A few love poems have been found, similar to these." Her gloved fingers trembled as she turned a page in her notebook.

"He wrote them for her," Aedan murmured.

She glanced at him swiftly, her heart pounding. She knew it was true — inexorably, startlingly true. Aedan mac Brudei had written those lines for his beloved Liadan.

A pull unlike any she had ever felt, a magnificent, engulfing power, drew her toward him. She wanted to be bold and wild. She wanted to be wanton with him again, as she had been before, and sink into his arms forever. She wanted to be his beloved.

"Aedan —" she began.

"Mm?" He looked up at the clock on the mantel. "Good Lord, it's late. I need to take these maps out to the work site." He stood. "Thank you for showing me your work. Fascinating, truly." He inclined his head.

If he felt what she felt, he gave no sign and chose not to act on it. Perhaps she was wrong after all — perhaps he did not share her feelings at all.

Then she realized that the laird of Dundrennan would not want her as she wanted him. Of course he had loved her freely and divinely, but he was a man, after all, and she had offered herself to him in a very wanton manner.

Cheeks burning, she stood, hastily putting her notes away in her leather writing case. Aedan watched her, his expression unreadable, curious, thoughtful.

He did not seem inclined to make any affectionate moves toward her now, she thought. Obviously he had not come to the library to declare his burning, undying devotion.

She had been every bit the little fool yesterday. Once again she had fallen in love impulsively, with utter trust and naïveté. Apparently six years of sorrow and penance had not taught her to guard her eager little heart any more carefully.

Stepping back, she felt flustered and breathless, swamped by disappointment and acute embarrassment. "It is very late," she agreed. "I promised the ladies I would join them for tea. Lady Strathlin . . . Meg . . . said she and Mr. Stewart would be leaving with the children for Strathlin Castle tomorrow, and I wanted to say goodbye. And I . . . I must return these parchments to the folio." She bound the silk packet with ribbon as she spoke.

"Leave them," Aedan said. "I will put them back."

"Thank you. I . . . I must go. Good day, sir."

"Mrs. Blackburn," he murmured. "I —"

She glanced up at him. "Yes?"

He began to speak, and the sound of a door closing made her nearly leap out of her skin. Amy Stewart stepped into the library, the wide flounces of her blue gown sweeping the carpet gracefully.

"There you are, Aedan!" she said. "Mr. Campbell has been looking for you — he says you have some maps he needs."

"Aye," Aedan said while looking at Christina, "I'll be there directly."

Amy came toward them. "Good afternoon, Christina," she said pleasantly.

Christina murmured a greeting, then excused herself quickly. Turning, she crossed the room, aware that Aedan watched her.

Had she stayed, had Amy not entered, she might have thrown herself on him again, desperate for his love, eager for the secure and marvelous circle of his embrace. Her anchor, her rock.

But his neutral manner today, after yesterday's passion, only proved that it was not meant to be — that he did not want it as much as she did. She wanted love from him, wanted to give him her own love, but as laird of Dundrennan, he could not reciprocate. Love of a physical nature, yes, he gave that gladly and skillfully — but not the love of the heart that she now craved from him.

Hearing Amy chatter and laugh with

Aedan, Christina exited through the glass-fronted doors and took the hallway toward the foyer, intending to return to her room before tea.

Love. She almost sobbed aloud. Entering Dundrennan, with its nearly magical weaving of legends and dreams, she had somehow been waylaid by love. She could not deny that to herself.

Pausing at the stairs, her hand on the newel-post, she remembered that Aedan had kissed her in this place, late one night. That melting, glorious power rushed through her again with the very thought, and she leaned her head against her hand and sighed out.

Straightening, she covered her face and attempted to compose herself. She would keep silent about her feelings, for she did not think they would ever be returned as she hoped, as she might dream. At least when she and Aedan posed for John, she could be close to him. In that fantasy world, her dream could exist, and she could be in love with him as the princess and he her prince.

But soon the dream would end, and she would wake one morning knowing that the time had come for her to leave Dundrennan — and Aedan — forever.

Chapter Twenty

Through the slick of heavy silk under his palms, Aedan felt the warmth of her body. He savored the feel of her natural curves under his fingers. She looked up at him, motionless, beautiful.

"Spectacles," he reminded her.

"Oh." Christina lifted the frames from her nose and set them on a table. Aedan gathered her close again, spreading his fingers across the small of her back.

"Good," John said. "Hold that, now."

Her hands rested on his chest, and she leaned into him, so that her torso met his, with only thin fabrics sandwiched between her belly and his. Her breasts were soft and full against his chest. Stirred and awed by the freedom of touch that their posing sessions allowed, he felt his body arouse and shifted his hips to retain his dignity.

Frowning, he felt tempted to throttle John for thinking up this situation. The posing sessions night after night for over a week taxed his control immensely. Her slight weight against him, her warm, firm body, the play of textures under his hands, the soft thickness of her unbound hair, all set him afire. He ached to kiss her as thoroughly as he had done before, burned to continue what they had begun the other afternoon in that ancient storage chamber. Her half-closed eyes and soft breathing, her subtle fragrance — flowers and warm woman — made these hours of posing sweet torture for him.

How long could he pretend that she meant little to him, that he was impervious? He felt tested beyond his mettle. Christina had seeped into every part of him — blood, bone, and being.

Yet he could not finish what had started between them. He knew that intellectually, though his blood and his heart urged him to pursue it and continue it far into the future.

"They meet secretly in her bower and are about to be parted," John said as he drew on the paper leaned against the easel. "The princess knows she must marry her father's choice for her, but she cannot bear to be parted from her Druid lover. They ache for each other. I want to show that."

He ought to throttle the lad, Aedan thought.

John seemed absorbed in his drawing, his chalk dashing as sheets of paper flew off the easel, slid untidily over the table. He began one new sketch after another, hardly stopping. Aedan had glimpsed elegant studies of faces, hands, and drapery, and several of full-length couples, their bodies joined like rising fountains, passion and love translated into fluid dark lines.

"Beautiful, that standing pose," John murmured as he glanced toward his models. "The princess gazes up at him with her heart in her eyes. The prince cannot resist her charms. They are enchanted, swept up in the magic."

"Oh," Christina said in a breathy voice. Aedan felt her desire, suddenly, like a flame stoking his own.

John came toward them, reached out to adjust his sister's gown. "Christina, it would help to see more of your shoulder here . . . a graceful, expressive line along the shoulder and throat. It's less than you'd show in one of your dinner gowns, actually. Good." He retreated to his easel.

Aedan had seen countless feminine bosoms bursting from countless dinner dresses, but he had never seen a sweep of skin as alluring as the slender curve of Christina's shoulder emerging from that drape of cream silk. He stood silent and motionless, though every part of him demanded he take her, kiss her, taste, touch, and thrust into her luscious body.

He cleared his throat and tried to angle his pelvis away from hers. Contact would be disastrous indeed, he thought, for he wore only a simple skirted tunic of red wool.

"Tip your head toward hers, Aedan," John said. "Better. Ah, the very picture of true love." He nodded to himself as he drew.

Seeing Christina's eyes close in a sort of ecstasy, Aedan wanted to kiss her so much that he trembled with it. A light sweat broke out on his brow. This modeling venture had been a colossal mistake, he told himself.

The only sounds were the whisper of chalk over paper, the sputter of a candle, the sound of breathing. He thought he would go mad. His body heated like steel in a forge, and he could only stand there like a blasted statue.

" 'Struck deep to her soul, the winsome creature smiled,' " John said after a while, reciting Sir Hugh's poem while he drew.

Grateful for the distraction, Aedan listened. John had a rich voice, and he knew the poem well. He understood its meter, its meaning, and every verse was beautifully inflected.

Aedan had not heard *The Enchanted Briar* spoken aloud in a long time and had not read his father's poem in years. Now, as John's voice wove the story fresh for him, and Christina leaned in his arms, Aedan understood the poem as he never had before. He felt the characters and themes come to life in a tapestry of words, threads of destiny, passion, and poignant emotions.

" 'She lay among the briars, lost to him, oh! Lost,' " John recited while his drawing hand swept over the paper. " 'Fallen among the wanton blooms, the cruel thorns . . .' "

Still and silent, Aedan sensed Christina listening as intently as he did. He held her while her brother spoke the last verse, sounding like a bard.

Oh! My love, come back to me
And oh! My love, come home.
But she drifted moorless upon that distant sea
Where no soul sails, but for the last time.

Hearing a sniffle, Aedan looked down. Christina's eyes welled with tears. "That always makes me cry," she whispered, chin wobbling.

Unable to resist, he kissed her brow quickly in sympathy, inhaling the sweet womanly fragrance of her hair. She sniffled again.

John continued to sketch, then looked up. "I know you two are not the fondest of friends," he said, "but I must ask you to pretend to kiss, if you would. Aedan, draw her to you. Christina, lean back and look as if you are . . . well, enraptured. But remember, sir," John added good-naturedly, "she is my sister. This is only for the sake of the painting."

"Of course," Aedan murmured. His heart slammed.

John dropped his chalk, stood. "I left some sketches in the dining room, where I was working earlier — I've started to transfer some of these scenes to the walls. I'd like to look at one of them for this pose, so I'll go down and get it. You both need some rest anyway." He grabbed his cane and hastened from the room. The door swung shut and clicked into place.

The silence was heavy. Aedan straightened, fighting the burden of his control, for his body thundered, his blood pounded. As he started to release her, he found that he simply could not.

"Damn," he breathed, an apology of sorts, and pulled her to him to kiss her soundly and thoroughly. She opened her lips beneath his in passionate welcome, tilting her head as she fit her mouth to his. A fierce hunger overtook him. He kissed her, slaked, drew back, delved again, helpless as a drunken man.

He cupped her face, and she rested her hands at his waist, leaning back her head. Taking her with his mouth, then his tongue, he could not quench his thirst for her, no matter how much he tried. His hands trembled on her body, slipped over silk as he took her by the waist.

As she pressed against him, he could not hide how profoundly he wanted her. Pulling her forward, he arched into her and let her feel his erection and his obvious, mounting desire. She moaned into his mouth and gave a sensuous movement of her hips.

Dimly he heard the rhythm of John's foot-steps outside. Again he kissed her, deeper, open, and felt the delicate, wet caress of her tongue upon his own.

Then the door handle turned, and the candle flames vanished in the draft as John entered, cloaking them in sudden darkness. Aedan felt ecstasy tear through him, goad him onward, but he ended the heartrending kiss and drew back.

While John lit the candles, Aedan resumed the pose, sensing Christina trembling. His mind was fogged, so that he could not remember their exact pose. Drawing her to him, he touched her cheek gently with his right hand, and with his left hand he captured her fingers against his chest. His heart pounded furiously under their joined hands.

John looked up. "Oh," he said. "You changed your position. I like this one even more."

"Today I started working on the dining-room wall," John told Christina later, after nearly an hour of posing, when she and Aedan had taken another break from standing together in stillness. The tension between them remained high, her body throbbing rebelliously, his hands upon her hot enough to burn.

"Yes, so you said," she answered. "I haven't seen it yet."

"I transferred several drawings with Miss Amy's help. She's an eager apprentice. Lady Balmossie watched us and even assisted. We made quite a little party of it."

Laughing, Christina looked at some drawings on sheets of brown paper, glued at the edges to form large cartoons. Using the point of a steel compass, he had punched tiny holes around each sketched figure. Once they were tacked in place on the mural, he had pounced chalk or charcoal in little bags, tracing over the punch marks to transfer the outlines onto the wall.

Christina nodded while John talked about the transfer technique that their father had taught him. She relaxed as she sat on the table. Hearing the turn of a door handle, she glanced up and saw Aedan emerge from the little sitting room.

Deep within, something turned in her, bounding in response to the mere sight of him. He had changed out of the red tunic and back into the black jacket and red plaid kilt he had worn earlier that evening at dinner, when they had gathered in the breakfast room — in temporary use as a dining room until John finished his murals. They had shared a simple supper of vegetable soup, roast fowl, and lemon pudding. She particularly remembered the pudding, for she had inadvertently spilled some on her blouse and brown plaid skirt.

Now, as Aedan came back into the room, she rose from her seat, gathering the trailing skirt of the ivory silk gown.

"I'll change, too." She moved toward the sitting room.

"It's very late," John said. "I'm sure no one would notice if you slipped back to your room in costume. Everyone is asleep but the three of us."

Christina thought of the tedium of dressing again in stays, crinoline, petticoats, blouse, velvet waister, and skirt, just to go to her room and take it all off again. "My skirt does need cleaning. Perhaps I could leave my things here and ask one of the maids to take them to Effie MacDonald for cleaning. It's laundry day tomorrow. If you think it would be acceptable."

"Of course." Aedan took off his black jacket and slipped it gallantly over her shoulders. "John and I will keep your secret."

"Thank you." She gathered his coat around her, breathing in its spicy, earthy scent, resonant with the strength and mystery of the man who wore it. Going to John, she kissed him good night.

"I have some studies I want to finish," John said. "I'll stay up here for a while, I think. Good night."

Christina nodded and went through the

door that Aedan opened for her. He followed behind her, carrying a lit candle in a brass dish. In the hallway, she turned toward the staircase, but he touched her arm.

"Over here is an access to the steps that lead past our rooms." He guided her toward a narrow door and opened it to reveal the dark, curving stair. He moved ahead of her, holding the candle high. "I'll go first, in case you should trip in your long gown and wee slippers. Careful, now."

She lifted the trailing hemline to descend carefully, while Aedan led the way, candlelight illuminating the stone walls. The wedge-shaped stairs were steep, the stairwell a dark abyss. She managed easily in the simple gown and slippers, glad to be without the hindrance of a crinolined skirt. Trailing a hand along the wall, she listened to the quiet cadence of their footsteps and the shush of silk over sandstone.

At the landing before her door, Christina paused with her hand on the old iron latch and looked up at Aedan. The solitude was a powerful force, and his kisses still steamed through her blood. She felt a fierce urge to step into his arms passionately. Her hands shook from it.

But she could not succumb to the lure of the physical again. Years ago, she had foolishly mistaken infatuation and youthful, lusty appetite for love.

What she felt for Aedan was wider, deeper, everlasting, she thought. It hardly mattered if she had known Aedan MacBride a day, a month, a year, or a lifetime. She loved him. The certainty filled her, stunned her. Strangely, she felt as if she had been born loving him and had needed only to find him.

But she did not think he shared it. Perhaps one person could be lost in love's current while the other merely floated upon its surface.

Tipping her head against the door, reluctant to go inside, she gave him a puzzled little look and summoned courage for the question that burned inside of her. "Sir Aedan," she began. "I must ask you . . . something."

"What is it, Christina?" The quiet sound of her name on his lips, in that confined and private space, was compelling.

"Are you . . . still impervious, as you said once? Each time we . . . touch, is that the temptation of the moment and nothing more? I must know." Her heart pounded with the boldness of her question, phrased so indirectly. *Do you love me as I love you?* She wanted to ask. *Or have I been foolish?*

He sighed low and did not answer, only setting the candle in a wall niche. She watched him, feeling all her need, all her uncertainty, center in her eyes.

"Christina," he murmured. "Come here,

lass." He drew her into his arms.

Denied too long, desire and joy welled in her. She gasped out and looped her arms around his neck as his mouth sought hers.

Strong and giving, hot and immediate, one kiss bloomed into another, his lips sure and hungry over hers. She grabbed at the buttress of his arms as her legs turned fluid and faltered.

He lifted her until her feet cleared the stone, and she shared with him a vibrant rain of kisses. She felt as if a new language had emerged between them without words, employing only emotion, easily understood through silence and caresses. What had begun when she had met him, nurtured in secret meetings and inspired by posing, now burst full flower within her.

Floating in his grasp, she sensed the dizzy fall of the stairs below and their soaring rise above. Caught in that spiral draft, Aedan was her anchor point. She wanted to be that for him, as well, hoped she could be.

Sliding her fingers through his raven-dark hair, thick and soft, she touched his cheek, whiskers like sand beneath her fingertips, and kissed him again. He set her down and slipped his hands over her back, rounded her waist, skimmed over her breasts. Even through layered cotton and silk, she felt the startling tingle, and her soft moan echoed in the stairwell.

The silken gown was only a thin layer between her body and his, and she arched and pressed against him, seeking more closeness, desperate for no more barriers between them.

With utter certainty, she knew what she wanted, what she had to give him. Consequences would come later, but she could not think about that now. She understood there might never be a future with him.

But in the spark and fire of the moment, love was a tangible thing, a gift that she must share. Holding on to it in secret would only cause her pain. She had to give herself to him.

And selfishly, she craved a memory to take with her into her lonely future. She had kept little of beauty in her heart from her earlier tragic experience.

And here, as in the souterrain, she and Aedan were isolated. No one else used these old steps. The knowledge that they would not be discovered excited her, gave her a wild sense of freedom, urged her onward.

His hand traced gently over her breast, and she rested her hand on his to tell him that she wanted him to touch her there — anywhere. She kissed him, not wanting this to stop. She felt his breath, his heart, racing as fast as her own.

Her fingers traced along his bristly jaw, found the shell of his ear, followed that with her lips. He groaned, low and deep, and framed her head in his hands, kissing her so deeply that she opened her lips for him, tasted him, pleaded for more.

Turning her so that her shoulders and back braced the oaken door, he tipped back her head and kissed her jaw, found the arch of her throat, his tongue light now over the hollow of her throat, then her breastbone. The gentle tease of his breath falling into the cleavage of her breasts, filling the silk with heat, swept her toward a sort of madness.

Sliding her fingers through his thick hair, she breathed out in joy at the tender touch of his lips on her earlobe, the warm shock of his hands cupping her shoulders, his fingers sliding downward, to the low curve of her neckline.

His fingers shaped the swells of her breasts. She sighed, feeling his lips so marvelous upon her. Swaying against him, she felt graceful, beautiful, cherished — she felt wanton, and she loved the sense of that freedom in her.

His fingers slipped inside her gown and chemise to find her taut nipple, sending a lightning spark through her. The echo of her gasp whirled into the stairwell. He dipped his head, and his lips heated her breasts through the silk. With his hand on her thigh, he floated her gown upward, so that her legs, in silk stockings and garters, encountered the thick wool of his kilt.

As his fingers trailed up her leg and rounded over her hips, she pushed at his kilt until she felt the hard, warm rasp of his muscled thigh against hers.

He broke away from her suddenly, smacked his hands flat against the door behind her. "Christina," he rasped. "I cannot —"

She silenced him with her lips. "I want to, and so do you," she murmured.

Aedan groaned, took her mouth deeply, pulled away again, like a drowning man fighting for air. "This is madness, what I feel for you. I cannot explain it, I swear. But I will not disgrace you like this."

"This is not disgrace," she whispered against his cheek. "I have lived through disgrace, and this is different. This is — joy, the only real passion I have . . . *ever* known," she said, knowing suddenly that it was true.

He shook his head. "You do not understand," he said, his voice ragged.

"I do," she said. "I do understand — as much as I need to just now. Please, love me. . . . Let me love you. . . ."

He made a low moan and murmured something she did not quite hear, for he took her lips with his fiercely then. Lifting his hands from the wall, he caught her to him with one arm and touched her breast with the opposite hand, kneading, teasing, so that his touch fired deep inside her, made her tingle and ache. She budded hard through the fabric, crying out with the craving.

He slid his hand down, bunched the silken skirt of the gown and slid his hand underneath and upward, delving beneath cotton and lace until his fingers gently caged her breasts, one and then the other, and coaxed the rosebud swelling of both nipples. She cried out softly as a current shot straight down between her legs. Sliding her thigh up over his, she felt his woolen kilt slipping upward and his bare leg pressed under her own.

While he kissed her lips, his fingers left her breasts to slip lightly down over her abdomen and lower, beneath loose cotton and silk. The touch made her moan, and she swayed, seeking more from him, much more.

Her hands caressed his back, his shoulders, his chest, and she explored his astonishing male firmness, iron muscles, wide shoulders, long back and arms, his hands sinewed and strong and so very kind and knowing upon her body. She slid her hand over the rock-hard flatness of his abdomen and sifted over woolen folds, seeking him, as he sought her.

His sure fingers dipped inside her lightweight drawers, cupped, slipping upward, where she was slick and aching for his touch, so that she moved with his gentle stroke, burning for him until she wanted to weep, until she arched and cried out and pure exquisite feeling burned clean through her.

She found him, velvet hard and taut, took him in the warm, tight sleeve of her hand and pleaded silently with her body against his. With widened, careful hands, he lifted her again, pushing the softness of silk and wool and cotton away until skin met skin, until he slipped inside of her.

This felt right, so very right, and she moved in unison with him and whimpered soft, ragged, secret sounds. She felt held by enchantment, passion drunk and drowsy with love.

Hidden with him in the swirling stairway, no rules, no doubts existed. Here they could have their secrets. Here they could allow each other freedoms of body and soul that they could not acknowledge elsewhere. In this place, she was loved and she loved. Here, his passion was the fiery twin to her own.

Out there, she had no such certainty.

He kissed her, drew out of her, wrapped his arms around her, his breath fast and furious. Brushing back her hair, kissing her brow, he began to whisper an apology.

She shushed him with a simple, lingering kiss, and unlatched the door behind her.

After slipping inside, she closed it silently, firmly, and pressed her brow against the wood, trembling. He stayed there a long moment, leaning against his side of the door. She felt the tug of his presence on her soul.

Then he was gone, and she felt that, too.

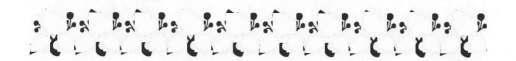

Chapter Twenty-one

After smoothing her dark green skirt and putting a hand to the thick knot of her dark hair, Christina flexed her trembling hands. She hurried along the upstairs hall, certain that Aedan would be at breakfast at this early hour, as usual. Smiling to herself, she thought of intimacies and wondrous secrets last night, and did not regret a moment of it. What they had done would be considered wrong and shocking if it were ever discovered, but she knew that loving him could never be a shameful act.

Last night, when she finally drifted to sleep, she had dreamed that Aedan came to her as the prince, and she was Liadan. They wore archaic tunics, but this time the garments were not costumes. Everything in the dream had a strangely precise authenticity, as if she and Aedan were those long-ago lovers.

Inside a stone tower, in the moonlit darkness of a fur-lined bed, Aedan had made such tender love to her that she had awakened beneath her quilts whispering his name, her hands flexing to hold him. That yearning still lingered like a deep ache.

She would see him soon. Blushing, she opened the door of the breakfast room. Morning light poured through tall windows, enhancing the cheerfulness of flowered chintz and golden oak.

But Aedan was not there. Without his presence, the room seemed suddenly less bright. She looked around and saw Mrs. Gunn and MacGregor standing near the window.

"Mrs. Blackburn, dearie, good morning," the housekeeper said. The butler bowed slightly, murmuring in soft Gaelic.

Christina greeted them and took a plate, serving herself from the warming dishes and salvers on the buffet, as was the casual custom at Dundrennan in the mornings.

"Looks like sun all day, and none o' them thunnerplumps we've had lately," Mrs. Gunn said, pausing by the window. "Will ye go to the hill again? Tam took Sir Aedan oot in the carriage, but if ye'd like the gig, MacGregor will send for a groom."

"Oh, no, thank you. I'd enjoy walking on such a fine day." Christina took her seat with MacGregor's silent assistance. He poured coffee for her and set down a little pot of the thick cream that she liked. Then he put within reach a plate of her favorite currant muffins and a bowl of fresh berries.

She smiled at him, grateful for the gestures that made her feel as if she belonged at

Dundrennan. "Has Sir Aedan left for his work site?" she asked Mrs. Gunn, as Mac-Gregor left the room.

"Oh, no, he's gone wi' Miss MacDonald and her grandmother to the train station in Glasgow and from there to Edinburgh. Lady Strathlin and Mr. Stewart went with them. They all have business in the city today," Mrs. Gunn said.

"He's gone?" She hid her plummeting disappointment. "I knew that Lady Strathlin and Mr. Stewart were leaving, for they bid me farewell yesterday . . . but I did not know Sir Aedan was also taking the train this morning."

"Aye, he's gone for just a few days," the housekeeper replied.

"And . . . did you say the laundresses went with him?" She found that surprising and puzzling.

"Och, aye, he's great friends with them, wi' being engaged to t'other Miss MacDonald and all."

Her stomach flipped. She had forgotten about his previous engagement. "The other Miss MacDonald? Oh yes, I believe something was mentioned of that," she said casually.

"Aye, Dora's cousin Elspeth, and a bonny lass she was. I thought he'd die o' the grief after she passed so quicklike. And what a shock 'twas, so soon after Sir Neil was lost in the war. Miss MacDonald were nae suitable wife for a laird and baronet mebbe, but she was a sonsie lass, and we all loved her well."

"I see." Christina sat very still, her fingers resting on her cup, the heat searing her through the fine china.

"Sir Aedan wasna the heir then, and he could marry as he liked. Aye, that were so sad." Mrs. Gunn sighed as she checked the dishes in the warmers. "We hoped he might wed Miss Stewart someday," she confided. "But I think that willna happen."

"Oh?" Christina said carefully.

"Aye well, the laird doesna bother anyone wi' his troubles. All I know is that Miss Stewart says Sir Aedan is a braw lad, but a dullie, and she likes him better for a cousin. Cut him free, she has, to set her sights elsewhere."

Christina blinked at Mrs. Gunn over her coffee cup. "Oh?"

"Well, she's a sonsie lass herself — isn't she? — and does wha' she pleases. Too much the wee lark for his broody hawk, do ye ask me. 'Tis better this way. He may never marry, our laird," Mrs. Gunn said, shaking her head. "Ye'll have heard o' that naughty curse."

"Yes," she said quietly. "I've heard."

"Well," Mrs. Gunn said, clearing her throat as MacGregor came back into the room. "Enough o' that. Sir Aedan says ye've made good progress on that wee hill, Mrs. Blackburn, and he says he hopes ye'll finish the rest quicklike."

"Finish quickly? Oh . . . I suppose . . . I shall."

Mrs. Gunn smiled, her round face and vivid blue eyes kind. Christina knew the housekeeper was oblivious to the blow she had just delivered. So he hoped she would finish quicklike, indeed — and be gone from Dundrennan.

Dear God, she had been wrong, so foolish, so very naïve. He had dallied and tasted and satisfied his hunger, and now it seemed he was done with her. No wonder he wanted her gone from his house quickly.

Steaming temper rose in her. *Fine,* she thought. She would happily arrange to leave. Let Sir Edgar take over the excavation. Her work on Cairn Drishan was almost done, after all. She would pack her things and leave, wishing only that she could go before Aedan returned. And may it please him no end, she thought.

"Mrs. Blackburn, dearie, will ye return for luncheon, or shall I have Cook pack a basket and send a gillie to the hill wi' it?" Mrs. Gunn asked.

She scarcely heard. Aedan had left without a word to her, and Mrs. Gunn's remarks revealed that he regarded Christina as someone who had overstayed her welcome.

Despite wild, wonderful kisses, despite his passionate response when he had made love to her, it had been lust, after all. Only that.

Loving him, she had prepared herself to accept even that from him, but the truth cut too deeply. Her cheeks burned with mortification. She had behaved indiscreetly once again. Would she ever learn to trust her head and not listen to her heart?

When she saw him again, she would put a good face on it and show him only dignity and aloofness. She would not hide, as she had done years before. She would not feel ashamed of doing what she had done out of love.

And she would leave as soon as she could arrange it.

"Mrs. Blackburn?" Mrs. Gunn awaited her answer.

"Lunch? Oh . . . yes. I'll come back to the house, thank you. I've work to do in the library."

"Pity, on such a bonny day." Mrs. Gunn turned as the door opened. "Good morning, Miss Stewart. Ye're up early today!"

Amy entered the breakfast room, her gown a fetching swirl of flounces and ruffles in a pastel tartan glacé that suited her blond coloring beautifully. Looking up, Christina smiled a greeting, although inside she felt plain and mousey by comparison. Amy always seemed to glow with verve and confidence.

And just now, Christina felt very plain and unwanted indeed.

"Good morning," Amy returned. "I thought to catch Cousin Aedan before he went to Milngavie. Have I missed him?"

"Och, he's long gone." Mrs. Gunn served Amy some coffee.

"I wanted to go to Edinburgh, too. It would be so nice to visit with Aedan's sister again." Amy put some fruit and a bit of bacon on a plate and took a seat.

Christina looked in dismay at her own generous helping and felt piggish for a moment. Then she picked up her fork and deliberately tucked into her meal with an appetite she no longer felt. She could not allow herself to feel bad about any of the choices she made in life, she admonished herself, the large or the small ones. She had done only what she felt was right.

"I'll be modeling for Mr. Blackburn again today," Amy said, smiling across the table at Christina. "I have so enjoyed that. Your brother is so charming. We have had the most delightful conversations. He has such a nice laugh, and he has such interesting stories to tell. He told me that I am a perfect model." As she spoke, Amy seemed to brighten.

Christina smiled. "John has a very discerning eye and does not compliment freely. You can be very flattered."

"But he did not want to use me for the

princess. He says you are perfect for her. How very flattered *you* must be."

"Well, John has a certain physical type in mind to suit his vision. He thinks of the princess as dark, and I am of dark Celtic stock, while you must have a good deal of Norse in you, with that stunning blondness."

Amy patted her hair. "Well, my grandmother was Norwegian."

"Oh, Mrs. Blackburn, there's a letter for ye. I nearly forgot," Mrs. Gunn said, sifting through some mail in her pocket and handing Christina a brown envelope. "It has a fancy seal."

"It's from the National Museum of Antiquities," Christina said, slitting it open. "Oh, it's from Sir Edgar."

She read it quickly, her heart pounding. "Oh my! He expects to arrive here sometime in the next few days." She swallowed hard.

"Och, Sir Edgar Neaves, here? Sir Aedan willna like it, but what can we do?" Mrs. Gunn threw up her hands. "The laird isna here, and Sir Edgar will be here any day. We canna put the man oot to find a bed in a tenant's croft!"

"He could stay at Balmossie, I suppose," Amy said.

"But he's come to look at Cairn Drishan, and Balmossie is several miles from here," Christina said.

"True," Amy said, frowning. "Well, we have no choice but to be polite and hospitable. He's sent here by the government, after all, and that's near enough to the queen, I suppose. We'll just have to be nice to him and show him that old hill, and maybe he'll come and go before Aedan returns."

Christina watched her steadily. "What would happen if Sir Edgar is still here when Sir Aedan comes back?"

"Oh, I would not like to see that," Amy said ominously, while Mrs. Gunn shook her head in fervent echo. "But it's too late to reply to Sir Edgar and too late to send word to Aedan. Sir Edgar will be here before then."

"Sir Aedan said he'd be gone a few days," Mrs. Gunn said. "And there's no way to tell when Sir Edgar might arrive."

Amy's frown cleared. "I'll send Cousin Aedan a note. But if Sir Edgar comes in his absence and we are chided for it, you and I will just smile at Aedan sweetly, and he'll forget his displeasure with us." She wiggled her pale brows. "Although Aedan is less susceptible to that than other men," she added with a little pout.

Christina nodded silently and sipped her coffee, scarcely noticing that it had grown cold and was not sweetened. She doubted anything in her life would ever seem sweet to her again after last night's flood of pure joy and the small, hammering blows that her heart had endured this morning.

"John." Christina knocked on the dining-room door. "It's Christina." Her brother had spent much of the last week shut up in the dining room, emerging now and then to accept trays of food and tea from Bonnie Jean or to speak briefly with Christina in the hallway. He had not requested modeling from his willing subjects in the household; nor had he invited anyone in to see the progress of his mural.

Earlier that day, Mrs. Gunn had reported to Christina that Mr. Blackburn had neither left the dining room nor slept in his bed for two nights. "Och, mistress, and ye know the Jeanies need to do the dusting in there," she told Christina. "And he keeps asking for eggs — raw eggs!" She made a face and shook her head.

Assuring the housekeeper that the dusting could be skipped for a few days, since the dining-room furnishings were draped in sheets for now, Christina promised to investigate the situation.

"John," she said again, knocking harder.

Finally the door opened, and her brother stood in the shadowed gap. "Christina! Did Gunnie send you here to see if I was still alive?" He grinned. "Tell her I'm fine, though in a fair seizure of inspiration. Did you bring food?"

"No." She held up an envelope. "I had a letter from Uncle Walter. Well, Aunt Emmie wrote it for him. May I come inside?"

He hesitated, then stepped back, opening the door. Christina walked in, struck at first by the utter change in the room, its highly polished mahogany table and chairs and cherry sideboard, draped in white like an assembly of ghosts. Two ladders and a stepping stool were arranged at various points around the room. Brushes, paints, rags, a palette, chalk pieces, small jars, and various art materials were scattered over the table. A bowl filled with unbroken eggs sat beside a second bowl, gleaming with egg whites and surrounded by a mess of eggshells.

The large cartoon sketches, glued together from several smaller pieces, had been haphazardly tossed on the table surface. An open window, its draperies shoved back, lace curtains billowing, blew fresh air into the room.

"Thank goodness you have good ventilation in here," Christina said. "You always need that when you're painting with oils and turpentine — though it smells quite clean in here."

"That's because I'm not using oils this time. I'm using egg tempera on the wall, as the medieval artists used. Look." Taking her shoulders, he turned her toward the wall.

"Oh!" She gasped, astonished and pleased by what she saw. She walked forward to look more closely.

The rather ordinary landscape background painted by the previous artist had been transformed by the addition of figures and a charming array of detail. In the background and middle ground, here and there, castles perched on hills, farmers worked in fields, shepherds tended flocks of sheep, and herdsmen goaded cattle along a path. Mounted warriors splendid in shining Celtic armor rode along a winding road emerging from a forested part of the background.

What caught her attention immediately was the foreground image of the prince and princess meeting for the first time. They faced each other in profile and gazed into each other's eyes, their hands joined.

The sight thrilled her, yet she also felt the dull stab of lost joy. Aedan mac Brudei must have gazed at his Liadan like that, long ago — but Aedan MacBride would never again gaze at Christina with such adoration in his eyes.

"It's beautiful, John," she murmured. "Really extraordinary. What a wonderful idea to paint Dundrennan's sleeping-beauty legend here. When it is done, it will be glorious."

He smiled, arms folded. Dabs of paint colored his fingers, marred his white sleeves. His cravat was askew, his dark brown curls wild, his jaw whiskered and in need of a shave. He leaned on his cane as if very fatigued. Circles smudged his eyes, but his gaze sparkled with excited inspiration.

"I am just now seeing how wonderful this could become," John said. "It could take me the better part of a year to finish it the way I'd like. I hope Aedan will not mind."

"A year!" Christina looked at him. "You know it must be done as quickly as possible. The queen visits in a few weeks."

"I will not compromise the mural, now that I know what it could be like," John said, shaking his head. "But I can have the figures and architectural elements sketched in, and I can apply color washes to the figures within a few weeks. It will at least look presentable by then."

"The queen will not mind a mural in progress, I'm sure."

"Because of the eggs, I must work much faster than usual."

She looked askance at him. "Eggs?"

"I am trying a bit of an experiment." He held up a hand. "I know — many a painting has been ruined by experimentation. But I feel certain this will work. I cannot apply oils to the plaster ground — the result would be disastrous. I've decided to use the medieval technique of egg tempera. Some of the Pre-Raphaelite Brotherhood tried their hand at it, with good result. None of them tried it on the larger scale of a wall mural, though," he added, frowning. "Still, I sent word to Father to ask his advice."

"I know you had a letter from him last

week, though you mentioned only that he asked after my health and my work here — you said nothing of egg tempera!" She smiled. "Is it working?" She noticed that only a few areas looked finished.

"It shows real promise. The egg gives the paint a wonderful richness, a sheen like oil color. But it dries very fast, so I have to paint quickly. And Mrs. Gunn is complaining about the number of eggs I need," he added.

"Sir Aedan will be glad to hear that it is moving quickly. And when he sees what you've been doing in here, I doubt he will care how long it might take. It's marvelous."

She looked again at the exquisite main image of the prince and princess. Though the figures were sketched and then washed in pale color, the drawing was precise. Realistic in the faces and hands, there was a fluid, decorative use of line in the bodies and draped costumes, showing the elegant and masterful control that characterized John's best work.

"Now, what of your business here?" he asked. "You said you had a letter from Uncle Walter."

"Aunt Emmie wrote it for him." She showed it to him, and he scanned it quickly. "He's not doing well, John. He can hardly hold a pen, and she says he shows no interest in reading history now — that is so very unlike him. Though he still seems strong, she says she fears he will not last the winter."

He handed it back to her, looking grim. "Perhaps you had best finish up here soon and go home to them. He will want to hear about your Pictish house, I'm sure, with its cellar and all. That will bring back some of the spark in him. He loves to learn about new discoveries."

"You're right. I should go to him. Except for you and your work here, there is . . . nothing further for me here."

John looked down at her for a long moment. "Nothing?" he asked gently. "When does Sir Aedan return?"

He said it so gently that Christina felt sure he knew that something had happened between her and Aedan. "I — I do not know. Edgar will be here any day. I do know that."

"Well, then, I believe you have a decision to make."

"What do you mean?"

"I think you know what I mean, princess." He took her elbow and guided her toward the door. "And now, out you go. I must work alone. And you have a great deal to do, too. Uncle Walter will be so happy to know you've found proof of his theories about Celtic Scotland and King Arthur."

She shook her head. "I do not think that hillside proves any of that after all, John," she said. "I was wrong. Hopeful, but wrong. It's a Pictish site, and that's wonderful. But there is no indication of anything more magical than that."

He smiled. "You've found some magic here, I think."

"The ancient site is a very exciting find, but it's not going to yield any extraordinary treasures." She smiled wanly.

"I'm not talking about the hillside. I may be busy during your posing sessions, my dear, but I am not a blind man. There is something very magical for you here — and for the laird, too. I've certainly done my best to encourage it."

She gaped at him. "You — oh! I see it now, you rogue."

"I'm amazed you hadn't noticed before. Both of you are distracted when you are with each other. You scarcely notice anyone else. Certainly not the artist who is nudging you together." He wiggled his eyebrows.

She tilted her head, curious. "What have you noticed?"

"Look through my drawings, my dear, and you will see it for yourself. The laird is in love, I'd guess."

She frowned. "I'm not so certain of that."

"Ask him when he returns and perhaps he'll tell you — if he is an honest man, and I think he is." He smiled and shoved her gently through the doorway. "Send someone with a tea tray, if you will. I'm starved." He winked and closed the door.

Chapter Twenty-two

A blazing sunset illuminated the city of Edinburgh, touching reflected fire to countless windows, reddening house façades, highlighting the rugged outlines of the castle and hill. Aedan stood watching the changes in sky and town, shoving his hands deep into his pockets. From Doctor Connor MacBain's front window in his house on the slope of the Calton Hill, the view over most of Edinburgh was expansive and stunning.

Aedan gazed at the castle on its high, black rock and the rugged cone of Arthur's Seat, the great hill that sheltered the city from winds and pocketed fog on wintry days. Below, he saw the long ribbons of streets and buildings and the moving flow of carriage traffic on Princes Street opposite the drained loch, a small valley now filled with bright gardens. He could see part of the long slope of the High Street, which divided the city, and clusters of tenement buildings, closes, and narrow streets. Laundry hung like pale, tiny tiles, and people moved about like so many bustling ants up and down the innumerable inclines.

"Lovely, isn't it?" his sister asked.

He turned to see Mary Faire entering the drawing room where he stood. Her wide skirt of dark brown satin complemented her slender figure and gleaming black hair. Quietly she closed the door of Connor's examining room, where Dora and Effie MacDonald were closeted in consultation with Mary Faire's husband. She crossed the room toward Aedan. "I love this view of the city at sunset — the colors are so vibrant and the silhouette of the castle so powerful, watching over us all."

"Beautiful, aye, but I prefer a Highland sunset."

"You always did." She slipped her arm into his. "It's good to see you, Aedan, and I'm glad you brought Dora here."

"Does Connor think he can help her?"

"I think so. He'll explain when he's done examining her. And it was good of you to bring her here and offer to pay any expenses on her behalf. That is the generous, warmhearted little brother I remember."

"I haven't changed," he answered pragmatically.

His sister angled a little to study his face. "Oh, I think you have. For a long time, you seemed determined to keep others away. You built a wall around yourself, especially after Neil's death. It grew higher and thicker after Elspeth, and then Father, too, passed on. But

366

you're breaking out of that at last."

"I didn't realize . . . I had done that," Aedan said quietly.

"Yes, to some extent. I haven't seen you for several months, but you seem changed now. I thought perhaps that you might have fallen in love with someone. Only that would soften a lad like you. Is it . . . Dora, perhaps? Or dear Amy?"

Laughing a little, he shook his head. "Both Dora and Amy have stolen someone's heart, but not my own." His own belonged to Christina now, but he was not about to admit that to his sister. Difficult enough, he thought, to acknowledge it to himself.

"Well, you've definitely changed for the better, my dear. When I saw you last spring, you were brusque and cold, glowering and rumbling like a bear disturbed in his den."

"You might do that, too, if you lived at Dundrennan, with Amy and Aunt Lill going full bore with painters, carpenters, and upholsterers," he drawled.

Mary Faire laughed. "I'm sure of it — neither you nor I would have much patience with that."

Aedan smiled faintly and looked over his sister's head as the sunset fire deepened to purple. "I built that wall for a reason," he said. "You know I felt as if Neil's death, and Elspeth's, too, were my fault." He was surprised how easy that was to say, after years

367

of carrying it about inside.

"Aedan, you were not even there. Neil died on a battlefield half a world away. And we all knew the hazards of that dreadful war when he left Scotland. I saw it for myself. Connor and I met there, on one of those horrid battlefields."

He nodded. "Even you were there, and I was not. I should have gone, but I chose to stay here and pursue my engineering work. I might have saved him — pulled him out of the way or taken that lethal wound myself. You know what an impulsive, idealistic lad he was."

"And you were the levelheaded lad who saw the importance of staying home with our ailing father, when both your brother and sister had trotted off to jump into a pointless, brutal struggle. You saved Father, I think — added years to his life. If anything, Neil's death is on my hands," she added softly.

He reeled at that, drew back to look at her. "Yours? Why on earth would you say that?"

"You know they brought Neil into the field hospital where I was working — I had just met Connor that morning, I remember, for we had a fierce argument, silly as it seems now, over bandage supplies. But I could do nothing to save my own brother, could scarcely make him comfortable while Connor tended to him and while Neil . . . died. If it was anyone's fault —" She stopped.

He put his arm around her. "You did your utmost. It was in God's hands. I know that now. You had best remember it, too."

"As for Elspeth's death," she went on, "I know you think the curse brought that on when you became heir to Dundrennan. Is that why you think your fiancée met tragedy?" She peered up at him.

He shrugged a little. "I've certainly wondered."

"Of course. Anyone would. But Aedan, you are a pragmatist in most things. Surely you realize that it was only coincidence. And besides, you were not the laird then."

"No," he said slowly. "But I am now."

She glanced up at him. "So there is someone."

"If there were, what does it matter? I will not risk that dreadful curse again. Love and happiness are not for me."

"What if you are wrong?" Mary Faire slipped her arm around his waist. "I think sometimes we can hold on to pain and fear as familiar things in a world full of the unknown, when all we need to do is let go and . . . well, free ourselves. Miracles do happen."

He was silent for a moment, thinking, hoping. Finally he nodded. "As always, you are the steady, wise one." He kissed the top of her head. "Miracles, is it? I promise to consider that."

"Good," she said. "Now, tell me — what is the state of things at Dundrennan? Will the house be finished by year's end, as Father's will stipulated?"

"It might be done in time for the queen's visit," he said, more brightly than he felt. Aedan still did not know if he would be able to keep the estate, though he had not yet told his sister the full truth of the ancient find. "The house looks marvelous."

"Marvelous? I thought you hated chintz."

He grinned. "I'm growing fond of it. And the mural in the dining room promises to be a beautiful thing. Father would have been very pleased."

"What about the old wall you discovered on Cairn Drishan?"

"It may be the location of an ancient settlement. That is yet to be determined. Mrs. Blackburn has not finished her work with that, and the museum will send others to investigate."

"Mrs. Blackburn?"

"The antiquarian sent by the museum, Christina Blackburn, has been digging in the hill. Her brother is the artist who has taken over the mural project. And Mrs. Blackburn is posing for the figure of the briar princess, I . . . well, you will be surprised, but I am posing for the prince in the painting."

Mary Faire smiled in delight. "You? I must meet this Mrs. Blackburn if she talked you into that. She must be rather wonderful to convince —" She looked at him closely. "Aedan Arthur MacBride . . . are you smitten with your Mrs. Blackburn?"

"Smitten? A laird of Dundrennan? Hardly."

"Stop hedging. Is she the one who has changed you so?"

"Oh, I doubt —" He stopped, realizing that he did feel different — lighter within, made of finer, kinder stuff in thought and emotion, finding it easy again to show that he cared about others. He laughed more, too. Felt younger and less burdened overall, yet with the hard-won wisdom gained of experience.

Watching the sunset glow pour through the window, he felt that incandescence within himself. Love filled him, and he knew it, and at last must face it. Though he might not be ready to take the risk, he suspected it was far too late to choose.

"I believe their consultation has come to an end," he said, turning as he heard a door open. Voices and laughter sounded out in the hallway.

"Oh, Miss MacDonald, Mrs. MacDonald, please come in," Mary Faire said, stepping forward to welcome Dora and Effie into the drawing room. A tall, fair-haired man accompanied them. Aedan strode forward to greet them.

"Thank you for seeing her, Connor," he said.

Blond and handsome, his appearance more like a Viking marauder than a studious physician, Connor MacBain smiled. "I think we have good news, Aedan. It's very possible that I can help Dora." He smiled at the girl and indicated to Aedan that he wanted to speak to him privately. They strolled together to the other side of the room. "Dora has cataracts of the eyes, an unusual condition in a girl so young and otherwise robust."

Aedan nodded, glancing across the room at the women, who chatted together while Mary Faire rang for refreshments.

"How would you treat such a condition?" Aedan asked.

"Generally the cataracts are treated by couching — slipping the tissue downward with a probe," Connor explained, "but I have had good success in removing the clouded tissue with the delicate use of certain instruments. The operation requires ether, which has its risks. I explained it to her and asked her to think about it."

"If anyone can help her, it is Connor," Mary Faire said quietly, coming toward them. She took her husband's arm.

"Dora will do well with the treatment, I think," Connor said. "She's young and healthy."

"And I'd like to try it," Dora said, turning toward them. The light of the sun turned her red hair to molten bronze and shone upon her strangely veiled eyes. Seeing the pretty glow in her face, Aedan realized it was hope.

"If you decide to do this, Dora," he said, "anything you need will be provided. I will see to it."

Effie MacDonald smiled, seated beside Dora. "Ye're a dearie, Sir Aedan, and always were. And lately yer kind heart shines a wee bit brighter than it used to. I'm glad to see it."

"I was just telling him the same thing, Effie," Mary Faire said. "He claims it's stuff and nonsense, that he hasn't changed a bit, but whatever has happened to Aedan has been for the better."

The old woman nodded. "Aye, and about time, too. Now, tell me," she said, pointing toward the gathering darkness through the window, "is it too late to get some of that fruit ice cream I was promised for coming all the way to the city?"

Chapter Twenty-three

Sheep wandered the slopes, black-faced with dingy fleece, munching grass, while the gray clouds rolled overhead. Christina glanced around as she stood on a high slope of Cairn Drishan. A strong, cool wind tugged at the brim and the ribbons of her hat.

She wished she could just toss away her bonnet and let the wind tousle her hair. Craving that sort of freedom, she realized what she really wanted was the freedom to tell Aedan honestly what she felt for him and how much Dundrennan meant to her now.

Coming to Dundrennan to investigate his discovery, she had discovered love instead — and she had failed to keep it, once again. And she did not know how to save it.

Soon her life would return to its previous dull, safe state. Edgar would arrive to take over the excavation on the hill, and she would go back to Edinburgh, leaving Aedan and her dreams.

The sky grew darker, and the wind felt laden with rain. To the west, a distant loch shone like a pale mirror, and the hills merged in the gathering mist. Christina breathed in deeply of the primeval beauty that surrounded her. She did not want to leave Dundrennan and all that it had come to mean to her.

Southward, she saw Aedan's crew, tiny figures along the raw strip of the road. The red steam engine glinted like a drop of blood. Nearby, a man in black sat on a gray horse.

Startled, she recognized Aedan. He must have just returned from Edinburgh, she thought. Her heart quickened, and she hoped he might take the path toward the hill where she stood, but he turned Pog and disappeared from sight past an outthrust of the ridge. Disappointed, she turned away to climb the slope with the aid of MacGregor's walking stick.

Reaching the level of the excavation, she looked out over the moorland from that higher vantage point. She could see Pog grazing now in the small yard beside Effie MacDonald's house.

Moments later, a red-haired woman in a tartan shawl came out of the house, followed by Aedan. Christina realized that the girl was Hector's daughter, Dora. They walked together across the yard, obviously talking.

Then the girl stopped and threw her arms around Aedan's neck, clearly kissing him. He embraced her, and they resumed walking, their arms looped, heads close together.

Christina whirled away, feeling struck to the heart. Of course Aedan knew Dora well — he had been engaged to Dora's cousin Elspeth. And Mrs. Gunn had mentioned that Aedan had taken Dora to Edinburgh for some reason.

Suddenly, seeing their closeness, Christina felt isolated from him and his life, and that realization hurt deeply. Perhaps Aedan saw her as simply an interlude, a passionate pastime. Perhaps he had charmed her and used her only in order to win her influence to save his road. Perhaps he was a cad after all.

And she had been foolish indeed to let herself dream and to let herself be hurt again. This time the wound went very deep, for she had given her heart away in full. She walked away, digging the tip of the walking stick into the earth.

Angus Gowan and his sons arrived on the site, shovels in hand, calling to her. She waved and settled down on a boulder, taking her memorandum book and pencil from her skirt pocket. Opening her book, she reviewed her notes and measurements.

She smiled when Angus greeted her, and she discussed the weather pleasantly, but all the while she felt hollow inside.

Aedan saw the rain miles off, streaming down from sky to earth in a darkling mist. He paused to watch it as he climbed the hill.

Then he adjusted his hat, shrugged his shoulders in his frock coat, and continued up the incline.

Seeing the Gowans digging in a corner of the foundation, Aedan raised a hand in silent greeting. Christina sat on a rock, intent on writing something in the little notebook on her knees. Deep in concentration, she did not look up at his approach.

She wore the veiled black hat again, he saw, with a trim jacket and skirt of dark gray that matched the leaden color of the old stones. The wind battered at the hem of her skirt, and he glimpsed her petticoats, a red one layered among the white. Her feet, snugly tied in black boots, peeked from underneath.

He knew the body beneath that neat outfit intimately now, and his body surged to think of it, and at the sight of her. He wanted to sweep her up in his arms, spin her around, tell her how much he had missed her, how much he loved her.

He quickened his step, then hesitated. He simply could not act on his impulses, regardless of how much he wanted to do so.

But now he understood why his parents had flown in the face of Dundrennan's curse. Love had overpowered tradition and superstition. Love had overtaken him, too, and was about to topple him. He was on the verge of telling Christina exactly how he felt, and damn the consequences.

If a remedy existed for the cursed lairds of Dundrennan — and their doomed wives — surely it could be found only through love, not fear. Did he have courage enough to take the chance?

He strode forward. "Mrs. Blackburn," he said, without waiting for her to acknowledge him first, as was proper.

She barely glanced up. "Oh," she said. "You're back."

"Aye." He frowned slightly at her coolness. "I came in from the train station in Glasgow and have not yet been back to Dundrennan. I hoped to find you here. I've been in Edinburgh for a few days," he added unnecessarily, when she did not look up.

"Mm, so I heard." She turned a page in the notebook and wrote something. "I hope your trip was pleasant."

"It was." He narrowed his eyes. She was upset about something. Her knuckles were white on the pencil, and through the veil, he saw hot pink suffuse her cheeks.

What an idiot he had been to forget, he thought, that the last time they had met, he had taken her roughly against a wall. He had not stayed to comfort her, or to apologize, or to confess that he loved her.

True, she had shut her door firmly afterward, accepting no apologies. And he had forgotten about his plans to leave early the next morning for Edinburgh. He had hoped that a few days apart would give them both time to think, to let ardor cool. In that time, love had taken full hold of him.

Now he saw that such was not the case for her. She had a right to be angry with him, after all.

"Well then," he said awkwardly. He wanted to apologize, explain himself, confess his love, but the words would not come. He wanted to pick her up bodily and kiss her, carry her down into the souterrain and show her just how deeply he felt about her.

But he would do nothing of the kind. The underground chamber was covered in a tarpaulin weighted with stones, and the Gowans stood nearby, shovels idle while they watched the laird and the antiquarian with unabashed Highland curiosity.

And Dundrennan's curse still existed, he reminded himself.

Angus's brown and white spaniel came out of nowhere to nose at Aedan's legs, begging to be petted. He leaned down and ruffled her head and shoulders, then sent her away. Christina ignored the dog, just as she was ignoring Aedan.

The *scritch scratch* of her pencil and her air of deliberate indifference nearly drove him mad. But he was not willing to go away quite yet, though she clearly wanted that.

"How is the work coming along here?" he asked.

"Fine," she answered, still scribbling.

"Have you made much progress?"

"Some." She turned a page. "The mud has been troublesome from all the rain — though I know you are anxious for this to be finished and for me to leave here."

"I'm not anxious for you to leave." He wanted her to look at him, react to his words, but she remained silent. She jotted something down, and he was tempted to snatch the pencil from her. "What are you working on there?"

"Notes."

"I can see that. Well, then. So you've made some progress. Have you opened the clay pots yet?"

"No. I am waiting for Edgar."

Dear Edgar. He nearly bit his tongue to avoid saying it. "I was sure you might open at least one of the pots. I thought you were eager to see what is inside them."

"Not so eager as I was." She turned another page. "I will wait."

"I thought perhaps there might be something of real value in them." Too late, he realized he had said the wrong thing, for she glanced up with snapping eyes — but at least she looked at him.

"Must there be something glittery in those pots for them to have value? That is not a king's treasure house. It is a storage room. A plain little cellar. If I never went down there again, I suppose you could hardly blame me."

He keenly felt the reference. "Christina —"

She stood, slammed her notebook shut. "I suppose if that storage chamber were King Arthur's own pantry filled with King Arthur's own soured beer, that would not interest you! It must have gold and jewels to be of value for you!"

He stared at her. "What on earth is the matter?"

"I think you could care less about this place, unless it holds a fortune that can be claimed for Dundrennan."

"That's ridiculous," he growled, moving toward her.

"I should have listened to Edgar, who said that historical significance would mean little to you, for you only care about your highway. He warned me that you would try to convince me that this was a worthless site. In his most recent letter, he said that if I find anything of importance, to be sure to protect it until he arrived."

"Charming man," he snapped.

"He should have warned me to protect myself." Her eyes flashed behind the veil and behind her eyeglasses.

"That," he said, "is an unfair sentiment, madam." He reached out for her, no longer caring that the Gowans watched avidly now.

Christina sidestepped his grasp. "You

should know that Edgar will be here soon, in a day or so. He sent word while you were in Edinburgh. Mrs. Gunn has readied a room for him."

He glowered at her. "I do not want him at Dundrennan. I thought that was obvious."

"There is nowhere else for him to stay."

"Milngavie has a good inn. Tell him to go there."

"Why must you be so difficult about him?"

"I've told you why. Among other reasons, he covets Dundrennan's collections." He had already explained to her that Neaves's dogged persistence had pressured and overexcited his father enough to trigger the final fit that had caused Sir Hugh's death. Aedan did not want to detail that again.

"Edgar's interest in Dundrennan is understandable. He's a museum director."

"He also covets you, madam," he ground out.

Her glance was keen through the netting. "If he chooses to visit me, even court me, I do not think it is your concern."

"I do," he snapped.

She huffed in reply and stalked away, skirt blowing out behind her in the increasing wind. Within moments, raindrops began to fall, cold and fat and fast.

Aedan waved to the Gowans, calling for them to climb into the souterrain for quick shelter. They nodded and clambered inside, whistling for the dog. Aedan grabbed Christina's arm.

"Go down into the souterrain — it's closest," he ordered. "I left Pog at the bottom of the hill. I've got to get her."

Christina pulled away from him, skirts whipping, and picked up her walking stick. "I don't mind the rain. It's not lightning, after all. I'm going back to Dundrennan. You can go to Effie's house if you like. No doubt you will be warmly welcomed there." She said it with odd emphasis and marched down the slope.

Aedan went after her, hard put to keep up with her irritated speed. "What is the matter?" he demanded. "You've achieved your goal up on the hill. You've proven the wall is ancient and stopped my road cold." He felt irritated himself now.

"That was not my goal," she said, hurrying onward.

"No? This place will be regarded as a triumph among scholars. Your name will be associated with it forever. And there will be no damned road through here."

She stopped, turned. He saw fierceness in her and winsome beauty, and the combination struck him to the heart, took him down like a felled tree. Instantly remorseful, he reached out a hand. She pushed him away with the walking stick.

"There is no need to swear," she said. "And I doubt a woman's name would survive in the annals of historical research. Cairn Drishan will be recorded as Edgar's find, and you well know it. But none of that is important to me. Furthermore, I never intended to stop your road. And if I have accomplished anything at all here, it is only in making yet another mistake!"

He blinked at her. "What are you talking about?"

"Nothing," she said, while the rain whipped at them. She turned, digging the stick furiously into the earth as she walked.

Bewildered by her outburst, he hurried after her. Where the slope eased into the moor, she took off running, using the stick to propel faster. Raindrops struck the earth, driving hard.

He dashed to untie Pog's lead from a shrub, mounting quickly. Fighting the wind, he turned the horse's head and cantered after Christina as she ran along the moorland road toward Dundrennan. Pog's hooves were fast and sure on the graveled top coat, and he caught up with her in moments.

Aedan wanted to drag her up into the saddle, kiss some sense into her, and finally explain himself. He reached down for her, but she batted at his hand.

"Let me take you home," he said, riding alongside.

"I want to walk."

"It's raining."

"I like it. I am not a hothouse flower."

"You are more like a prickly briar," he groused. "I will not ride off and leave you marching through a thunderstorm." Rain soaked them both now. Stubborn girl, he thought irritably. If he had not sent Tam ahead with the carriage, he could have thrown her into it.

"I've been out in rain before."

"You'll ruin your hat," he pointed out.

She put a hand to the black brim. "I have other hats."

"Not as fetching as that one," he drawled.

She gave him a dark look through the veil and hastened off again. Pog snorted, and Aedan urged the horse in pursuit.

"Ride with me," he said. "Mrs. Gunn will serve me up for supper if bonny Mrs. Blackburn develops a head cold from getting soaked through."

She lifted her chin, the swath of veil sparkling with rain. "It is not proper for a lady to share a horse with a gentleman."

"You shared other things with me," he growled.

"Well, I will not share that horse with you," she said, and she stalked onward.

"I want to talk to you," he said moments later, when he cantered up beside her. She ignored him, walking at a fast pace.

Thunder rumbled, and far off, lightning brightened the sky. Pog danced sideways, and

Aedan lost his patience.

"Christina Blackburn, come up here now, you wee bit fool." He leaned down to extend his arm through the driving currents.

She stopped, looked up at him, and then held up her hand with an air of resignation. Leaning down, he grasped her by the arm, and she placed her foot on his as he pulled her up behind him. Sitting sideways, she wrapped her arms around his waist.

Twisting to see her face just at his shoulder, he tilted the brim of her hat and lifted the damp, smoke-colored veil to look into her bespectacled, beautiful eyes. He saw traces of tears on her cheeks.

"Mrs. Blackburn —" He hesitated. *I love you*, he burned to say. *I love you*. "You're wet as a frog," he said instead.

She made a weary face, and he laughed, leaning toward her. He meant to kiss her endlessly, as he wanted, as she deserved, amid the rain and the thunder and the pounding of his own heart.

"Christina," he said. "I —" God, he could not say the words.

"Halloo! Mrs. Blackburn!"

Aedan jerked up his head to see a closed carriage hurtling toward them. A man's arm in a black coat waved from a narrow window. Then a top hat showed.

"Damn," he muttered. "I think dear Edgar is here."

Christina gasped, looked around. "Oh! It *is* Edgar!"

The vehicle, a hired chaise by the look of it, drew up and stopped. The top hat poked partway through the window, and a smartly gloved hand and cane showed.

And he saw a face he remembered all too well, slickly handsome, masking a sly and covetous man. Aedan scowled.

"Christina!" Sir Edgar Neaves called out. "My dear, what are you doing out here in this weather?"

Aedan leaned to look at her. "Christina, my dear?" he murmured. "He's a familiar fellow, isn't he?"

"So are you," she retorted. "Oh, Edgar, what a surprise!" she called back pleasantly, as if she stood in a candlelit ballroom and not clinging to a man on horseback in the pouring rain.

"My dear girl! Have you had an accident?"

"I'm just caught out in the rain, sir." She smiled.

"And who is this fellow? Your rescuer?" Edgar looked at him with cool blue eyes, his long, perfect features pulled in a critical frown. "Are you Dundrennan's factor, sir? I hardly think you should ride with the lady like that, even if she was caught in the rain. I shall have a word with the laird of Dundrennan."

Aedan removed his hat. "Then have that

word with me, Sir Edgar. I am the laird of Dundrennan, Sir Aedan MacBride."

"Great heavens, Sir Aedan, I did not realize! We've met only briefly, once or twice. You looked like a farmer or a laborer, sir, in that exceedingly plain suit and . . . low bowler."

"I sometimes do a little idle work about the estate," Aedan drawled. "Just now I was assisting the lady, who was walking back to the house when the rains hit."

The rain increased, slanting so hard that he nearly lost his apparently unfashionable bowler. He put a hand up to save it, feeling absurd as he sat in the rain exchanging pleasantries with a man who sat neat and dry inside his carriage.

"Thank you for assisting my fiancée." Edgar smiled, showing long, perfect teeth beneath his long, perfect nose. Aedan felt a primitive urge to put his fist through that chiseled countenance.

He glanced at Christina, whose cheeks flushed. "Ah, fiancée," he said expansively. "May I extend my congratulations, madam. Sir." He touched his hat.

"I never accepted his proposal," she said between her teeth.

"But he did propose," Aedan answered in a murmur, sending her a stony glare. "He knew you well enough for that."

"You know me better," she said.

"Ah," he replied. "That I do." He did not vary his stare.

Edgar beckoned as lightning split the sky. "Christina, come into the carriage." He opened the door from inside. "Driver, help the lady," he directed.

Aedan noted that Neaves had no intention of helping her himself. The rain might have spoiled his top hat, frock coat, and pale kid gloves. As the driver got down from his perch, Aedan slid a leg over the horse's head, dismounted, and lifted Christina down to the muddy ground himself.

With a quick, almost frightened glance, she grabbed her bedraggled skirts and climbed into the carriage with the driver's help. Edgar slammed shut the door and nodded farewell.

As the carriage rolled off toward Dundrennan, Aedan sat his horse, rain dripping from his hat brim, and watched them go.

"My dear, your gown is a dreadful mess," Edgar said as he handed her a folded carriage rug. "I would kiss you, but we will save that until you are presentable. Whatever possessed you to climb into a saddle with MacBride? He ought to know better than to share a horse with a young lady."

"He meant only to save me from a drenching," she answered, drawing the rug over her skirts. Sniffling, she dug into her pocket for a handkerchief, found none, and dabbed at her nose with her gloved hand. "Excuse me," she said.

Edgar made a disparaging sound and handed her his handkerchief. "You are always forgetting something," he said, "either gloves, or handkerchief, or losing your spectacles." He tilted his head. "Although you are always fetching, regardless. It is good to see you again." He smiled.

"Thank you, Edgar," she murmured flatly.

"I am anxious to hear about your discoveries here. I read your letters carefully, but you gave little detail away. Saving the best to surprise me, are you?" He smiled.

She used his handkerchief. "I told you as much as I know about the hillside. I sent you the measurements and sketches of the foundation walls, the dimensions of the souterrain, the number of clay jars in it, their shape, and the nature of their decoration."

"Have you found any artifacts yet?" he asked. "Have you instructed your workers to dig farther to look for valuable pieces?" He leaned forward. "Did you open those jars yet?"

"No, I decided to wait —"

"Yes, wait for me, as you should."

"— I decided to wait until digging revealed more of the site," she said, bristling. "If you believe me to be an incompetent, sir, why did you send me here?"

"My dear, you can be so prickly at times,

but that's just your charming feminine nature. You are not incompetent, of course, and you have the Reverend Carriston to advise and guide you. Have you written to ask the reverend's assessment of this? I am curious to hear his opinion."

"I have not troubled Uncle Walter with much of this as yet. He is ill, as you will recall."

"Indeed. A pity. Tomorrow we will go to the site and have the men dig deeper. Perhaps there is something to bring out."

"You would do that so soon? I proceeded slowly, thinking caution the wisest course."

"It is in some things, but I will decide what is best now that I am here. You ought to return to Edinburgh in the next day or so, my dear. I told Lord Neaves that you would call on him in his office at the museum. My father is anxious to learn more of our progress. If your father can accompany you, all the better."

"Father is still in Italy," she murmured. Lord George Neaves, Edgar's father and the high director of the museum, was a close friend of both her father and her uncle.

"Dear Christina," he said. "I confess I am anxious to know if you have considered my proposal, and if you are ready to give me your answer." He smiled confidently — smugly, she thought — and crossed one gloved hand over the other on his knee.

She hesitated. "Oh, Edgar. You've only just arrived, and I'm chilled through. I really need to rest."

"Of course."

"And we will have time to talk. I wish to stay at Dundrennan for a little while longer." *I want to stay here forever,* she thought. Even a few minutes with Edgar, after their separation, made it profoundly clear that she had made a grave error in allowing him to court her. He seemed even more imperious now that she knew Aedan.

Needing affection, and doubting herself greatly, she had accepted Edgar's criticisms and controlling ways as the best that she deserved after her tragic marriage. Edgar was fond of her in his way, but now she knew, really knew, what love could be.

She watched the rain, unable to look at Edgar. Even if staying with Aedan was impossible, she knew with chilling certainty that she could not be with Edgar in the future.

"Why do you want to stay here?" Edgar asked coldly.

"I am translating an early document from the Dundrennan Folio, which my uncle worked with years ago. It's not done."

"Oh." He leaned back, looking at her with interest. "Are these pages of any historical significance?"

"So far, they are just part of the family records." She watched the angled, silvery rain.

Smooth thou, soft thou, she heard in the rhythm of the carriage wheels. They were the ancient, timeless words of a lover. *Smooth thou, soft thou, well I love thee under the plaid.* . . .

Chapter Twenty-four

"A pity Miss Thistle is not here," John murmured to Aedan while they sat at a game of cards with Christina and Amy. "It would be such a diversion for her to meet Sir Edgar. Perhaps we should invite her for tea tomorrow."

Smiling, Aedan tossed down his next card. "What a truly excellent idea," he said in a droll tone. "Thistle has been languishing in her palm tree in the conservatory at Balmossie House, hoping for an invitation to Dundrennan. She would adore Sir Edgar."

"She might particularly enjoy his hat," John said.

Aedan grinned as he examined his cards. Beside him, Amy giggled and turned to look at the man who strolled the drawing room arm in arm with Lady Balmossie.

"Stop behaving like bairns," Christina said tersely.

"Well, he's an insufferable boor," John said, low enough that only they could hear him. "He's spoken only of himself all evening. Lady Balmossie told him that he was a blatherskite, and he did not even realize she called him a braggart." He laid down a card after Amy did. "Seven of hearts. Trump suit. That stops your eight of clubs."

"I am allowed to lay mine down if I want to clear my hand," Amy insisted primly, while John reached out to spin the round painted tray used to play the game Pope Joan.

"Minx." John wiggled his eyebrows at Amy.

"Will you need me to model again soon?" Amy asked.

"Not quite yet, sad to say," John replied, and Amy blushed. "Though I might need Aedan and Christina for one or two more sessions, if that could be arranged."

"Perhaps," Christina murmured.

"When might the mural be done?" Aedan asked, glancing at Christina. Her mood had been subdued ever since she had returned in Edgar's carriage.

"Several months at least," John answered. "Such things take time. But I will have the color washes done for the queen's visit. The finished project will take longer."

"Of course. Take as long as you need, sir," Aedan said. "It promises to be an extraordinary piece of work."

"How wonderful to have you both here for an extended stay." Amy smiled, her glance trained on John. Aedan watched with interest, remembering Amy's earlier confidence to him.

"Thank you, Miss Stewart," John said. "Although I believe my sister plans to return home to Edinburgh soon."

"Sir Edgar feels I should return, now that he is here," Christina said. "There seems little reason for me to stay."

Aedan frowned. He could think of many reasons for her to remain, none of which he could voice here. "What about the translation?" he asked. "You will want to finish it."

"That will be done very soon." She finally looked at him, and he felt it like a blow to his midsection. He was sure he saw need, and fire, spark in her eyes.

"We will be sorry to see you go, Christina," Amy said.

"Indeed," Aedan said, as Amy deposited a card. He resolved to find a chance to talk to Christina soon, tonight. He hungered to hold her, to make love to her again in that hidden stairway — but she had to want it, too.

She looked enticing tonight in the brown plaid skirt and a matching bodice, her shining hair pulled back in graceful wings, her bare shoulders like silk and cream. Knowing the taste of her, the feel of her, beneath those fetching garments, he pulled in his breath sharply.

A slow burn filled her cheeks, and her eyes glimmered. Aedan was sure she felt more than indignance toward him. Tonight he would sort this through with her, he thought, remembering that John had said he needed them to pose again.

Christina laid a card on the table. "Knave of hearts."

"Oh! Christina won 'intrigue' in this game," Amy said. "So she gets some game counters." Dipping her fingers into the tray, Amy rained mother-of-pearl pieces into Christina's hand.

Aedan turned his own card over. "Queen of hearts."

"Good! That is 'marriage,' in Pope Joan," Amy said.

He turned to Christina and held out his hand. Silently, she dribbled several mother-of-pearl slices into his palm, and his closing fingers brushed her gloved ones.

"Excellent," he said.

"No laird of Dundrennan ever wants marriage," Amy teased.

"There is a first time for all things," he murmured, calmly rearranging his cards.

"Both of you seem stiff and tense tonight," John said. "We need something vibrant and full of passion. Whatever is the matter?" He peered around his easel to frown at Aedan and Christina, who had joined him, in costume, in the long gallery.

"I suppose we are both tired," Christina said. "It is late."

Aedan glanced down at Christina, who

stood rather woodenly in his arms while gowned in the cream silk with a red tartan shawl tossed over her shoulders. Aedan wore a hauberk of chain mail over the red tunic, with a sword from his father's collection attached to his belt. The weight of the steel mesh pulled on his shoulders.

"Aye, we're tired," Aedan said. "Let's get on with it."

"What I want to show here is the moment when the prince discovers his beloved in the briars," John said. "This one is the most emotional and dramatic of these scenes, I think. Stephen painted the princess sleeping in the rose briar, and though it was passionately rendered, it was a passive pose. I'd like something more dynamic."

Aedan felt Christina tense in his arms. "Yes, a new variation would be good," she said.

"I thought perhaps he could discover her? . . . but how? . . ." John frowned thoughtfully, looking through a sheaf of drawings.

"You need to show urgency and danger," Aedan said. He scooped his arms under Christina and lifted her high. Gasping, she looped her arm around his neck. "You could show the moment when he takes her from the briar, before he tries to revive her."

"As in Sir Hugh's poem," John said. "Bring out the prince's desperate grief and determination to save her — excellent." He adjusted their pose and returned to his easel.

"Are you comfortable?" Aedan asked Christina as he held her.

"Very. But how long can you really hold me like this?"

Forever, he thought. "No need to worry. If my arms get weary, I will simply drop you to save myself the trouble."

"Oh," she said in a small voice. He huffed a laugh.

"Hush," John said. "Christina, try to look unconscious."

She drooped her head back, and her soft, loosened hair swept over his arm. Aedan caught his breath, held her closer.

"Very good," John said. "I'll paint the prince climbing Cairn Drishan, I think." He drew intently for several minutes, working fast and free with the chalk. Candlelight flickered, and rain drove against the windows.

" 'She lay among the briars, lost to him, oh! Lost,' " John recited in a quiet baritone. He continued through the last few verses of the poem, and Aedan heard Christina sigh softly.

The sight of Christina collapsed in his arms reminded Aedan of the painting he had studied for six years and of the times she had lain in his embrace. A strange magic seemed to work its way through him, an urge to hold her and protect her, though there was nothing to save her from but himself.

"John," Christina said, "have a heart. Sir

Aedan has been holding me for a long time."

"It's no hardship," Aedan said.

"Put her down, if you like. I have what I need now. Thank you — that's all for to-night." John sifted through his drawings, murmuring to himself, on fire with creativity despite the hour.

Removing weapon and chain mail, Aedan dropped the hauberk with a heavy chiming sound into the wooden trunk with the rest of the costumery. He laid the old sword on the table and turned.

Christina stood looking out the window, the Highland tartan drooping on her slender shoulders. He walked toward her.

"You look fatigued," he murmured.

She nodded. "I should go to my room."

"I'd be happy to escort you there."

She glanced at him. "To see me safely down the stair?"

"If you like," he answered, watching her steadily. He wanted to be alone with her, wanted to sweep her up in his arms again and carry her off. Perhaps the medieval costume he still wore made him feel virile, forceful, and passionate beyond the bounds of his usual somber self. Or perhaps it was his very real need to unburden his heart to her and to feel her love wrap around him.

Dear God, he thought, watching her. He adored her. She stood all unmoored and simple in her plain gown and Highland blanket, her shining dark hair bedraggled, her face somewhat forlorn just then. Love filled him, flowed over, poured full from his soul.

Quietly magnificent, the sense of well-being and balance, of a generous, fulfilled heart, could hardly be a curse. Loving her like this could only invite joy upon joy.

She glanced at him. "What is it? Why do you look at me so?"

I love you. The need to say it set him on fire. He leaned toward her. "Mrs. Blackburn —"

She watched him, eyes intent and beautiful.

He gestured toward the door. "Shall we go?" he murmured.

She nodded and put her hand upon his arm, as if he were about to escort her to dinner. They bid John good night while he was still working on a drawing. Aedan picked up a flaming candle and then opened the door for Christina.

In silence, he conducted her to the narrow door in the hallway and stepped inside first, so that if she tripped or fell on the steps, he would be there to catch her.

Candlelight flickered on the stone walls as they went down the steps, their feet quiet on the stone. He wore the tunic, and she wore her medieval gown; he realized that neither of them had noticed or had worried about changing.

Each step took him deeper into the secluded spiral of the stairwell with her. He had not been on these steps since the night of their last encounter, and the very air seemed charged with the lightning ecstasy of those moments. He felt it infuse every part of him, quickening his breath, making him hard and fervent for her.

Soon he could bear it no longer — the silence, the tension, the raw need. His feelings fought for expression. He turned, holding the candle out in its dish, and waited as she glided down to the step above where he stood. Being taller, he faced her directly, and he reached out.

Pulling her close, he kissed her, hard and fast and swift, holding the candle out in one hand, the other arm snug around her waist. He kissed her breathless, kissed her until he felt the tension drain from her, until she sagged her weight against his chest in surrender. Soon her tongue danced over his, and her hands came up to frame his jaw. He partook, as she did, of what swirled between them like slow honey, never wanting to stop, never wanting to let go.

But the candle sputtered and dripped wax on his hand, and he pulled back at last, resting his brow against hers, his heart hammering while he caught his breath.

I love you. He ached to say it, while she looked at him, silent and curious. Instead, he took her hand and led her downward, past her doorstep, where they had made love once. He drew her along with him to his own landing, where she had fallen one night on his doorstep and where his own heart had fallen like fruit from a tree.

Opening the door, he stepped back, waiting, blood and heart pounding. Christina stepped into the room, which was shadowy and warm with a newly laid fire. Shutting the door, he set down the candle dish and turned toward her.

A step, a cry, and she flowed into his arms. Wild with need and a joy that felt strange and new, he kissed her with the deepest hunger he had ever felt. She bent like a willow, graceful and supple, and he felt her give in to the need, as he did.

He had desired other women, had made love to them when circumstances allowed; years ago, he had lost his young heart to Dora's pretty cousin Elspeth, and they had tumbled together in heather and hay whenever chance allowed. Later, he had developed the wry, distant veneer that kept him safe from onslaughts of the heart and the vulnerable emotions that went with them.

But he had never felt like this, never. He was filled with a pure, bright, burning need to lose himself in her and to share it with her. Once he had believed he could never fall victim to this. Now he knew that love could happen in an instant, like the sudden dazzle of a sunbeam.

He had first dreamed of her years ago, when she was but a likeness in a painting, the one that overlooked them now, its presence lush and provocative. But she was real and warm under his touch, a thousandfold more seductive, and his body grew hotter and more firm as he absorbed the sight and feel of her.

Reaching out, he touched the glint of the fire in her hair, traced his fingers over her smooth shoulders. She leaned back her head, her throat beautiful, her hair rippling, swinging, and he kissed her cheek, her throat, felt her lips upon his jaw and soft upon his ear.

Questioning but silent, he pulled back to look down at her, and she gave her answer, leaning forward to kiss him, deep and open. He knew then that she wanted this as much as he did. He took her plaid, let it fall to the floor, then removed her little spectacles carefully. He kissed her eyelids, one and then the other, and then she looked up at him with honesty and gentleness.

He fell, once again, in love with her. The painting on the wall was but a dim, lovely shadow of the woman before him.

His mouth moved over hers, succored, withdrew, discovered again. She seemed to melt in his arms and under his lips. Deftly he untied cotton and lace and silk and floated them to the floor.

She stood unashamed before him, her body

marvelous in the warm gold light, satiny and beautiful. His own body grew hard and full, and he ached to lose himself in her softness.

When she reached for him and tugged at his tunic, he removed it quickly, let it drop away. He slid his palms along her waist, following the curves to span her hips, then upward around her ribs, his hands gliding over her breasts. He felt her falter, heard her soft, breathy gasp as she surged toward him, pressing her body to his, seeking his mouth with her own.

Lowering her to the floor, he lay with her on a pool of discarded silk and wool. Tracing his lips over hers again, he slipped his mouth downward, kissing, nibbling along her throat to her breasts. He sensed her heartbeat quickening like his own.

Loving her was not wrong or shameful. Loving her, he felt clarified and whole. This was no risk, he told himself — this was salvation in itself; it was bliss and forgiveness and nurturing. He could not stop himself, for an inexorable current pulled him onward. He thought it drew her, too, in its swift path.

Lying with her on the pool of fabrics, sensing the warmth of the fire on his back, he lifted slightly and traced his lips over her shoulders, over the living silk of her breasts, where the nipples pearled as he fitted his lips first to one, then the other. She arched, her arms encircling him.

Her breasts filled his palm, and he tasted her, then traced his mouth lower over her tight abdomen. Slipping his fingers downward over smooth, taut skin, he found her nested heat, clefted and honey slick. He touched her within, caressed her there until she shivered, until she undulated in a bold, moaning dance that he longed to join.

Her fingers smoothed over his back, over his buttocks, around and over his abdomen. He felt the hot leap of desire when her hand sheathed his erection. Fingers like warm velvet soothed over him, measured the span, teased until the burn grew so hot he could not bear it. Trembling, he pulled her to him, delving into her mouth with his tongue, tasting her, but desire overtook him, throbbed for release.

Supporting her hips with his hands, he rolled her gently to her back and she drew him downward, curving toward him like one cresting wave meeting another. He surged into her, losing himself in the sumptuous heat that wrapped so exquisitely around him. She moved with him, crying out softly when he did. He knew then that all her secrets were his now, and his belonged only to her.

Taking his weight on his hands, he arched to thrust deeply into her, riding a powerful cadence, for what shook his soul now spilled through his body, unstoppable, ecstatic.

I love you, he wanted to say. *I love you.* His

body said it, his hands, his lips, his heart brimmed with that gathering force. He felt the love flowing from her like a fountain to envelop him, comfort him. Nor did she say it, though it resonated between them like the strings of a harp.

He gathered her close, curled with her beside the fire, drew the plaid over her softness, and kept silent. For a long while he studied the fire and watched the shadows while she slept, and he made a silent promise, with his lips against her hair, to find a way for them to stay together forever.

Sliding out from his embrace, Christina slipped out of Aedan's large, comfortable bed, then pulled on her chemise and the silk costume. She had slept only a little, waking in his arms without regrets. Her body ached sweetly in secret places, and she smiled to herself, remembering.

She tugged the quilted coverlet high over his bare shoulder, for the room was chilly with the approach of dawn. Admiring the gleam of dawn light on taut skin sliding over the muscled firmness of chest and abdomen, she yearned for him again. She wanted to feel his arms around her, meet the passion of that hard and powerful body. But she stepped away.

He loved her. She felt it, though he had not said as much. She had known it through

407

his lips, his touch, the pattern of his heart-beat under her hand. Love had shone clearly in his gaze. More than passion had urged him to take her in his arms, had helped to make her feel so splendid, so wanton and willing.

But now, she knew she must leave. She could not be found in his bedchamber. Gathering her things quickly and silently, she kissed his cheek as he slept unaware. Then she went barefoot to the door and climbed the stairs, cold stone underfoot in the secret, shared passage that was theirs alone.

She would not stay until he woke, nor ply him to declare his love for her. She would not ask of him what he could not give her freely.

Chapter Twenty-five

"Interesting," Edgar said, turning on his heel, his cane pressing into the dirt. Although he did not need the support as John did, he lounged elegantly upon the silver handle. "This is a nice find, Christina, but it seems to be of fairly minor significance. Ruined walls and a storage chamber with a few pots are all things we've seen before."

"It is significant," Christina replied firmly. Guiding Edgar around the site, listening to him complain about the mud and the primitive conditions, her patience was sorely tried. "The pots in the souterrain are rare examples of early Celtic work, with beautiful animal designs. And the provisions in the jars will very likely tell us more about this ancient society."

"True, the pots are pretty, and they will make a curious exhibit, once they are cleaned and emptied."

"You cannot mean to simply dump them out!"

"Someone will list their contents and then dispose of any useless goods. The contents are certain to be spoiled."

"I'd like to open them myself, here on site. They could suffer damage if we move them to Edinburgh first."

"Here?" He looked down at her. She realized, suddenly, how very long his nose was. Its design suited his tall, aristocratic appearance. He was exceptionally handsome, with brown hair, blue eyes, and elegant features, but he made her think of a long-legged spider. Odd that she had so long denied how uncomfortable he made her feel.

"Edgar, you know the newest methods of archaeology advocate painstaking work and careful records. I have done that here."

"I've always recommended careful working methods, though I see no harm in removing the items from the site to examine them at our leisure in the museum. It's tried and true."

"But usually items are not even catalogued properly. The Danish approach of careful labeling is very sensible. We must dig slowly through the entire site, listing and sketching everything here, in situ, and then again in the museum. I'd like to finish my work here before we move the pots — or heaven forfend, discard anything."

"The new scientific methods are useful with fragile fossil layers. But man-made artifacts can easily be removed from the earth and transported for study. You can hardly expect me to sit in the mud and the rain," he added, looking with disdain at her skirt and earth-stained hem. "We'll take the jars back to Edinburgh."

"But, Edgar —"

"My dear, we need not stay here to empty pots or dig with spoons or scrub stones, or whatever else you've been doing. Later, I'll decide how to manage the pots. And I think we should call them the Dundrennan Vases — it is less mundane than 'pots.' "

"They are pots," she said truculently.

"Nonetheless, we can create an interesting exhibit, if somewhat thin. Pity you found nothing more here. Perhaps some of these old stones should be transported as well, to appease curiosity. I shall talk to the museum board about opening this site to the public within a year or so. Many would travel to see Dundrennan, I think. This place could become quite an attraction. An inn might do near here, perhaps even a resort hotel someday." He turned. "The landscape is rather spectacular."

She frowned. "Sir Aedan would not approve of tourists here."

"He has little choice now." Edgar waved a hand. "This place is a national treasure. The ruin isn't very romantic on its own, but we could make it seem so. The walls could be a Pictish foundation, after all. Ah! I have it. We could claim that this was the home of that sixth-century Dalriadan princess — you know, the one in Sir Hugh's poem."

"Yes," she murmured. "I know the one."

"Mr. MacDonald says that there is an old rumor that King Arthur's gold is hidden in these hills," Edgar said. "It's hardly believable looking at this paltry ruin, but it is a pretty fairy tale, after all. We could stir up public enthusiasm by hinting at ties to the days of the actual King Arthur and his twelve battles." He slid her a quick look. "What do you think, my dear?"

"Uncle Walter devoted his life to studying that subject, as you well know," she said. "I hardly think you can dismiss those theories as unscholarly fairy tales. It is perfectly feasible for the historical King Arthur to have had some contact with the Scots in this area."

"Christina, there would have to be some irrefutable proof of that, and there is not. This site is hardly Camelot — look around. But fairy tales attract tourists, and tourists have money, and that would greatly benefit the museum." He raised an eyebrow. "Perhaps you could write up a little pamphlet about the Pictish influence in this area."

"All of this is very hasty, Edgar. We have scarcely begun the excavation."

"Since it's clear the site will yield only ordinary things, I am simply putting a more exciting face on it, for the good of the museum. Sir Hugh generously provided a condition in his will to allow our involvement." He smiled.

"I heard something about that," she said, staring at him. "I wondered if some compromise could be reached."

"Why would the directors compromise, when a prize like Dundrennan is in the offing? Oh, by the way, I shall need to see the notes you've made. You may make another copy for yourself, of course," he condescended.

"Perhaps your secretary can rewrite my notes," she said, thinking of the hours required for such a task.

"Oh, no, the fellow is much too busy," Edgar said. "You have little to occupy your time, now that I am here to oversee the excavation." He took her elbow to stroll with her beside the low, crumbling wall. "And besides, you will be returning to Edinburgh within a day or two."

She knew now that she could not bear to leave Aedan. Not yet, not after last night. There were feelings to sort through, things to be said. "I've decided to stay here for a while longer . . . to help with the site," she told Edgar.

"Well, if you really feel you must be near me, I suppose you could stay for a few days," he said indulgently. He looked down the slope. "Ah, here comes our Highland work crew."

Christina turned to see several men walking up the hill.

Her heart leaped as she recognized the man in the lead. "Sir Aedan has brought Hector MacDonald and the Gowans. The men have done the digging up here."

"Good. I'll speak to them about clearing this mud. And I want them to shovel down a few feet more in the interior of the house to determine if there is anything buried here."

"Shovel the interior?" She stared at him. "But we must go carefully through that area, or lose the chance to discover more about daily life at the time this house was in use. That sort of evidence is so fragile. Edgar, as a historian and an expert in early medieval culture, you cannot be so callous to that!"

"Of course. But Scotland is rather full of old walls. We have no guarantee yet that this place is even Pictish. Further digging might tell us more, of course, but it still could be —"

"Merely a black house, perhaps?" Aedan inquired as he strode toward them. "If this place is not that important, Sir Edgar, then you will have no objection to the road going through here as quickly as possible."

Edgar spun to face Aedan. Taller and thinner than the laird of Dundrennan, he seemed pale and bitter compared to Aedan's honest power and dark beauty. Christina gazed at Aedan, feeling overwhelmed, suddenly, by a desire to run to him, to stand in the lee of his solid strength, rather than here with Edgar's sharp fingers pressing her arm.

Aedan inclined his head. "Mrs. Blackburn," he murmured, and she read something deep and compelling in his vivid blue eyes. Then he looked at Edgar, and a muscle flashed in his jaw.

"Sir Aedan," she said quietly. Behind him, Hector and Angus nodded and tipped their hats to her.

"Sir, your highway cannot go through here yet," Edgar said. "You will have to find an alternative."

"Without a road over the hill, the two sections of highway down on the moorland will be rendered useless," Aedan said.

"I cannot help that," Edgar said.

Aedan put a fist to his waist, the wind whipping through his hair. "Luckily, we have an alternate route — the other side of this hill. I've directed my crew to prepare the other slope. Blasting will begin soon, then digging and topping."

"There must be no explosions near this site," Edgar said.

"If these walls are unremarkable, that will not matter," Aedan said. "And since the other side of the hill is also on my estate, I am well within my rights to do what I want there."

"It is not advisable," Edgar barked.

"If you object strongly, sir, then read this." Aedan pulled a folded letter from his pocket. "An order from the Parliamentary Commission of Roads and Highways. This road must be completed by mid-October. I've obtained permission from the commission to do whatever is necessary to complete the route for the queen's use. And I intend to cut a path on the other side of this hill."

"I warn you, sir, that would be a mistake. I remind you that Treasure Trove Law protects this place. And we still require your men to dig out this area, so you will be shorthanded until the museum sends some assistance here. I trust your hospitality will be extended to that group when they arrive."

"There is a good inn at Milngavie," Aedan said. "You will all be comfortable there. However, Mrs. Blackburn is welcome at Dundrennan for as long as she likes."

"Mrs. Blackburn will return to Edinburgh soon," Edgar said.

"Oh, will she?" Aedan asked, looking at her quickly.

"No — I have decided to stay for a bit," she said.

"Then it's settled." Aedan nodded.

"Nonsense," Edgar said. "There is no reason for you to stay, Christina. You have plenty to keep you busy in Edinburgh."

"Let the lady decide for herself," Aedan said.

"The lady," Edgar said, "will listen to me. We have been courting a fair amount of time, sir, so please do not interfere. If I may be so bold as to hope, the lady may soon consent to be my wife. Of course she will listen to me now." Edgar touched Christina's elbow in a proprietary way.

She frowned at him and stepped out of his reach.

"Oh? May he be so bold as to hope?" Aedan asked mildly.

"He may hope all he likes," she snapped, feeling irritated with both of them. One loved her and would not admit it. The other was incapable of real love, despite his proclamations.

She turned and snatched her walking stick from its position against a rock. "I'm going back to Dundrennan. You two can stay here and sort this through." She strode away.

Aedan caught up with her quickly and reached for her arm before she could avoid him. "Wait," he said in a low growl. "Tell me you don't want to be with that blatherskite fool."

She snatched her arm out of his grasp. "And which fool should I be with?" she whispered fiercely just beneath her breath. "You, a man who wants me, but does not want me? Or him, with his lofty opinion of himself? I'm leaving. You and Edgar can stay here and lob rocks at each other, for all I care."

She strode away without looking back, and suppressing the sob that rose in her throat. Her feelings for Aedan had grown deep and dominant, and her respect for Edgar had quickly diminished. But she could not side with one over the other, and she could not bear to see them snipe at each other. She dreaded the inevitable confrontation that must come over the matter of Dundrennan, the site — and her, as well.

For though she knew her own choice, she was not certain that he would claim what she would so gladly offer him.

"Beast and behemoth are here, lad," Hector told Aedan, pointing to the ox-drawn cart lumbering toward the earthen slope, drawing the steam shovel on the flatbed. "And Rob has already set another charge of black powder."

Aedan glanced at the wide, zigzagged path that climbed the opposite slope of Cairn Drishan. The new, raw-cut road had been grubbed free of undergrowth and marked by wooden stakes. High on the hill, Rob Campbell stood with a few men. Seeing Aedan and Hector below, the young engineer lifted a hand.

"We'll clear out of the way when he gives the signal," Aedan said. "Tell Donald Gowan to keep the behemoth at the foot of the incline. We don't want the ox hurt by debris or the engine scratched." Hector nodded and trotted off to give the order.

Sighing in exhaustion, Aedan wiped his forearm across his brow and surveyed the road. His crew, and he himself, had worked day and night to advance this far in just a few days. Most nights he had stumbled to his bed very late, after quick, cold meals on covered trays left out for him. One night he worked so far past midnight that he had slept by Effie MacDonald's hearth.

He had hardly seen Christina since the day he had met her on Cairn Drishan with Edgar. Three times he had gone to the excavation site to consult with Hector and the Gowans and had seen Christina there, but they had spoken no more than a greeting. Edgar had been there each time, talking with Christina. She had looked mildly pained, as if Edgar had become a pest — or perhaps, Aedan thought, that was his own interpretation.

And each time Aedan had left the site, he had nodded curtly to Christina, avoiding her somber, beautiful gaze. As he walked away, he had felt her watching him, and he had ignored the urge to turn around.

He had made a mistake, he thought, in giving way to his passions — in letting himself fall so deeply in love. Christina had a life of her own, a suitor, and she must return to that. And Aedan must retreat into his safely secluded heart.

For a little while, he had set himself free, but he had forgotten, essentially, that he could never allow himself to fall in love. For Christina's sake, he could not.

Edgar might be an arrogant boor, but he was wealthy, socially prominent, a handsome fellow, and willing and able to marry Christina. He loved her as much as he was capable of it, and his scholarly interests matched her own.

Aedan's own fortune had dwindled with the vast expenses of the house. Nor did he have a bookish bone in him, despite a taste for poetry. But he longed for Christina, the urge burning all the hotter as he drew back.

Loving her, he owed her his honesty. He must tell her of his feelings — it seared in him to do that — but he had to explain that he could not risk claiming a life with her, because he loved her.

Not eager to voice the finality of that, he had kept silent.

The afternoon heat had grown stifling. Aedan wiped his brow, then drank from a silver flask. Lemonade laced with whisky, he discovered — Effie's donation for a long day's work that would once again go deep into the night. Sighing, he stuck the flask into his jacket pocket and looked up at the ominous sky.

"Damn this rainy luck," he said as Hector came back to join him. "The highway will never be finished if the weather continues to plague us with water and mud."

"Mebbe the queen can float to Dundrennan," Hector said.

Aedan smiled. Hearing Rob shout that the fuse was about to be ignited, he stepped behind the protection of the steam engine with Hector. Rob and the others ran to join them.

Moments later, he felt the rock shiver under his leaning hand as the powder ignited and watched dirt and stones spew outward. Aedan thought of the blast weeks ago that had torn open the other side of the hill, exposing the ancient wall.

That previous blast had initiated events that had sent deep and everlasting shocks through his life. He knew, now, that he would never be the same. And he wondered what this explosion would bring in its wake.

Chapter Twenty-six

"One of the Jeanies should be here soon with tea," John told Christina. "I asked that it be brought here for Aedan and me. Perhaps you'll join us, Christina." He crossed the room, leaning heavily on the ivory head of his cane.

Seeing how much her brother relied on the cane today, she knew that he had taxed his strength while painting the mural. Christina sighed and turned to glance at Aedan, who studied a partially finished section of the mural.

Surprised to find Aedan here when she had entered the room a few minutes earlier, Christina felt almost shy near him. With so much unsaid between them, they had exchanged banalities — the weather had been pleasant, but the rain would likely resume soon, and the nights were growing darker more quickly these days.

All the while, she desperately wanted to be alone with him, to tell him how she felt. She needed to feel his arms around her.

Smoothing her hands nervously over the

bell of her dark green skirt, she smiled at John.

"I just took tea with Lady Balmossie and the others," she said. "We missed you — both of you — up in the sitting room. Thistle was with us today," she added.

"Oh? How did she agree with Edgar?" John asked.

"She seemed to fancy him. He had to run and change his coat after she put cake in his pockets." She smiled at the memory of Edgar fending off Miss Thistle's attentions.

"Fickle lass," Aedan drawled. "I thought she preferred to mess my coat."

John laughed and turned as a knock sounded on the door. "Excellent! Tea at last." He went to the door and opened it.

"Good afternoon, John." Sir Edgar stood in the doorway, then strode past John without invitation. "Ah, Christina! Miss Stewart said I might find you in the dining room. And Sir Aedan is here, too. Good afternoon, sir. You've been scarce lately."

"I've been rather busy, blasting the hills," Aedan said. He crossed his arms and leaned against the table, which was covered in cloths and the chaos of John's art materials.

Edgar did not answer, simply turning away. "Ah, the mural!" He looked at the two walls that now held elaborate compositions, partially completed in line and color. "Yes, quite interesting."

John limped forward to stand between Edgar and the wall in a protective manner. "It is not ready to be seen. I've asked that my privacy be respected in here until the mural is finished."

"Yes, so I heard," Edgar said without remorse. He turned a slow circle, looking at the walls. "But we are old friends, after all, and your sister is here, as is the laird. I assume your ban does not apply to me, either. This is marvelous," he murmured. "But will you have it done in time for the queen's visit?"

"It will be presentable by then," John said curtly.

Edgar strolled to look at the other wall. "You are fortunate that I am here, for you may need the good opinion of a director of the National Museum of Antiquities. We are considering having a large mural done in the Industries Hall."

"I had not heard," John said.

"Yes. And you have a certain gift. I think you should submit sketches for the Industries project. I can recommend you to my father, who is heading that committee. Winning such an assignment would be a plum for you, and it would greatly boost your artistic career."

"That is very kind of you, Edgar," Christina said, while John murmured quiet thanks.

"I am certainly glad to help." Edgar joined his hands behind him as he strolled beside the wall, studying scene after scene. "Ingenious, really. The pictures have a medieval sense. You are depicting the legend of the Dundrennan princess, I see."

"Aye," Aedan said. "But I believe Mr. Blackburn does not care to have his mural examined too closely as yet."

"Oh?" Edgar peered closer at an image of the prince and princess — Aedan and Christina — facing each other, hands joined. They stood framed in a medieval arch. Edgar frowned.

"So, Christina," he said, turning, "I see that you and Sir Aedan posed for these figures."

"Yes," Christina answered.

Edgar narrowed his eyes. "But, my dear," he said smoothly, "you promised me that you had reformed your behavior."

She stared at him, speechless. She remembered that when Stephen's painting of the briar princess had been exhibited at the Royal Scottish Academy, Edgar had been instrumental in having the picture taken down early, ending her public embarrassment.

Silently she looked away, feeling her cheeks burn.

"That was not gentlemanly." Aedan stepped forward.

"Considering her unfortunate experience in the past, I cannot approve of her posing. And with a man — most unseemly."

"No one asked for your approval," Aedan answered.

"Edgar," Christina said, "there is no harm in this at all. John is creating a beautiful artwork in this mural. I'm proud to be part of it."

"Lady Balmossie posed for the princess's mother, as you can see," John said, pointing to one of the figures. "And Lady Strathlin herself consented to model for a mere serving maid — that lovely blond lass, there. If such illustrious ladies had no objection to modeling for this, you cannot criticize Christina for doing so."

Edgar frowned, strolling beside the wall until he came to the last scene, a simple penciled sketch on white plaster of the prince lifting the unconscious princess in his arms. Slipping a monocle from his pocket, Edgar leaned forward.

"Really, Christina," he admonished.

Aedan strode toward him. "Sir, the artist values his privacy, and the models object, as well. I'm sure you understand." He gestured toward the door.

Ignoring the obvious hint, Edgar inclined his head. "Sir, I've been hoping to speak with you. Now that you will be unable to meet the conditions of your father's will, we must arrange a meeting between your advocate and the museum's advocate to discuss the terms of the transfer of the house."

Christina gasped and hurried toward them. Aedan reached out and took her elbow, his hand tightening on her arm.

"All conditions will be met," he ground out.

"But the renovations are ongoing, and the mural is not finished yet, either," Edgar said. "And now that the ancient walls have been discovered on the property, that voids your claim to the house, according to your father's wishes." Edgar smiled, his smugness detached rather than hostile.

"You said yourself it had little significance," Aedan pointed out. Christina looked from one man to the other.

"Regardless, it remains a historical site," Edgar said. "But all is not lost. We at the museum are not so heartless as to take away your ancestral home. The museum board discussed the matter before I came here. They urged me to make an offer to you."

"What offer?" Aedan asked in an ominous tone.

"Dundrennan's historical collection belongs in a museum, not hidden away from the public."

"You know I will not sell my father's collection."

"The costs of these renovations must be enormous. Your father's fortune dwindled in the years before his death. One wonders how you pay your creditors."

Christina heard Aedan intake a breath

sharply. "That is none of your concern. I have the funds."

"Not for long, I'm sure, once the remodeling is done. We would not render you penniless as well as homeless. The board members wonder if you would be generous enough to donate your father's historical memorabilia collection to the National Museum of Antiquities of Scotland. We do not offer you a fee, but we do offer to take the care and maintenance of those objects off your hands. In return, we would relinquish our claim on your house."

Aedan frowned. "My father wanted those objects kept here."

Christina looked up at him. "It is something to consider," she said quietly. "House the collection in the museum and save your house. Please, Aedan," she added in a fervent whisper.

Aedan studied her for a moment, his black brows lowered over cool blue eyes. "I will think about it," he told Edgar.

"The directors are not unanimously agreed about this," Edgar said. "I could be persuaded to vote in favor of this compromise, and I can convince my father to vote for it, as well. Then the vote would go your way and the house would remain yours."

Tipping his head, Aedan considered him. "And what," he said, "might be your price for that vote, sir?"

Christina felt a chill suddenly as she saw Aedan's hard, stony glare and Edgar's harsh returned gaze.

"Stephen Blackburn's painting. You own it, sir. I want it."

Christina gasped. "What?"

"I will not sell it." Aedan said flatly.

"I suggest that you give it to me, sir, in return for my influence. It is not much to ask."

Silence filled the room. Aedan stared at Edgar and drew Christina close to his side, his fingers firm on her elbow.

"The painting is not mine," Aedan said. "It belongs to Mrs. Blackburn now. And I doubt she will give it to anyone."

She stared up at him in astonishment, then looked at Edgar. "But why do you want that painting?"

Edgar smiled and walked toward the door, which John yanked open for him, clearly wanting to see the man exit.

"My dear," Edgar said with a little bow, "that image of you should belong only to your husband. Since I have long hoped to be that someday — despite your reluctance to commit to it — I thought to have the painting myself, to contemplate our happy wedding."

"That," she said, "will never happen."

"No?" He smiled again. "Sir Aedan, if you want to keep this house, I suggest you let that painting go to me — and relinquish your hold on Mrs. Blackburn. She seems almost to have fallen under a spell of some kind since she came here. She has reverted to her formerly rebellious nature. My dear, I regret to see the weak side of your character returning. I thought you had cast that off when Stephen died."

"Edgar!" Christina said, stunned.

Aedan left her side to stride angrily across the room toward Edgar, who ducked quickly through the doorway. John lunged forward, too, but Christina hurried to catch them both. She caught John's sleeve and grabbed Aedan's arm. Her brother turned back into the room, muttering under his breath, but Aedan jerked away from her, stepping forward.

Once again she pressed on his forearm, the muscle hard under her palm. "Aedan, please. Edgar is not worth it," she said.

He looked down at her with cold, angry eyes and stopped. Ahead, Edgar breezed down the hallway, swinging his cane, and disappeared around a corner.

"Not worth it? At least you realize that now," Aedan said.

She nodded. "I know you have been trying to tell me that since we first met."

"Indeed, madam," he said. She felt him fuming and wanted to offer her solace, but his glance was hard and cold.

She rested a hand on his arm. "Aedan,

thank you for the painting," she murmured.

"No one should have it but you," he said.

"As for the rest, I want you to know that Edgar presumes too much. I have never formally promised to marry him."

He watched her for a moment. "Perhaps you should."

"What!" She stared at him.

"He loves you, in his way — he's devoted to you. And he can offer you a great deal. A wealthy scholar, an eminent man, and free to marry. Charming as you are, you could no doubt reform him from a pompous ass into an obedient husband."

"How absurd. Do not swear at me. And I do not love him." She felt her gaze transfix his, felt herself melt into that. Helpless against the pull, she leaned toward him. "Not at all."

The anger dissolved in his voice, his eyes. "In my family, madam," he said slowly, "love is not a condition for marriage."

"Rather the opposite, I know," she said, hurting suddenly.

He did not reply, but stepped into the corridor quickly, striding down the hall toward the main staircase.

Christina stood in the doorway, feeling as if her world had tipped wildly, as if she could not find her balance.

"Christina," John said. "Go after him."

She blinked, looked at her brother, then gathered her skirts and hurried down the hall. "Aedan," she called. "Aedan!"

By the time she reached the stairs, she heard the slam of the great oak door echoing in the foyer. When she got to the door, MacGregor hastened to yank it open for her.

Outside, she saw only the empty drive, but she heard Pog's hoofbeats echoing somewhere along the wooded lane.

She turned back and entered the house, aware that MacGregor and Mrs. Gunn watched her as she walked past, their gazes concerned and sympathetic. Summoning dignity, she headed upstairs to the dining room to seek out her brother's secure, unquestioning company.

Moving the magnifying glass slowly over the fragile vellum, Christina studied the phrases crammed along the margin of the second sheet. All afternoon, she had carefully copied the words into her notebook in pencil, not daring to use pen and ink near the old page. She was also careful to wear white cotton gloves whenever she handled the delicate vellum.

For weeks, Christina had gone through the marginal notations painstakingly to decipher the areas of tiny, nearly illegible script. She had flipped endlessly through the pages of Sir Hugh's thick Gaelic dictionary, seeking the oldest Irish root of each word she transcribed. Where the correlations were not obvious, she had relied on logic and intuition to discern the meaning.

Finally, she had come to the end of the text. When it was done, she planned to transcribe and translate it all again, to be sure her interpretation was as close as possible. Then she would send a copy to her uncle Walter Carriston to ask for his opinion. She hoped that the ancient verses, never before translated, would stir his interest and improve his spirits, which in turn might benefit his health.

Glancing around the quiet, lamplit library, she wished she could share her discovery with Aedan, too. For the last two days, while she worked in the library or watched Edgar supervise the clearing on Cairn Drishan, she had hardly seen Aedan.

He was still spending long hours at the site of the alternate road, returning too late to share formal meals with the others. Christina suspected he deliberately avoided meeting Edgar, and she wondered if he avoided her, too.

Though she longed to see him, she hesitated to seek him out alone. After the clash in the dining room with Edgar, and after their exquisite, impulsive lovemaking several nights ago, she knew that hot, deep emotions had to be addressed. What existed between her and Aedan had grown too powerful to treat with silence, or even to express with passionate, fevered lovemaking, secret and eloquent. The time had come for truths.

In the last few days, she had come to a realization, and she wanted to tell Aedan what she fiercely believed. Love — true love, soul deep and profound, such as she felt for him — could heal all wounds, break all spells. She wanted him to believe that, too.

But she knew he had to realize it for himself.

Sighing, she rubbed her weary eyes, then reviewed her penciled translation once more, wanting to be certain that it was correct. Though composed about thirteen hundred years earlier, the ancient words still seemed fresh and immediate. The verses astonished her and touched her deeply.

The hope and despair of the sixth-century author rang clear in every phrase, as did his eternal passion for his lost beloved. Christina was utterly certain that her translation was right, and she was sure that the poet was Aedan mac Brudei himself, the Druid prince of Dundrennan's legend.

She traced her fingertip along a verse she had copied:

In dark of night and light of moon,
I, Aedan mac Brudei of Dùn Droigheann,
a prince of Dál Riata, write these words.
I summon thee, Liadan, Daughter of the Bear
To hear me through the mist.
Come to me, my heart.

Shivers cascaded through her, crown to foot, sensual, strangely provocative, for she sensed the strong power of the words. Reading the lines again, Christina suddenly realized, with a startling shock, what the poet had intended.

Wondering if it could be so, she removed her eyeglasses and leaned close to study the aging brownish ink, where his passion still resonated. Heart beating fast with excitement, she looked at her penciled translation.

Liadan, hear me. Come to me, my heart.

"Oh, my God," Christina whispered. Her hands trembled. "It's a spell . . . a magical incantation."

Mouthing the words, feeling something magnificent behind their simplicity, she felt the magic ripple through her, a poignant stirring of her heart. Tears pricked her eyes.

Writing down a spell or a charm would have been forbidden to Druid initiates, she knew from her research and discussions with her uncle. Not only did they protect their secret rituals, but they believed that the written word had force enough to transfix magic in eternity.

Yet Prince Aedan had inscribed, in his own handwriting, a charm to call a lost and wandering soul back to the realm of the living. Loving Liadan, he had risked all for her.

In her hands, Christina held his heartfelt effort to save Liadan's life. According to the legend, the princess had fallen into a deep and endless sleep. Sir Hugh's poem claimed that the princess had fallen victim to the evil enchantment of a rival king. Perhaps she had been ill or injured, Christina thought with a more practical bent.

Now Christina sat reading the words he had penned in secret so long ago. Like a tangible force, Aedan mac Brudei's love for Liadan reached out, flowing through her, heating her blood, stirring her soul. In her mind, his voice echoed across the centuries — and he spoke in Aedan MacBride's quiet, mellow tones.

Sitting there, stunned, she could almost feel the Druid's hand touch her own, warm and firm and impassioned, like the brush of Aedan's own fingers over hers.

Her heart quickened; her head seemed to whirl. The magic in the old verses swept through her, a profound, loving force, so irresistible and deeply comforting that tears began to stream down her cheeks.

Journeying upward, come again down
Journeying outward, come again in
No peril shall befall thee on hill or in heather
Come again homeward, safe to me.

Chapter Twenty-seven

Rousing from rapt concentration, Christina noticed twilight shadows gathering in the library. She turned up the wick of the little oil lamp on the table, its odor lightly pungent. Hearing footsteps, she glanced up.

Amy, Edgar, and Lady Balmossie entered the enormous room to congregate by the fireplace, chatting. When Amy invited her to join them, Christina declined politely and returned to her work.

Touching a hand to her brow, she began to copy the Druid's verses yet again, wanting to confirm her translation. With other people now in the room, the strange magic of the poem faded, but she remained convinced of her conclusions.

"Something certainly has your attention," Edgar said.

She looked up. "Good day, Edgar. Yes, I'm working on that translation I mentioned to you."

Nodding, he stood over her, hands folded behind him. Lady Balmossie and Amy remained seated near the fireplace, and Amy began to read some poetry aloud to her aunt in a soft voice.

"You missed tea, but Mrs. Gunn said you were studying in here, so I was not concerned," Edgar said. "I wanted to tell you that I went to the excavation site today and told the Highland workers to bring the vases up tomorrow and box them for shipment. We will transport them to Edinburgh by train, but they will have to be carefully wrapped, of course."

"I wish you would not move them yet," Christina said. "I'd like more time to examine the pots in their original setting."

He shrugged. "We've seen enough of the Dundrennan site for now. You have thorough notes and sketches. And you can look at the pots at your leisure in the museum."

"I do not think this is a good idea, Edgar." She really did not want to argue with him. For now, she just wanted to be left alone with her translation and her discovery.

"Is that the document from the Dundrennan Folio?" Edgar asked. She nodded, and Edgar came around the table to look at the page over her shoulder.

Murmuring over the parchment's age and condition, he leaned a hand on the table beside her own. "Fascinating," he said. "A military roster. And there are additional lines in the margin."

"Yes. I've translated some, but not all of it." She did not offer to show him what she

438

had found. The verses were too precious, too intimate and personal, to share with anyone but Aedan as yet.

"Some of this is in Latin, I see," he said.

"No, Gaelic — Old Irish, really."

"That is Latin," he said, pointing with one finger.

She stared at one of the cramped and indecipherable lines in the midst of the roster. Suddenly it shifted and made perfect sense, as if it were a moving puzzle. "Oh, I see! I had thought it was Gaelic like the rest of the inscription, but the words are blurred here. Yes, it could be Latin. D, U . . . X . . ." She frowned.

"*Dux bellorum*," Edgar said. "This is a military roster, so *dux bellorum* makes perfect sense. It's the title of a military commander. A warlord in the earliest documents. The term fell out of use and became 'grand duke' in later ages."

She stared up at Edgar, feeling the blood rush in her ears. "Of course! *Dux bellorum* was used by the ancient chroniclers Nennius and Gildas to describe Britain's greatest warlord, Arthur. I had not seen it on this list before now."

"The term might have been used rather broadly for warlords in the early centuries," he said. Edgar was an expert on knights, armor, and medieval weaponry. Although well versed on Arthurian matters, too, he was among the scholars who disdained Walter Carriston's theories about King Arthur in Scotland. That had always been a point of intellectual tension between Christina and Edgar, as she embraced her uncle's work wholeheartedly.

She sat up straight, her thoughts sparking. "Perhaps it refers to Aedan mac Brudei, the Druid warrior prince who became the ancestor of the Dundrennan MacBrides. Thank you, Edgar. I missed that reference."

"You've been working too hard, Christina."

She frowned. "Perhaps so." She put away her notes, feeling uncomfortable with his cool blue-eyed stare.

"Sir Edgar, come listen," Amy called. "You wanted to hear me read some of Sir Hugh's poetry. Christina, will you join us?"

"No, thank you. I'm rather tired." She smiled.

"I'll be there in a few moments, Miss Stewart," Edgar said, and he turned back to Christina. "You promised to show me your excavating notes. Are they here?"

"Yes, but — I think I'll do some reading in my room this evening. May we go over the notes tomorrow?"

"Of course, my dear. The responsibility of this excavation has strained your fragile feminine nature. I'd like to see your notes before the jars are removed. If you can leave them for me now, I'll read them and leave them for you here on this table."

She nodded, her attention distracted by her great desire to work with the Druid's verses and her disappointment that she could not continue with Edgar hovering over her. Reaching into the leather case that held her writing materials, she took out the journal that held her notes on Cairn Drishan and tucked the notebook with her translations into the case, pausing to wrap the parchments in silk once again. Edgar took the memorandum journal and wished her a good night before he joined Amy and her aunt.

After returning the parchments to Sir Hugh's study and leaving her leather case in the cabinet with them, Christina left the library, bidding the others good night.

As she opened the door, she heard Amy begin Sir Hugh's epic poem about the Viking invasion of Scotland. Considering the poem's length, they would be sitting there quite a while, Christina thought, glad she had not stayed to listen.

Climbing the main stairs to her room, her thoughts raced. *Dux bellorum . . . Liadan nighean Math-ghamhainn . . . Daughter of the Bear . . .*

Then she stopped, hand on the banister. "*Dux bellorum . . .* a great leader . . . and 'Artorius' in Latin means 'The bear!' "

Suddenly it all became clear. King Arthur was linked to early Scotland — and the evidence existed in the Dundrennan Folio. Now, standing there, her mind racing, she realized that there might be further evidence on Cairn Drishan.

Some of the clay vessels in the souterrain carried the design of bears, she remembered. Until now, she had not taken the mental leap to connect the bears on the pots, Liadan's epithet as Daughter of the Bear, and the alternate meaning of Arthur's name.

Now she had to know for her uncle's sake — and for the sake of Dundrennan and its laird — if she was right.

Running upstairs to her room, heart pounding, she changed out of her black slippers into leather brogans and snatched her black hat, gloves, and half-length cape. She would have to go up to Cairn Drishan now. Edgar had asked the Gowans to move those pots in the morning.

With Edgar occupied in the library, her brother busy in the dining room on his mural, and Aedan out somewhere working on his road, Christina had the perfect opportunity to search for a clue.

Hurrying downstairs, she grabbed her walking stick and made her way out of the quiet, dim house, striding out over the moor.

Under a mother-of-pearl moon, through purple twilight, Christina reached the top of Cairn Drishan. A pale flash brightened the sky, and she heard a distant rumble. Pausing beside the ancient wall, she felt a slight tremor underfoot.

Not thunder and lightning this time, but a far-off blast, she thought. Aedan and his men must be setting charges along the new section of the road. As the sound and shaking faded, the wind whispered quietly around her again. Then she heard the muffled chug of the steam shovel.

Even now, Aedan was on the other side of the massive slope, only a mile or two away. She wanted to go and find him now, to tell him about her discoveries and her hopes. But she had come up here to look inside the souterrain, and that had to come first.

Aedan might not share her excitement, and with good reason. Thanks to his father's will and the ancient find, his hold on Dundrennan was already precarious. A discovery of this magnitude would topple Aedan's claim on his own estate entirely.

Frowning, feeling torn between her love for Aedan and her love for her work, Christina walked to the souterrain and removed a corner of the tarpaulin. She climbed down the wooden ladder, stumbling a little in the dark pit below, groped around to find the candle and matchbox kept there, and lit the flame.

Looking around, she breathed a sigh of relief. Angus and his sons had not yet moved the pots. Oblong and waist high, they were stacked two deep against the far wall. The rest of the little chamber was empty, the walls faced with mossy stones, the floor packed earth, which the protection of the tarpaulin had kept dry despite the rain of the past weeks.

Kneeling, Christina moved the candle slowly to examine the clay jars. Their shoulders were decorated in brownish paint, showing a variety of decoration — chained loops, swirls, key mazes, and elegantly contoured animals. Some of the jars bore fat handles in clay. All of them were sealed with thick wax.

Two pots, placed together, carried depictions of bear-like creatures. Scuttling over to them, heedless of her skirt in the earth, Christina examined the designs more closely in the candlelight. The abstract linear images were certainly bearlike.

Setting her candle dish on the ground, she tipped one of the pots cautiously and found it was heavier than she thought. Reaching into her reticule, she removed her little sewing scissors and attempted to remove the waxen plug.

Overhead, she heard the muffled noise of yet another blast on the far side of the hill. The ground beneath her shook a little, dirt and small stones spitting down around her. The candle fell over and went out.

In dense blackness, she fumbled for the

taper, inserted it in the dish, then relit the wick. The souterrain bloomed with light once again.

When she saw Aedan next, she must tell him that the blastings, even so far away, did indeed affect the ancient site. But the underground chamber was snug and well made, lined with heavy stones. She was not concerned about collapse, for it had stood secure for centuries.

After some tugging and a few inarticulate groans on her part, the plug finally cracked loose from the rim, allowing her to pull it up in one piece.

Then she reeled backward. "Ohhh!"

The odor was awful. Holding her nose, she approached the pot tentatively, afraid to bring the candle close in case the substance ignited. Peering inside, she saw black muck and replaced the plug quickly.

Turning to the second bear-marked pot, she began to work at the wax seal, which was stubborn. Changing the angle of her assault, she saw a single word painted over one of the lugs.

Or. In Gaelic — and Latin — it meant gold.

She sat back, her hands shaking. The pot had been here all the time, mixed with the others, and no one had noticed its tiny label. Gold and a bear — had she found King Arthur's gold?

Hardly daring to hope, she struggled with

the seal, then popped it with a flourish and a small cry of triumph. A sweetish smell wafted out — nothing fermented or rotted, she realized with great relief. Leaning forward, heart slamming, she held the candle high and saw the glint of a thick, golden substance.

She poked at it with the tip of her sewing scissors. It oozed lazily. Honey. The pot was filled with honey.

Gold, indeed, she thought. And bears with honey — how very apt. Sighing, she replaced the plug, then sat staring at the pots for a moment, greatly disappointed.

Crawling from one pot to the next, her confidence higher now that she had the knack of popping the seals, she opened one vessel after another, peeked inside, and replaced the wax seals.

She found oats preserved so fresh and dry that they sifted through her hand, and folded cloths of a beautiful weave that she dared not touch in case they disintegrated. She discovered desiccated root vegetables, dried meats, and more honey. Several of the pots held wine and beer, only two of which smelled sour.

But she found no treasure of gold or precious items, and nothing to hint at links with Artorius the Bear, *dux bellorum,* or Aedan mac Brudei and his Liadan.

Sighing, convinced that the evening's mission had been a failure — but for the fact that she now knew what was in those pots — she wiped her gloved hands on her skirt and rose to her feet. There was no more she could do here tonight.

Blowing out the candle, she set it on the little stone shelf Hector had placed there and went to the ladder. As she put her foot on the bottom rung, she heard the crunch of stones above, near the lip of the opening. Wondering if the explosions had loosened something, she paused.

Then she saw a man appear beside the opening of the souterrain, his lean form silhouetted against the violet sky.

Edgar.

In the darkness, he would not have seen her yet. She stepped away from the ladder and walked backward, shaking with a sudden, unreasonable fear, though she knew that he was no threat to her.

Then she saw his boots and trousered legs as he began to descend the ladder into the souterrain. With nowhere to hide, she knew he would find her.

And this was only Edgar, after all, who could be selfish and annoying but had never meant her harm. Lighting the candle again, she stepped forward in silence.

He leaped, startled, and stepped down to the earthen floor. "Christina, there you are! I came as soon as I could."

"Came after me? How did you know I was

here? I — I wanted to study the pots again before they were moved."

He stepped forward. "I read your notes."

"The excavation notes? But why would you come here, Edgar?"

"Not just the excavation notes. I read your translation, as well. That cabinet is shamefully easy to open."

"You opened Sir Hugh's cabinet? Why?" His tone seemed odd, his expression unusually intent. Aware that she was alone with him in this strange, eerie place, she felt suddenly wary, although she had never feared Edgar before. When she had been here with Aedan, she had wanted to stay forever. Now some sense told her to leave, quickly and urgently.

"My dear," he said. "Did you think the true meaning of *dux bellorum* escaped me? I am familiar with your uncle's work on Celtic Scotland, and I know all there is to know about the historical King Arthur, the supreme *dux bellorum* of Dark Age Britain. I am an authority in such military matters."

"Yes, I know that. But what do you expect to find here? You said yourself there was nothing significant in this site."

"I suspect I came here tonight for the same reason you did, my dear, I came to find the gold. King Arthur's gold."

Edgar walked toward her. Christina eased toward the ladder. But he reached out and snatched her wrist in a sudden and painful grip, yanking her toward him.

"Come here," he said, and he drew her to the far end of the chamber, where the cluster of jars stood in darkness. Taking the candle dish from her and grasping her wrist tightly, Edgar moved the light over the vessels.

"When I first came to the hill," he said, "I admit it was a disappointment. I hoped you would unearth something here, but you fussed about with toothbrushes and new methods, delaying everything. I thought to take the vases back to Edinburgh and examine them at my leisure there. I knew you were looking for the gold, too — you had to be. Your uncle would have put the idea in your head as soon as he learned you were coming to Dundrennan."

"Actually," she said, tugging, "he never mentioned it."

"No? Sir Hugh himself told me about the gold. He was certain that it was on his estate somewhere, and he regretted never finding a clue to its whereabouts. I convinced him that a codicil to his will would protect any treasure that might be found later. Of course, I was determined to find it myself, if it existed."

She blinked. "The codicil was your suggestion?"

"Of course. I had Sir Hugh's ear by then. He was a brilliant man, but not a practical

449

one. He was relieved to have a sound plan to protect the historical worth of his estate. When his son blasted through the hill and found the wall, I was delighted — I knew it might lead to the treasure at last. Of course, I could not appear too eager, so I sent you here first, to clear the way."

"So you always thought the find was important, even though you said otherwise."

"I did doubt it lately — until I read your notes tonight," Edgar said. "There are some intriguing coincidences between the local legend and this site and now that ancient document you translated. The meaning isn't clear to me yet, but it has to do with King Arthur — and so it must involve that lost treasure."

"Edgar, there is nothing here. I have looked. And the translation has nothing to do with any of this."

"Perhaps not, outside of the reference to the Daughter of the Bear," he said. "Curious little document, though. Why do you suppose the MacBride ancestor wrote those very strange charms?"

"I have no idea," she said firmly. She wanted to keep secret the magical intent of Aedan mac Brudei's phrases. Having felt their mysterious force, she must protect that power and the purity of that ancient love from Edgar.

"Why do you want to find this gold so

very much? You are a wealthy man, after all."

"A man can always use more, my dear. Ask Aedan MacBride — it's said he has little left of his inheritance," he added. "But it's not fortune I want. Imagine a treasure hidden by King Arthur's own hand! It would be the most important historical discovery of our age." He smiled coldly. "I want the glory of that, quite simply. I do not want your uncle to take it, or you — God forbid a woman should be given credit for such an accomplishment. Nor should it be attached to the memory of Sir Hugh. No, this must be my find. I have dreamed of it all my life, since I first read of King Arthur's deeds when I was young."

"But you did not want to do the work of finding it yourself."

"Of course not," he said easily. He considered the pots. "Now, tell me — did you open these? What did you find?"

"I found nothing that would interest you," she said sharply.

He sighed. "I see I must find it myself, without your help." He glanced at her in the darkness. Suddenly he looked sardonic and truly dangerous.

How could she have been so wrong about him? All her life she had trusted too well, too quickly. Aedan loathed Neaves, and her brother disliked him, too. Both had tried to

451

warn her. She knew about Edgar's lesser qualities, but she had refused to accept that he was capable of real cruelty or wrongdoing. She had refused to see Stephen's darker qualities, too, and it had ruined his life and nearly ruined her own.

Now she would pay, for Edgar could not let her walk away unharmed from this night. He was an academic to his core, but he was mad with it, keen for a glory he had not earned.

He twisted her arm to pull her closer, shining the candlelight over the pots. "The clues are all coming together now, like a puzzle to be solved. It's as if the gold was meant to be found at last. And I mean to be the one to do it."

A shiver ran through her. Mad as he might be, Edgar was right. Destiny had arranged this, somehow. Every step of the way, from her arrival at Dundrennan, she had felt the workings of magic, and not only in the Druid's incantations. Here at Dundrennan, she had felt the profound magic of true love. She had found her heart and the true home of her soul.

No matter what happened this night, she would never leave Aedan and Dundrennan — never. Nor could she allow Edgar to harm them or steal Aedan's chance at happiness.

"Curious," Edgar murmured again, thoughtfully, then bent toward the pots.

She tried to pull away from his grasp. "I really must go now. Do what you want here, but it's very late, and we will be expected for supper. And we should not be here alone."

"It's best we're alone, really. You cannot go anywhere now, my dear. I never wanted to hurt you, but if you cannot help me, you shall have to be silenced somehow. This magnificent discovery depends on it." He glanced around the dark and eerie chamber. "I suspect this place is not safe — at least, not safe for you."

Chapter Twenty-eight

"What?" Aedan called over the rasp and groan of the steam shovel. Hector hollered again, and Aedan strode toward him.

"I said," Hector called as they neared each other, "I saw Sir Edgar walking up to Cairn Drishan a bit ago!"

"Why would he come out here so late?" Aedan asked, startled.

"Most likely to fash ye over summat that doesna please him," Hector said. "He wants Angus and his lads on the hill at screech o' day to move those pots."

"Damn," Aedan muttered. "We do not need his harassment now. His business can wait until morning."

Hector glanced up. "Ye'll see him back at the hoose soon enough, for the rain is here again, and we'll have to give this up for the night. We've had a curse o' rain lately."

"It's sprinkling," Aedan said, holding out the palm of his hand to feel light raindrops. "We'll work as long as we can."

"Aye then," Hector said. A grinding sound emanated from the mechanical monster behind them. "Robbie Gowan!" Hector called, turning toward Angus's older son. "Back that beastie up, if ye will. The damn shovel is striking the rock there. We'll take it from a new angle." The young man complied, calling and coaxing the oxen until the cart holding the steam shovel backed up.

Gazing at the harsh profile of the peak against the darkening sky, Aedan frowned thoughtfully. He wanted to know why Edgar Neaves had come out to the hill so late at night.

Turning, he saw that his work crew was busy, some men still digging and grubbing, some overseeing the noisy, finicky steam shovel, others inspecting the results of the most recent blasting. After several minutes, Aedan realized that Edgar had not headed for the construction site.

Raindrops fell thicker, fatter, soon increasing to a downpour that began to soak through his vest and shirt. Aedan swore low in exasperation. Grabbing his jacket, he shrugged it on as he walked toward Hector MacDonald and Angus Gowan.

"We'll have to stop work for the evening after all, with this rain," Aedan told them. "Tell the lads to turn off the steam shovel, if you will." Hector nodded and ran off to do so.

"Sir," Angus said. "Did the mistress come up here?"

Aedan stared at him. "Mrs. Blackburn? I

thought it was Sir Edgar Neaves who came up the hill."

"I did not see him, but I saw the mistress earlier. She was climbing the other side of the hill."

Aedan frowned. "Odd," he murmured. "Are you sure?"

"I am sure that Sir Edgar does not wear a lady's skirt," Angus answered. "If he came later, then they are both there now, by the old wall, for I am not seeing anyone leave the hill."

Aedan turned before Angus finished his sentence. Instantly alarmed and greatly suspicious, he headed for the rough upper slope that led toward a high peak of the hill. From there, he could see the site of the excavation.

Slanting rain and deep shadows made the climb treacherous, and Aedan went hand over hand, placing his booted feet surely and rapidly, climbing over the toothy rocks even as fine sheets of rain turned every surface slippery. But he went upward without hesitation, knowing that this was the quickest way to reach the excavation site — and Christina.

A cold feeling in his gut told him to hurry.

"Where is it?" Edgar muttered, prying off one waxen lid after another. He had cracked a few of the pots, and the contents lay strewn on the ground. Three candles flickered inside the chamber now to afford him more light as he examined the pots.

Huddled in a corner, her hands tied with rope that the work crew had left there earlier, Christina watched Edgar silently. He had tied her wrists in front of her and bound her ankles, with polite apologies and a stiff tug on the ropes.

Since then, he had looked inside the pots as she had done. But he had dumped some of contents on the floor, tilting jars and tossing things about impatiently.

While the rain beat on the tarpaulin, open enough to let in drizzling rain, Christina sat amid multicolored patterned weavings, piles of spilled grain, sloshes of wine, and an ooze of honey, which dripped from a crack in one of the pots marked with the bear design.

Her heart broke to see the destruction, and she ached to think what might happen if Edgar found what he searched for.

"Where the devil is it?" Edgar muttered. He yanked out a cloth that shredded as Christina watched. He threw it aside.

"Edgar, please stop," Christina said. "Think of the immense historical meaning of these things —"

"What is missing from this batch is far more important," he answered. "That gold must be here somewhere. After the princess fell into her sleep, or whatever happened to her, King Arthur himself sent the mourning prince a gift — isn't that the legend?"

"Something like that. But a magic spell was laid over the treasure. It will never be found until the princess wakes, or so Sir Hugh wrote in his poem."

"Yes, I've read it countless times. 'Deck'd in raiment of the sun. A mighty horde of treasure bright . . . Hidden forever in perpetual night . . . so long as the beauty sleeps.' That gold has to be here somewhere." He looked around, frantic.

"It is not here, Edgar," she said wearily. "I have looked."

"I hoped to trust you with the first part of this task, but you have not managed it well at all, my dear."

"How kind of you to point it out," she said sourly.

"I will not give up, now that this Pictish site has been found." He pried at the lid of another jar. "For years, I studied your uncle's work and read every word Sir Hugh wrote. So I was certain there was a strong connection between Arthur, the Scots, and Dundrennan. I wanted to find it for the world."

"But you agreed with the scholars who dismissed my uncle's work as preposterous," she argued.

"Well, I didn't want to ruin my own good reputation," he said pragmatically. "But privately, I suspected that he and Sir Hugh were both right. Arthur was here in this region of

Scotland, at least for a short while."

"My uncle would have appreciated your support as a museum director. He would have benefited greatly from your goodwill."

"But he became a laughingstock for his Arthurian theories! I could not associate myself with that — I needed the proof first."

"All you needed was a little courage of conviction, Edgar. You might have seen things very differently, had you done that."

"But it's so much easier this way."

"Let others do the work, and you take the credit? How can you live with that?"

"How could I resist? Guilt and conscience are tedious on a frequent basis, I find." He slapped a waxen seal into place impatiently and popped free the next one. "The evidence is too compelling to overlook. Dundrennan is near Loch Lomond, which your uncle identified as a site of one of Arthur's famous twelve battles. The lands of this very estate could have held one of Arthur's strongholds or the fortress of one of his supporters."

"The prince, Aedan mac Brudei?" she asked breathlessly.

"It could be. The Dundrennan legends support that. King Arthur would not have gifted gold to just anyone, you see. Put that together with the mention of *dux bellorum* and . . . and it all makes sense. That gold was given to Aedan mac Brudei, just as the stories claim . . . and this structure probably belonged to that prince. Therefore, it is most likely here somewhere. If not in the storage chamber, then somewhere above, inside those walls."

"If all you ever cared about was making a magnificent discovery," she said, "then that means you never truly cared for me at all." She hoped to distract him from his destructive course with the jars and perhaps remind him of his humane side — if indeed he could reclaim that at all.

"You're a bonny wee fool, Christina," Edgar said mildly. "Have I not been devoted to you for years? I fell under your spell the moment I first saw you." The way he said that sent revulsion shuddering through her. "I have been very sincere about marrying you. A pity you could never agree to it."

"And now?" she asked. "You've tied me here — you've threatened me. Will you not let me go, for love's sake?"

He sighed, set down the wax lid, and came toward her, bending down to one knee. Reaching out, he stroked her cheek. "So lovely . . . something so innocent about you, despite your . . . luscious appearance and your . . . lack of good judgement at times. I fell in love with you years ago, my dear, when I saw Stephen's painting. My God, what a seductress you are in that image. I knew one day you would be mine," he murmured. "I cannot resist your power. Dear Christina," he said, sliding his fingers into her hair.

He forced her head back then, kissing her suddenly, his mouth moist and eager, his lips working heavily over hers. His tongue plunged into her mouth.

Nearly gagging, she turned her head away, her hat sliding askew, the satin ribbons dragging at her throat. Edgar grabbed her by the shoulders, growling in his passion, pulling her toward him. She booted him in the stomach with her joined feet, knocking him backward.

"Edgar," she gasped, "stop!"

He gathered himself up, and when he snatched at her again, she kicked harder, knocking into his legs. Struggling, she slid down the wall, her petticoats frothing around her ankles.

"Christina, my dear, please —" He groped for her, pulled her toward him, his hand closing at her waist and inching toward her breast. "We could do this together, you and I. It would be a brilliant triumph of scholarship and a brilliant match. All you need do is . . . give me your trust, your belief."

"Edgar, leave me be —" she began. A movement in the shadows caught her attention. Suddenly, behind Edgar, who still clawed at her, she saw a lean, athletic figure.

Aedan's face looked hard and dangerous, his jaw tight with anger. Growling, he snatched Edgar and dragged him off Christina.

Edgar whirled and struck out, and the two

men grappled until Aedan grabbed Edgar by his carefully tied stock and gave him a solid punch upward to the jaw. Edgar sank to one knee, groaning. Aedan hauled him upward again and held him by the collar.

"Touch her again," Aedan growled fiercely, "ever, and you will die, I swear it." He shook Edgar almost easily, although the man was taller, and threw him back. Edgar's back struck the wall, and he slumped, then lost his balance and fell to one knee.

Christina struggled to her feet, leaning against the wall, her skirts more a hindrance than her roped wrists and ankles. "Aedan," she gasped.

He glanced toward her, and Edgar leaped for him, his hands like pale claws at Aedan's throat. Christina cried out just as Aedan broke Edgar's hold and shoved him backward. Grabbing Edgar by a handful of his brocade vest, he pushed him again, so that Edgar's shoulders hit the wall. Advancing, Aedan pinned him to the wall with a forearm, using his body to block Edgar's flailing arms and legs.

"And as for finding King Arthur's gold," Aedan said in a vicious tone, "that right is reserved for me and mine. So says the legend. When the princess awakes, they say" — he shoved Edgar hard against the wall again — "the gold will be found. Not until then. Certainly not by you!"

As he spoke, he tore off Edgar's cravat and used it to bind the man's wrists, forcing Edgar into submission. Now the taller man seemed to cower, trying to hide his face, as if he had no real spirit for fighting.

Christina hobbled a few steps to come closer. "Aedan, how did you know Edgar wanted to find King Arthur's gold?"

"I heard what you and Edgar said," he replied, tying the knots tightly around Edgar's wrists and forcing him to sit. "I was coming down the ladder. Neither of you noticed me."

"Then you saw him kiss me and saw me fend him off, and you did not come to my defense immediately?" she asked indignantly.

He glanced at her. "You defended yourself quite nicely, Mrs. Blackburn," he said dryly. "If you had needed help, I would have interfered. I thought you might want to pummel Edgar a bit before I took over."

She opened her mouth to reply when Edgar lunged, bowling Aedan to his knees. They rolled to the ground, Aedan beneath, and Edgar threw a knee into Aedan's stomach and wrestled away. Grunting, Aedan dived for the other man, who slithered past him and grabbed the ladder, attempting to scramble up the rungs, his wrists tied but his legs free.

Standing, hopping about, Christina shrieked as Aedan threw himself toward the ladder, reaching to pull Edgar down. Attaining the top of the ladder, Neaves butted his head against the tarpaulin to push it aside and make his escape. Rain dripped from the heavy cloth as he shoved against it.

Then a gush and a monstrous sucking sound as a deluge of rain and mud poured into the souterrain like a black waterfall. The thick cascade blew Edgar and Aedan back and collapsed the ladder. Muck rushed into the chamber, dousing the candles, crashing into the cluster of pots, shattering them.

Christina screamed as the flood tore through the chamber and poured toward her. Choking, gasping, suddenly all she could see was darkness. The force struck her hard against the wall, and she felt her head hit hard, so that all sound and motion seemed to stop for an instant. Then the mossy stones behind her gave way, and she felt the wall somehow shift behind her, beneath her, and the ooze swept her with it, through the wall and into the earth.

Helpless, she went into that nightmare abyss like a doll in a current.

The mud took him with all the force of a water beast, picking him up, whirling him, spewing him out again. He slammed into a wall, dropped into ooze, came up on his hands and knees. Coughing, groping in the blackness, he felt the stones in the wall like a welcome anchor in a storm.

"Christina!" His voice echoed strangely. "Christina!"

Staggering to his feet, he groped his way along the wall. A few steps later, he fell over what he realized was Edgar's body, slimed and motionless. Aedan knew almost immediately after grabbing the man's shoulders that Edgar was lifeless. Somehow he had died in the onrush of mud and water — perhaps he had fallen and broken his neck. Propping the body against the wall, out of the muck as much as possible, Aedan sighed heavily and turned again, searching through the darkness, unable to see or to orient his location in the chamber.

"Christina!" he called. Silence. He called again, nearly sobbing out her name, desperate for her answer. Only silence.

Feeling his way along the wall, moving through heavy mud, he suddenly felt his arm plunge into a depth of darkness. Somehow the stones in the wall had tilted, unbelievably, into earth. He realized there was a hollow space in the hillside, behind the wall of the souterrain. He stepped through.

The force of the mud had broken through the wall into what appeared to be a second chamber, for Aedan struck stone overhead. Too tall for the space, he could not straighten completely. Lifting his hand, he felt a ceiling made of earth and rock, its pattern deliberate and man-made.

He edged forward, then stumbled over something in the pitch blackness. Dropping to one knee, he explored with his hands, his fingers realizing what his eyes could not see.

"Christina," he murmured.

She lay on her back in mud, unmoving, silent. Under his hands, her head lolled, her arms sagged, but he could find no obvious wounds, no broken bones. Gently he scooped under her head and shoulders and gathered her to him as he knelt, terrified that he would discover what he had found with Edgar.

Then he sensed the faint rhythm of her breathing. He sighed in utter relief, but realized she was unconscious. He needed to find out the nature of her injury. Groping in his inner jacket pocket, he found the silver flask, a slender candle stub, and a box of matches, items he often carried when working late hours.

Leaning her weight against him, he touched off a match and lit the candle wick, which sputtered and flared into blessed light. He set the taper on a protrusion of stone, noticing that the surrounding walls of the close space were lined in stone like the outermost chamber.

The light spilled over her face. Mud spattered and strangely serene in his arms, her features were peaceful, her eyes sweetly closed. He stroked his fingers over her cheek and saw a cut and a bruise on her temple. The force of the mud slide must have thrown her against stone, rendering her unconscious, then knocked her through the hidden doorway like a battering ram.

He looked around. The door, made up of several stones backing a single slab on its opposite side, had been disguised as part of the wall of the storage chamber. The onslaught of mud had tilted it inward. The second chamber was tiny, lined in stone and filled with a profusion of objects, so many Aedan could hardly take it all in — pots, stone carvings, what looked like a bench, harnesses hanging on the wall, and something that looked like a chariot, wicker sided, iron wheeled.

And gold. He saw it glitter and wink all around him in the feeble candlelight. Bowls, vessels, gleaming torques wrought for a man's neck, hammered armbands and wristlets stacked haphazardly. Gold shaped an engraved bowl, glittered in a jumble of wire-wrapped handles in an array of daggers.

Blinking, stunned, he looked at it for only a moment — the woman in his arms was far more important to him just then. She was breathing steadily, if shallowly. He could not see her eyes, and that sight would be more precious to him right now than an ancient king's ransom. He bent down.

"Christina," he whispered. "Christina, my

love." He kissed her brow, her eyelids, her soft, unresponsive mouth. "Wake up. Please. Oh God. Please wake up." He felt desperation rise in him like a tide, felt his own soul surge within him.

"I love you," he whispered. No words had ever come more naturally, more truthfully, to his lips.

She did not stir, scarcely breathed. Desperation gave way to determination, and he felt sheer will rise up within him. "Come back," he said firmly, and he framed her face with his hands. "Come back."

Come homeward to me.
Drawn forward like a boat slipping inward on the tide, she moved through darkness, through peacefulness, feeling lazy and languid, content to follow the stream that carried her forward, had carried her for ages. Centuries might have passed, or mere moments — she did not know. Outside the span of time, caught in the dark void, she had floated, lost, forever.

She heard his voice, her beloved. His love surrounded her, gathered itself into substance like a silvery ribbon, wove itself into a sparkling net and drew her along with it. Slow, steady, the force kept her safe, kept her from slipping into the void. That compassionate strength had not forgotten her, had loved her forever, had found her at last.

His magic drew her upward, upward. She climbed as if on the earth, swam as if in an ocean, rose on a carrying wind, and then she soared, borne on the breath of a flame.

Come again homeward, safe to me.

My love, she tried to say, *I hear you.*

She felt his touch upon her cheek, and she opened her eyes.

He smiled, her beloved, his eyes brilliant blue in candlelight. His love overflowed her, warm, golden, and healing. She lifted her hand to touch his face in wonder.

He kissed her fingers as she traced his mouth, his smile. He bent toward her.

"I love you," he whispered. "I always have."

Epilogue

"Mrs. Blackburn," Aedan murmured, seating himself carefully on the edge of the bed, so that Christina would not jar where she lay. "There you are, awake at last. We've been worried about you. We thought you might sleep forever." Smiling, Aedan leaned down to kiss her cheek. His hand slipped over hers.

"Come now, I've only slept the afternoon," she murmured as she gazed up at him with a slow smile, her cheeks pale, without the subtle pink glow that he so loved to see. She glanced past him toward the doorway, where John, Amy, Mrs. Gunn, and Lady Balmossie stood clustered together. Christina wiggled her fingers in a feeble little wave.

"Och, she's still tired, puir wee lass," Mrs. Gunn said. "But 'tis good to see her with her eyes open."

"Come. We'll leave her to rest," Lady Balmossie said.

"Not Aedan," Amy said. "I think he should sit with her for a while and read her poetry, talk to her. Christina needs to feel safe after that awful experience. She was ill for days, and she slept so long that I was afraid she might never recover —"

"Hush, my dear girl," John said affectionately. "She's well now, and she's quite safe. Come along. I want to show you something — I've nearly finished your portrait in the mural," he said, and Amy gasped in delight. John pulled the door partially closed as he spoke.

Aedan glanced over his shoulder. "He left it open a bit. I suppose that's for propriety's sake — since we're alone together, you and I." He brushed a waft of dark, glossy hair away from her forehead. "But I think we'll be proper . . . at least for now." He raised one brow. "I cannot guarantee it later."

Christina smiled up at him, her eyes a clear, sparkling hazel. "Sir Aedan," she said, her voice sleepy. "I think I adore you."

"Is it so?" He smiled a little and tucked the covers higher. "And I feel the same about you, Mrs. Blackburn."

"Christina," she whispered.

"Christina," he repeated, leaning down to kiss her lips. Her eyes drifted shut, as did his, and he felt her mouth move beneath his, gently. Though he knew she was weak still, his body responded deeply to her kiss, like lightning all through him. His heart and breath moved faster, but he drew back, wrapping her hand in his, kissing her knuckles.

Her smile was content, even serene, but

471

her eyes danced with a little mischief as she watched him. She lay propped on several pillows, her dark hair flowing loose, her prim white bedgown embroidered around its high-necked collar.

Chaste and lovely, she looked younger and lighter somehow, Aedan thought, as if years and cares had washed away while she slept. The bruise on her brow had faded in a week's time, and she was pale and seemed thinner. She wore an air of peacefulness that seemed new, and that glow suited her beauty very well.

"You've missed quite a bit this week, while you've been lazing about and dreaming," he murmured.

She laughed, breathy and quick. "I've heard more than you thought I did of the conversations around me, though I often felt too sleepy and vague to answer. And the dreams were very nice, might I add."

"Good," he said, holding her hand, stroking her fingers. "Hector and the Gowans have been clearing the mud out of the souterrain all week. They've made a path through to the second chamber, and we've done what we could to clean the area and protect it for now, until you are strong enough to get back to your work. You should have seen Hector when he first saw that gold," he added wryly.

"I remember a little of that, I think, when you carried me out of there. I seem to recall that Hector nearly crowed with delight." She smiled, but it was quickly followed by a sigh.

"The gold was found, but I'm sorry to say that your pots were destroyed. The men have collected the shards as best they could. The mud slide was the result of weeks of rain, the excavation, and the blasting. We kept the explosions small, but sometimes mud slides and landslides cannot be avoided."

She nodded, and smoothed her fingers over the back of his hand. "Poor Edgar," she whispered.

Aedan brought her hand to his lips and kissed it again. "I'm sure he died very quickly, my love. It's ironic that he never lived to see the treasure he coveted."

Christina sighed. "I know he had ill designs, but until that day I never thought him a bad man, just arrogant. He must have been a bit mad. You tried to warn me."

"I knew, deep down, he could not be trusted."

"But it was not the gold he wanted, not for himself. He wanted to be the one who discovered the only real evidence of King Arthur in Scotland — or anywhere, for that matter. He knew that the Dundrennan legends offered the best hope of finding something. The temptation drove him to what he did."

"Ironic, as I said. Now you will have the credit for this amazing discovery. Have I told you that we've heard from the museum? Several, in fact, including the British Museum and the Louvre. We will have a contingent of historians here within the week. I made it clear to each of them in my reply letters that Mrs. Christina Blackburn will be in charge of the operation to explore the find of the century."

She tilted her head as she looked up at him. "We have found treasure, but we do not yet know if it belonged to King Arthur."

"There must be some basis for the long-standing tradition. Remember the legend — that 'mighty horde of treasure bright,' and so forth," he said, quoting from his father's poem.

"We do not yet know if this is that horde. Still, Uncle Walter will be delighted with it, whether the find proves his own theories or not."

Aedan nodded. "If your uncle is strong enough, my dear, I wish to arrange for him and your aunt to stay at Dundrennan. My sister is a nurse and her husband a doctor. We shall invite them at the same time, to have their skills available."

"Oh, Aedan, thank you. Uncle Walter will find the strength for this journey, I'm sure. I can hardly wait to go up to Cairn Drishan and see these things myself. Perhaps I'll be strong enough this evening. Or tomorrow."

"Not just yet, my lass. And when you do

go, I'd rather carry you up that hill myself than have you walk it so soon after that head injury."

"I'm perfectly fine," she said. "Really, I feel wonderful."

"Do you, indeed?" he murmured, and he leaned down, his hands on either side of her, to kiss her cheek and nuzzle the silken cream of her throat. "You do feel rather wonderful," he murmured.

She laughed and looped her arms around his neck. Holding her, he closed his eyes, cherishing their embrace. She felt thin and fragile under his hands, and he laid her back down gently.

"Tell me something," he said, "so that I will not seem an ignorant fool when I correspond with the erudites at these various museums. Could this chamber be a tomb?"

"It is more likely a treasure room, though I have not yet seen it in detail. But from what we saw that first night — and I remember little of it — and from what I've heard over the week, it sounds like a hidden safe room. Souterrains are sometimes multichambered. There might even be a whole warren of underground rooms and passages inside that hill, possibly a tomb as well. We will have to excavate it carefully, and that will take a very long time." She looked at him. "I'm so sorry."

"Sorry? This is an astonishing discovery."

"You may well lose the property now, according to the laws of Treasure Trove and your father's odd codicil. This is a historical find of huge importance, whether Arthurian or not."

He frowned. "Well, I am hoping that Edgar was right about the compromise the museum is willing to make." An inner instinct told him that a solution existed and would be found. He realized that his sense of dread about losing his home had vanished, replaced by a feeling of security and guarantee.

"Oh," he said. "I brought something out of there to show you. It's the only thing I moved, but I thought you might want to see it in particular. I left the rest of that fine stuff in place — all the little silver bowls, enameled brooches, golden buckles, silver and brass helmets, brass shields, and so on."

"Stop," she said, laughing. "I cannot bear it. I want to see it for myself, so much. Let's go tonight. Would you really carry me all the way up the hill?"

"Hush, you," he said wryly. "I will not. Now look at this, for I think it might keep you content for a day or two." He stood to fetch a box from the table where he had set it, wrapped in cloth. After coming back to the bed, he sat again on its edge.

The box, when she dropped away the cloth, was of hammered and chased silver, trimmed with engraved brass panels, its base large enough to fill Aedan's two spread hands.

"Oh!" she said in delight. "It looks like a reliquary box, meant to hold a religious object or something very precious." Christina gently lifted the latch. Inside was a book with a cover of delicate silver over leather, holding bound parchment sheets.

"I have no gloves on," Christina said. "I should not —"

"It will not suffer from your touch this once. Go ahead. I think there is something important in there."

Gingerly she lifted the volume and opened the fragile pages with care, studying them in silence. "These first few pages look like the muster roll in the Dundrennan Folio," she finally said.

Aedan peered at it. Like the military roster in his father's library, the page was covered in neatly written columns. He could tell that it listed names. "Can you read it?" he asked.

"It's an early genealogy of your family, I think," she said tentatively, turning another page. "Yes, there — Aedan mac Brudei, see it? And — oh!" She gasped, tipped the book closer. "Here is her name, too. *Liadan nighean Math-ghamhainn*, Daughter of the Bear . . . Oh, dear heaven," she added softly.

"What?" Aedan leaned over her shoulder.

"It describes her. . . . Listen to this. 'Liadan, Daughter of the Bear, wife of Aedan mac Brudei, mother of Artorius the Fair, mother of Cunedda, mother of Niall, Diarmid, Aengus, Ivor, Brithnic, Eiri, and Ealga the beautiful.' "

"Good heavens," Aedan remarked, genuinely surprised. "She lived to have . . . nine children with Aedan?"

Christina stared up at him. "If so, then she did not die as a young woman and a bride."

"Unless she fell into that deep sleep when she was nearly a grandmother."

Christina shook her head, then looked up with tears in her eyes. "Aedan, look at this." She pointed to some lines of text.

"My love, I cannot read Old Irish," he said gently.

"It says, 'Liadan, natural daughter of the Bear, the *dux bellorum,* the great Artorius.' "

"Artorius . . . My God! Arthur was her father?" Stunned to his core, Aedan peered down at the elegant, tiny Celtic lettering.

"He must have been. Oh, Aedan!" A tear slid down her cheek. "Here is more. . . . 'Liadan, natural daughter of Artorius the Bear, and her husband, Aedan mac Brudei, elders on our council of war.' She sat with her husband on a council of warriors!"

"Well, as the natural, though bastard, daughter of the great Arthur, she certainly had the right. Perhaps she was even a warrior herself," he mused.

"That's very possible in ancient Celtic society," she said. "But it's wonderful to know that she lived to be an elder. So Princess Liadan did not languish and die young after all." Laughing and crying all at once, Christina looked up at him. "Aedan, you know what this discovery means."

"My head is reeling with meaning, my dear," he drawled.

"The legend of Dundrennan is wrong."

He felt his own throat tighten. "Liadan did not die tragically, lost forever, as the stories claim."

She nodded. "She was a happily married woman who lived a full life as a mother, a wife, and a counselor of her people."

"My God," he said. "The events of her life may have happened as the legend says — she may have had an illness or an injury, as you did. But no one ever knew the true ending before this."

She smiled through bright tears. "His magic worked, after all. He did bring her back. She lived."

"His magic?" Aedan tilted his head, puzzled.

"Aedan mac Brudei wrote the verses on the folio page after his bride became ill." Looking up at him, her lips wobbled. "He used the charm of writing to weave a spell of love and healing to bring Liadan back. The power he summoned must have been very strong — this document proves that she did wake up, after all. And they lived a long and wonderful life together. He loved her so much," she added, sniffling. "So very much. And she loved him desperately, as well. She wanted so much to come back to him. I'm sure of it."

"He loved his princess more than his life," he murmured, brushing his hand along her cheek, wiping her tears with his thumb. "Nothing could keep them apart. Nothing could ever separate them. Two halves of a soul, they were, and compelled to come together again."

"Oh, Aedan," she whispered, "that is so poetic."

He half laughed, watery and low, for he could not speak just then. Drawing her into his arms, he held her silently, caressing her head. She sniffled, her damp cheek to his, and he kissed her again, soft and deep.

"We'd better put this book away before it's ruined by both our tears," he said in a droll tone. Reverently, he took the volume out of her hands, folded his clean handkerchief around the silver cover, and replaced it in the reliquary. His mind was spinning. He took her hand, never wanting to let go.

"Aedan," Christina said slowly, "you know about Treasure Trove, which governs historical finds on Scottish soil."

"Aye," he said. "All that we found will go to the museum."

"Except in cases of inheritable goods. Then

Treasure Trove does not apply."

He blinked in surprise. "Inheritable goods?"

"That book is a record of your ancestors, and it establishes that the treasure belonged to Aedan mac Brudei and thus to his heirs. You are his direct male descendant. So I think the conclusion must be that all of this belongs to you — and to Dundrennan. All of it. The government cannot claim it from you. And it is entirely yours, for these goods were not listed as part of your father's estate."

"My God." Stunned, he shoved a hand through his hair, glanced at the reliquary, then at her again. "I could never keep that treasure. The gold of Dundrennan belongs to . . . to Scotland. To the whole of Britain."

"And it belongs to you, too," she said. "No matter what solution you finally choose, your troubles are over, I think."

"My troubles were over," he said, leaning forward a little, clasping her hand in his, "the moment you walked through the doorway of Dundrennan House."

"If only you had known," she said, smiling mischievously.

"Aye," he murmured. "So," he went on, drawing back a little, "does this mean that the curse on the lairds of Dundrennan is broken, now that we know the princess did wake after all?"

"Oh, yes, I think the spell is broken at

last," she breathed, her eyes sparkling with tears. "And with the lifting of the curse, what does the current laird want in his life?"

"Happiness," he said, touching her cheek. "And contentment with his true love." He tilted her chin and kissed her lips, long and slow. Then he drew back and touched her nose.

"Why, madam," he said. "You're not wearing your spectacles."

"They were lost in the mud."

"So they were. Have I told you that my brother-in-law is a physician in Edinburgh? He specializes in the conditions of the eye. I'd like you to consult with him. My wife should not have to purchase her new spectacles from an itinerant merchant."

She stared up at him. "Your wife?"

"Aye." He smiled gently. "Will you marry me?"

"Ever the pragmatic Sir Aedan," she said, laughing. "No romantic proposal or declaration of undying love for you."

"My darling," he murmured, "there will always be romance and undying love in this house — and wherever we make our home." He swept his hand lovingly over her head. "Although once we are married, we will not have to take our trysts in the hidden passages of Dundrennan House. Pity, that. It was rather delicious."

"We could still do that," she said, and she

slipped into his embrace.

"We could." He chuckled, then sobered, framing her face to kiss her, pulling back. "My dear, I want to marry you most desperately. I truly love you with all my being. That is, if you will have the laird of Dundrennan."

He felt suddenly anxious for her reply, for he had laid himself open to her, as vulnerable as he had ever been, could ever be. Yet he knew that this was love at its most true, and he felt privileged to be blessed with it. He wanted to be with her forever. She was the missing part of his soul, now reclaimed.

"What, marry the laird who swore never to fall in love?" she whispered, her lips but a breath from his.

"The very one," he said, "until he found his beloved."

"Mm . . . but are you not promised already?"

"Amy will not have me." He touched his nose to hers. "She thinks I am dull."

"And so you are." She nipped his lower lip. "But I love a reliable, earthy, strong, quiet man." She pulled away to regard him for a moment. "What of the young woman I saw you kissing not long ago? Miss Mac-Donald?"

"Ah, Dora. I took her to see Connor in Edinburgh. She has a serious eye condition, but Connor thinks he can help her, thank God. She was ecstatic at the news and was only thanking me."

"Oh, Aedan. I thought — well. I trust you will be her benefactor? I would expect it of you." He saw her eyes twinkle.

"Certainly, though Amy may have to do without a few yards of tartan and chintz, so that I can divert funds for Dora."

She slipped into his embrace again, kissing his cheek, his chin, his mouth, until he pulled back.

"Christina, you have not yet answered my question. Will you marry me? I have much to recommend me. I come of very good family. My father was a famous poet. And he would have unabashedly adored you."

"Hm," she said, and she gave him a coy and luscious smile, her eyes shining. "What else recommends you?"

"Well," he said, "the queen will be visiting my home in two weeks. Perhaps that will impress you. And I come of sound lineage. Have I ever told you my middle name?"

She shook her head.

"It's Arthur. A traditional family name."

"There must be a reason for that," she said, and he laughed. "Aedan Arthur Mac-Bride. A wonderful name that you must pass on to your son someday."

"I shall," he whispered, nuzzling her cheek. "With your help."

"Indeed, I would love that." She nibbled at

his ear, and he felt a swirl of excitement and deep, abiding love. "And what else do you have to recommend you, sir?"

"This," he said, and he wrapped her in his arms, kissing her hard and fast, deep and endless.

About the Author

Susan King, a Ph.D. candidate in medieval art history at the University of Maryland, took time off from her dissertation to write her first historical romance, *The Black Thorne's Rose*. A native of New York, she currently lives in Maryland with her husband and their three sons. Be sure to look for her next historical romance, coming soon from Signet. Susan loves to hear from her readers. She can be reached at www.susanking.net.